Publius Cornelius Scipio

The above image was produced by the author using computer manipulation to produce an image of Scipio at the age of seventeen when he first enters this story.

The cover image is by the artist Terry Culkin it depicts Scipio in his prime using a famous but broken marble bust as a guide.

MY FRIEND SCIPIO

This book is dedicated to
Publius Cornelius Scipio Africanus
Valeria Pulcher Laelia
Laelia Julia
Caius Laelius Sapiens

CONTENTS

Prologue	Page 6
Chapter 1 AN ALL TOO COMMON ADVENTURE	Page 7
Chapter 2 SPRING TO SEPTEMBER 2007 218BC	Page 12
Chapter 3 OCTOBER AND NOVEMBER 218BC	Page 44
Chapter 4 BATTLE OF TREBIA DECEMBER 218 BC	Page 61
Chapter 5 AFTER TREBIA, SATURNALIA END 218BC	Page 71
Chapter 6 SPAIN & ITALY LAKE TRASIMENE 217BC	Page 81
Chapter 7 OUR ARRIVAL IN ROME 217BC	Page 106
Chapter 8 CANNAE, JOY & DESPAIR 216 BC 538	Page 126
Chapter 9 ROME IN TURMOIL END OF 216BC 538	Page 157
Chapter 10 LIFE ON THE HOME FRONT 215BC 539	Page 165
Chapter 11 EVENTS IN ITALY 214BC 540	Page 180
Chapter 12 PUBLIC LIFE 213BC 541	Page 184
Chapter 13 MY BROTHER IN LAW CONSUL 212BC 542	Page 191
Chapter 14 BEREAVEMENT 211BC 543	Page 199
Chapter 15 INTO THE FURNACE 210 BC 544	Page 216
Chapter 16 BEGINNING OF THE BEGINNING 209 BC 545	Page 231
Chapter 17 THE BATTLE OF BAECULA 208 BC	Page 260

Chapter 18 I LEARN THE MEANING OF COMBAT 208 BC   Page 272

Chapter 19 THE AFTERMATH OF BAECULA 208BC 546   Page 278

Chapter 20 THE BATTLE OF THE METAURUS 207BC 547   Page 284

Chapter 21 THE BATTLE OF ILIPA 206BC 548   Page 296

Chapter 22 MY FRIEND THE CONSUL 205BC 549   Page 322

Chapter 23 THE INVASION OF AFRICA BEGINS 204BC   Page 347

Chapter 24 UTICA AND GREAT PLAINS 203BC 551   Page 359

Chapter 25 ZAMA 202BC 552   Page 385

Chapter 26 AFRICANUS   Page 406

Chapter 27 HANNIBAL   Page 420

Chapter 28 CAIUS LAELIUS   Page 426

Chapter 29 LEGACY   Page 433

APPENDIX   Page 436

PROLOGUE

I will not discomfit my reader with extravagant claims and proofs as to the veracity of my tale, for in 2007 mankind believes science has answered all the great questions, and cleverer men than I would counter every evidential proof I might bring forward. My digital camera and the tablet, which so amazed my Roman friends have long since lost their power, their memories and pictures. Perhaps it is better they have, since all accused of falsehood and forgery would be, yet my memory remains clear. To share my experience is my only aim.

It is enough, and more, for me, that I have lived another half a lifetime in another time and another place, that I have loved and seen another two children grow and also loved my Roman wife. That I have this tale to tell at all, and again I have my own, or should that be my old life back, my first daughter too, who has now become my second daughter. That I have learned that everything and nothing is real, that space and time are mysteries yet.

That I have a son of thirty years and a daughter of thirty five years, two thousand years dead, who I know to be alive in another realm, me too in fact; that I will die who am both ninety nine apparently and also just fifty one years old and yet am living, always somewhere, and may even find myself again in that maze we call universe and time. These gifts from God, or fate, or nature as the case may be and the tale itself, are more than are given to most men, as far as I can tell. And for these gifts, providential, I heartily give thanks and share.

CHAPTER 1 - AN ALL TOO COMMON ADVENTURE

Life running a small advertising agency was getting hard. Big companies with powerful brands still valued the creative excellence and experience of the large agencies, but the advent of that superb tool, the Apple Mac computer threatened the livelihoods of smaller agencies. Now anyone could produce finished artwork for their brochures or press advertisements, and deal direct with printers and publishers.

That their own expertise was in the garage, or hotel, restaurant trade or some such thing, that they had little or no understanding of how advertising works mattered not a jot; to many clients, all they saw was a reduction in costs. No consideration that the advertising might not work, effectiveness is hard to count, to quantify, without the more sophisticated tools available to the major players, not so the bottom line; the bean counters would approve the instantaneous improvement through cost cutting and if sales fell off a cliff further down the road, due to ill conceived, but cheaply produced advertising, then blame the sales reps!

Besides which I was becoming tired of the rat race. Was this what life was all about? What about my dreams, my passions, had I taken life by the balls and lived it to the full? I'd tried I reflected, but perhaps I hadn't always seen the way clearly. As a youngster I'd loved sailing boats, raced dinghies and devoured books by Clare Francis, Robin Knox Johnston, Shane Acton, Joshua Slocumb and others.

Subsequently, other, possibly even more exciting activities had come along and taken my attention too, skydiving for example; I was once the youngest skydiving instructor in the land and ran a full time parachute centre in my twenties.

Then there was motor-sport, I'd competed on two wheels and four and even won a minor motorcycle racing championship, but the dream to sail about the world, maybe my first love, came back to me now, after fifteen mostly office bound years promoting this product, that product.

I'd enjoyed the challenge and the travel, even had an affinity for some of the products, and the clients in the automotive and motorcycling world too. Enough though; life is short, or so I thought. In any one time zone that's true enough.

As I looked into the matter and weighed the effects on my beloved daughter, now living with my former wife, I realised that it was achievable, without necessarily losing touch. Flights home were cheap from many places, marina prices fell dramatically in winter. Perhaps my daughter could visit me in the Mediterranean in summer and I could fly home to visit her in winter, take her skiing as we'd always done.

Boats I found were plentiful, the French were turning them out in their thousands. Not that I particularly wanted a plastic boat, but supply and demand and all that, meant second hand boat costs generally were not prohibitive. If I could buy a tough steel yacht outright, and rent my home out I might just survive financially as well as physically.

Some years ago I took the plunge and found my boyhood dream was no longer an uncommon adventure. Boat gypsies abound, we're very much a minority, but there are still thousands of us around the world at any one time. There seem to be a great many boats that live in marinas and go nowhere most of the time, but everywhere I've stopped I've met, at least a few, like minded travellers.

And so, to me at any rate, my life was changed, quite different from the lives most people live on land, commuting to an office or factory. Quite different from the life I'd been living for fifteen or more years. This new, altered reality swiftly became a normal thing for me and I realised it was also like that for those around me who felt the same way. I'd joined a new community of travellers on the high seas.

I was innocent enough to start with and troubles there were aplenty. Three boats were surveyed before the right one came along and then she lay in Ireland. Anxious after all the delay to get her home by Christmas I naively sailed her across the Irish Sea in December!

After a period of making improvements and repairs in Gravesend and London I finally set out to explore my world, my passion for history a driving force, to see the lands of the Norse Sagas and the monuments of Greece and Rome.

The first day out, from South Dock Marina in London, the roller reefing on the forestay failed to work properly, a navigation light went out and in the morning the anchor winch just plain broke. Repairs were made at Harwich before a mighty North Sea storm brought enough water aboard to put out half the electrical devices, mostly pumps! To Lowestoft then and more repairs.

Soon the teething problems lay astern and Norway and Sweden came and went, then Denmark, Germany, Holland and France. From Guernsey thence to Brittany, Biscay, Spain and Portugal. Sojourns on the Guadiana and the Gualdalquivir, Seville with its history of the Moors, Columbus and all the other attributes that great city has to offer.

Then on to Cadiz – Phoenician, Carthaginian and Roman Gades as it was once known, with more recent history of Armada and Essex. I explored all these places, before sailing on to the next, all the while expanding my knowledge and firing my historical interest even more.

I'd seen the stone age sites of Menorca and the forts St Philip and Marlborough, whose sieges occasioned Byng's downfall, the homes of Nelson and Collingwood and then returned to Fuengirola to see my young English daughter on holiday there, before wintering in Almeria with its amazing Moorish Castle.

After all this, some eight thousand miles of sailing, anchoring and entering a hundred harbours, I felt my apprenticeship was over; that next year, year three already, how time flies, I was ready for Sardinia, Corsica, Elba , Italy and Sicily. They called to me, together with the historical periods I loved the most. The sailing part was easy now, I respected the dangers, but had confidence in myself and my boat, yet nothing at all could have prepared me for what was actually to happen.

CHAPTER 2 - SPRING TO SEPTEMBER 2007 (218BC)

I sailed from balmy Almeria at the end of February 2007. A gentle northerly breeze helped me out to sea, the sun shone on the Moorish castle high on the hill and glinted on the wavelets. The Cable Ingles, the old overhead railway on mighty steel girders that once brought ore to be loaded down enormous chutes into the waiting cargo ships beneath, shrunk from view behind me. All was serene as I came around to a beam reach and headed for Cabo de Gata.

My immediate aims were to coast up to Cartagena, New Carthage as once was, the one time base of the mighty Carthaginian general Hannibal. I was in no hurry, several overnight stops were planned en route to Cartagena and I had delightful company for the next four days, a charming friend from Finland, who, sadly from my perspective, would jump on a train at Cartagena and then fly home.

Cartagena itself was something of a disappointment, excepting a Roman amphitheatre there was not so much to see from its illustrious, historic past. This region had once become the focus of Carthaginian operations by way of compensating themselves for having lost control of Sicily in the First Punic War and then Sardinia and Corsica, which were also snatched by the Romans after Carthaginian infighting and their own mercenaries destabilised those islands too. To add insult to injury the Romans, sensing Carthaginian weakness also demanded a greater financial tribute than previously agreed.

The Romans were in for a shock; although the Carthaginians had long traded on the Iberian peninsula, the Carthaginian general Hamilcar Barca had new ideas. He had effectively been forced by the Carthaginian government to surrender Sicily after someone else's naval defeat, whilst as yet undefeated personally on land. He had now made it his mission to re-grow and re-establish Carthaginian might and power in this fertile region endowed with so many natural resources.

His surname, Barca, translates as Thunderbolt, he and his sons Hannibal, Hasdrubal and Mago, his young brood of lion cubs as he saw them, bred, in his mind, to defeat Rome lived up to the name.

He would set about conquering the local tribes and enriching Carthage in order to re-arm, whilst endowing his men with confidence and experience. First he took his young son Hannibal, the eldest of the three, with him, having made it a condition of passage that the keen, excited youngster swear an oath of lifelong enmity to Rome on the blood of a sacrificial victim. A sacred oath Hannibal maintained fidelity to his entire life.

He was also accompanied by his oft forgotten son in law, another successful general in his own right Hasdrubal, known as 'the Fair' who would, following Hamilcar's death, found the City of New Carthage. The port city which Hannibal would later use as his launch pad following the death of Hasdrubal the Fair. The Carthaginians had what today, we might call strength in depth.

In 221BC Hasdrubal the Fair, the founder of New Carthage had been murdered by a Celtic mercenary. The, soon to be feared throughout the Roman world, Carthaginian general Hannibal, had taken command by popular acclaim of the army and had made the city his base. His predecessor Hasdrubal the Fair, had been married, by Hannibal's father Hamilcar, to Hannibal's sister since at least 237BC.

Hasdrubal the Fair, should not be confused then with Hasdrubal Barca, a brother of Hannibal and yet another Carthaginian general who would play a starring role in the Second Punic War on which the curtain was about to rise. Before his murder Hasdrubal the Fair had further extended Carthaginian power in the regions around Cartagena and had reached an agreement with Rome, a treaty in fact, which, although unratified in Carthage itself limited Carthaginian conquest to a boundary along the Ebro river.

It's doubtful if this treaty was ever intended to be anything more than a delaying tactic. The Carthaginians in Spain were deeply endowed with ambition and the desire to make Rome pay, not only for the defeat in Sicily, but also for the opportunistic breach of the original treaty that cost them Sardinia and Corsica and many talents of silver into the bargain.

Upon taking command in 219BC Hannibal had promptly invaded the territory of the Olcades, whose capital Carteia was within the agreed, by the Romans anyway, Carthaginian sphere of influence, (that is south of the Ebro river) but, which lay in an area not yet fully controlled by the Carthaginians until this point. Having succeeded, Hannibal would soon turn his attention to the city of Saguntum.

Saguntum had recently made an alliance with Rome, yet was south of the Ebro. The treaty between Rome and Carthage, made at the end of the First Punic War, which Rome had already abused by seizing Sardinia and Corsica and demanding a greater tribute from Carthage, also stated that neither party should interfere with the allies of the other party.

Nothing in the said treaty specifically differentiated between existing allies or future allies. Saguntum had not been allied to Rome when the treaty was agreed and so there was sufficient ambiguity to create a perfect recipe for disagreement, differing interpretations and renewed conflict.

My own mood was more subdued when I sailed, alone once more from Cartagena and heading for the Mar Menor. Not long out of Cartagena, with the autopilot doing the work and feeling slightly sorry for myself I was brought back down to earth by an alarm and an on screen message that said the rudder was inactive. Oh great!

I pulled everything out of the aft cabin, no mean feat since it had become something of a dumping ground and kit store. Alongside the grab bags were three folding bikes (a long story), sun awnings, a kite, canoe paddles and tender oars, plus all manner of spare clothes, a volley ball, football, softball set and other toys for my daughter, waterproofs, life jackets and lifelines, shoes and all manner of detritus not used every day. The wheelhouse looked like a poorly organized stall at a village jumble sale by the time I'd pulled all this stuff out of the aft cabin and raised the floor panels of the cupboards running across the transom.

To find what? Well nothing, thank goodness I suppose, the rudder worked and everything was still attached, there was no pool of hydraulic fluid. I put everything back, it was hot and I was sweating and also cursing.

Naturally I'd hoped to find the problem and that it should be easily curable of course, but no. I put the autopilot back on and it worked for a while then the alarm went off again, the message the same as before. "No it isn't you stupid machine" I replied verbally to the screen, "the rudder is fine and you've just been moving it". I opened more lockers, pulled out more items, spare hoses and pumps, I traced the entire course of the back up steering cables, but nothing was interfering with them or chafing.

I was getting tired and irritable, but at least there was no danger. I removed the autopilot control unit and put some Vaseline in the multi-pin connector and put it back. That did it. That was all it took, a bit of Vaseline to cure a poor connection and hey presto the various parts spoke to one another again. No need whatsoever for all that previous labour! I started to believe in my problem solving abilities once more at least and then anchored in the Mar Menor.

There, in that picturesque lagoon, almost an inland sea, I endured a gale for two days and two nights, frequently fifty knots or more and on two occasions I saw gusts over sixty, the most I'd ever seen in an anchorage. It was tiring and stressful, the shallow water ensuring the boat was getting shaken constantly, I worried that something would break, or the anchor would drag. I tried to stay awake throughout; on the one hand that was impossible, on the other I woke frequently anyway with the noise and the turmoil all around.

I left the Mar Menor, despite its many attractions and a free display by the Spanish Air Force Aerobatic Display Team with little affection to coast to Barcelona, Narbonne, Montpelier, Marseilles, Toulon, Cannes and Nice. I judged St Tropez as being too expensive to consider a stop; out of my price band! Eventually I'd planned to progress to Genoa, Pisa, maybe visit Elba and possibly Corsica and Sardinia.

Things went well for a couple of weeks, some long hops, some short ones. A lazy sailor by nature, something I justify on the basis of needing to stay fresh and alert, I used the autopilot extensively; solar panels and a wind generator plus a bank of six large batteries, four exclusively domestic deep discharge batteries, made this modus operandi both possible and practical.

Early in September I heard an alarm once more, coming from my satellite navigation system. This time however the message read 'No GPS Data' and where the speed and position had been there were now asterisks. No panic there then, I'd lost count of the number of times the GPS had lost contact with one or two satellites and therefore reserved judgment on giving me our position. It always came back as new satellites were detected.

I would simply continue on my merry way, sailing on a compass heading and within five minutes or so the GPS would have found new satellites and would be talking to me and to the rudder once again. My position was approximately forty three degrees, twelve minutes north and six degrees, nine minutes east, I was off the coast some way out from St. Tropez as I had no intention of stopping there and I was thinking about a possible one night stop at Frejus or Cannes.

Not being worried about my position and having become a little blasé about the GPS, (not least because I had three back ups!) I allowed my attention to be distracted by a strange looking ship that was approaching from over the horizon. The ship was inshore of me and heading in the opposite direction along the coast. I'd seen a few historical replicas already on my travels and despite the distance guessed that this was another.

In Gothenburg there had been a replica Swedish East Indiaman setting out on its maiden voyage as I sailed in, a happy coincidence and I'd seen a Viking longship, in Kalmar, there had been a reconstruction of a 12th Century cargo ship I'd seen in Scandinavia too, genuine historic boats abound in The Netherlands, whilst off the south coast of Spain I'd seen a galleon which reminded me of, and was I think, a replica of Columbus's Santa Maria, although this one was motoring! In Lagos and Almeria there had been replicas as well, Faluccas I believe.

I reached for the binoculars. Now that's really quite a replica I said to myself, I knew from a television documentary I'd seen some years ago that someone had reconstructed a Greek warship of classical times, a trireme as I recalled, with three decks of oars, each manned by a single rower and I'd seen the movie Troy with its vast fleet of mostly computer generated warships, but this was impressive!

A quinquereme, had three banks of massive oars, not dissimilar from a trireme, but rather bigger, the two upper banks of oars were wielded by two men each and a third, lower bank had shorter oars handled by a single rower. Since the rowers were effectively in groups of five, two, two and one the ship was called a quinquereme.

The boat that I saw must have been at least forty five metres long to my ten and a half. Excluding the mast, it probably rose nearly four metres above the water too with its various decks.

A huge bronze prow for ramming and a single square sail furled to an enormous spar completed the picture. They must be making a movie, and a big budget one at that. I'd worked as an extra, in film and TV, from time to time and I knew how the movie industry could throw money around, but even so, this was a big investment, in people as well as in materials.

A ship like that might have four hundred and fifty people aboard, rowers, marines, officers, that's even if it wasn't part of a fleet transporting an entire army, which this one was it would turn out later. 'A remake of Cleopatra' I wondered, that was the first of several assumptions which would all turn out to be well wide of the mark.

A second ship appeared and then a line of them, how do they do that? Surely they can't have built six. I threw a glance at the GPS, still nothing there but I was too fascinated by the sight that greeted my incredulous eyes to think the unthinkable yet.

By the time Publius Cornelius Scipio's fleet had grown to thirty five warships I became very scared. 'Am I scared of getting in the way of the movie or am I scared for my life?' I wondered. Well the latter actually; when you see a Roman fleet with weapons of war bearing down on you it's a terrifying sight, whether you hope they're just replicas or not.

Unfortunately, my senses, logic, experience and the still redundant GPS screamed silently, yet eloquently, that this was no mere movie and no hallucination either, something totally unexpected, inexplicable and yet inescapable was happening. By the time I decided to turn tail and flee some sixty quinqueremes were bearing down on me.

I'm not a scientist, I've heard the expression worm hole, no idea what it means, I think I heard about a rent in the space time continuum, both probably terms I'd heard in a movie or from a book I read somewhere in the deep distant past; at this moment, the deep distant future. That would have been science fiction, with the emphasis on fiction, or a fantasy type movie. These things simply don't happen in real life.

In the spring of 218BC Hannibal began an offensive against the Vaccaei, the towns of Hermandica and Arbocala specifically, the latter of which mounted a stern defence but still fell. Fugitives of the Olcades and those from Hermandica induced the Carpetani to join them and attack Hannibal's column near the Tagus river.

Fortunately for me, I had studied both Livy and Polybius. The knowledge I had from those studies would prove instrumental in saving my life and in building the most important friendship in my new Roman life.

At his next battle Hannibal revealed the first signs of the genius which would perplex and dismay mighty Rome for years. His enemies, one hundred thousand strong, were tempted to cross the Tagus in pursuit of Hannibal's seemingly defeated, heavily outnumbered army, which had retreated across the river without leaving obstacles in their wake, deliberately as it happened.

The jubilant pursuers were duly ambushed and went down to a heavy defeat themselves. The Carpetani surrendered, leaving all the peoples south of the River Ebro under the sway of Carthage. With one notable exception, Rome's buffer state, the city of Saguntum.

Before Saguntum fell, Rome, cautious by nature, had sent envoys Publius Valerius Flaccus and Quintus Baebius Tamphilus to Hannibal to tell him to leave Saguntum alone since it was a friend and ally of Rome. Hannibal had declined to see them, continued the siege, already begun by this time and had written to his supporters in Carthage to ensure the Romans would be rebuffed there too.

Rome's envoys travelled in person to the city of Carthage itself, in North Africa, modern day Tunisia, where despite the efforts of a Carthaginian politician named Hanno, who wanted peace with Rome, they were duly rebuffed, the majority having been swayed by Hannibal, his friends and his letters.

Publius Valerius Flaccus and Quintus Baebius Tamphilus were disingenuously informed that the Saguntines had started the hostilities and that Rome should let it be, keep out and respect the treaty agreed with Hasdrubal the Fair! Everything south of the Ebro, belonged to Carthage.

Saguntum fell, with much bloodshed, and the news reached Rome at about the same time the two envoys finally returned with the Carthaginian government's rejection of Rome's demands. Rome had, somewhat optimistically, demanded Carthage leave Saguntum alone and surrender the person of Hannibal to Roman jurisprudence.

Although Hannibal's family, named Barca, had their enemies in the city of Carthage their supporters were more numerous and more powerful, Hannibal would not be given up and therefore must be backed up.

Publius Cornelius Scipio the father of that Scipio I would come to call friend, had been allotted Spain as his theatre of operation for 218BC and Tiberius Sempronius Longus, had drawn Africa and Sicily. Lots being the way these things were decided amongst elected Roman officials in the Republican system of the time. Both men being the consuls for 218BC.

Rome despatched a second, larger, more prestigious, delegation to Carthage, consisting of Quintus Fabius, Marcus Livius, Lucius Aemilius, Gaius Licinius and Qunitus Baebius. This second attempt at diplomacy offered Carthage a final opportunity to avoid war with the state which had defeated it the first time around in Sicily and which had gone on to make inroads into what we now call Sardinia and Corsica, previously, also within the Carthaginian sphere. Carthage detested Rome with a vengeance and in fact it was vengeance that Hannibal sought.

Despite experiencing defeat at the hands of Rome previously Carthage placed its faith in Hannibal and once again tried to argue the legality of his attack on Saguntum. Rome's envoys duly declared war and travelled onwards to Spain in person, there seeking to find allies against Hannibal. After what had seemed a promising start they ended up with none, this in no small part due to what the local tribes people saw as Rome's abandonment of Saguntum to its bloody fate when it mattered. Dithering in other words.

The envoys began their return to Italy and Rome via Gaul where they again looked for allies to prevent Hannibal passing. They met with no success there either, despite the fact that Massilia, modern day Marseilles was ostensibly friendly to Rome.

By the time the envoys returned to Rome the consuls had left for their own spheres of operation. Their demands having been contemptuously rejected, Rome raised fresh troops and a new navy for what would come to be known as the Second Punic War, the longest and bloodiest of the three wars the two states would fight.

My friend Scipio's father had been elected consul for 218 BC at the outbreak of this, the Second Punic War. A war which his faction was strongly in favour of. The Roman strategy called for a two-pronged attack on the Carthaginian possessions, more or less simultaneously, in Africa and in Spain.

The attack on Spain was to be led by my friend's father and his uncle. At this time my friend was just seventeen years of age, we had not yet met, but he was now eligible to serve in his father's army and sailed for Spain alongside his father and uncle. Rome did not anticipate a war in Italy, she intended to fight Carthage in Iberia and North Africa. Hannibal had other ideas.

A Roman citizen of sufficient status was expected to serve at least ten campaigns in the legions, which in effect meant ten full years under the standards. Scipio's uncle Gnaeus Cornelius Scipio was also an officer in my friend's father's army. Scipio senior's army, destined for Spain, reached Massilia in September of 218, at the same time as Hannibal reached the river Rhone on his way to invade Italy, where he would run rings around the Romans and inflict heavy losses there for near seventeen years, but that, as yet, lay in the future, his, and mine bizarrely.

The Scipios had sailed with their army from Pisa with the intention of confronting Hannibal in Spain, they were already too late. The Roman fleet stopped at Massilia for supplies only to be told that Hannibal's army was already crossing the River Rhone on its march into Italy.

Reports vary but it's not impossible that Hannibal crossed the Pyrenees heading for the Rhone with close to sixty thousand men, having left thirty thousand Carthaginian soldiers to defend their hard won possessions in Iberia, those forces being split between Hanno, south of the Ebro and Hannibal's brother Hasdrubal in the foothills of the Pyrenees.

Publius Cornelius disembarked his army and marched west to meet Hannibal in battle. Unable to do so he returned to Massilia and re-embarked his army, whereupon he ordered all to go on to Spain under the command of his brother Gnaeus Cornelius, whilst he, at the same time, returned to organise the defence of Italy. I would find myself a prisoner taken along to Italy too!

Having turned tail to flee I wondered if I could outrun the Roman fleet. The wind had been abeam, almost Francesca's best point of sail, a beam reach. A one hundred and eighty degree turn would also mean a beam reach, just with the wind on the other side, still coming from the land. A wind like that was of little help to a quinquereme with it's one large square sail, it pretty much needed a following wind and so the fleet was rowing.

My boat, when I purchased it, was chosen for comfort, space and safety, not speed. On a beam reach with three of my four sails flying I could achieve an average of just over five knots in a calm sea with a decent breeze. On a straight beam reach there was no point flying two foresails as one stole wind from the other. If I sailed closer to the wind I could go faster, fly the genoa and the staysail together, the slot effect might get me up to six knots, but turning closer to the wind would also take me towards the shore and closer to the track of the Roman fleet. I wasn't so sure about that.

I knew I'd been spotted and my craft must have looked very strange to a Roman observer indeed. The fact that I could sail forwards in a cross wind probably perplexed the Romans, but I cannot have looked like much of a danger, and indeed I was not. I noticed that their speed had increased. My mainsail, genoa and mizzen sail were all pulling and I knew that starting the engine would only increase my speed marginally, hull speed is hull speed, it's not a boat that can plane!

I guessed the nearest quinquereme was making about seven knots to my five and a half. My hope was that the rowers would tire before they had me in range of their ballistas, or catapults, or whatever shipborne artillery they carried. If they aimed at a capture they probably wouldn't want to sink me. I knew their ships had been copied from a Carthaginian example captured some years before.

The Roman ships had not quite achieved the excellence of the Carthaginian originals, they were usually made of cedar from the Lebanon and were heavier, even though the Romans when they took the Carthaginian ship apart to study it had labelled every component, then duplicated them and built their ships from what we today might call a kit of pre-fabricated parts.

The major improvement made by the Romans to their copies of Carthaginian warships was a thing called a corvus, meaning crow, or raven. The Romans were experts at land based warfare, not naval engagements. The corvus was a sort of gangway that could be swung over the deck of an enemy ship. It had spikes beneath it and when dropped hard onto the wooden deck of an enemy vessel it would hold fast enabling the Romans to swarm across and fight as they would on land, close quarters with their deadly, short stabbing swords and shields. It did require getting more or less alongside however and I wasn't planning on letting a Roman warship get that close to me.

If they wanted to study how my boat worked they'd have to capture me and I had no desire to be captured. I had an idea that I wanted to lose myself in the Rhone Delta. If I accepted I'd travelled two thousand years plus into the past, my charts would be useless, but the Delta would have myriad small channels and tall reeds, I hoped, where a boat with a shallow draft might get in and hide. I guessed a quinquereme would draw at least three metres, I drew around half that.

My calculation that the rowers would not be able to maintain seven knots for an extended period proved correct, before long the distance stabilised and I was ready to start my engine should the breeze fail. I took a course seaward of the Ile Du Levant and the Iles D'Hyeres, Scipio's fleet divided, most went between the islands and the shore, a few others kept me in sight.

Through my binoculars I had a much better view of them, I hoped, than they of me, I didn't know if they had telescopes and I found it hard to look away, they of course knew much less about me, if only because my craft would appear so peculiar to Roman eyes and I had studied my history, one cannot study the future.

West of Toulon and clear of the headland Scipio's fleet began its turn north towards Massilia, rowing more into a headwind as they did so. Only one quinquereme continued to follow me, clearly Hannibal, news and resupply were far more important than I was. The mouth of the river Rhone was scant thirty miles from Marseilles on my charts, but my charts were, out of date, the wrong way around if that makes sense, I figured the Camargue which spread towards modern day Montpellier would be marshy and contain many channels. At least, that's what I was banking on.

By turning some degrees to starboard and setting a course for the western extremity of the Camargue I was able to add my staysail to the genoa getting a slot effect from the two sails which saw my speed increase to six knots. An hour or so later the quinquereme giving chase gave up on me and set course for Massilia.

I gradually rounded up to the north and as I grew closer to shore took down all sail and motored. I was well west of the Rhone mouth as it is today, so I motored east, towards danger but hoping to find a place to get in and hide. Without the need to think about sailing I was able to watch my depth sounder and with the alternator generating power I could turn on my radar to try and better ascertain the shape of the coast now that I had no usable charts to find a channel big enough to allow me to get in, yet small enough to hide me. The radar wasn't in fact a great deal of help, the land being so low and flat.

I was busy watching not only the depth sounder, and the radar screen but I was also scrutinising the shore with my binoculars. I approached a couple of likely looking channels, only to find them to be effectively dead ends. It was also apparent to me that my masts would give me away.

My masts were not very tall, and they were wooden, nonetheless they would stand out, they had lights and aerials on them, spreaders, radar reflector on one, radar on the other and being made of solid wood they were far too heavy for me to lower on my own, despite both being mounted in tabernacles. Maybe I could rig some way to winch the masts down, but it would mean designing a system from scratch, making it and then trying to attach everything solo. I ruled it out, this was not an eventuality even I had planned for. Marinas had cranes for that kind of thing.

At the third time of asking, in the approaching gloom of dusk, I found a channel I could follow far enough and which was twisty enough that my hull and superstructure at least were hidden from view by the reeds, both from the sea and the land unless someone got very close.

Those masts were still a worry but it would be dark soon. I was tired and hungry. I dropped anchor. I know today that my location must have been what is now called Grau de la Dent, I'll never know for sure what happened on my return, just as I'll never know for certain how I went back in time to begin with. However, if I wasn't discovered I knew from what I had read that the Romans would soon be moving on; in fact, it suddenly occurred to me, did I not have both Livy and Polybius on a tablet somewhere on board?

Yes I did, I decided to re-read both, at least the most relevant bits as speedily as possible. I'd skip over the pre battle speeches and the like, which may have only existed in the minds of the ancient writers anyway, who wished to enthral their audience with the drama of it all, or big up their friends or heroes. I'd just concentrate on the order of events, the actual battles and their consequences and hope the ancient historians had got most of it right!

I certainly already knew that Scipios fleet, if my guess was correct and that was what it was, would leave after some days, under the command of Gnaeus Cornelius Scipio Calvus, (called Calvus, meaning bald to distinguish him from another older Gnaeus Cornelius Scipio, known as Asina meaning Jackass!).

Roman names fascinated me, even if Romans' propensity for giving offspring the same names as the parents sometimes gave the study of Roman history great potential for confusion! That Scipio named Jackass had been in command of, and had lost the first ever fleet the Romans sent to war. They lost that fleet to duplicity, through a clever Carthaginian stratagem which outwitted that Scipio soon thereafter to be known as Asina, during the first Punic War.

Never ones to give up, the Romans built more ships, changed the way ships fought at sea with their corvus and still won the war though, and largely thanks to a naval victory at that. I knew that in the end they would defeat Hannibal too. The Romans viewed themselves as warriors, giving up was anathema to them. Hasdrubal and his son Hannibal doubtless felt the same but there were many in the Carthaginian government who were minded more like accountants, did the sums add up? Was it worth the fight in economic terms. Never a consideration for a true warrior.

Anyhow I digress, I knew that the fleet, if it was what I thought it was, together with its embarked army commanded by Gnaeus would sail for Spain after failing to bring Hannibal to battle and that Publius, his son, and some others would return to Italy to organise the defence, whilst Hannibal would be on his way to cross the Alps. In other words this particular hotbed of activity would soon be left in peace once more.

What I would do then I had no idea, but actually by then I wouldn't be making decisions for myself anyway, I'd be a captive. Not knowing that, and feeling that I was dealing pretty well with an impossible situation, which I doubted other yachtsmen in the noughties had faced, I made a couple more arrangements.

Basically I lowered the tender, mounted the outboard and made sure it was fully fuelled, if surprised I could take off quickly in the tender. I could not raise the anchor and motor the yacht away anything like as fast, I was relying basically on not being found, but at least there was a semblance of an escape plan if the worst came to the worst.

By the time the tender was prepared it was truly dark. I drew the curtains, closed the cabin doors, risked one small interior light, prepared some food and finally got some sleep. I did not sleep well, but it was better than nothing. I'd found my tablet before going to bed and with my six bladed wind generator still turning, thankfully almost silently unlike some of the three bladed examples I'd come across which sounded like a turbine engine on full power, I'd been able to quietly charge the tablet fully whilst I rested.

At first light I had some cereal and started brushing up on my Roman history and a bit of Latin, well I knew quite a lot of modern Italian and many of those words had a Latin root, but if I needed to talk my way out of anything it wasn't going to be simple! Thankfully I'd downloaded a ton of books to my tablet when I bought it, books are heavy and they take up a lot of room on a yacht. The tablet held a veritable library. One of the downloads was some basic Latin. You'd almost think the universe had a plan!

My laptop and digital cameras which got used on an almost daily basis were already charged. I hid them as effectively as I could in case of intruders, not that an intruder would know what to make of them! My main camera a Nikon D7000 already had some long range shots of quinqueremes, now that would cause a stir if I ever returned to my own time!

On arrival in Massilia, having received news from local sources that Hannibal had already crossed the Pyrenees and reached the River Rhone, a sceptical Publius Cornelius Scipio immediately despatched a reconnaissance force, reckoned by Polybius to be three hundred of his bravest cavalry supported by an unquantified number of Celts as guides. Their brief was to ascertain the veracity of these reports which suggested Hannibal's army had moved with superhuman speed.

Hannibal, likewise, heard reports that the consul had landed at Massilia, he too despatched a force of cavalry in the form of Numidian horsemen to reconnoitre the situation. Polybius numbers this force at five hundred.

Whatever the true numbers, the two cavalry contingents would run into one another and meet in a small battle or a large skirmish. We are told that the Carthaginians lost some two hundred men before fleeing back to camp, Roman losses were not much less, however the pursuing Romans would ascertain that Hannibal had already crossed the river, before returning to the consul with this disturbing news.

Publius promptly marched his entire army out to meet Hannibal in battle, but as mentioned earlier in this narrative he was already too late, by the time he reached Hannibal's abandoned camp Hannibal was well on his way to the alpine passes in a region known then as 'the island', being the confluence of the Rhone and Isara rivers, the Isara being the river which we know as the Isère, not far from the town we call Grenoble.

On his return journey from this expedition the consul recalled the strange ship his fleet had sighted and lost, he sent his scouts out on the coast side, into the marshes as well as ahead as the army marched back to Massilia. Luckily for me his scouts were instructed to take the crew alive in order to ascertain information about both the strange boat with its fore and aft sails and its presence in these waters at this time.

With my curtains drawn I sat silently below deck revising my schoolboy Latin on my tablet which was still plugged into the power via an inverter and occasionally reading chapters of Polybius and Livy to vary things and maintain concentration. Once in a while I would venture gingerly into the wheelhouse to get a good look around, for several days all had been quiet.

I could have ventured out to sea again I realised, but where would I go in the ancient world? Would I miraculously reappear in my own time. Whenever I slept or even just dozed off I dreamed that this was the dream before waking to find myself in marshes which bore no resemblance to my charts or indeed to the Times World Atlas I also kept aboard.

Seemingly lost in these thoughts I felt one side of the boat dip slightly 'this is it' I thought 'someone has just climbed aboard. I normally kept my tablet, and indeed other electrical devices not specifically designed for a life at sea in waterproof plastic pouches. The pouch for the tablet had a lanyard I wore around my neck. Tucking the tablet into its pouch and then under my shirt I ventured into the wheelhouse. I'd kept the canopy at the rear unzipped and strapped open to facilitate a quick escape into the tender, but of course it had also made entering easy for Publius's scout.

For a moment we just stared at each other, no doubt the scout had never seen anyone dressed the way I was in my Craghopper trousers, button up shirt and deck shoes and I'd certainly never met a Celt in service to Rome. Also in trousers and wearing a short sleeve tunic of some sort, I was more concerned by the size of his arms!

He had two mounted colleagues on the bank armed with bows as well as long cavalry swords. Resistance as they say was futile, the scout who had swum out to Francesca for stealth pointed to his comrades, clearly indicating that I should swim to shore. It was scant yards, the current had kept Francesca parallel to the bank.

They clearly didn't see me as a threat and were under orders I later discovered to deliver me to the consul unmolested. I swam as instructed, it didn't seem to be a good idea to try and demonstrate the tender and outboard! Just do as you're told.

Had speed not been an issue they would doubtless have made me, a prisoner, walk to Massilia, but time was an issue and the ability to move quickly without losing the prisoner should they happen upon any Carthaginians might have entered into the equation too. I found myself mounted behind the lead scout. We rode slowly out of the marshes before galloping for Massilia once on firmer more open ground.

As the four of us rode into Massilia we were the subject of some speculation, but people watched as we passed and then returned to their own business. I was taken to headquarters immediately, where I was to be taken straight into the presence of Publius Cornelius Scipio, consul of Rome and commander of the legions here present.

The consul was in conference with his brother Gnaeus, his now just turned eighteen years old son, also Publius Cornelius Scipio stood off to the side listening respectfully. The consul and his brother were discussing the war in Spain, Gnaeus was to sail onwards with the army with the objective of defeating the Carthaginians left behind by Hannibal under the command of his brother Hasdrubal.

Events were moving quickly and the army was, even at that moment re-embarking on the sixty quinqueremes. Publius Cornelius had commandeered a fast merchantman to transport himself and some chosen officers and his son to Pisa from whence he intended to take over the Roman legions already based in northern Italy to meet Hannibal as he descended from the Alps. Decisions were being taken with care, but without delay.

We were in the house of a wealthy merchant, a house either commandeered or offered to curry favour, or maybe because it would likely have been commandeered anyway. The Latin for merchant came to mind, 'mercator sum, merchant I am'. A story started to form in my head. The truth being too far fetched, even for a superstitious people like the Romans.

The consul came straight to the point "Who are you and what are you doing here?"

" Mercator sum consul."

The use of the title consul might have been a mistake, it was meant as a sign of respect.

"Unde?" "Where from." At least the Latin was undemanding so far.

Was Britannia known as Britannia so early? I racked my brains.

I wanted to say the tin islands, but I had no idea how to say tin in Latin, insulae meant islands I knew, the word was also used for apartment blocks in ancient Rome although I wasn't sure if they had those yet either, then it occurred to me, Herodotus, he predated this period, what did he call them?

"Cassiterides.

"I seek new markets, the Carthaginians do not keep agreements."

Maybe a statement of dissatisfaction with Carthage would be enough to keep me alive!

At that moment a tribune, or other officer, I wasn't yet conversant with the ranks, reported that the embarkation was complete. I was placed under guard in a side room, a bedroom in fact where I could at least take the weight off my aching legs and think.

The guard, thankfully, was outside the only door. My tablet was still pressed close to my chest, beneath my shirt in its waterproof pouch. I quickly began work on the further Latin vocabulary I would need for the story taking shape in my head. A story which I hoped would both save my skin and make me useful, important even.

Knowledge as they say, is power.

The consul went down to the harbour with his brother to see the army off, on its way to Spain, he left his son to deal with the merchant whose house they had used, to brief those joining the ship for Pisa and to pack his own and his father's possessions. The harbour was so crammed and chaotic that the consul's ship would be made ready once the fleet had sailed, departure for us would be at dusk at the earliest, or at dawn the following day if the pilot felt it was too dangerous to depart in the failing light. I say 'us' but at this point my fate hung precariously.

Curiosity was gnawing at Publius Cornelius Minor, he fulfilled the tasks allotted to him efficiently and correctly, but promptly returned and instructed the guard that he had need of conversation with the prisoner. I heard the brief conversation between him and the guard, giving me just enough time to turn off the tablet, already in silent mode and return it to its pouch and do up my shirt.

"Why did you not sail away when you had the chance?"

"I seek contact with Rome." It was the only thing I could think of to say, but how else would I survive in the ancient world unless I got in with someone, and if you're going to join forces and you know who the eventual winner will be it make sense to try and ingratiate yourself with that faction. Furthermore, although I didn't love certain aspects of Roman culture I had to accept that I was in a completely alien world, one with different standards and ideas. I did admire Roman achievements.

"Why so? You are unlike any merchant I have ever seen, I don't believe your story, you may be from the far islands we have heard tell of, but there is more."

In for a penny, in for a pound, I didn't think that a claim to be from the future would be wise, not yet at least and maybe not ever, so I hedged my bets. Romans did believe in mysticism, seers, prophets, that kind of thing, at least most did from what I'd read, then I remembered, the Sibyl, the Sibylline verses, of course they believed, a claim to know the future, especially if my 'prophecies' came true would make me useful.

"I see the future. I know things that will be useful to you Publius. Your father is even now watching your uncle depart to fight in Spain, you and he, with a chosen few, will sail for the Padus to take command of the legions in the north of Italy. It is the beginning of the longest and greatest war Rome will ever fight. Hannibal will cross the Alps, you will be the hero who eventually defeats him, you will take the cognomen Africanus, you will be remembered throughout human history."

" Nonsense, my father will defeat Hannibal and my uncle will conquer Spain, it will all be over come Saturnalia."

I could not help but compare his optimism with that shared by the soldiers on both sides in World War One, it will all be over by Christmas! Bizarrely, the stories told to me by my own grandparents were some two thousand years ahead of me now, I must not allow my mind to wander, what happened here and now would determine my fate of that I did have a premonition! Well, a sense of certainty, or an instinct for survival at least.

"Take note of what I tell you Publius, I can help you fulfil your great destiny. Ask yourself how I know your name, your father's name and rank, how do I know that Gnaeus is sailing for Spain, how do I know your father's plans to return by ship to Italy to take command? Have I not been held captive by your scouts, was I not brought straight here, you can see I struggle with Latin, how much could I have learned, how do I know these things?

"It is written and I have read it." That at least was true!

"I will tell you now what will happen next, keep me close Publius, you will see that all I predict comes to pass, you will find the knowledge that I have and the advice I can offer invaluable, just listen to me now, keep me safe it will not be long before you see the veracity of what I have to tell you.

"The journey back to Italy will be uneventful, your father will take command of raw troops, currently commanded by the praetors. Hannibal will not only cross the Alps successfully despite losses and battles with the local tribes, but he will have already rested his men and then conquered the Taurini. He will also have made overtures to the Gauls of northern Italy before your father can bring him to battle.

"Buoyed by his cavalry success here your father will throw a bridge over the river Ticinus and fight another cavalry battle which will come to be known as the Battle of the Ticinus.

"Rome, having expected to fight in Spain and Africa, not on Italian soil will recall your father's colleague Tiberius Sempronius Longus, currently he is in Sicily planning to invade Africa, that will not happen.

"Things will not go well for either your father nor for Gnaeus after some initial successes in Spain, nor will things go at all well for Tiberius, but you will cover yourself with glory. There is so much more I can tell you. Ask yourself how I know the name and whereabouts of your father's co consul, watch what happens, keep me safe and keep me close, you will soon realise that I speak truly, that I am your greatest weapon and support. Hannibal will go down to defeat, but not soon, not at all soon."

"How will I cover myself in glory so rapidly then?"

"At the battle soon to come at the Ticinus your father will endeavour to keep you safe with a small group of cavalry to act as your bodyguard observing the battle. Your father will be wounded and surrounded, he will fall from his horse, those with you will think of their safety and yours, they will hold back. However, you will gallop to the consul's aid, the men with you will be shamed into following you, you will save your father's life an event that will shape your life in both war and politics. I will say no more, these things shall come to pass then take me as your counsellor and you will understand everything I promise."

CHAPTER 3 OCTOBER AND NOVEMBER 218BC

I could see both doubt and wonderment at the possibilities. The idea that he might eclipse the reputation and nobility of his scions was something most noble Romans espoused, if only in dreams and ambitions. Publius wanted to believe. This was the moment, it might never come again.

"Swear to protect my life, to be my friend and I will reveal to you how I know what I know."

"You ask a great deal as a prisoner!"

"Publius, there is more than your life and destiny at stake here. We have to do this now whist we are alone and whilst I have something to show you that will soon cease to function."

"Very well, I don't know why, but I have a feeling this is the right thing to do, they say Hannibal swore an oath of eternal enmity to Rome, if my swearing will lead to his fall it's a good bargain, you must first swear to Sancus, the God of good faith that what you tell me is true, I will swear to the same god to be your friend and protector, may either or both of us be made sacer, outcasts of all the gods should he prove false."

"I swear to Sancus that the testimony I give to you Publius Cornelius Scipio shall be the truth, the whole truth and nothing but the truth." He couldn't know that I'd lifted it!

"I swear to the ancient God Sancus to be the faithful friend and protector of, what is your name?"

"Mal... no, I needed a Roman name and then it occurred to me that if time were indeed circular, without beginning or end then this had already happened, more than once in all likelihood, didn't Livy or Polybius name a friend of Publius Cornelius Scipio Africanus, could that friend be me?

If I could only think of the name; if I used it and he responded that he already had a friend by that name I'd know it wasn't me, but if the moment passed unremarked it would be a sign, an almost certain sign that events would follow their intended path, that fate, deja vu, time were all linked somehow.

Had there been a first time when these things were decided? No time for philosophical, mental debate, what was that bloody name? Call me Laelius, it came in a flash."

"I swear to Sancus on penalty of being made sacer to all the gods and the ancestors that I will be a faithful friend and protector of Laelius for as long as we both shall live, that I will listen to his advice, trust in his honesty and weigh what he tells me in all my decisions.

"Good enough?"

"Good enough

"You'd better sit down, I have evidence that what I say is true and I have sworn."

I took the tablet out from inside my shirt and quickly took a photograph of him.

"What are you doing?"

"We're friends now, trust me."

I turned the tablet around to show him the picture.

"What is this?"

He started to rise.

"There's more" I said opening the Latin translator thank all the gods already downloaded.

"This is how I learn your words, this is my language, this yours."

I opened Polybius.

"This" I said, "is a history of ancient Rome."

"What do you mean ancient Rome?"

And so we came to it, life or death in all probability.

"I'm from the future Publius, this is from the future, more than two thousand years into the future. What is happening here, now to you is ancient history to me and luckily, for both of us, ancient history is my passion."

"You expect me to believe this?"

"My life depends upon it, why would I lie to you? Have you ever seen anything like this before? Did you see my ship? Have you ever seen its like? The knowledge I've already displayed, have you thought of a better explanation? It's true Publius, I am a visitor from the future, at least I hope I'm just a visitor."

"It's true I don't have a better explanation and this, this will be useful."

"It won't last Publius."

'Explaining electricity, batteries, satellites would be far too difficult' I thought.

'I need to explain the limitations without getting bogged down.'

I brought up a map of the world.

"This is a map of the world, in the future, in my time the tablet would show us our exact position at any time, already it is failing, it doesn't show our position. Soon it will fail completely, it's out of its time, it doesn't belong in this world."

I realised that I had a portable solar charger for such devices on board Francesca but there was no going back now.

"There are several books on here, but two are crucial."

I showed him how the pages turned.

"Two complete books written by your countrymen AFTER the war, a history of the war just now beginning. I've read them, Publius this is how I know what will happen, the events that will happen now. What happens to you.

"I have read them both twice over, but I cannot remember everything and in part the authors disagree on the exact sequence of events but I believe the important facts are all here. I need writing materials Publius, I need to make notes before my tablet dies and it will die soon."

"How did you get here? When will you return?"

"Publius, I don't know, I wish I did, the gods willed it, an accident, I don't know, I don't know if I can return to my own time, my world, my family, my daughter, my friends, I may be trapped here. I think I have to build a life here and what will be will be."

"I can get some wax tablets. How do you know it will die, just because it has travelled in time?"

"I know how it works Publius, it needs something from my time to maintain it, it will die and soon."

I didn't hold out the hope of the solar charger, we certainly wouldn't be going back anytime soon.

"Wax tablets I can get quickly and easily, I will bring some, make a start, I don't know what we may have aboard in the way of scrolls, paper, ink, but I will find out. Can you keep it alive until we reach Italy?"

"I'll try." I said turning it off to preserve the battery I'd make notes of the key points I could remember on the wax tablets at least and try to fill in the blanks on a book scroll if Publius could produce the goods in time.

"I will arouse less comment if I'm dressed in Roman clothes." I pointed out.

"That I can take care of right now. I'll return with clothes and tablets of my own immediately"

He said it with a conspiratorial grin. At least the Roman aristocrat has a sense of humour I thought with no small relief.

"Then I have to explain to my father that I believe you will be of use to me and that I want the responsibility. I will not reveal the oath or the truth of what you've told me though, he will think I'm mad simply for wanting to keep you close. You may have to be regarded as my slave, can you cope with that?"

"No" I answered honestly

"A free man can be a servant, counsellor, friend. A freed man will always be a former slave, my standing in Rome will matter to me. It's within my gift to help you become the greatest Roman of your age. I will not be known as a slave, you are my sworn friend, you must find a way."

We reached the Padus in the third week of October by my reckoning and I believed from my reading that Hannibal would very soon appear on the northern Italian plain. Had Scipio senior returned with his army instead of sending it on to Spain, then maybe the threat might have been nipped in the bud whilst Hannibal's greatly reduced, half starved army was in no fit state to fight.

Now, we had to locate the praetors, take over command and this meant moving east and north before marching west along the northern bank of the Padus river, the modern Po to meet Hannibal not far from where the Ticinus joins the larger river. I knew that battle would take place in late November and I started to prepare Publius junior.

In the interval I knew that Hannibal would rest his men, take the capital of the Taurini at what we now call Turin and that as a result he would also receive at least some supplies and tributes from other local tribes cowed by the fall of the Taurini capital. In short he would grow strong again. Furthermore the survivors of the alpine crossing were by definition the strongest, ablest and most determined warriors in the Carthaginian army.

Still, I didn't believe I was here to change the course of history and I was in no small way concerned to simply survive. My friend Publius had convinced his father to let him take care of the strange prisoner, I wasn't privy to the conversation, but Publius senior seemed to have lost interest in me, he had more important things on his mind, whilst my obvious good standing with Publius junior meant the few soldiers with us also left me largely to my own devices so long as they knew where I was.

One morning awaking from dreams I found myself looking around the room for a power socket to recharge my tablet, now down to twenty percent, before reality struck me forcefully.

The eighteen year old Publius proved to be as popular amongst his men as the young Hannibal had been amongst his soldiers, the same I thought as the young Alexander The Great in his time. That at least boded well for me.

I tried to stay close to my new friend other than when he spent time with his father, I didn't want to draw attention to myself from that quarter, nor did I want my friend's father asking him difficult questions about me, to fade into the background with everyone except young Publius and his immediate friends, that, despite the age difference, was my strategy for survival.

We marched across Etruria, the old Etruscan lands in a north easterly direction from Pisa towards Mutina, better known to me as Modena the home of Ferrari. All was not well in this region either although things were calm.

Roman colonies in the lands of the Boii at Placentia and Cremona had caused sufficient ill feeling that a revolt had occurred. The Roman legions opposing the Boii had been ambushed and retreated to Mutina. However, at the time we arrived there was an uneasy peace.

Publius senior relieved the praetors Lucius Manlius and Caius Attilius of command and marched his somewhat raw and somewhat dispirited army north west for Placentia, modern Piacenza where intelligence suggested we would find the camp of Hannibal.

In fact, having crossed the Padus at Placentia we needed to continue west along the north bank of the Padus river until, as I had advised Scipio the younger, we came to the tributary known as the Ticinus.

Hannibal was close now and the consul, as predicted, and without urging from his son, who was testing what I told him, decided to have his engineers throw a bridge over that river in order to advance to battle as swiftly as possible. Then, to bring the engagement on even more swiftly, he intended to take his proven and rapid cavalry, together with light armed javelin throwers ahead on reconnaissance, leaving the still raw legions who fought on foot with shield and sword in camp to the rear.

Scipio junior was clearly minded to question his father's decision, change the course of events and I made it clear to him that such a move was not credible in one of his age who had yet to see military action. I also suggested that I believed I had not been put in this place to change the course of history, it had already happened as far as I was concerned and who knew the consequences of any changes we might make.

In addition I pointed out that his father's time was not yet at hand, that we knew the outcome already. An outcome which would raise my friend's standing, an outcome which, if he did want to meddle with history, the gods and the universe would be more likely to succeed once he became a war hero. The Romans do love a war hero I suggested, he agreed with that anyway.

I had been given a horse and I accompanied the younger Scipio, but without shield, armour or weapon. I was amazed at the way the Roman's took 'throwing' a bridge across a river as a given, nothing remarkable, neither Livy, nor Polybius had made a big thing of it either.

The consul's light armed infantry, the velites could be relied on to move rapidly with us, but they were skirmishers, facing Carthaginian cavalry in a major engagement, could they be relied on in such a battle? Naturally I knew the answer, I felt for them.

As predicted young Scipio was assigned a small troop of cavalry, effectively a mounted bodyguard and we were placed where we could observe, on a small hill to the rear, from which place we could also escape if such need arose. The consul was, as we would say in my time, a belt and braces man in that regard although he had considerable confidence regarding the outcome, largely based on his experience in Gaul, confidence which was, I knew, misplaced.

Hannibal also faced us with a force which was largely cavalry, also supported by light armed foot soldiers, the most notable difference being that they outnumbered us substantially. The ancient sources say two to one and I could believe it. Numbers meant little to Romans, even at this relatively early stage in Roman history they could and had defeated far larger forces through superior discipline and often superior equipment. Unfortunately, I knew this was the cream of the Carthaginian army, experienced, hardened by their alpine crossing and buoyed by recent success. For all I knew we'd survive, I shuddered.

The consul had become aware of the Carthaginian force before he saw it due to the dust kicked up by the horses. He had stopped and chosen his ground knowing that Hannibal would come on. So far, so good. He was however overconfident after his cavalry success at the Rhone. He placed the javelin throwers front and centre ahead of his Gallic cavalry in squadrons with passage ways for the velites to retire behind the cavalry having discharged their missiles. He anticipated skirmishes to start the battle a cautious testing. What was to come was anything but.

Behind the Gallic cavalry the consul based himself with his Roman cavalry, the cream of which formed his bodyguard and around them were some allied cavalry, Italian but not Roman.

Hannibal too had a mixture of troops and even though he outnumbered us this was not his complete force. In his centre he placed Spanish cavalry, men whose horses had bridles, on both wings were his Numidian cavalry with simpler harnesses, but men who had been on horseback most of their lives.

The anticipated testing skirmishes failed to materialise, many Roman cavalrymen had velites riding behind them whilst those who had moved to the front were overawed by the heavy cavalry charge bearing down on them at speed, Hannibal was in no mood for caution, especially given his numerical advantage.

A handful of our velites discharged their weapons to little or no effect. The Roman cavalry tried to move to the attack but with their own velites falling back between them and some still hampered by passengers so to speak they could not move in a coordinated fashion and certainly could not achieve any sort of a coordinated charge.

The Romans' horses were as confused and panicked as their riders, many Roman cavalrymen and all their passengers dismounted to fight on foot, but with each Roman cavalryman deciding for himself whether to fight on foot or in the saddle chaos ensued. Nonetheless, the battle ground on in a kind of stalemate, probably for about an hour, maybe more but like a gripping movie time passed unnoticed like the Numidian cavalry moving around the wings to threaten the Roman rear.

Soon they were attacking the Roman and allied reserve around the consul, we saw Scipio's bodyguard form a ring around him and we saw him fall from his horse, since no Carthaginian had been close enough to land a sword blow we knew he must have been struck by some sort of missile. I looked to Publius, he looked to the commander of his bodyguard who shook his head, Publius spurred his horse, the keenest of his men followed hot on his horses hooves and soon the entire troop was streaming down the low hill towards the embattled consul.

Their charge out of the blue, at a full gallop threw the Numidians into confusion long enough to rescue the consul and for most of the Romans and allied cavalry to escape, the Gaulish cavalry were soon fleeing too, those who had lost their horses after dismounting and nearly all the velites were slaughtered. The Carthaginian pursuit was thankfully half hearted, they stopped to finish off the Roman forces left on the field and to take equipment.

I imagine they thought they would finish us soon enough although Hannibal must have realised that most of our infantry were still in camp, it became apparent later that Hannibal still anticipated a larger battle with the infantry of both armies coming to blows.

What we came to regard as the first battle of the Second Punic War, Hannibal regarded as nothing more than a major skirmish. The wounded and humbled consul needed to think and reorder his forces. He had, had confidence in his cavalry, he had less confidence in his raw dispirited infantry. A pitched battle of a more conventional nature was not on his agenda for now.

Quite naturally Publius was concerned for his father and gave no thought to me, had I wanted to I could quite easily have escaped, or even tried going over to Hannibal, the idea of meeting that great general tempted me for no more than a second or two. He was unpredictable and although history is written by the victors, quite likely of a cruel disposition, certainly a ruthless one.

I rode with the tired, bloodied crowd of men, bitter at their defeat, grateful to be alive, worried for the future, anxious to make the relative safety of the camp. A camp which offered some small protection with the infantry still fresh, but untested and men who would be shocked and dismayed to see a much reduced force and a wounded consul return. Morale even among those, as yet unaffected soldiers would be an issue. In reality our retreat was only just beginning.

We were in camp scant hours, the camp was west of the Ticinus, by retiring quietly in the night we could possibly cross the bridge of boats and cut the bridge away to delay pursuit. This plan was put into effect and our destination was given out as the army base at Placentia on the west bank of the Trebia, opposite the town of Placentia, south of the Padus River.

The idea of telling the men was so that they could find their way back if separated or delayed and in fact, so well constructed was our pontoon bridge that some six hundred men were left behind as a rearguard to destroy the bridge as we continued. Some were engineers, others were there to protect the engineers whilst they did their work.

That force would succeed in its tactical objective, but all of the six hundred were doomed to death or slavery. Having made camp at Placentia, Publius sought me out.

"I've never seen my father so dispirited."

"Nonetheless, he will recover in mind as well as body thanks to you, the men are impressed too, everywhere you are on everyone's lips, your rise starts here. Your father will award you the Corona Civica, you will not accept it stating that the survival of the consul is its own reward.

"A war hero is greatly admired, a modest war hero is even more greatly admired."

Hannibal will have learned of our plans from the men captured at the bridge on the Ticinus, he'd not baulk at torture and someone at least in the six hundred would talk. Knowing that we would be south of the Padus and wishing to cross that mighty river unmolested Hannibal would actually march west in search of a place where his engineers could construct a bridge. We would have a few days respite, for the consul to begin to heal and make his plans.

Word reached us that the co consul Tiberius had been recalled from Sicily and was on his way north with his legions. Like all Roman commanders he had absolute belief in his own abilities, Roman superiority and he wanted all the glory of defeating Hannibal for himself. The Achilles heel of the Romans at war. Tiberius would arrive in weeks however, not days.

Soon Hannibal arrived again, having marched swiftly eastwards along the southern bank of the Padus he made camp a few miles away, paraded his full army and offered battle. Scipio declined to leave camp and that night a couple of thousand of the Gauls with us slaughtered the guards, took their heads and went over to Hannibal.

Hannibal naturally would reward them and send them out to recruit more Gauls to his cause. I knew this of course, I hadn't issued a warning because I didn't believe I should materially alter the course of history. I didn't know why exactly, I just felt it was important, even in the details. With our cavalry depleted, our morale low and our infantry untested we did the only sensible thing, although it stung and hurt morale still further. We slunk away once more that night.

Realising that we would be vulnerable to Hannibal's cavalry on the open plains we crossed the river to the eastern bank and then headed south along the Trebia, until we reached high ground unsuited to cavalry and chose a place to build a proper Roman marching fort with ditches and spikes, palisades and ramparts.

Our site provided us with a water source in the form of a clear fresh stream, drinking water upstream, latrines downstream. We lost some stragglers and were lucky that Hannibal's Numidian cavalry did not catch the main body. We learned later they had delayed to look for spoils in the camp we had deserted.

The fort was rectangular and entirely wooden, the men slept in tents within it, the consul's quarters were at the centre. Since we were not under attack virtually all the soldiers were put to work in the construction or gathering wood, although many of the materials needed had travelled with us. The fort went up in an unbelievably short time, just hours, although, partly to keep the men occupied and fit, improvements were made daily, for some days.

We had water, food had to be rationed and foraging parties were sent out but life began to take on a routine which was of itself reassuring. The badly wounded had either died or been left behind, those with less severe wounds were healing and regaining their strength. Men who had distinguished themselves received awards and Publius modestly and very publicly declined to accept his decoration endearing him even more to the men than before.

CHAPTER 4 THE BATTLE OF THE TREBIA DECEMBER 218 BC

Tiberius Sempronius Longus together with his consular army arrived in mid December, not the ideal time of year for warfare and not a time of year when the Romans normally chose to campaign. This was different though, now the war was in Italy and one consul had already been defeated and wounded.

Tiberius had relocated his army from Sicily in the far south to our camp in the far north in something around forty days, a not inconsiderable achievement in its own right. His men, on the whole, had not been under the standards long, but nor had they suffered the humiliation and confusion of defeat. The mood in the hastily enlarged camp grew more optimistic, only I knew what would follow.

Tiberius had transported a part of his army part of the way by sea, but lacking sufficient transports to do the entire job and perhaps not trusting everything to the vagaries of the sea in winter he had marched one body of troops past Rome in person. This was a break with convention, but seeing a Roman army march north in good order, combined with the Roman belief that their infantry were close to invincible had lifted spirits in a city mourning the loss of pride it had suffered at the Ticinus.

Other troops were left to find their own way to the rallying point Tiberius had chosen at Ariminum. Rimini on the east coast of northern Italy to you and me. Tiberius, believing that men in small groups could move swiftly and sustain themselves more easily, living off the land, or more likely receiving help from Roman farmers along the way, farmers who would happily help a dozen men but would be less inclined to feed a hundred at a time, had made his men swear an oath to meet him at Ariminum in a month. This meant marching more than thirty kilometres a day every day, but his men achieved it and many seemed to have enjoyed it. Most arrived fit and well.

From Ariminum they still had a march of around three hundred kilometres to our camp. If good judgement and organisational abilities are key to good generalling then Tiberius was doing well, so far. His eagerness to fight and claim the glory was no different from that of any other Roman magistrate.

Hannibal had been reinforced by Gaulish warriors, but a few had approached us too. The Gauls were comprised of many tribes, only Vercingetorix would succeed in uniting them but that was in Caesar's time, still way off in the future.

We took some of them in, but not too many, the duplicity of the Gauls who had killed our guards, beheaded them and taken their heads to Hannibal was far from forgotten. I realised that already I was thinking in terms of 'them' and 'us', but I was still intent on the idea that I had no place meddling in history, rather that I already had a role in that history and it must pan out as it should.

Hannibal was also cautious in his relations with the Gauls, the tribes were fickle and his scouts had reported Gauls visiting our camp. Shortly after Tiberius arrived Hannibal sent a force of some two thousand odd infantry and about a thousand Gallic and Numidian Cavalry to plunder the possessions of the Gauls he suspected of favouring us, who were living in the plains across the river from our camp, that is to the west and slightly north. They duly applied to us for assistance and Tiberius was only too happy to oblige them with a test fight against the famed Carthaginians.

Tiberius sent out a large cavalry force supported by around a thousand velites many riding two up. The Trebia was not yet swollen and was still easy to ford. The raiders were encumbered with plunder and divided into groups, they soon started to lose men and fall back. Our men chased them with enthusiasm but as they approached the Carthaginian camp they met more serious opposition and stalled.

Both sides now sent out reinforcements, but Hannibal did not want an unplanned battle he could not control and with men on horses as well as on foot the fight was fluid, complicated and different skirmishes were having different outcomes.

Hannibal formed up a line close to his camp, a line which could be defended by missiles from his camp on the higher ground behind it. Our men quite rightly feared to approach this line but each group of Carthaginians who got back close were taken in. Hannibal prevented any counter attack or sallies by his side with an iron discipline.

Enough of the surprised raiders had been killed for Tiberius to claim this minor event as a victory, proof of Roman superiority and so forth. I closeted myself with my new friend Scipio and told him I would reveal the course events would take, if he promised not to interfere, but to learn.

I told him that not only would the next battle be disastrous for Rome, but that more disasters would follow too. Even greater ones. It would be hard, very hard not to interfere. However, I promised him his time would come.

"Rome will not give you the command yet, nor are you equipped for command yet, it's only by watching, waiting, learning, growing, and developing a political following of your own in Rome that you can win this war. You will do it but this war will last for years."

"How many years?"

"Do you really want to know? Too much information at once might be overwhelming and disheartening, be assured we will win..."

"We!"

"Oh yes, I'm Roman now in corde meo certe.

"Let us concentrate on what will happen here, it will be grim but if you have any doubts left whatsoever about my information this will put them away."

I explained that Hannibal was already reconnoitring the plains in order to set up an ambush. Scipio countered that an ambush is not possible on an open plain and that the topography favoured the Roman infantry and the Roman modus operandi.

"Yes and Tiberius will think as you do, but he hasn't reconnoitred the plain, Hannibal has, Hannibal doesn't work on assumptions and nor will you when your time comes."

I offered to explain where and how the ambush would take place but only on condition that he must not pass the information on. It was an easy promise to make, given no one would take him seriously yet anyhow. I revealed that Hannibal had found a stream flowing across the plain, a stream that had cut a defile and the water had caused trees and bushes to grow sufficient to hide a large force under the command of Mago, Hannibal's trusted youngest brother, behind the Roman lines.

Scipio raised more logical objections.

"He would have to station them there unseen and he would have to know the date and location of the battle in advance."

"That's very true, he will determine both of those things himself. He knows how to bring Tiberius out of camp now and how to lead him to the place of his own choosing at a time of his own choosing."

I explained that the day would be cold and sleeting, the daylight short and that Mago with a picked force of a thousand cavalry and a thousand infantry would hide in the wooded valley the night before. In the morning the Carthaginian cavalry would break fast early and then attack our guards and lookouts with missiles.

"Tiberius will respond exactly as Hannibal wishes him to, he will lead his men out before they have broken their fast, the river can still be forded, but the levels are rising, our men will be cold, wet and hungry and marching through the sleet.

"Hannibal's cavalry will skirmish and retreat, skirmish and retreat over and over, we will follow to a place of Hannibal's choosing, leaving Mago and his forces in our rear, undiscovered. Whilst Hannibal's cavalry play games with us, his troops will be warm in camp by their fires filling their bellies with hot food.

"A large body of inexperienced troops like ours will take a long time to form up in their battle formation, they will be tired of the whole exercise, their officers will become frustrated and angry. Hannibal will let them take their time, the longer it takes, the colder they will become.

"Tiberius will be very happy at this point, believing he's done well to prepare his army so thoroughly and thinking that the tardy appearance of Hannibal represents uncertainty in the mind of his enemy, not that he and his men are warm, comfortable, fed and ready to attack without a long, cold, tedious march through the sleet and snow in soaking garments.

"When Hannibal does come out our men will do surprisingly well, but our system doesn't work so well when attacked from the rear. Ordinarily cavalry should protect the wings, but Hannibal will have men and cavalry behind us already.

"Furthermore we will have just two thousand horse on each wing and our missiles will have been largely spent in the early skirmishes, Hannibal will have hoarded missiles, and he has his lethal Ballearic slingers with a great store of projectiles, our cavalry will not acquit themselves well, but they will in fairness be in an untenable position.

Their horses made all the more nervous by the smell and sight of the elephants, strange to them, but not to the Numidian horse, with which Hannibal will also reinforce his wings. It is on the wings and then in the rear that the battle will be lost to us.

"Tiberius and ten thousand of our best Roman troops will actually cut through Hannibal's centre, mostly Celts, but stiffened by a troop of his Libyans, the rest of whom will face our allies on the wings. This small victory in the centre will be a remarkable feat of arms under these conditions, however all the rest of the army will be lost, all of them."

"You are telling me we will lose more than thirty thousand men in one day!"

"I'm afraid so, a few of our cavalrymen will get away as well as the ten thousand, not our finest and bravest equites though. The ten thousand will be Roman; allied infantry will suffer the most, recruiting more may prove difficult in future and after this defeat yet more Gauls will flock to Hannibal.

"You must understand why this war will last for many years. Hannibal may be a military genius, but you Scipio will defeat him, in a very real sense you already have, but there is unimaginable pain to endure first. I wonder if the universe sent me here to keep you on your true path."

"We cannot afford such losses."

"I don't think it's wise of me to reveal everything, you may lose heart, there's worse to come, much, much worse, but understand this, the Romans are true warriors..."

"And Hannibal isn't!"

He interjected forcefully, but I continued in a measured tone.

"He is, so are his brothers, but not all Carthaginians are, they regard war as a business, the numbers have to add up. They are not like Romans, ultimately you and Rome will learn how to fight Hannibal, ultimately his own people will let him down, but that time is not yet. Not by a long way.

"Have faith in your people. Rome will be the master of the world for an age, Rome is still in the ascendency, like you Rome is a youth, full of vigour and ambition. Carthage has been a great power for a while now. This war will be the making of us, the beginning of the end for them, but first the pain, Rome will be tested and forged in the flames of this war. Two great generals will be remembered, Hannibal and the man who defeats him, that's you my friend."

Of course events fell out as I predicted. There was much tearing of hair and clothes in Rome apparently, but not immediately Tiberius sent word, but minimised the size of the disaster, downplayed his own rash actions and the extent of our losses. Claimed the action was inconclusive and that the weather had prevented him from taking outright victory. The truth would out.

Having broken through Hannibal's centre Tiberius and his ten thousand made no attempt to rejoin the fighting, the wings of the Roman army had collapsed first, although not until after stiff resistance against the major part of Hannibal's crack Libyans and the Ballearic slingers, cavalry and elephants.

It's easy to forget in the misery of defeat how well those cold, hungry men fought. It's doubtful that Tiberius could have turned the battle by wheeling his ten thousand and rejoining the fight, our infantry outnumbered Hannibal's infantry and despite the cold were probably better disciplined, They were certainly better equipped, but what ifs don't change anything.

Tiberius and his men re forded the Trebia and made base back in Placentia, leaving the rest, mostly our Italian allies, to their bloody fate. Some survivors turned up at our camp later. Hannibal's Gauls and the one troop of Libyans in the centre had sustained heavy losses against our legionaries and Hannibal did not push his luck by chasing Tiberius.

We were in no position to know Hannibal's losses, I believe they were significant, but Mago had left the result of the battle in no doubt I believe and Tiberius's men had already done a superhuman job without trying to fight on.

The loss of so many allies weakened our army and our standing, the victory for Hannibal, the signal it sent about his strength, his genius and our weakness swiftly replenished his losses, whatever those losses may have been on that fateful winter solstice. Hannibal's army would soon be sixty thousand strong. Warriors flocked to join him and to revel in Rome's anticipated downfall.

CHAPTER 5 AFTER THE TREBIA, SATURNALIA AND THE END OF 218BC

Whilst Hannibal's army rested and recuperated following the exertion of battle Scipio senior ordered the retreat of those of us remaining in his camp. We went first to Placentia and thence on to Cremona in order to spread the burden of feeding the remaining parts of the two consular armies, through the winter, between the two colonies.

Winter in the ancient world was not considered to be the season for warfare, but Hannibal's cavalry ranged far and wide in northern Italy, terrorising the people and seizing supplies. We were able to defend the magazine near Placentia, but that at Victumviae surrendered after initial resistance and was duly plundered and sacked as though it had been taken by storm not by agreement.

Tiberius, to his credit, braved the journey to Rome despite the risk of capture by Carthaginian cavalry and organised the elections. The new consuls for 217BC 537 would be Cneius Servilius Geminus and Caius Flaminius. In the case of Flaminius this would be his second consulship, a rare event indeed. Tiberius returned then to winter quarters at Placentia.

The new consuls would take over at the start of the year, auguries would be taken on New Year's Day, each consul elect would sacrifice a garlanded and drugged pure white bull, sacred rites would be performed within the temple of Jupiter Optimus Maximus, Jupiter, greatest and best, Rome's most important god; oaths would be taken and a great feast would be held.

Each new consul was to be given a consular army and the recruiters were hard at work. The consular armies would comprise two Roman legions of four thousand two hundred infantry and three hundred equites or cavalry. Each would also have two alae, an ala being in effect a legion of socii, in other words Italian allies. The ala at this time was not a small cavalry unit as in the imperial period, it was in effect another legion, in fact larger than a Roman citizen legion, it could contain as many as four thousand five hundred allied infantry, each man equipped with the same weapons and armour as a Roman legionary plus an Ala fielded nine hundred cavalry in support.

Thus the consular army of Caius Flaminius comprised eight thousand four hundred Roman legionaries and nine thousand allied legionaries that is seventeen thousand four hundred infantry in total plus two thousand four hundred equites, nineteen thousand eight hundred men in total. For reasons not shared with young Scipio or myself, the army of Cneius Servilius Geminus had an extra one thousand six hundred cavalry, giving him an army of twenty one thousand four hundred men.

Total Roman military strength excluding the remnants in the north and the army in Spain then totalled thirty four thousand eight hundred foot soldiers, six thousand four hundred cavalry, a total of forty one thousand two hundred men at arms for the defence of Italy, split not quite equally between two commanders. The recruiters had done well. Roman allies, especially those further south, who had only long range news reports, not always accurate, had responded well.

Hannibal meanwhile had an army which had grown to something like sixty thousand, twenty thousand of whom were really crack troops, experienced, confident and victorious. To see the new consular armies would fill anyone with confidence and pride but were either of those Roman armies of roughly twenty thousand to come on Hannibal's sixty thousand individually.....

Whilst these events were taking place in Italy, let's not forget that my friend's uncle had sailed to Spain with the original army of Publius Cornelius Scipio, my friend's father. Gnaeus Scipio had landed initially at the port of Emporiae, a little to the north east of modern Barcelona. The Carthaginian forces closest to him were commanded by the Carthaginian general Hanno, who had remained on the Iberian side of the Pyrenees. It's hard to know how much information each commander had received.

Gnaeus was shrewd and had formed alliances, as well as using force where necessary, to start securing the coastal regions. Hanno would have been wise to join up with Hasdrubal, his supreme commander based in New Carthage before offering battle, but instead chose to fight and went down to defeat. Gnaeus continued to Tarraco, modern Tarragona, where Hasdrubal arrived too late to defend the city and duly retreated back to New Carthage.

Gnaeus had not only won the first battle of the war in Spain, but he had also succeeded in recruiting from some of the Spanish tribes and had cut off communication links and potential supply lines between Hasdrubal and his brother Hannibal in Italy.

Publius Cornelius Scipio, consul until the end of the year when he would become proconsul, continued to recover both physically and mentally from his disastrous year in office. My friend and I prepared to spend a delayed Saturnalia in Cremona whilst awaiting the consul or proconsul's next move, depending on his title when he made a decision, or when Rome instructed him and depending also on what news came from Spain. News which when it did come would finally give everyone a lift.

The battle of the Trebia had caused no thought to be given to the Saturnalia celebrations which would normally take place on the solstice, but the consul and others around him felt the festival should not be abandoned in case it angered the god Saturn in whose honour it was held. There were also those who equated the Carthaginian god Ba'al Hammon with Saturn and wondered if the god had not shown favour to our enemies. Better to appease the god and bring him back to our side.

Then there were those who just needed the release after all that had taken place, a day to drink, forget rank, party and put recent tragedies and losses out of mind. December 25th was chosen. I took part but endeavoured to appear to drink more than I actually did, I had no desire to lose my self control or get carried away with loose talk, only young Scipio need know what I knew and even him I intended to drip feed.

Before the feast a bare headed priest had officiated at the sacrifice, we had no statue of the god to unbind, but in most ways the rites were observed. Gifts were exchanged, Publius gave me a hunting knife, a gift of some value.

I pointed out to him that I had nothing to offer, even the clothes I stood up in were courtesy of him. Publius laughed and told me that the lower the value of the gift the higher the esteem in which the recipient was held, so no gift at all must mean I held him in very great esteem indeed.

"However" he continued "We must do something about your position here, I can give you some money surreptitiously, but if you are paid by me openly you will always be seen as my servant rather than my friend or colleague. You cannot become a citizen easily, but in time I may be able to help there. Although the cursus honorum will probably never be an option.

"In the meantime I will talk with my father about putting you on the army payroll, You may be able to save some money with the legionary bankers, more importantly if I can persuade pater that you should have some rank, even if only an honorary rank then you will be entitled to a share in any spoils given to the men and officers. That may prove valuable when we turn the tide.

"If you can save enough you may one day be able to buy land and land is a prerequisite to any kind of position in society. You will need my patronage for many years if you are to establish yourself."

I assured him that he would need my counsel for many years too, that this was just year one of a great war, and I added, there will be a third and final war with Carthage even so.

It was ironic that the long string of defeats of the Second Punic War would occasion a number of religious changes within Rome, from fear, superstition, loss of confidence and the perceived need to appease any and all gods who might be displeased, for there had to be some explanation for the continuing disasters.

At Saturnalia everyone was considered equal, even slaves, although no one was brave enough to pretend equality with Scipio senior. Young Scipio was selected as the King of Saturnalia, a peculiar kind of honour, not least because of Romans' abhorrence of the title Rex, or King. The King of Saturnalia was something else however, in a way it made young Scipio the master of ceremonies, which despite the supposed equality of all meant he could give humorous or embarrassing instructions to guests which they would have to carry out, to the merriment of everyone else.

I would have preferred to keep a low profile, but as the friend and confidant of young Scipio I was to be beside him at the feast. Which in fact, if I did nothing to disgrace myself would also mean that social acceptance of me would grow too. The event was a universally male one, I supposed life in the armies of Rome was almost universally male all the time, although if an army remained in one place long enough camp followers would be sure to appear.

When towns were sacked soldiers would take women and do as they would with them. In non military households from those of tradespeople, to patrician or wealthy plebeian homes women did play a major role in the family, some indeed wielded a degree of power or influence, but Roman law favoured men.

Women could be married off to forge political alliances, some would love, or grow to love, their husbands and be loved in return, for others marriage was a form of servitude. The husband and father was the paterfamilias and his word was effectively law within the family, even to the point that technically he could execute his wife.

That didn't happen in reality, but in law the paterfamilias had absolute power, some exercised it wisely others had no awareness of the feelings of wives, or indeed of their own children. Possibly the wife of a common butcher, baker, shopkeeper had the most freedom in practice, or perhaps even the practitioners of the world's oldest profession.

With the army in town the wives of the men of Cremona, like me, kept a low profile although the taverns did a good trade, as did the women to be found in the taverns. I found myself missing female company and the greater equality of my own times.

There was little to be done about it for now. I considered carousing in town with the men, but doubted it would end well if I did. For all that I missed conversation with women, probably as much as the physical contact I was still struggling to converse at all. I knew I must concentrate on learning and wait to discuss anything of a personal matter with Scipio until the bond was stronger.

In the modern world I'd been divorced, so fidelity to a twenty first century wife didn't play a part in my thinking and technically if I formed any relationship with a Roman woman it would certainly predate any relationship I'd had in the modern world! In addition if I married whilst here, by definition I'd be a widower if I ever found my way back, not that anyone would know.

In many ways it was good that Scipio was universally acclaimed by the men as the king of Saturnalia, ordinarily lots would have been drawn, the clamour for Scipio reinforced the affection and now growing esteem with which he was viewed. At the Ticinus he had saved the consul's life, then declined to be honoured, at the Trebia he had fought shoulder to shoulder with the Roman legions in the centre, the only place on the battlefield where Roman arms proved superior to those of the enemy.

He had learned how a disciplined force can cut its way through even the worst situation if the men hold together and fight as one cohesive unit employing the tried and tested techniques of the Roman army. Stepping, thrusting with the enormous shields, pushing the enemy back, crushing and compressing them, restricting them, holding the line precisely and stabbing forwards between the shields with those deadly swords before heaving themselves forwards over the bodies once more.

It was bloody and tiring, but effective, the greatest danger when the front rank exchanged places with the second rank to effectively take a breather. The hastati and principes formed the two front ranks once the skirmishers had retired, they might exchange places several times if necessary or the third rank the triarii could be brought into play at the front, unless the enemy got around behind, which was not supposed to happen!

In the normal course of events the legions anticipated a victory without need of the third rank, the principes in the second rank being the finest soldiers in each legion. Trebia though had been a long drawn out, hard slog, every man had seen action, had had to kill or be killed. In the case of the allies, most had been killed.

Of course the Romans in the centre hadn't faced the slingers, cavalry or elephants, but nonetheless their achievement gave everyone hope and Publius Cornelius minor had been a part of it, not just a credit to himself, but increasingly a Roman warrior with an understanding of the vagaries and difficulties of warfare. A leader in the making.

On the last day of December news came from Spain, good news Gnaeus had established himself in the coastal area down to Tarraco, he had defeated Hanno at the battle of Cissa killing six thousand Carthaginian troops and capturing another two thousand including the general.

He had won glory for himself and his men, now blooded, were victorious and confident. In Hanno's camp he found much of the Carthaginian wealth in Spain that which had been plundered from the Spanish tribes. He had options now, to be generous to his men, to send plunder to Rome, or to use it to win the tribes to his side.

Better yet, in a way, Hasdrubal, the brother of Hannibal had not yet been defeated, there was still an opportunity for redemption, if not glory, for Publius Cornelius Scipio Senior and those close to him. On his last day in office Publius announced his desire to depart for Iberia, Hispania as we knew it, and join with his brother Gnaeus.

I had no way of knowing if he had secretly messaged his supporters and relatives in Rome concerning this decision, but soon good news arrived from that quarter too. Publius Cornelius Scipio was appointed proconsul in Spain and was to receive reinforcements to take with him before departing. That Rome could create two new consular armies and reinforce us was nothing short of a miracle of organisation.

The defeat of Carthage in Iberia would eliminate any chance of resupply for Hannibal from that quarter, might well divide opinion in Carthage, shake Carthaginian confidence and self belief, in short turn the tide, whilst the defence of Italy was now the province of two new consuls with two shiny new armies.

I alone knew that it would not happen in that way. I kept both my thoughts and the knowledge I held to myself, kept my own counsel for now.

CHAPTER 6 SPAIN AND ITALY LAKE TRASIMENE 217BC

Hasdrubal, like his brother Hannibal was no respecter of the convention that campaigning was only for summer. Bringing up eight thousand infantry as well as a thousand horse he attacked the Roman fleet anchored at the mouth of the Iberus River, the Ebro that once, and not so long ago, had been the contentious border between Carthaginian and Roman influence.

Roman success under Gnaeus had led to a relaxation of standards amongst some ships' captains and some mariners were caught ashore and killed. Gnaeus, hearing of the attack, brought up his forces and Hasdrubal retired. Nonetheless the Roman fleet also retired back to Emporiae to prevent further losses. Having garrisoned Tarraco, Gnaeus, with the larger part of his forces, pulled back to Emporiae with the fleet also.

With Gnaeus having made winter quarters Hasdrubal again came out and instigated a revolt of our new allies the tribe of the Ilergetes, notwithstanding the hostages given into the care of the Romans. Together with the aid of the Ilergetes our more faithful allies found themselves being raided and plundered. It would be a winter without much peace.

Gnaeus would succeed in capturing the capital of the Ilergetes and taking much silver before re-admitting them back into alliance, he would also besiege the Ausetani for some weeks despite the deep snow.

Eventually that too was successful, as were other Roman attacks against Hasdrubal's allies such as the Lacetani who had endeavoured to raise our siege upon their neighbours. Finally Gnaeus and his forces were able to return to the relative warmth of winter quarters for some rest.

Meanwhile in Rome and much of Italy many signs were interpreted with pessimism, sacrifices were made, statues dedicated, oaths taken to calm the gods or win them over. I alone knew that this was the start of Hannibal becoming the Roman bogeyman, the great superstitious fear for Romans and their children for generations to come. Even once defeated he would become the monster hiding under the bed to Rome's little ones, even long after his death.

The remainder of the army at Placentia had fallen to Flaminius by lot and he instructed that it should meet him at Ariminum to unite with his forces on the ides of March. I reflected that in many years to come the ides of March would become famous for other reasons to do with Rome.

Flaminius departed in secret for his province, having made himself somewhat unpopular amongst his peers by supporting a new law put forward by a tribune of the plebs named Quintus Claudius. This new law limited the size of merchant ship a senator might own for the transportation of his own produce. It being already required that senators income be derived from their land, not from trade which was frowned upon and the province of lesser men.

Senators nonetheless did not like any laws which might in any sense impede their ability to grow their wealth. Although not greatly supported the plebs enacted the law.

Rumours were started that the auspices had not been correctly taken at the inauguration of Flaminius, superstition and gossip boded ill. 217 BC or the year 537, being the year of the consulship of Geminus and Flaminius as we knew it was off to a shaky start.

There was always tension between the plebs, many of whom were in every sense noble Romans, and the patricians, almost exclusively considered noblemen. This however was different; men believed that not only had Falminius waged war on the senate, something approved of in varying degrees, but that he had also waged war on, or at the very least, shunned, Rome's gods!

It was decided in Rome that Flaminius having slunk away must be recalled. He was caught up with at a sacrifice where the victim's blood had been scattered about and the whole affair constituted yet another bad omen. Despite all the political and religious machinations, of which there were more than I recount here, Flaminius received two legions from Sempronius, the former consul and two from the praetor Caius Atilius.

This army then proceeded on its way, through the Appennine mountains without the new consul returning to Rome to officiate at the Latin Festival as convention obliged and as the embassy had instructed.

Knowing that Gnaeus Cornelius Scipio would win a naval engagement against Hasdrubal, before Publius arrived, which would lighten the load and improve the mood in Italy, I decided that the time to reveal the fresh disaster about to befall Rome at Hannibal's hands in Italy was now. I also had to ensure that my friend was not tempted to leave for Spain with his father.

For Scipio, the future Scipio Africanus, conqueror of Africa to fulfil his destiny he would have to become a consummate politician as well as a brilliant general.

"We must stay in Italy". I told young Scipio.

"I was wondering about the right course of action, the temptation to go with my father, to fight alongside him and my uncle once more is considerable, but I had a foreboding about this moment."

"Each of us has a destiny Scipio. Your father's destiny and that of his brother lies in Spain. My destiny is to be forgotten" I whispered to myself.

"Whilst your destiny is to defeat Hannibal, conquer North Africa and be remembered for all time!

"In order to do that you must climb the cursus honorum, only as an elected official can you command the armies you will need and to achieve your destiny as it is written, you will need to achieve high office, in advance of the traditional age too.

"You will face opposition in certain quarters, Rome is political intrigue and political intrigue is Rome. You must gain followers, adherents, clients, make familial alliances, it's the way Rome operates. Furthermore you must do it now whilst your military reputation is strong in people's memories, they have much else to think about, what happened last year will soon count for less than it does right now.

"Your father and Uncle will send some good news from Spain, for now at least, but things will fall out badly for Flaminius and Geminus"

"I wondered when you were going to tell me, you don't yet trust me not to interfere do you?"

"It's not that, there will be fresh disasters here in Italy, next year too. I'd prefer you had some good news to temper the bad at least. You will fight in the greatest defeat Rome will suffer from the time of Brennus and the battle at the Allia."

"Jupiter and Mars, is that the good news to temper the bad! You bring me continual pain, perhaps I should cast you off."

"Hear me out Scipio, hear me out. There will be another huge defeat at a place called Arausio more than a hundred years from now, but Rome will come back from that as well, as she did from Brennus and will from Cannae."

"Cannae?"

"The greatest battle of this war, barring your eventual victory, will take place in Apulia in the south, it will be Hannibal's finest hour and Rome's darkest moment in more than a generation, that will happen next year, in the year 538 as you know it, which will be the year of the consuls Caius Terrentius Varro and Lucius Aemilius Paullus. However, it will be the high water mark of Hannibal's achievements. Roman losses are reckoned at anything between twenty thousand dead and eighty thousand."

"Eighty thousand is just not possible"

"For me it's not just possible, it has happened. This battle has been studied, discussed and held up as a lesson for military students for two thousand years by my own time. You must be ready to play your part, which will again allow what glory can be achieved to fall on you.

"Looking at the figures for those who returned to the standards I think personally that Roman losses could be around seventy thousand, most, but not all dead, that includes those too maimed to ever fight again, some allies who will survive but escape and slink home vowing never to fight for Rome again and those sold into slavery.

"You should know that the dead will include a consul in office, many consulars and perhaps fifty men of senatorial rank, that there will be hardly a family in Rome untouched and not mourning. Rome will sink to its lowest ebb, there are even suggestions in ancient writings of human sacrifice to appease the gods.

"Rome will decide not to ransom several thousands of survivors despite an offer from Hannibal. You must not be in that group! The feeling in Rome is that the cost of the ransom will enable Hannibal to pay his soldiers and that men who've surrendered and not worth ransoming.

"My personal view is that Rome needs experienced soldiers, that many who surrendered had little choice in the matter and that the sale of slaves will help fill the Carthaginian's coffers anyway.

"Nonetheless, that is how it happens and we should seek to change nothing, maybe the senators were right. That's not our concern. Our concerns are with your destiny, political success at an early age, that you should survive the battle and famously rally a band of survivors, including a group of young noblemen minded to escape the country and offer their services to a foreign king!"

"It sounds both unbelievable and yet all too real!"

"Fabius will create time for Rome to recover her strength after the defeat at Lake Thrasymene something that is soon to happen, for all that he will be pilloried and abused for it. The epithet Cunctator will be given to him as an insult but will ultimately become a badge of honour and although he will not be dictator again his advice will be followed after the defeat, massacre really, to come next year at Cannae. A similar state of affairs will arise then after Cannae with fabian tactics once again being pursued whilst Rome recovers her strength.

"This fabian approach works to our benefit since it creates time for you to establish yourself politically, not only will you ultimately win the war, but before defeating Hannibal you will also win a stunning victory in Spain.

"Just as Hannibal's tactics will be taught two thousand years into the future as an example of how to defeat a larger force, even though weapons and warfare will have changed beyond all recognition, Fabius too will be recognised for the creation of a strategy that is still employed in my time, we have a name for it which will mean nothing to you, we call it guerilla warfare.

"It's a strategy by which general engagements are not fought but hit and run attacks on supply lines and the like weaken an otherwise powerful enemy. Fabius too has achieved immortality, but you will be the more famous.

"The war will continue for some fourteen more years, much of it a stalemate, but these first three years are those in which a new, even more formidable Rome will be forged, from the fires of defeat. Victory and empire will arise, a new world order will be established and you will be the single most important player in the game. That's the good news, for you and me at least.

"Hannibal has a strategy and it's not a foolhardy one, I think he is still working it out even now, but it misses an essential point, one I've touched on before, the essential difference in character and thinking between Rome and Carthage.

"From all that I've read, and I have read extensively, I believe that Hannibal never had the intention to besiege Rome as some of his officers will urge him, or has learned from experience by now that siege warfare is not a Carthaginian speciality.

"Saguntum may have fallen, but Hannibal nearly fell in the taking as well. It was a salutary lesson and there have been others since. For all that Rome will be in mourning after her unimagined and unimaginable losses at Cannae, she'll never throw open her gates.

"Hannibal's aim is, or will become, to destroy the alliances, federation, whatever you want to call it which binds most of Italy to Rome, gives her wealth and power. He will want to make another city pre-eminent in Italy thus neutering Rome's power and he will want that city to be loyal to Carthage, such that Carthage is the world's only great power.

"It would suit Hannibal's purpose that this new capital of Italy not only be allied to Carthage, but that it be a port city in close contact with Carthage.

"Which would you choose?"

"Neapolis?"

"Yes, that will be Hannibal's first choice but Neapolis was a Greek settlement and has been loyal to Rome for more than a hundred years, she won't open her gates either and although Hannibal will defeat the Neapolitans in a cavalry battle he will again have no means to take the actual city.

"Where next might he try?"

"Capua?"

"Precisely, Capua is a river port, but thanks to its tributaries the Volturnus is quite navigable to and from the sea up to Capua. In addition Capua is an anomaly, her senatorial class have close links with Rome, some are married into the great families and partake in Roman politics and lawmaking.

"However, although the common man in Capua has some rights, they exclude the full citizenship. The public mood in Capua is divided by class and circumstance and therefore ripe for conquest, giving Hannibal an opportunity to further divide and conquer, enabling him to take both a port and an entire region which is fertile, productive and wealthy.

"His aim will be to supplant Rome as Italy's first city with Capua, an intoxicating prospect for Capuans. The wonder is that although some other Italian tribes and cities will also ally themselves with Hannibal, much of the Roman federation of allies will hold firm. This will be the stalemate that will provide time for you to grow into your destiny and turn the tables.

"However, we must return to the here and now and ensure that events turn out as they always seem to have!

"Flaminius will make camp at Arretium, between Faesluae and Lake Thrasymene. Geminus will base himself at Ariminum. Hannibal will set out to defeat Flaminius first, by bringing his entire force to bear on our forces whilst they are split."

Publius sighed.

"Rome will learn, but more importantly, you will learn. Hannibal will move south travelling between Pisa and Faesulae."

"That's marshland, it's treacherous, disease and mosquito infested, that's madness."

"Precisely, no one will expect it and Hannibal will place his cavalry at the rear to prevent his own Celts from backing out. Still, no one will anticipate the move, it keeps him well to the west, a long way from the army at Ariminum and will allow him to surprise Flaminius.

"Hannibal will lose many pack animals and some men, he himself will get an infection and lose the sight in one eye, but nothing will stop him. It will take four days and nights, virtually without sleep, to cross the marshes, but it will be done and he will rest his men before moving on.

"He's been told that Flaminius is impetuous he will bypass Arretium and lay waste our lands to the south of the town and to the north of Lake Thrasymene. Messengers will alert Geminus and he will march out to join Flaminius, sending his cavalry ahead lest he be too late. Good decisions on the face of things.

"However, Hannibal will be too quick for Geminus, he'll draw Flaminius after him along the north shore of the lake. He will be lucky with the weather, a fog will add to the confusion of our men, but for the most part the credit belongs to Hannibal."

Scipio was rocking from side to side, sighing unconsciously and muttering "Jupiter" and "Mars".

I continued.

"Hannibal will make a camp at the end of a valley where an advance can easily be thwarted by his crack troops. He will also make the camp visible to draw Flaminius on towards him. During the night before the battle he will send his Gauls and his cavalry into the wooded hills at the point where our forces will enter the valley, Hannibal's Gauls and cavalry will be concealed there until needed to block our escape.

"His light troops will be hidden along the heights overlooking the plain and even his heavy infantry at the head will have a slight height advantage. Fires will be lit in the night to give the impression of distance, it will be a near perfect trap.

"Flaminius will advance into this ambush despite the fog, a group of Carthaginian skirmishers will tempt him to move forward at speed, stretching the line still further. Our men will be strung out, communication will be impossible, there will be no time to form up, it will be pure bloody hand to hand fighting, our men will find themselves assailed from the front, the rear and the side suddenly and simultaneously.

"Hannibal will use trumpet signals to order the attack, no need for visual communications. On the fourth side our men will meet only the cold waters of the lake, those driven to the lake still alive will mostly drown weighed down by their armour. Fifteen thousand will be killed there and then.

"Our vanguard, realising there is no going back will escape through the forest, but Flaminius himself will die on the field. Around ten thousand of our men will escape in the fog and make their way to Rome, another six thousand or so survivors who escaped in the fog will be captured by Maharbal the day after the battle on the guarantee of release if they lay down their weapons. Hannibal will not feel bound by the promise of his officer, they will be sold into slavery.

"On the second day after the battle the four thousand cavalry sent ahead by Geminus will be intercepted and killed to the last man. Twenty five thousand Romans dead or sold as slaves, the greatest tragedy of the war so far."

"We will not be at Trasimene as it's called in my day. The ancient sources reveal next to nothing about your activities this year, but I think I know what you must do nonetheless.

"This is only the second year. I am sure you are wise enough to realise that if you personally are to win the war for Rome, then by definition those commanders who precede you are bound to fail"

"I understand you don't want to reveal all, it makes you valuable" He said bitterly.

"It's not that at all. I think in truth, you know that."

"Spain then?"

"No, by the time your father arrives Gnaeus will have won a naval engagement and won over more allies."

"My father needs a victory himself." he sounded despairing.

"He will do well. Carthage has sent more ships to reinforce Hasdrubal, there is still much to do and time to do it."

The senate had provided twenty ships for the passage of Scipio senior to join and reinforce Gnaeus, aware of the wealth Spain had to offer and believing correctly that should Carthage win the war in Spain she would be able to send supplies, men and money to Hannibal by sea.

Much the same logic as had prompted Carthage to send ships to Hasdrubal, although Carthage also placed a high value on her gold and silver mines in Iberia. The war in Spain may have been far from both Carthage and Rome, but it was crucial to events in Italy.

The reunion of Publius and Gnaeus was to be a joyful one, two Roman generals who for once didn't want all the glory for themselves alone. They made a formidable combination, only I knew that neither would survive the war. Although from what I'd told him Publius had a shrewd suspicion, but chose not to think about it.

Publius Cornelius Scipio the elder arrived in the province with his twenty new warships plus another ten already in Rome's possession and a great many transports full of supplies plus eight thousand infantry. He docked at Tarraco and believed that in Spain anyway the gods were with Rome.

Now it was his turn to cross the Ebro, the brothers made camp about forty stades, roughly five miles from the portentous city of Saguntum close to the Temple of Ahprodite by the sea. Our fleet was travelling with them thus protecting us from attack by sea and transporting vital supplies. The Roman camp was both defensible and allowed for the necessary communication with our ships.

Hannibal, not trusting the local tribes when he'd departed from Spain had taken the sons of the leaders of local tribes as hostages and placed them in Saguntum. Seeing a Roman army and a Roman fleet so close a Carthaginian traitor succeeded in duping the commander of the garrison and placing the hostages in Roman hands.

My friend's father Scipio senior ensured the boys were returned to their families, thus contrasting Roman attitudes with Carthaginian. Rome's position was strengthened, but could not in reality be viewed as secure with Saguntum and New Carthage still strongly garrisoned by the Carthaginians under the command of Hannibal's brother Hasdrubal.

The dreadful defeat at Lake Thrasymene in Italy would happen in June, by the time the Scipio brothers crossed the Ebro and restored the hostages to the tribes it was already time for them to think about winter quarters. Such was the state of affairs in Spain, Rome had made a statement of intent, but little more.

The greater part of Roman success in 217BC in Spain was occasioned by Gnaeus on account of his naval victory and his efforts to make allies, or cow those tribes not disposed to ally themselves. He'd ranged far and wide north of the Ebro and had even been to the island of Ebusus, Ibiza as I knew it to bring as many as possible of the local tribes into the Roman sphere.

I spoke with Publius Cornelius Minor once more.

"Following the disaster soon to come at Lake Thrasymene back in Rome Quintus Fabius Maximus will be appointed pro dictator."

"What do you mean pro dictator?"

"Effectively dictator, but the measure should be adopted by a consul or consuls and Flaminius will be dead, Geminus cannot be contacted with Hannibal between Ariminum and Rome, so the senate will take the actions it feels necessary and will appoint Fabius as what it will call pro dictator. Strange times for Rome to be sure, such is the fear there that the walls will be strengthened and even bridges will thrown down to make the approach to Rome more difficult.

"Not everything will go Hannibal's way at this point, he will besiege Spoletum and sieges not being such a speciality for Carthage as for Romans with their superior engineers, better equipment and tactics Hannibal will be repulsed. This will give him pause, an immediate attack on an even larger city such as Rome will be postponed.

"Hannibal will, however proceed into Picenum, country full of grain and other supplies easy to plunder, his troops will again be rested, fed and ready for more. They will then lay waste to much countryside considered Roman. Our allies will suffer; after Picenum will come the territories of Pretutia, Hadria, the Marsi, Marrucini, Peligni, even down to Apulia around Arpi and Luceria.

"Gneius Servilius Geminus will indulge in some small fights with the Gauls, of little consequence, but on hearing of the disaster at Lake Thrasymene will march to protect Rome. Our new pro dictator meanwhile will call the senate into session and blame religious shortcomings rather than a lack of judgement for the failure of Flaminius.

"Games and temples will be vowed and more. The Sibyllene books will be consulted and auguries taken anew, all under the direction of the praetor Marcus Aemilius and Lucius Cornelius Lentulus, the pontifex maximus."

"I know who they are!"

"Sorry"

"Fabius will be told to take over the army of Geminus and to levy whatever troops, citizen and allied he feels necessary to face Hannibal. Two new legions will be raised even freedmen will be admitted to make up the numbers and Fabius will march out to meet Geminus. The meeting will be effected and Fabius will take command of all land forces, Geminus will take control of our ships patrolling the west of Italy, for the rest of this year anyway.

"Proclamations will be issued demanding all allied citizens gather in fortified places and the countryside be laid waste to deny food and supplies to Hannibal. Some will obey, others will not fully comply. Hannibal and his army will not starve, or even go hungry.

"Unfortunately, further ships sent from Ostia to resupply your father and uncle will be captured by the Carthaginian fleet prompting Fabius to march for Ostia to arrange a pursuit.

"As I've said Fabius will become famous right down to my own time for what have come to be known as fabian tactics, although it's more of a strategy in my view. Be that as it may, these tactics will not be well received in Rome although they are absolutely the right tactics at this moment, they will be viewed as cowardly at home.

"Remember that Fabius has raw troops who are all too aware of the stunning victories Hannibal has already achieved, even over Rome's famed infantry. Fabius will shadow Hannibal, keeping wherever possible to high ground and always making secure camps in places that Hannibal will not attack.

"What Fabius will do is to attack Hannibal's foraging parties, still trying to kick the Carthaginians in the stomach so to speak. Casualties amongst the Carthaginians will be light, but Fabius will be a constant source of annoyance and will cause Hannibal to constantly need to watch him."

"He should be a damn sight more than an annoyance."

"Well, that of course is the mood in Rome too. Shadowing and building unassailable forts is difficult and time consuming, Hannibal will get ahead of Fabius, he will plunder around Beneventum in Samnium and then the wine country in Campania believing that this will provoke the Romans to make an all out attack.

"Hannibal will endeavour to leave the Falernian plain by one of the few mountain passes, in search of good winter quarters. He will choose the pass by which he entered the plain, presumably because he knows how the land lies there.

"Fabius is no fool, he will anticipate correctly and occupy the pass. This should in theory put Hannibal in a difficult, even near impossible position for a less cunning general. With some four thousand troops guarding the pass twenty four hours a day Fabius will build a fortified camp where the balance of his men can rest safely.

"Unfortunately for us Hannibal will out general Fabius as he's out generalled every other Roman sent against him; at least this time our losses will be fewer. The Carthaginians will attach torches to the horns of a herd of oxen and drive them up the ridge adjacent to the pass in the dark of night. Seeing what they believe to be the enemy circumventing their position the troops in the pass will attack up the ridge where they will be met by a hail of javelins and those who do make the top will find only oxen, the javelin throwers having fallen back in the dark.

"In the meantime of course the bulk of the Carthaginian forces will have taken the pass with a straightforward march up the centre.

"In his camp Fabius will see the torches and hear the sounds of fighting, but he will not lead his troops out for fear of chaos and defeat. In the morning the Carthaginian javelin men who drove the oxen up the ridge will be exposed by the light. Although the Romans who were guarding the pass will attack them, Hannibal will react with speed and efficiency sending his light armed Spanish Caetrati, men used to fighting and skirmishing in mountainous terrain to rescue them.

" The Caetrati under their captain Viriathus will return with the javelin men and at the same time, they will inflict surprisingly heavy casualties on the four thousand Romans set to guard the pass. Viriathus will personally inflict another heavy loss on Rome next year at Cannae, the defeat I've tried to prepare you for, but things in Spain will be more of a stalemate. Your uncle currently controls Catalonia, the region north of the Ebro, thus preventing Hasdrubal from resupplying his brother from Spain and that's crucial.

"Your father and your uncle will strike out south of the Ebro, they will bring some of the Spanish over to us and garrison two of the ports, but Hasdrubal will still hold New Carthage and more besides, although he will have problems with some of the Spanish tribes in areas he considers Carthaginian. Next year, the year 216BC, as I know it, 538 to us, here and now, will not decide a great deal in Spain, but it will be the most disastrous year yet for Rome and Italy.

"That said, with hindsight, sorry, with the benefit of my own hindsight it could be said to be the high water mark of Hannibal's success.

"The tide will turn, slowly, but it will turn. Hannibal and Carthage will believe that Rome must surrender, when that doesn't happen Hannibal will move first against Neapolis and then Capua as we talked about, and here is where we find the real difference between Rome and Carthage. The Carthaginians will do little to help Hannibal; in my time we use an expression 'out of sight, out of mind'.

"Carthage expects Rome to do what it would do, cut its losses, give in to the inevitable, but Rome is not Carthage, Romans see themselves as warriors not accountants, Romans do not count the cost, they fight, which is why Rome will grow to be the greatest empire the world has yet known, and you Publius will play no small part in that, you will defeat Rome's greatest enemy."

"If you are right I will be the greatest Roman of all time!"

"Perhaps we shouldn't get into that; an empire that lasts more than a thousand years will have many heroes, but you will be in that band of immortals, not I.

"Fabius's defeat at the pass, where he really had Hannibal at bay will be a major humiliation. Fabius will be mocked for following Hannibal around like a slave carrying books to school for a young nobleman. This in turn will lead to more rash mistakes by our side in the conflict in Italy.

"When Fabius returns to Rome for religious duties Minucius will disobey his orders and attack Hannibal. The Carthaginian forces will be spread out foraging and Minucius will win what he will describe as a battle outside the town of Gerunium which Hannibal had intended to use as winter quarters.

"News of this great victory will cause rejoicing in Rome, Minucius will be the hero of the hour and will be raised to equal status with Fabius. A tribune of the plebs, one Metilius, I expect you know him too, will pass a foolhardy law making the imperium of the master of the horse equal to that of a dictator. In short a return to power split equally between two men, the same as having two consuls really. Which is fine in peacetime or when faced with lesser enemies but it defeats the point of having a dictator in an emergency!

"In fact the great victory of Minucius is actually just a large skirmish in the first place, exaggerated out of all proportion for his personal glory! Hannibal will not be materially weakened nor will Rome's position be materially improved.

"The result of this new law will be that the army will once again be divided into two, Minucius will be lured into a trap, his army will be severely mauled and he will be rescued by Fabius, the man he will have disobeyed and effectively tried to usurp.

"This is what's happening in Italy right now! We have other things to deal with.

" After rescuing Minucius and restoring his own reputation, Fabius's fabian tactics as we call them in my time come into play once more. We Romans will avoid a direct battle and continue to harass Hannibal's foraging parties and to do no more than skirmish.

"At the end of 537 Fabius and Minucius will return to Rome. The army will be left under the command of the surviving consul Geminus and Marcus Atilius Regulus who will be elected suffect consul after the death of Flaminius.

"The thing is Scipio that neither Polybius nor Livy, the writers I rely on for most of my information reveal much if anything about your activities this year, but for you to fulfil your destiny you must be a military tribune at Cannae next year and you must have begun building a political power base in Rome, that is where we must be this year.

"We must say goodbye to your father and travel south to Rome down the east side of Italy, well away from Hannibal and his army whilst they cross the marshes and lure Flaminius into the trap at Thrasymene.

"Let Fabius shadow Hannibal whilst Rome absorbs what's happened and licks her wounds. You must make contacts and forge alliances of your own whilst your valour on the battlefield is fresh in the memory. You must begin your climb up the cursus honorum. Your father will release you for this I'm certain.

"It won't be a simple matter, there will be factions and whilst Fabius is doing the right thing it will be difficult to support him whilst he's being mocked. We have on our side the knowledge that he will come to be revered for his wisdom later, so we must not be in the faction which openly opposes him, that way, when the mood changes you will be seen as a wise head on young shoulders.

"Your main objective is to build alliances with the great families, in particular you must confirm your childhood betrothal to Aemilia Tertia Paulla the daughter of Lucius Aemillius Paullus and set a date for the wedding, that too will keep you in the public consciousness.

"Your soon to be father in law will be consul next year with Caius Terrentius Varro as his colleague. Varro will survive the defeat at Cannae by the skin of his teeth, very sadly Paullus will not live to see you marry his daughter if it's not done quickly. Neither will Geminus survive he will be killed by Viriathus. You will avenge all, but you need to gain political power and influence. That is what this year is about for you.

"By the way, why is Aemilia called Tertia when there is no mention of sisters in my sources?"

"Two girls were stillborn, she was named Tertia in their memory, a strange idea, but in certain respects it's a family which sets its own standards and does things its own way."

"Do you know her well?"

"Enough to respect her, I like her too actually, it's a political alliance, but I'm well satisfied with the prospect. I believe she's very fond of me too."

"It will be a long, happy and fruitful marriage and your youngest daughter will become a very famous Roman in her own right, but that's another story. We have work to do."

CHAPTER 7 OUR ARRIVAL IN ROME 217BC

So it was that as Hannibal set out on his destiny, to lose an eye to infection crossing the marshes and yet still achieve another stunning victory at Lake Thrasymene, killing a Roman consul and wiping out virtually an entire Roman army. Our small party took the byways to Ariminum, using a route which would more or less become the Via Aemilia in the next century, from here we could join the Via Flaminia to Rome or proceed further south to Ancona, the town founded roughly two hundred years before by Greek refugees from Syracuse.

We chose to go by way of Ancona and take the old salt route west to Rome from there, in this way we kept a greater distance between ourselves and the war, but a bigger reason was to arrive in Rome unremarked and unexpected. The surprise arrival of the proconsul's son and war hero, would help to begin the process of building a reputation, status, public and political standing.

We were a small group, a young nobleman, his friend, four servants all armed and two bodyguards, barely enough to stave off an attack by bandits, let alone a scouting party. Nonetheless, for once I felt safe and confident.

I trusted the men around me and I knew that Scipio was destined to live to fifty three, so he wasn't going to die on this journey, which boded well for the rest of us! Although his death was some thirty four years hence its date and the fashion of it would not be facts I'd likely share with him, but that decision was for the distant future if at all; do many of us really want to know the date of our own death in advance and count down the days I wondered.

Confident that we'd make it safely to Rome and looking forward hugely to seeing the eternal city, even if it wasn't yet at its zenith I enjoyed the journey. They were long days in the saddle, but to keep the horses fresh we went at walking pace and watered and fed the animals wherever possible. I've always liked horses and felt a kind of bond with my mount. More sentimental than the average Roman!

In addition I've always loved Italy, but the Italy I'd come to know had autostradas, traffic and modern buildings with less grace and beauty than the ancient villas, or even some humble farmsteads. Here and now, there was no pollution, there were no discarded plastic bottles, wild flowers grew in abundance, the air and the water were pure.

The food we ate was not so different from much of that I'd had on my boat, where cold food allowed one to snack whilst still keeping watch, so bread, cheese and olives were staples. We drank our wine watered in order to keep our wits about us and had cured meats and occasionally fish with beans or polenta, depending upon where we stopped. I regretted that the modern Italian staple of tomatoes, pomodori, had not yet found their way to Europe!

The conversations were light hearted but helped me work at my Latin, something greatly needed, especially given I would meet more of Scipio's circle in Rome and would need to give good account of myself or I'd damage his credibility. This was my only real cause for anxiety or trepidation on the entire journey.

I wasn't sure but I felt that along the way we should construct a policy about what to say about me and my presence in his entourage. We needed to stick to the truth where facts could be checked, but the full truth might be going a bit too far!

Fortunately my friend Scipio would be the master of his father's house, with his father overseas, his word would be law, the slaves would be cautioned about loose tongues and I would go nowhere without an escort. Those of Scipio's friends whom he wanted me to meet would, initially at least, be brought to the house.

Even his mother would effectively be subordinate to her own son, although fortunately things would turn out well for me with both Publius's mother and his betrothed. At this point however I was still somewhat apprehensive.

The twisting route, especially for the first half of the journey meant that we would cover some four hundred and fifty miles on horseback. Roman legions would happily march twenty miles in a day and then build a fortified camp before retiring for the night. At least, those legions which were properly generalled would do so.

For me, twenty to thirty miles in a day, with the luxury of a bridled horse was a challenge. Men were certainly tougher then! Although I wondered if it was really just my generation that had started to go soft.

My grandfather had joined up in 1914 and spent most of his war in the western trenches. He'd been blown up and put in a coma, stripped and unceremoniously dumped, naked I might add, with the dead bodies, a telegram sent to grandma. It was only as he was being heaved into a mass grave that someone said "ere Sarge I don't think this one's quite dead".

After a stay in hospital it was back to the wet, rat infested trenches. There was no recognition of post traumatic stress in those days. The ulcers on my grandfather's legs, caused by the years in those waterlogged, vermin infested ditches never healed either, he changed the dressings daily until he died in his nineties and worked as a plumber until he was sixty five.

Yes, grandad could have held his head up in this company. I may have sailed thousands of miles, much of it solo, but I was as soft as a baby's bum by comparison. The journey took a little over two weeks. Usually we found an inn or someone happy to accommodate a nobleman with a small party. A couple of nights we slept under the stars, wrapped only in our cloaks, our bags for pillows. At least we found soft, fresh grass and were able to build a fire.

Scipio asked me to teach him something of my language. I thought it a crazy idea at first, but he pointed out that it would enable us to communicate in the presence of others without their understanding, something which would prove useful as it turned out. Furthermore the act of teaching him became a two way street and helped improve my grasp of Latin, something which at this juncture was still very rudimentary indeed.

We rode in pairs, the two bodyguards rode in front of Publius and me, and the four servants rode behind. The act of trying to learn each other's languages helped the miles pass by and, for me anyway, diminished the awareness of the soreness in my backside and thighs!

Some seventeen days after we set out the city of Rome hove into view, we closed the distance somewhat but decided to make an early start the next day. Arriving early in the day would allow for some of the necessary discussions and arrangements to be made, not least concerning me and accommodation and explanations!

It was early June, the disaster at Lake Thrasymene was still some two weeks hence, the news would take a couple of days more to reach the city. Time enough to make a start on our own project whilst there was still some semblance of normality.

As we entered the city, which looked impressive and attractive from a distance I was struck by the noise, the smells, the graffiti and how drab most of the buildings looked. Things were better when we reached the Palatine, but I was reminded of the supposed quote, at the end of his life, of the future Emperor Augustus: 'I found Rome built of bricks, I leave her clothed in marble'.

As a dutiful son Publius's first call was upon his mother, although it was also the most practical since we would be living at the house on the Palatine, could immediately hide me away and explain how the land lay to Pomponia.

As wife of a patrician consular and the daughter of a plebeian consular Pomponia was very cognisant of her status. It would help our cause also that she had a foot in both camps so to speak, plebeian and patrician. The house was immaculate and the slaves happy, but fully aware that they needed to perform their duties quietly, efficiently and without gossip. Their personal hygiene was above reproach too, which wasn't always the case in some of the houses one visited.

Caesar's wife and more especially his mother came to mind although the fact, known only to me, that Publius would father Cornelia, the mother of the Gracchi also chimed. Cornelia, who, in the not so distant future would, for long afterwards be held up as the ultimate example of how a Roman woman should conduct herself, was of course influenced by her grandmother Pompomia's example.

That was all in the future for now, how very strange it all felt, this jumble in my mind of history yet to happen. Aristocratic Roman women who embraced Roman ideals, only the very occasional few rebelled, seemed to have a most rigorous code of behaviour.

Pomponia greeted her son formally being in the presence of others, mostly unknown to her and the two whom she did know were servants, emotions were not displayed to servants. Although she hid it well, her delight on seeing her son was apparent to me nonetheless.

Fortunately Rome was a melting pot of cultures, Greeks, Jews, Arabs, Celts and Gauls, Germans et al, so another strange looking outsider would cause less comment than might otherwise have been the case.

At least I was dressed in a somewhat Roman manner. I have to admit to wearing two tunics, one of linen under one of wool. I had also been given a heavy hooded cloak known as a birrus which certainly helped. The spring weather was not especially cold, but the nights sleeping under the stars were cloudless and the temperatures had plummeted.

Naturally I didn't wear the hood up to greet Pomponia. In my saddle bags I also had a normal cloak or chlamys which fastened at the shoulder with a brooch I still have to this day.

I remember thinking I'd never get used to the combination of bare legs and cold weather. Of course in the summer I came to feel somewhat differently! What we, in my day and age, call trousers were the mark of a barbarian to my new friends, so no possibility there. I never got used to loincloths either and frequently went without.

Having grown up in the age of the mini skirt it was interesting to see that the majority of women on the street wore long tunics and we men the shorter variety. Of course aristocratic women such as Pomponia wore long dresses known as stolas. An extensive wardrobe, one that even extended to embroidered items, was one of the few luxuries Pomponia allowed herself, although always modest in style.

Pomponia wore limited jewellery and had her hair up in a bun, where more liberal women wore a range of rather more exuberant eye catching styles which sometimes included golden hairnets and jewels.

Many aristocratic women employed a slave for the sole purpose of cosmetics and hairdressing. Although said slaves would also dress their mistress and generally developed an intimate relationship of sorts. Stockholm syndrome or something like it I supposed, not something I'd want to have to try and explain! Heated curling tongs it also turned out, didn't get invented after the discovery of electricity!

Pomponia's style lent her a stern appearance, I soon learned that she was quite a gentle creature once you got to know her and any friend of her son's was a friend of hers fortunately.

The servants and bodyguards were dismissed to their various quarters or duties, leaving just the three of us in the atrium. Publius instructed Pomponia and myself to follow him into the tablinum, essentially his father's, and for now, his office, explaining that our voices were less likely to carry from there and that a lot needed to be done and more yet to be explained.

A messenger was to be sent to the house of Aemilius Paullus to request an appointment. Another servant was to be sent out to purchase several changes of clothing for me. Publius himself had plenty of spare tunics, but his build was a bit slimmer and fitter than my own, nor did he want me wearing anything of his father's.

Pomponia, allowed herself to show no hint of impatience or undue curiosity, but there was an almost audible release when Publius began to explain what had happened and who I was, although the latter explanation omitted much, whereas the description of events in the war was fully detailed. Publius did not want his mother to view me as a prisoner who'd used a silver tongue to get around her son.

My tablet now had a dead battery and a story about a traveller from the future was not on the agenda. That I had the second sight was a good enough explanation, were one to be needed, where Pomponia and Publius's friends were concerned.

Publius explained to Pomponia that I was a trader he had met in Gaul, no mention of capture, I was clearly positioned as a free man who had taken the Roman name Caius Laelius. Furthermore Publius explained to his mother that, even if she doubted the ability of prophesy my knowledge of geography and of Carthage, its ways and attitudes had been of immense help to him, and would continue to be of assistance, even if my Latin was extremely rudimentary. He explained that it was for these reasons that he regarded me as both an honoured guest, to be helped and protected, and as a close personal friend.

My status in the house thus assured I was shown around, allocated a bedroom with a writing desk, writing materials and leather buckets for my scrolls. It was decided that I should write a record, not only of my 'predictions', but also a history of the life and achievement's of Publius. If any of those writings turn up one day it might put the cat among the pigeons!

In addition I was allotted a personal manservant, a Greek, technically a slave but one who'd sold himself into slavery under particular conditions and who would one day be manumitted or purchase his freedom back again.

Publius advised me not to go out unless it was with him, however, he made it plain that I was not a prisoner and should I wish to explore, or visit the market when he, Publius was otherwise occupied, that my manservant Leander could and would both accompany me and arrange an escort for our security.

Publius would introduce me first, and for the time being at least, to only his most trusted friends. His first priority personally was Aemilius Paullus and Aemilia Tertia, he wanted me to meet the latter who he knew would respect his wishes and privacy, he did not want to try and explain anything about me to the former, not least because I had already foretold the death of the man he was wooing as a future father in law.

It was arranged that Publius would visit the house of the Paullii alone during the afternoon, there would be time for a private conversation between ourselves regarding that visit over vesperna, the evening meal. Two hours after sunset we were to visit the temple of Jupiter where we would meet three of Publius's closest friends. The purpose of the meeting being to enlist help in the political arena and start to establish Publius as a leader.

Night time meetings in the temple of Jupiter would become a frequent and regular occurrence. They would one day become part of the legend that Scipio himself was divinely inspired, or even that divinity flowed in his veins. I had forgotten about this legend regarding my friend until Publius informed me of the location of the proposed gathering thus reminding me of a detail I had forgotten up to that point.

Pomponia did not dine with us that evening, I assume by arrangement of her son, even so we talked in hushed tones.

"I had a very satisfactory afternoon, Paullus was delighted to see me, possibly a little relieved that I intended to wed his daughter in the near future, although he's never had any cause to doubt mine or my father's sincerity. The dowry will be substantial. I'm tempted to say it will help with my campaigning politically, but in point of fact I will protect it for Aemilia.

"Whilst I have every confidence in all that you've told me, and indeed all has come to pass the way you said it would, one cannot be certain that what you call history will not change this time around. Should I die in battle Aemilia will find her dowry intact and returned to her.

"We will marry in the confarreatio tradition, there will be no divorce. The date will be the thirteenth of September 538. I will need the support of patricians and of the people. I will develop the notion that I'm associated with Jupiter, beloved by patricians as Rome's greatest and best, but also beloved of the people by the god's association with justice.

"June is a propitious month to marry, but it's too late for this June, a wedding next June was the other consideration, this June would allow Paullus the opportunity to see his beloved daughter married however the thirteenth of September is the anniversary of the founding of the temple of Jupiter.

"If you are correct about this battle of Cannae in August it will be barely a month after the death of her father, an indecently short mourning period. Nonetheless I have much to do in the meantime, I must ensure Paullus appoints me as a junior military tribune, I must garner support and a wedding will divert attention, so September it is.

"I hope I can protect Aemilia and help her recover from her loss."

"Bring the wedding forward to this June, give her father this joy, furthermore Aemilia will be established under your hand, before the death of her father, it's safer for you, safer for her and I might add safer for the dowry since inheritance won't come into the picture!

"You will be busy, but you have time to marry and furthermore, make it known to Paullus that you wish to serve as one of the fourteen junior military tribunes and as your father in law he will certainly make it happen, which is the major thing you can achieve at this stage anyhow.

"Lastly, if Aemilia were ever to discover that her father's death were foretold, your setting a wedding date after that tragedy and so soon after as well would be a source of pain for her."

"You wouldn't reveal that you'd foretold it."

"Certainly not, of course not, not intentionally anyhow, but things get out and I have a feeling you will come to confide deeply in your wife, secrets are an error. She will be a powerful ally and a support to you. I've no doubt that this union will bring you joy as well as political benefits"

"You're right, I should have discussed these things with you before I went, I'll do as you say and arrange another meeting with Paullus tomorrow, in fact I'm looking forward to being married, I just want to keep my mind on the task at hand."

"You will and the war has some years yet to run, there's a time and a place for every purpose under the sun. You say you will protect Aemilia's dowry in case I'm wrong and you die in battle, you can also protect your line and create a legal heir before Cannae. I'm not wrong though."

Two hours after the sun set we found ourselves in the dimly lit temple of Jupiter awaiting the arrival of young Fabius Maximus, son of the dictator, Lucius Publicius Bibulus and Appius Claudius Pulcher, all destined to be junior military tribunes at Cannae and all destined to survive and join forces with Scipio at Canusium.

That was for the future. The founding of the Jupiter Club was the business of this night, brothers in political ambition, in arms and in religion. The Three Musketeers, who were also actually four came to mind, but I restrained from plagiarising the one for all bit! I wasn't sure that I was to be a full member, but it turned out I was, so that made five anyway.

Publius led the meeting, he told them that Rome's interests and theirs aligned, that they were the future and that they should work together to protect their own interests and those of their nation. Rome had never faced a greater danger, but that he believed this war would be the making of Rome and the making of himself and his closest friends.

"When Carthage falls and it will fall" he told them "Rome will become the greatest power on this earth, the middle sea will be known as mare nostrum, Latin will be the universal language and Roman law will govern all. Ours is a great destiny, one that is already written, but there is fire and blood, and pain and suffering to pass through first, we will be the ones to keep Rome on her true course. This will be our time, our pain, but also our glory.

He explained that he had met me in Gaul, introduced me as Caius Laelius and stated that my knowledge of Carthage and it's ways were a sort of secret weapon and that, into the bargain, everything I prophesied had come to pass.

"Swear an oath of allegiance to each other, to this brotherhood and in time I will reveal much more" he promised.

Oaths were taken, in Jupiter's name of course, and individual sacrifices promised, to be made privately before the next meeting. The Jupiter Club was thus formed and a date two weeks hence set for the first proper meeting when actions and responsibilities were to be allotted. In the meantime the founding members should consider potential friends and allies to nominate for membership.

"In a few days, maybe a week or so, there will be terrible news of the loss of a consular army entire, with the consul himself dead on the field at a place called Lake Thrasymene. A cavalry force sent by his colleague to reinforce the consul arriving too late to assist will also be lost, in its entirety shortly after. Rome will raise the greatest army she has yet put in the field, we will, all of us excepting Caius here, who has another role to play, serve in that army, but that is not where this journey ends.

"We meet in two weeks to discuss these events and our reaction to them, we can also discuss how I know these things, but remember, your oath commits you to secrecy, break that oath and you will no longer be my friend and he who is no longer my friend becomes my enemy."

As we walked home Scipio whispered to me "the die is cast, you'd better be right."

Two weeks later Rome was in mourning for the loss of its consular army at Lake Thrasymene and of the four thousand cavalry sent to reinforce that army.

The consul Gaius Flaminius had been consul before, not always popular amongst patricians as he had been a tribune of the plebs, he had nonetheless led a Roman army to victory over the Insubrians, given his name to the Via Flaminia, one of the greatest Roman roads and had been a popular governor of Sicily. For all that he'd made ghastly errors, he died fighting for his country and was mourned deeply by the people who almost universally adored him.

It was against this backdrop that the Jupiter Club held its first real meeting. Appius Claudius Pulcher, son of a former consul as we all knew, but also a future consul himself and the future father of yet another consul, as was known only to me was the only founding member to bring a new recruit. He had with him one Lucius Furius Philus, son of that Lucius Furius Philus who'd been consul in 136BC and whose son would also be Lucius Furius Philus!

It was as august (a name not yet coined of course) a body of men as one could hope to find at such a young age. Before the year was out we would add a Claudius Marcellus, a Pomponius Matho and an Atilius Regulus. The family Metellus, after some debate was not invited to join.

As I was only too aware, the only nobody was me. That a Caius Laelius would one day be a consul was not something revealed in my notes on Livy and Polybius and if I had ever been aware of the fact it had long since escaped my memory.

There was some discomfort within the group that things had come to pass so precisely as foretold by Scipio, right down to the exact timing.

"I took a chance" he admitted to the others, "I believe our friend here has the second sight. He told me I would save my father's life at the Trebbia, which could have been a self fulfilling prophesy, except that my father might not have needed saving, I might not have been in the right place, or I might not have had the means to save him.

"Laelius is my oracle, as a devoted follower of Jupiter I believe he was sent by the god to save Rome, through us. The gods however do not help those unwilling to help themselves, to put their lives on the line and make the necessary sacrifices.

"Two weeks ago you all swore an oath, all save Lucius here, I ask you to swear that oath now or to leave without rancour on the promise of complete discretion."

Lucius Furius took the oath, this was a group of his contemporaries he was most anxious to be allied with.

Scipio continued.

"This current disaster is hard to bear, sadly it is prophesied that a still greater disaster will weigh on us next year. It will not be the only tragedy we have to endure and I have not pushed Laelius to give me the whole story as I fear it may seem too great a burden to bear. I also believe that what is written is written, but that does not exonerate us from doing our duty.

"Laelius tells me that the war will last some seventeen years in total. If we take Rome's declaration as the start date that means the war will last another fourteen to fifteen years. I shall be thirty three or four when the war ends, with a complete Roman victory I might add.

"A complete victory over Carthage will be the making of Rome. I spoke of these things at the previous meeting Lucius when we agreed to form the Jupiter Club. Rome will raise the greatest army it has yet assembled next year, we must all be junior military tribunes. That is our starting point, there is much to do beyond that.

"I will reveal what we need to do and what will happen on a need to know basis, Laelius has warned me repeatedly about trying to use his prophesies to change events, to go against the gods' wishes would be to court disaster when we know that ultimate victory will be ours.

"Know this, we few here are the guardians of Rome's destiny, the future of the world is in our hands. We, in our prime, will shape the world, but the foundations are being laid here, in the temple of Jupiter Optimus Maximus this very night.

"Oh and by the way, I'm getting married..."

Over the course of the coming months Scipio revealed to the club members Hannibal's advance into the Ager Falernus, Fabius's success in hemming him in and Hannibal's brilliance in breaking out.

He released the information I'd given him ahead of events to build faith amongst his disciples, but always with too little time for them to alter the course of events should our associates be tempted to break their oaths. Given that messages had to go by courier not by telephone it was easy to maintain this drip feeding of news ahead of the actual events and thus protect said events from unwanted interference.

Members of the club largely forgot or chose to forget that the information supplied by Scipio all came from me and the manner of his revelations, always after dark in the sacred flickering torch lit atmosphere of the temple imbued him with an almost godly knowledge. That he was their leader was never in doubt.

Rome roiled and groaned, grieved and lamented the loss at Thrasymene, only for the cavalry disaster to be revealed scant days later. The senate was in session daily. The dictator was duly appointed and dispatched with his master of horse.

At each stage Scipio revealed not just Hannibal's escape from the trap laid by Fabius, but also Minucius exaggerating the success of his skirmish and then leading his men into the folly from which Fabius would rescue them.

CHAPTER 8 CANNAE, JOY AND DESPAIR 216 BC THE YEAR 538

By spring of 538 we were nine in number Caecilius Metellus had been asking questions but was not deemed suitable to be invited. To the original group of nobles, that is Scipio, Fabius Maximus, Bibulus and Pulcher had been added Philus at the first meeting and over the course of the next few meetings, as mentioned, we had inducted a Claudius Marcellus, a Pomponius Matho and an Atilius Regulus.

Although present from the start I was the least notable ninth member, but the one with the knowledge I consoled myself. I'd been making good use of the desk and writing materials in my bedroom. Sometimes I'd remember a detail from Livy or Polybius in the middle of the night and in these cases I'd always rise and record it, lest it be forgotten by morning.

Varro and Paullus had been elected consuls as predicted which helped keep my reputation or, more to the point, Scipio's reputation unsullied by error! Hannibal had also made his winter camp at Geronium in Apulia as predicted.

In June Scipio wed Amelia Tertia in the old style that brooked no divorce. It was a joyous day for Aemilia and Scipio in particular of course, but all the members of the Jupiter club were present along with extended family on both sides.

Paullus was as proud as a peacock and about as happy as a man can be. Consul, the proud father of the bride, an important man, indeed a ruler in one of the world's two most powerful city states watching his legacy grow. It broke my heart that I held the knowledge of his death in less than two months time.

The wedding feast lasted most of the day, with delicacies my modern mind and heart disapproved of from stuffed dormice to stuffed songbirds. That there was a kind of iced cream which was every bit as delicious as a modern Italian gelato was impressive, it was enjoyable and yet it took me back to other times and places I thought never to see again.

My melancholy was noticed by Valeria Pulcher, sister of one of the founding members of the Jupiter Club. She had been watching me quite unashamedly, some would say blatantly, but with the self assurance of a high born Roman noblewoman. Pulcher himself had clearly been questioned and occasioned an introduction.

Valeria it seemed was already aware of my weakness with Latin and my prowess at prediction. She was an interesting character, educated, but not just educated, she had a deeply enquiring mind, a fierce intelligence, a desire to matter and although it hadn't seemed so at that first meeting, the ability to be incredibly subtle as well as effective. Her Latin was as superlative as her Greek. Owning no Greek marked me out as an uneducated outsider, but no matter, I wasn't about to wrestle with that too.

Appius Claudius Pulcher might not have been as rigid in keeping his vow of secrecy as should have been the case, but his sister would in no way risk the family reputation. In fact she was on a mission to be an influencer of events and from that stemmed her interest in me and my relationship with Scipio. I might be a complete outsider and a nobody, but I was involved in events and she wanted answers.

In my own day and age Valeria would certainly have been considered far too young to be a potential wife, for almost anyone, let alone for me! However, in Roman society where girls could be betrothed at twelve and married scant years later it was most unusual for a woman of twenty to not be spoken for. Such was her bearing, self confidence and knowledge that I took her to be at least that if not a year or two older, when in fact, as I would discover somewhat later she was actually a mere seventeen.

Her force of character and her father's unusual, not to say surprising unwillingness to force anything that might upset her on his favourite daughter had left her uncommonly free. Older Roman men, particularly those with social standing were quite able to marry younger Roman women in their own class. Obviously I possessed no such standing.

Valeria was slender and elegant, stylish but not overtly adorned, she could be both serious and joyful, she could also debate, delight, challenge, amuse and arouse. I was a mature and experienced man with a huge amount of useful knowledge and I had wanted female company so very badly, more than I fully realised, for so very long. I was now, and not for the last time, all at sea in her company.

Here came a young woman, not just beautiful but challenging, interesting, alluring and thought provoking. I had to force myself to concentrate, what to say and in particular what not to say. Difficult when an impossible dream and an impossible future start swirling unexpectedly and uncontrollably around one's mind. Weddings it occurred to me were often events leading to the start of another romance, why should the Roman world be any different in that particular.

With death a regular visitor to families in the ancient world and divorce for those not married in the confarreatio tradition being relatively commonplace, marriage between people with a considerable age difference was neither unusual, nor frowned upon. Wealth and status, allegiances between families were far more important, but of course I had neither wealth, nor status. I needed to put any crazy thoughts concerning Valeria and myself out of my mind, which I would have done if I'd known her true age.

After the feast friends of the bride and groom followed them in procession to their new home, watched them cross the threshold, offer libations to the household gods and disappear inside. We then made our own way home which in my case meant returning to the home of Scipio senior and Pomponia.

Pomponia had, drunk little at the wedding and comported herself exactly as would have been expected as the mother of the groom. In my time we hear much about Roman licentiousness and orgies, a far cry from my experience of the Roman elite. There was prostitution in the lower orders and I'm sure there were parties of a sexual nature in some quarters, but not in my personal experience or social sphere.

Drunk she was not, but emotional Pomponia certainly was. As the only non slave in the house the only person she could talk openly to about her feelings was me and that wasn't easy.

"My son thinks highly of you, yet you're a bit of a mystery to me. He says you know the future, yet you don't talk in riddles or puzzles or comport yourself like any oracle, you're not a woman like the Sibyl, not a priest, you don't live at a holy place, I've never seen you converse with the gods."

"Your son is a very special man, but you know that. I count myself most fortunate to know him and to be his friend. Be assured that I am his true friend and that I am in a position to help him. Do you need to know more?"

"I don't need to know more, but you can understand my interest I'm sure."

"I understand, but I don't know if I should tell you more about myself, facts are sometimes stranger than fiction. I was able to prove things to Publius which can no longer be proven to others, only the veracity of what I tell to Publius and to his close associates maintains me. I have no wealth, no status, no family, but I am useful, to Publius, to you in a way and to Rome. I will ensure things turn out the way they must. I didn't choose to be here, forces and events I don't understand myself brought me to this place.

"Rome and the world stand at a crossroads. The city has recently lost an entire consular army together with its commander. Rome will pick itself up, build a bigger army and carry on because that's what Rome does. However, this year there will be an even greater disaster, the greatest tragedy for Rome since the Gauls besieged the Capitol.

"Publius will be the new Cincinnatus, he will save Rome."

"He's too young."

"He is indeed, sadly he will not be by the time this war is done."

"You're scaring me."

"I don't think you scare easily Pomponia but curiosity has its price. We should talk about other things. Know this, despite the pain, and there will be much of it, nor will you personally be exempt from tragedy in the years to come, your son will be the greatest Roman of his age, an age in fact when Rome truly comes into her own. Your granddaughter will be famous and venerated too, your name will not be forgotten to posterity either, nor that of your husband or his brother.

"One little thing that might be worth knowing is that next year a law will be passed which will be known as the Lex Oppia. It will be a reaction to Rome's financial difficulties, but it will be aimed at the women of Rome.

"The wealth permitted a woman will be severely restricted, as will any display of wealth. As a true Roman you may feel that following Rome's laws is a duty, but be aware, you will be limited to no more than half an ounce of gold, multi coloured clothes like the stola you wore to today's wedding will be outlawed. Nor will you be allowed to travel in a vehicle drawn by an animal or animals although I think that particular measure will affect you the least.

"If you wish to preserve jewels, brooches, rings of particular sentimental value I should stop wearing them now, hide them away and hope your friends forget about their existence, better yet place them in Publius's care, I will warn him too for the sake of Aemilia Tertia, just not in the week of their wedding I think!

"This law will be repealed, but twenty years after it will be made, let me see, that's the year 559 I think."

"How can you know this? Such detail, such precise dates, Publius says you are never wrong."

"I hope I'm not wrong, there may be some small errors in the detail. If I tell you now how it is that I know these things you'll think I'm mad. Follow events, watch and you'll see that in the essentials at least everything I say comes to pass. That is not to say I know everything that will happen, there may well be some gaps, I'm sure there are gaps in my knowledge, but the general course of events I can foretell with a considerable degree of accuracy.

"In the years to come when we've been trusted friends for a period I judge sufficient, then I may reveal the truth to you, but only when I know that you are truly my friend and that you truly believe in me as your son does. There is nothing special about me Pomponia, but the circumstances that brought me to this place are somewhat inexplicable, not least to me, that alone is what is special."

The following morning Pomponia came to my room in person, where I was writing and trying to put my haphazard notes into some coherent order, in English I might add and announced that a messenger from Appius Claudius Pulcher had arrived to invite me to attend their house for the midday coena, that is to say lunch, and required a reply.

Trying not to sound or appear too excited I answered that I would be happy to go and would Pomponia be so kind as to send Leander to me to make arrangements for an escort as required by Publius when I went out and about.

On arrival at the house Leander and my escort were dismissed to the servants quarters to eat and I was shown to a dining couch set alongside another for the younger Pulcher whilst a chair was set beside the table for Valeria, not yet present.

"My father is away, so I'm master of the house, I hope you don't mind me inviting you like this."

"Why would I mind? We're both friends and friends of Publius, I'm honoured."

"The chair is for Valeria, I have to be honest Caius we're all a little nervous around you, Publius we've known most of our lives, his friendship makes you our friend too, his obvious respect for you commands our respect for you as well, but you are a mystery to the rest of the club, you struggle with our language and offer information that no mortal man should know in advance."

"I assure you I'm all too mortal, what do you prefer I call you?"

"Pulcher, everyone uses my cognomen."

"Well, I'm all too mortal Pulcher and not at all special, except and only in the strange way I find myself here. Yes I have a great deal of knowledge, which will be of use to you all and I believe I was put here for a purpose, I even believe I know what that purpose is, but do not think that I have any real power, I possess none in reality."

"I will repay friendship with friendship, trust with trust, fidelity with fidelity. You offer me friendship and respect as a respected friend of Publius I offer you the same, for much the same reasons."

"I'm glad we're having this talk, but I have to admit I'm not the person behind it. Valeria is most keen to converse with you and this is the only way, there will not be another event like yesterday's for a while I think and even if there were, people observe things."

"Brother, Caius."

Valeria swept into the room and sat upon the chair, giving no inkling that she'd been listening to our conversation, though we both suspected she had; she continued.

"I'm famished, I've instructed the servants to bring the food in and then return to the kitchen until they're sent for.

"Caius, I gather you make my brother nervous, she said with a smile."

That settled the eavesdropping suspicion then.

"Apparently so, although there's no reason for him to feel so."

"You do not make me nervous."

"I'm pleased to hear it."

"You do raise as many questions as you answer however, probably more."

"That which I feel able to reveal I will reveal" I answered.

"It may not satisfy however, you may need to be patient, get to know me better."

"Oh I intend to. I think Publius matters, I think my dear brother and the Jupiter Club matter."

I shot Pulcher a glance and he had the decency to look bashful, or perhaps it was just that he was simply too easy to read, especially by his sister.

"I think you too matter, in fact it may be that you matter the most."

"I assure you.."

"Don't."

She cut across me.

"Don't say it, I know my place, but I'm not a fool and I'm not an enemy. I can't take a place in the world of men openly, but I can possibly help in more subtle ways.

"My father has given me much freedom for a Roman woman, some would say too much."

It was her turn to glance at her brother.

"Some women are happy to be mere ornaments, some to simply breed the next generation for Rome, others are interested in fun, scandal, gossip, other shall we say pleasures.

"I want more. I realise that any contribution I make must be behind the scenes, I'm a realist, but I have a brain and I intend to use it."

"I have the greatest respect for women, in my own."

I stopped myself. It was Pomponia all over again, probing, wanting to know everything, but this lady attracted me and was single, out of reach as regards class and status but one can dream and still unaware of her exact age, I did.

"Let's eat, the fish is fresh this morning and our cook is excellent, you won't regret coming"

Thus Pulcher cut short the exchange. Not that it was long before Valeria recommenced her interrogation.

Over the course of the meal I explained the, by now agreed, version of events. I was a ship's captain, a merchant with knowledge of and a grudge against Carthage, that I had knowledge useful to Publius as a result and so on and so forth.

"But there's more" she said, "there has to be more, I just know it."

"As I told Pomponia, trust comes with time and experience. You will learn that I am honest and trustworthy, loyal and on the side of Rome and my friends. If I learn that the same is true of you, I may reveal more, in time."

I became a frequent visitor to the Pulcher household, my relationship with Valeria became warm but always appropriate, except maybe in thoughts and looks exchanged between us.

Publius reappeared on the scene after a week of enjoying married life and he and Amelia often accompanied me to the Pulcher household and indeed, many a time, he invited them and me to his new home.

In the meantime I lived in the house of his father under the care of his mother, who spoke to me more and more, helped me with my Latin, examined the strange indecipherable writing on my scrolls and gradually relaxed in my company.

I was blissfully unaware that she and Valeria were also meeting frequently and discussing the war, the Jupiter Club and their thoughts about me. In my own time their friendship might have been remarked on, but in Rome people were less divided by age than by class.

Publius was swiftly named as junior military tribune and the other members of the Jupiter Club were duly appointed as tribunes too. A four legion army was freshly recruited and began training. With Italian allied legions it would be an eight legion army, the greatest army Rome had ever fielded and more than a match for the barbarians, or so everyone believed.

I knew that the variety of soldiers in Hannibal's army and the different ways in which they fought, coupled with the experience, genius, leadership, determination and cunning of Hannibal himself would annihilate this mighty force. I kept my counsel, except with Publius and the Jupiter Club despite the increasingly pointed questions from Pomponia, Valeria and now Amelia Tertia into the bargain.

I needed to ensure that the Jupiter Club members knew their roles and that they all survived to rally the survivors as my history books had taught me they would.

Time was going way too fast, although I would depart to play my part after the departure of the others time was still short. Summer was upon us. Aemilia was with child, Rome was boiling hot and she retired to her father's villa in the hills above Rome in an area we now know as the town of Frascati.

Publius myself and the members of the Jupiter Club would hold constant discussions at the Villa. Pomponia and Valeria virtually moved in on the pretext of looking after Aemilia. She needed little looking after, but they were their own happy scheming triumvirate of beauty, allied to intelligence and ambition. Three veritable lionesses; Aemilia welcomed the other two as much as they desired to be there.

Writing this now in 2023, despite having started to write in 2007 and remembering the view from the villa I'm pretty certain that my sailing friend Hans from Groningen who now lives in a luxury ground floor apartment in Frascati is living over, or next to Paullus's villa and for all that his apartment is lovely it's nothing compared to the opulence I enjoyed there some two thousand, two hundred and thirty nine years before, or thereabouts.

It would be scant days before the tribunes left. The battle order of the army would be the decision of Paullus and Varro, the young men could not influence it even if they tried, Hannibal's battle winning strategy could not be altered either. All the boys needed to do, well no small thing actually, but what the boys had to do was cut their way out and get themselves to Canusium.

Given that Publius was attached to the first legion, Bibulus the second Pulcher the third and so on it was not as if they could easily work together to form a unit that would cut through. All I could do was explain how the battle would unfold.

It was vital that these young men, 'our boys' as I called them (probably due to watching too many World War Two movies as a child as well as to the age difference), should find a way to survive. In twelve, thirteen, fourteen years time when they would be in their early thirties these men would all play crucial roles in Rome's eventual victory. At least forewarned is forearmed as we say in the modern world.

Regarding the age difference, historians assert that I was about the same age as Publius, not so obviously although travelling backwards in time had somehow seemed to make me feel younger, even look younger I kidded myself.

My son and Scipio's grandson would one day meet Polybius and give him much of the information for his book, my son got his information from me and it in fact became the primary source for me to brief Publius and the Jupiter Club. Strange the fates are. Something I thought to myself very often over the years.

It always struck me as a great irony that in a roundabout way through my writing and notes, passed eventually to my son that I gave Polybius the information that would one day save my own life and keep history on track!

My son not yet born in 216BC, but who would be born, although in quite a few years time, would have access to my own histories. Histories written in modern English, a language he grew up with. He translated my scrolls into Latin for me and for posterity, his Latin being so much better than my own. He also of course heard my stories endlessly at social events as I became older.

Both his writings and my own seem to have been lost whilst those of Polybius survive. The universe it seems does have a plan. The books we have from ancient Rome, those that survived, were copied and re-copied over time so my scribblings and my son's are almost certainly lost. I want to say for all time, but when is that?

I digress though. I explained to the boys how the legions would face a convex front line, that Hannibal would place his best troops on the wings, I explained that Hannibal despite no longer having elephants, had superiority in cavalry and deadly Balearic slingers and javelin throwers.

I drew diagrams and explained how the convex line would change into a concave one and tempt the legions forward, how Rome's cavalry would be outfought, out-manned and outmanoeuvred. How the crack African troops on the wings would turn inwards and with the Carthaginian cavalry now free of opposition attacking the rear, the smaller army would in fact completely encircle the larger, restrict it, confine it and kill it on an industrial scale.

All I could tell them I told them, They knew that the Gauls were the weakest link and that both the Roman camps would subsequently surrender or be taken. They needed to cut their way through the Gauls, find horses if possible and whatever happened they had to make it to Canusium where I would be waiting to meet them and explain what had to happen next.

Leander and a couple of picked men were to accompany me to Canusium, there was no point in having more, capture would be a disaster, fighting was not an option, but we knew where Hannibal was and we could get to the rendezvous without too much difficulty. Unlike the boys.

I had about ten days at the villa with just the three women and servants for company. Naturally the women harangued me for information and the day before I left I decided it was safe to tell them. They could not influence the outcome and they would learn that my information was good, thus reinforcing their confidence in me. There was one enormous problem however.

How do you tell a newly married, pregnant young lady who has seen her husband and father go off to war, that only one will return?

I managed to get Pomponia and Valeria aside in the gardens.

"I'm going to tell you now what will happen. Then I'm going to tell all three of you together what will happen at the evening meal. I need your advice and your help and I'm trusting you. I believe it's certain that all the boys will survive, something which is in itself miraculous.

"Hannibal has a greater variety of weapons, he will defeat our cavalry and lure the legions forward, they will be surrounded and annihilated. It will be Rome's worst military disaster in a couple of hundred years.

"I say again the boys will escape and I will meet them and help them to not only make good their escape but to raise their profile, especially Publius's profile, but that brings us to Paullus."

"Ye gods."

It was Pomponia who spoke Valeria looked into my eyes, tears forming in her own. It was clear they believed that I truly knew, even if they railed against it.

"How do I tell Aemilia?"

"Tell it to her exactly as you just told us, honest, straightforward, sincere."

Again it was Pomponia, who spoke and who it seemed had started to grow fond of me. One day I would have to reveal that her husband and brother in law were to die too in far off Spain and that her son would be the only Roman prepared to go and avenge them. That would come soon enough, but thankfully not just yet.

Valeria was looking at me and nodding as Pomponia spoke.

"Aemilia is strong and we will take care of her."

I didn't tell it word for word over dinner, I let Aemilia know first that there was both good and tragic news for her in particular, but other than that I kept it factual and straightforward as before. She didn't faint or panic, she did weep.

"Did Publius know?"

"Yes."

"Why didn't he tell me?"

"That's my fault, mea culpa, there are good reasons I promise you and one day, when all of this is behind us I will explain those reasons to you Aemilia, to all three of you. On this I give you my word."

Thus it was that I committed myself to tell them whence I came, but not for some years at least.

"Publius loves you deeply, your marriage will last, you will have five children.

"Publius will be the greatest Roman of his age and one of the greatest generals in all history. You will be happy, you will enjoy greater autonomy and freedom than many a Roman woman.

"Many noble families will suffer loss at this battle, almost all in fact, senators and consulars, knights and ordinary Romans will fall, everyone in Rome will have cause to mourn someone, but the boys will return, your husband will return to father more children, you will know joy again."

I was tempted with the sunshine after the rain thing but had the sense to stop there. Pomponia and Valeria took over.

Next morning as I was preparing to leave Valeria came secretly to my room.

"What of us?"

To the point when she wanted to be!

"What exactly do you mean by that?"

"You and me, what awaits us?"

"I don't know Valeria, I don't know everything, that would be far too great a burden for any man. What do you want for us?"

"You've suggested that you were put here for a reason."

"Yes, I have to believe that to make any sense of it all, my life is not my own anymore."

"I too believe in destiny and I believe you are my destiny."

"What makes you believe that?"

"It's hard to explain, I could have been betrothed a hundred times, even from the age of twelve, yet from early on I've felt that I was important. Arrogant, hubris, pride, foolishness, yes, all of those things, but I have always felt I needed to wait for a sign, that somehow, somewhere something would happen that would show me my course.

"A huge risk, I gained a reputation for arrogance and standoffishness, my father was thought weak and overindulgent for humouring me.

"I could never shake the belief that I was waiting for someone though. There were noble Romans I was attracted to who would have loved to ally themselves to the Pulcher clan, the slightest hint from me and I could have been happily betrothed, even mistress of my own household and mother to children by now, but I waited."

"You think you were waiting for me then?"

"There's no other explanation, nothing like this has ever happened."

"Are you saying you want to marry me?"

"Yes, I am."

"Do you love me?"

"Is that important?"

"Yes, to me it's very important, where I come from.."

"Continue."

"I can't, not now."

"If you don't love me, then what else is there?"

"I didn't say I don't love you, or that I couldn't love you, I just believe it's my destiny. Many women have arranged marriages, most in our, my circle anyway, some find love later, some find only a degree of contentment, for some it's ghastly.

"I know enough of you to know that life with you would not be ghastly, I believe you're my destiny, that we will matter, our children will matter and I think we can make each other happy."

"I applaud your honesty. I can say that I fell in love with you at Publius's wedding, no doubt of it. If I love you but the reverse is not true you will hold all the power. That is not good for me.

"Nonetheless I can't deny my feelings and I cant deny that your assessment may be correct. Nearly everything I believed in has been shaken, tested or broken these last few years.

"We will talk about it when I return."

I kissed her lightly on the cheek. She threw her arms around my neck and hugged me tight without kissing me then let me go.

"Yes, we'll talk when you return, you have much else to think about I know, but think about me too, nay."

All three women saw us off. I let Leander lead the way and make the accommodation arrangements along the way. He was comprehensively briefed on where we were to go and by what route and by when we needed to be in Canusium.

The journey was not as enjoyable as the earlier ride to Rome. Cannae was to be a disaster on a massive scale. I knew only too well what was to follow.

I arrived in Canusium towards the middle of Quinctilis, that is July to you and me. I knew from my history studies, although I don't recall Polybius or Livy giving the exact date, that the battle of Cannae was supposed to have taken place on the second of August, that is the second of Sextilis as we called it then.

The problem for me was that the Republican Roman Calendar, predating the Julian, let alone the Gregorian calendar had only six months of thirty or thirty one days. In short the Romans were sixty one days short of a year! Luckily for me the seasons more or less coincided with the calendar in 216 BC which obviously wasn't always the case.

All of this haphazardness meant that I could predict accurately what would happen, but exact timings were beyond me. In fact I based the timing of my arrival at Canusium on the manoeuvres I expected the army to make, the distances involved and so on.

The crucial thing was that I not be late! In either sense of the word. Accordingly I arrived at Canusium near two weeks ahead of the battle.

Once there I sought out a noblewoman called Paulina Busa. I knew that at the end of the war she had been honoured by the senate for the aid she had given the Roman survivors of Cannae when they arrived, bloodied, often wounded, exhausted, hungry and although we don't like to admit it, somewhat frightened in many cases.

Our meeting was, how shall I put it, interesting.

A wealthy widow, Paulina Busa was her own woman. On the face of it a supporter of Rome and Roman laws and conventions, she was however, not one to be told what she could and could not inherit or how she should conduct herself.

"I cannot tell you how I know, but the gods speak to you now through me."

She laughed and I couldn't help myself, so did I.

"I'm sorry. I have to tell you things. You are someone who matters, if I can help you to be prepared then so much the better. I know you will do the right thing, believe me it is already written."

She simply smiled, ironically I suppose you'd call it this time. I persevered.

"You are aware that the army of Hannibal is in the region and that an even larger Roman army is not far away either."

"I am."

"A Roman victory is expected, it will not happen."

"Go on."

"Rome will win this war, but not for many years yet. A battle will take place at the settlement called Cannae which will be the greatest disaster for Roman arms to date."

No point muddying the waters with Arausio.

"There will be more defeats in the future too, but after this battle the tide will slowly turn in Rome's favour until eventually a complete victory will come about.

"From Rome's vast army some ten or at the most fourteen thousand will survive to return to the fight. Some four thousand anyway will arrive here at Canusium.

"The battle will occur approximately ten miles away from here, those who choose to make for Canusium will do so at night, most will arrive before sun up.

"Within the four thousand or so survivors who will arrive here will be a number of nobles, Publius Cornelius Scipio has sent me to you."

"Publius Cornelius Scipio is fighting in Spain."

She cut across me. She knew her stuff!

"His son Publius Cornelius Scipio has sent me to you, he and his friends are all junior military tribunes. I have reason to believe they will all survive. They will be crucial in defeating Hannibal when their time comes, it is vital that they survive and take command of this group of survivors.

"They will all need your aid Paulina, you are wealthy, but more than that you are respected, you have influence in this place. The town's leaders will be understandably nervous, they will fear that helping the remnants of the army will bring the full wrath of Hannibal down upon them.

"Trust me Scipio and his friends will rally the survivors, our task is to make sure those men are fit to march as soon as possible. They will be tired, hungry, mostly weaponless, demoralised, even scared, they will have seen more death, blood and terror in one day than most of us see in a lifetime.

"We must give them back their swords, their strength and their spirits."

"And you're telling me this why?"

"I know you will help Paulina, as I have said, it is written. By forewarning you I can help you to be more effective. Stockpile food and medicines, warn those with medical skill that you may need to call upon them, prepare to win any arguments about helping the defeated and defying Hannibal. If you can obtain them source weapons and armour too.

"All I'm really saying is be ready, I know you stand with us, I know you will do what's right, I'm just helping you to be prepared."

"Strange it is that you, a foreigner should speak to me so, and yet I too have had premonitions. It shall be done as you say, you should stay under my roof, my servants will also take care of your people and of your animals."

So it was that preparations were quietly made to welcome the survivors. I stationed the members of my small party at the entrances to the town each night and threatened them with every misfortune should they fall asleep in the late hours before dawn and we waited, and we waited.

On the fifteenth night after my arrival at about the fourth hour, chaos threatened to erupt. The first of the survivors staggered into the town. With the aid of Paulina, Leander and my travelling companions we were able to ensure they were admitted, although there was opposition from some of the townspeople they were taken unawares and we were prepared.

Finding greater comfort and shelter than the streets was no simple thing. Paulina convinced her friends first then went out and about around the town tirelessly persuading people to take in one here, two or three there, open their storehouses and stables if not their homes.

Those who opposed giving shelter to the fugitives soon realised that they had lost the argument and before too long the number of refugees was sufficient to brook no argument anyway. Tired and apparently broken they may have seemed yet many still had some spirit left and the will to survive was strong in them. They were not cowards who'd run away, no one escaped Cannae without being a fighter.

The members of the Jupiter Club did not arrive in one group as I'd hoped in my wildest fantasies. They'd been spread about in different parts of the field, each would have different recollections of the fight, each his own story to tell, stories of the heroism and self sacrifice of others, stories of men dying quickly and of men dying slowly in agony, clutching their wounds, foaming pink at the mouth, crying out the names of loved ones and of gods appealed to and gods cursed.

Nor did the boys arrive in quick succession and Scipio was the fifth to arrive, leaving me breathless with worry, for all I thought I knew.

Paulina was friendly with another widow of Canusium, there was no shortage of widows in Rome or Italy. Women who survived the perils of childbirth frequently outlived husbands. At my suggestion Paulina's friend was to take in Caecilius Metellus and his friends. Confident of their status they would take it for granted they would be accommodated in one of the more comfortable homes.

She was also instructed to set her servants, whilst delivering food and drink to listen to and report on the conversations amongst the young men until such time as Lucius Furius Philus could be insinuated into the Caecilius Metellus group to keep watch.

It was not long after Philus had settled into the widow's home that he returned stating that Caecilius deemed the war lost and was at that moment persuading his friends and fellow nobles to quit Italy and offer their services to a foreign king, which foreign king was the only subject of debate currently.

In the meantime the remainder of the Jupiter Club had elected to follow Scipio and Appius Claudius Pulcher, brother of the lady, girl almost, who had stolen my heart. I followed at the back of the group as Scipio, sword in hand, he'd not thrown his equipment away in flight, led the Jupiter Club entire down the street and burst in on Caecilius Metellus.

Though Caecilius and his friends were twelve in number to our nine, the shock of the intrusion and the sheer, blazing fury of Publius and his group stunned them to silence.

Publius delivered a very short and to the point lecture about the nature of what it meant to be a Roman, that the country was not lost and forced them at the point of his blade to swear eternal fealty to Rome on pain of death at his hand should any so much as think of wavering again.

All swore the oath, individually aloud and in front of nineteen other high born witnesses plus myself. Scipio announced that all those fit enough would march for Rome to reinforce the city, it being assumed that Hannibal would march on Rome once he'd finished with the two nearby Roman camps, dealing with the spoils and the captives.

I had assured Publius that Hannibal would not march on Rome, nonetheless that's where his reputation would be enhanced by events and he could not at this juncture claim advance knowledge of what would happen to any but the Jupiters anyhow.

I knew that Varro would also rally survivors, some ten thousand at Venusia compared with the roughly four thousand here at Canusium. I advised Scipio that we should probably not head straight to Rome but in fact that the correct thing would be to report to the surviving commanding officer.

Publius of course could not reveal how he knew Varro had survived, much less that he had ten thousand troops left scant thirty miles away. Fortunately this conundrum was soon solved. Varro had sent out horsemen in search of other groups of survivors and Scipio and Pulcher who were now undisputed commanders of our rag tag group were happy to march to Venusia and report to Varro for duty.

We would be in Rome soon enough and no one could accuse the tribunes of any wrongdoing. Details of the would be mutiny of Caecilius Metellus and friends was kept quiet to avoid division and against future need. Caecilius dare not cross the Jupiters now or in the foreseeable future.

CHAPTER 9
ROME IN TURMOIL THE END OF 216BC 538

Soon enough we found ourselves back in Rome, a Rome quite unlike the one we had left so recently, a Rome so very confident in her eight legion, two consul army just a few weeks ago, now roiling with grief, worry, fear and recriminations.

I, technically not a member of the army rode behind the column with Leander and the two servants who had accompanied me to Canusium. The survivors made as bold and proud appearance as they could but there was no hiding their physical and mental state, skinny and dirty, with sunken eyes and cheeks that were obvious in many cases. Missing armour and weapons had only been partially replaced.

A few who had acquitted themselves well, escaped uninjured and had held on to their equipment and spirits looked better. This certainly applied to the Jupiters. Caecilius Metellus and his friends, well looked after in Canusium, looked in good shape too, only a few of us knew of their spinal problems.

As the fourteen thousand marched into Rome, indeed as soon as we were espied approaching the city the population turned out en mass, not excluding noble families. "So few, so few, just look at them".

As men were recognised they were assailed by both their loved ones, but also by the loved ones of their friends, neighbours, colleagues and acquaintances demanding news. Occasionally the news was, "he's here somewhere", occasionally "I think he's a captive we may be able to ransom him".

Far too often the response was just a shake of the head or an expression of sorrow. Soon the roads were lined with grief stricken mothers, lovers and sisters tearing their hair and clothes and screaming through a miasma of tears, what menfolk they had left were holding them up or providing a shoulder to cry on. Too many had no one.

The so called upper classes tended to maintain their dignity somewhat better, but many a noblewoman was seen with tears streaming down her face being supported by and ushered away by her servants.

Barely a household was unaffected and as families grieved the senate ground into action. Senate sat each and every day for weeks. The Sibylline Books were consulted, a delegation was sent to enquire of the Oracle at Delphi, what did it mean, what was to be Rome's proper course of action, what gods had she offended and why were the gods favouring her enemies?

One of the accusations frequently made against Carthage was that they were barbarians who indulged in human sacrifice. Rome now sank to that very level of barbarity.

Four more deaths may have been seen as nothing against the killing fields and mass slaughter at Cannae. Nonetheless four innocent victims were buried alive, this was truly Rome's darkest hour. For all I had wanted to see and experience Rome I was sickened and stayed closeted with Pomponia.

Scipio returned to his new home and comforted Aemilia, but he was out and about daily getting all the news he could of goings on in the senate, sounding out the plebs and coming to me with questions. The only time I went out was to meetings of the Jupiter Club now reconvened in the temple of Jupiter Optimus Maximus.

Prior to each meeting Publius consulted with me regarding what to say to the members. There wasn't so very much to say in terms of what to do, what could we do that wasn't being done by those in power. A paltry two new legions were being raised and even this could only be achieved by breaking all the normal requirements; even slaves were purchased by the state if they were willing to fight and achieve freedom later.

What I knew I was able to tell the members. Firstly I knew that Hannibal would not attack Rome. Some of his officers wished it, but siege warfare had not been Carthage's most successful form of attack, either at Saguntum or since.

Hannibal would instead try to sap Rome's support, turn other cities and Italian tribes against her, set up a rival. By these means he intended to destroy Rome's power and her influence even if the destruction of the city itself was not an immediate option.

A messenger arrived, in fact a group of messengers sworn to return to Hannibal as captives came to the city with an offer to ransom the many captives Hannibal held. I had of course prepared the Jupiters for this event and also predicted the senate's response. Whilst I personally was sickened by the senate's refusal to save the men Hannibal had captured I could not help but admire Rome's determination and the message it sent.

Relatives of those not ransomed did not feel at all kindly disposed to the senate's decision, but in matters of war the senate held the power. Yet more families turned from hope to grief.

The disasters of 216BC or 538 as we knew it were not over. I had to advise that Spurius Postumius Albinus and two entire legions plus allies would be wiped out almost literally to a man in a forest ambush by the Boii. Spurius would die with his men and his skull would be gold plated and used in Boii religious ceremonies for many years to come.

Rome could ill afford the loss of another roughly twenty five thousand soldiers including cavalry and auxiliaries. In addition her military reputation was in tatters, it was not just Hannibal who'd found ways to defeat the mighty military machinery of Rome with her previously much feared legions of immovable infantry. Then there was the political upheaval that followed the death of Spurius who had been consul elect for 539.

There were only two things I could offer the Jupiters to try to shine a small ray of light in the gloom. One was that I was able to assure them that the Boii were well satisfied with their victory and had neither the energy nor the intelligence to follow it up. That and the fact that Hannibal would attack Nola and be repulsed by Marcus Claudius Marcellus and the Roman garrison he'd installed there in the nick of time.

Hannibal's hopes rested on the fact that a faction in the city were enthusiastic to betray Rome and go over to Carthage. Marcellus knew of the conspiracy and declined to take his men out and offer a pitched battle, knowing the gates of Nola would be closed behind him.

When Marcellus failed to come out Hannibal decided on a frontal attack on the main gates with what siege equipment and rams he had. Although Marcellus left enough men behind to ensure control of the city gates he led the major part of his force out when the besiegers least expected it and inflicted major losses on Hannibal's troops. Albeit not sufficient by any means to end the war, or take Hannibal out of the equation it was something of a morale booster at Rome.

I counselled the Jupiters to display joy at the victory and exude confidence. Even so the Saturnalia was a much reduced torpid affair with so many absent, never to return, whether dead or, something Romans perhaps dreaded even more than death, sold into slavery.

So it was that this terrible year finally passed away. It would be 213BC our 541 before Scipio would stand for curule aedile, more than two years hence and it would be 210BC or 544 before my friend would gain his first command and in tragic personal circumstances at that.

That's not to say that the next few years would be uneventful, far from it, there would be action on the field of battle in the Italian and Iberian theatres and a great deal of politicking for us in Rome, it's only to say that Hannibal's greatest achievements now lay behind him. He had subdued Iberia, crossed the Pyrenees, the Rhone and The Alps facing opposition at every step. Whilst still leaving substantial forces behind him to protect his gains.

He'd defeated Rome at Ticinus and Trebia. He had crossed the marshes at the cost of an eye and gone on to inflict another terrible defeat on the Romans at Lake Thrasymene and now he'd wiped out a vast Roman army at Cannae in a bloodbath to rival the mechanised killing seen in World War One.

Hannibal would remain active in Italy for years to come but fortune would gradually desert him. He and his brothers would achieve more victories, the pain was not over for Rome but the pendulum was at the very end of its arc.

I was able to advise the Jupiters, that just as Rome had other enemies, such as the Boii, Carthage was not immune from attack from other quarters either. I was able to predict that King Syphax of Numida would revolt against Carthage in a year or so and that forces which might otherwise have been sent to Hannibal would be tied up in Africa.

I was also able to prophesy that there would be good news next year from Spain. Publius Cornelius Scipio and his brother Gnaeus would have their moment in the sun, inflicting a heavy, if not conclusive defeat on the Carthaginians at Ibera.

Capua and Syracuse would go over to Carthage and this would be a blow, Capua being one of, if not the richest city in Italy as well as being a river port. Syracuse owning a massive and secure harbour would be valuable to Carthage too, but at least it wasn't a harbour on the mainland.

Neapolis, a far greater prize on the other hand, would stay loyal. Some southern Italian tribes would go over to Hannibal, but the Latins and Etruscans would remain loyal. The alliance that bound Italy to Rome was injured, but still far from dead.

On the home front as I thought of it Scipio and to some extent Appius Claudius Pulcher and the other Jupiters would start to make their names and their reputations politically, although none would achieve the level of popularity achieved by Scipio. Already a war hero, the good news from Spain of the success of his father and uncle would build support bordering on love for the Scipionic faction.

The following years would be momentous for me personally too.

CHAPTER 10
LIFE ON THE HOME FRONT 215BC

The fear in Rome gradually subsided. The fourteen thousand survivors of Cannae recovered their health and confidence, the two new legions were enlisted and were well on the way to being trained. Rome's resilience and self belief were remarkable.

At the beginning of the year Hannibal was in winter quarters in Capua, it was still a year of war, although inconclusive in Italy. Carthaginian forces tried to take Sardinia and failed. Hasdrubal tried to break out of Spain to come and reinforce Hannibal, but was prevented from so doing by my friend's father and uncle.

The battle of Ibera, once again near the Ebro River prevented Hasdrubal from moving east and raised morale in Rome, but still failed to end Carthaginian power on the Iberian Peninsular. Both Hasdrubal and the Scipio brothers had received limited reinforcements and both armies were about twenty five thousand strong. The Roman victory was largely due to Hasdrubal's Iberians in the centre failing to stand their ground.

Nonetheless losses on both sides were considerable, yet Hasdrubal escaped with his cavalry pretty much intact. The major effect of events in Spain and Sardinia was that Carthage failed to reinforce Hannibal, either from Spain or Africa, whilst at the height of his success and this may have turned the course of the war, with hindsight.

Early in the year as I'd prophesied tribune of plebs Gaius Oppius introduced his Lex Oppia, a sumptuary law, ostensibly to limit expenditure on frivolities in a time of war. How it helped the war effort was beyond me and beyond most of the women affected. It satisfied Rome's misogynists though and took people's attention for a while.

So far as I could tell, none of the women, certainly not the ones I knew anyway, were materially worse off. Naturally Pomponia, Aemilia Tertia and Valeria were forewarned anyway. Pomponia had simply secreted her jewellery and her friends and servants were fiercely loyal. Publius took care of his wife's treasures and Appius Claudius Pulcher took care of things for his sister.

It was the fact that women could no longer wear jewellery, or multi coloured garments in public that rankled the most with Rome's upper class women. They could not ride in a carriage either, except to attend religious ceremonies. Personal adornment and clothing was the way a noble woman proclaimed to the world that she was someone. They weren't happy. Only my little group knew the law would outlast the war and not be repealed until 559 and so they resigned themselves to it more than most.

Come spring, Hannibal had a second attempt to take Nola and failed once more, again being repulsed by Marcus Claudius Marcellus. These successes in Spain and Nola had a considerable, beneficial effect on morale but the situation was still precarious.

Later in the year Hannibal proceeded to occupy both Heraclea and Thurii and we besieged Capua, however the situation in Italy although it ebbed and flowed effectively remained at a stalemate once more come the end of the year.

The consuls for the year were Tiberius Sempronius Gracchus and, elected to replace the gold plated Boii trophy, the now deceased Spurius Postumius Albinus, was the saviour of Nola, Marcus Claudius Marcellus.

Marcus Junius Pera had officially been made dictator after the defeat at Cannae and it was his support that won Tiberius the consulship.

Nonetheless Quintus Fabius Maximus Verrucosus Cunctator was the man really in control and a return to avoiding major risk taking was very much the order of the day. As I had predicted to Scipio sometime before, Fabius was once again beloved of the people and the epithet Cunctator, intended originally as an insult, had become instead rather a badge of honour and respect.

Scipio and I, and indeed most of the Jupiters, spent by far the major part of the year in Rome. Meetings of the Jupiter Club took place weekly in the temple and Scipio and I met there also after dark whenever we wanted to talk privately. I also continued to teach him English and he helped me with my Latin.

We all kept abreast of events as they happened. My predictions continued to prove valid and I confirmed to Scipio that Syphax would turn on Carthage next year, again preventing reinforcements reaching Hannibal from Africa and helping his father's situation in Spain into the bargain.

Feeling secure that the year would end without anything decisive happening, and knowing that Scipio would not be curule aedile for a couple of years yet, we were able to talk about personal matters. It was important that Scipio's popularity and visibility should remain high and to this end he made sure he was seen with the Cunctator as much as possible.

Living, as I was, with Pomponia was very comfortable and allowed me much time for thinking and writing without the burden of loneliness, something which was a risk given my out of time, out of place situation and Scipio's happily married state.

My social life might have revolved solely around Pomponia and Scipio and Aemilia, but thankfully Valeria Pulcher had other ideas. I had decided that perhaps I was more besotted than in love and that her interest in me was more a kind of superstition than a passion, I'd also discovered her true age and my opinion of seventeen year olds was coloured by my experiences in the modern world.

Here girls were often betrothed or married at fourteen, sometimes younger. They grew up quickly and girls from noble families had a high opinion of themselves and their status, they knew their own minds early.

Given the need for high born Roman ladies to protect their virginity until married, then physical passion wasn't likely to enter into the equation. In my own time sex before marriage was not a rarity and some might consider it an essential before settling down and committing to a partner. Nor did magazines like Cosmopolitan seek to influence young women to save themselves. In 215BC things were somewhat different.

It wasn't long before I was receiving social invitations to the Pulcher household, whenever the father, Publius, was unavailable, but these events still presented no opportunity for private meetings with Valeria.

In March Aemilia announced that she would return to the family villa for her confinement. Pomponia announced that she would be going to keep Aemilia company and asked me to accompany her on the journey and to stay a few days at least.

I happily agreed to the change of scenery and a none too arduous ride in the spring weather. On the morning of our departure Valeria arrived at Pomponia's house in travelling clothes and accompanied by a few servants. She informed me that she would like to ride with me.

Clearly I was being manoeuvred by the ladies, but I was still drawn to Valeria whether I liked it or not, all the more so when I found myself in her proximity as now. We rode side by side and as the party became just a little strung out Valeria read me the riot act.

"I told you that I believed our destiny is to be together and you assured me that you had feelings for me. An alliance with my family is far beyond what you might expect, it gives you a chance to become someone.

"You must realise this, why have you not spoken to my father, or at least questioned my brother about these matters. You spoke about me having too much power because you believed your feelings for me to be stronger than my feelings for you but it's unbecoming for a woman in my situation to display her feelings and furthermore as paterfamilias in your own household you would hold all the power anyway.

"I insist you give me an answer, you who seem to think you know everything."

It was a strange feeling being told how the land lies by someone so much younger, but she was right. If I was to build a life in Rome being married into one of its most important families could only be a good thing, it would give me legitimacy, status, money and it would in some sense legitimise my friendship with Publius also given that I was currently a nobody.

It finally dawned on me that Valeria was a gift from the gods, or fate and that whatever her motivation she was clever, beautiful, on my side in effect and I knew she would be loyal. I could envisage happiness, a sense of belonging, a family of my own once again.

My life in the modern world hadn't been such a success in that area, twice divorced with one daughter who had come to have little time for me. I didn't want to be a three time loser, but fear gets one nowhere fast.

"Confarreatio?"

"Thank the gods, yes Caius, of course, if it can be made possible."

"Ah, yes I have to be a Roman Patrician first don't I."

"It's worse than that I'm afraid, you have to be eligible for high office too, I don't know that we can achieve that much, certainly not quickly, but we can get married and we can make our vows to one another."

Naturally it wouldn't actually be as simple as that either. I knew the younger Pulcher, we were by now firm friends but the father I knew not at all and if I were him I'd not be happy about such a union.

The age difference wasn't an issue in Roman culture, but class and wealth certainly were. Valeria was in his hand as paterfamilias. As Valeria had pointed out the paterfamilias held all the power in family matters.

That evening I had dinner with Scipio, Pomponia, Valeria and Aemilia, and I, uncomfortably for me, was the main topic of conversation. Clearly this was a conversation all the other parties had prepared for in the event that Valeria signalled my willingness to marry her. Schemers the lot of them!

"We all want this and I'm sure your brother will be with us on this won't he Valeria?"

It was Scipio who started proceedings.

"Oh yes, my brother will be all for it, if anything happened to Pater I'd be in his hand, but of course none of us wants anything to befall papa, we just have to convince him."

"I'm sure your brother will help, but we need arguments to lay before your father to convince him. For a start I will offer a farm as a wedding gift, trade is looked down on, land is considered honourable and a requirement for senatorial rank."

"I appreciate the offer really I do Publius, but aren't we getting ahead of ourselves, I don't actually hold the citizenship yet, to say nothing of equestrian rank; the senate, ye gods."

"You do have citizenship my father bestowed it upon you for your help in the campaign."

"No he didn't."

"Well, no, he didn't, but I can forge his signature well enough and mother has a spare seal, she doesn't admit it, but I know that she does."

He looked conspiratorially at Pomponia whose smile betrayed her.

"I'll make up the document with an appropriate date and we'll get it lodged, we'll just have to say we've been too busy and forgot, war and all, but with me vouching for you personally it won't be doubted.

"So, welcome citizen."

"Thank you."

"And, marry Valeria here and you can invest her dowry and with my gift you'll be a landowner too. As I rise up the cursus honorum I will be in a position to appoint you to tasks that will make your name and reputation as well."

"I think we're all aware of the benefits to me, it's the benefits to old man Pulcher, sorry Valeria, that are lacking and that's where it all falls apart."

"It's my wish to marry you, I will have to convince papa, probably I'll have to try and get at least partial approval before he even meets you, Pater never goes back on his word."

"And just what will be your strategy?"

"I have actually thought about that. Papa might refuse to give me to someone he didn't approve of, but he'd never force me to marry someone I didn't want to marry. That's his Achilles heel.

"He may be paterfamilias, but he's a bit of a softy in some ways. For a start, a united front from wife, son and daughter would give him pause, but we need to go further. Brother Appius will have to say that were I in his hand he would give his blessing."

"Yes, but you aren't."

"Wait, the thing is Pater is dismayed that I wasn't betrothed at fourteen and mama wants a grandchild, if I can convince everyone that I simply won't marry anyone else and that I'll wait until such time as I am in my brother's hand I think the wall will crumble.

"Mama, will beg papa to let me marry so she can have grandchildren, papa will not like the idea of not seeing me married in his lifetime, you and my brother can promise to advance Caius's career and at that point we throw in the wedding gift.

"We must all speak to Pater, before he meets Caius, I'm afraid the poor Latin in particular will make father wish he'd never consented, but if he has consented to the rest of the family and made an agreement with you Publius he'll see it through.

"Pomponia once I've spoken to mama, will you find a reason to visit and add your support?"

"Of course dear."

And so it was that Publius became a forger of documents, I became a Roman citizen and Publius Claudius Pulcher was bullied by his wife and children into consenting to a family marriage with a man of no family whatsoever whom he'd never met and a foreigner in reality to boot.

Despite all the obstacles the wedding was arranged quickly and took place in June, being the month of the god Juno and the most propitious.

My new brother in law left straight after the ceremony. He had been elected praetor and had the duty of visiting Sicily with a detachment of the troops who survived Cannae to try and influence Hieronymus the grandson of our loyal ally King Hiero II to stay loyal to Rome. The King was on his deathbed and his grandson was coming under the influence of Carthage.

Appius Claudius would fail in this mission and would be obliged to spend much of this year and next in Sicily. I was aware that he would return to be consul in 212BC 542 alongside Quintus Fulvius Flaccus and that he would take the fight to Hannibal, something that would lead to his demise in 211BC 543.

I wondered if he believed my predictions about Publius Cornelius being the man to defeat Hannibal and wanted the glory, or whether he just felt it his patriotic duty. I agonised about telling him about his own death, but, as with everything else it was already written, what if he didn't go to fight as a result, what effect would that have on history?

Valeria had promised her mother a grandchild and I was delighted to play my part. My son would take my name but would attract the cognomen Sapiens, the wise. I was creating a reputation myself for predicting the future, but ensured that Publius took the credit, only the Jupiters knew my full role. My son on the other hand did not have the advantage of having read what would happen, he earned his cognomen as Publius earned his, the hard way.

Valeria and I were not married confarreatio, that I might one day be important enough to qualify seemed highly unlikely back then, but our vows to one another were sincere, we would not divorce. Furthermore, I believe now that despite her reliance on superstitious feelings, she either loved me at the time or subsequently came to.

My happiness was quite equal to that of my friend Publius. The wedding was still seen as a sacred ritual, there were many guests, all dressed like ourselves to prevent evil spirits identifying the bride and groom as was the custom. A goodly number of witnesses also boded well for married life and all the Jupiters had brought family and friends to help make the event auspicious.

The bride had her hair dressed and parted by the hasta, (a tradition you don't want to know about) and finished with a wreath, veil and yellow hairnet, we wore chaplets of roses and when all was done made love for the first time on a lectus couch. Earlier in the day I had had to pretend to kidnap Valeria to convince her household gods, the Lares that she did not go willingly! I don't think it was a very convincing display.

We had purchased our own house on the Clivus Scauri, it was close to the Palatine but not quite on the Palatine, upmarket enough without breaking the bank. Well, it would have broken the bank, but with gifts of money from all the Jupiters, especially the brother of the bride we did not need to borrow and of course we now had a modest income from our own farm!

It was beyond belief, from fugitive, to prophet, to Roman citizen, house owner and landowner, married to a beautiful and intelligent woman from one of Rome's most prestigious and oldest families and with friends in many of the other great families.

I was beside myself and although there was the little matter of the war I settled oh so happily into married life. We visited our farm in July to make ourselves known to the manager, employees and slaves and for Valeria to go over the accounts, she had a good head for such things. Fortunately the farm was well away from the war and only a single day's ride from Rome.

Before we left there was an important meeting of the Jupiter Club. I say important, there was nothing we could do to influence the war at this point, but it was important that the group stayed together and remained convinced of outright victory. Appius Claudius Pulcher, my brother in law was slightly older than my friend Scipio and had already held the post of aedile before Cannae.

I knew that the battle of Zama would not take place until 552, some thirteen years hence, even to me it seemed incredible that Hannibal could hang on and present a threat for so long. I also knew that Scipio would lose his father and uncle to Hasdrubal in Spain and would have to take on the war in Spain before he took it to Africa.

The one tool I had to keep everyone believing in my calendar of events and their roles in the final victory was to continue proving myself, and Scipio, by pre empting every bit of news that arrived in Rome. I always briefed Scipio before each meeting so he could be the one to give the details.

Hannibal was to ally himself with Philip of Macedon, they would pledge mutual support against Rome. Hannibal would still be able to make his own peace with Rome, should he so desire, something we all knew he was never likely to desire, but were he to do so Rome would have to cede Corcyra, Apollonia, Epidamnus, Pharos and much more to Philip and Demetrius of Pharos.

It was a worthless bit of politicking. Rome would have to be soundly beaten to give away so much, maybe Philip thought Hannibal would soundly beat Rome. Whether he had much intention of making a significant military contribution was more doubtful, just hoping to pick up some of the spoils for minimal risk and effort.

Maybe Hannibal believed Philip would prove a worthwhile ally. If so he would be disappointed. Other than a few thousand Macedonian warriors who would eventually be sent to Africa when it was almost all over King Philip did very little.

The only disappointment for Valeria and myself on the home front was the fact that a baby was not on the way. I couldn't tell her at such a young age and so full of optimism that she would not have a son until around thirty years of age!

I didn't know why we had such difficulty, but I did know the date of my son's birth, roughly anyway, in advance. The universe and its plan once more I suppose. Daughters not being so well documented I had thought that maybe there would be a child, maybe more than one for us before too long, but in the event our first child, our daughter Laelia Julia, would not appear until Valeria was twenty seven.

CHAPTER 11 EVENTS IN ITALY AND ELSEWHERE 214BC 540

At the beginning of the year 540 I advised Publius that Carthage would persuade Syracuse in Sicily to revolt from Rome despite the attentions of brother Appius and Marcus Claudius Marcellus who would also be despatched to Sicily. I was also able to counter the bad with some good in that Hasdrubal would be sent by Carthage to deal with the threat posed by King Syphax in Western Numidia.

In Syracuse King Hiero II had passed away and his grandson Hieronymus had come to the throne. Syracuse was equipped with a powerful fleet and extensive defences designed by the famous Greek thinker and philosopher Archimedes. There hadn't been an immediate severing of ties but the new king Hieronymus had come under the influence of the anti Roman faction as I knew he would.

Although Hieronymus would be assassinated Roman and Syracusan preparations for war, much like events leading up to World War One where all sides prepared for war, made a war that could and should have been avoided more or less inevitable. The siege of Syracuse would commence next year.

In Numidia Syphax would not be comprehensively defeated and his ongoing fight with Hasdrubal would help relieve the pressure on my friend's father and uncle in Spain. In fact next year, in the year we call 541 Syphax would formally ally himself with Rome. So far so good.

The Carthaginian general Hanno, had some time previously had been ordered by Hannibal to undertake operations in Bruttium, modern Calabria, and to turn the people there against Rome and to raise reinforcements. He would now be ordered to return to Hannibal with those much needed reinforcements.

Hanno had been successful in the south and currently had an army consisting of the twelve hundred Numidian horseman he'd started with plus some seventeen thousand infantry many being Bruttians and Lucanians. Hanno had recruited enthusiastically as instructed.

For our part, the consuls for the year were Quintus Fabius Maximus, now known as Cunctator, who'd been pulling the strings anyway for the last couple of years and a re-elected, once again, Marcus Claudius Marcellus who would take the command in Sicily, with brother Appius put in charge of our fleet there.

In the field Tiberius Sempronius Gracchus, aedile two years ago, consul last year and master of the horse to the dictator Marcus Junius Pera after Cannae, was despatched from winter quarters at Lucercia to Beneventum. Quintus Fabius Maximus, son of the Cunctator, destined to be consul next year, was to replace the slave army in Lucercia with a smaller separate force.

This redistribution, primarily intended to try once more to trap Hannibal in Campania, was a most fortuitous event since only Publius, myself and the Jupiters knew that Hanno had been ordered to reinforce Hannibal at Nola by way of Beneventum. We also knew that not only would Gracchus prevent the reinforcements reaching Hannibal, but that the slave army would kill all but about two thousand of Hanno's more than eighteen thousand strong force.

Unfortunately Hanno himself was in the two thousand to escape. The battle would be a bloody slogging match. Hanno duly marched up the Via Appia to resupply Hannibal at Nola on the route that took him to Benevento.

Gracchus, now praetor arrived slightly ahead of Hanno and in view of the fact that the town already boasted a Roman garrison within its walls made camp about a mile from the town blocking Hanno's path. Hanno's scouts made him aware of the situation and he made camp about three miles from the town.

The battle took place the following day alongside the Calor River a tributary of the Volturno. Hanno did the conventional thing and put half of his cavalry on each wing, one of those wings being adjacent to the river, the other in the field. Gracchus promised his slave soldiers their freedom if the enemy were completely defeated with each slave soldier being required to bring him the head of a defeated enemy.

This second requirement almost cost us the battle as the slave soldiers were more intent on decapitating enemy soldiers and carrying their severed heads around with them than pursuing victory. Until their officers reminded them that ultimate and complete victory was the first requirement of the day.

Hanno's Numidian cavalry fought very well and it was only when the Roman slave infantry got its second wind, after being reminded that their liberty was not to be taken for granted on the basis of a trophy that Hanno's forces were routed.

At Nola Marcus Claudius Marcellus kept an unreinforced Hannibal out for a third time and retook Casilinum, before departing to take charge of the siege of Siracusa in Sicily. A great and oft overlooked Roman.

These events cost many people their lives and left us fully at war yet again, but like last year 214BC would end with nothing much changing as regards the big picture. As in many a major conflict however the tides would ebb and flow. Hannibal's position was materially weaker, but we were still committed in Spain and would soon be committed heavily in Sicily too. Publius's moment was getting closer but his time to rise to greatness was still not upon us.

At home Valeria and I were very happy, if still childless to the great disappointment of ourselves and her parents, who naturally blamed me. Sperm counts not being available I had no defence.

CHAPTER 12 PUBLIC LIFE 213BC 541

The cursus honorum which translates more or less as the course of honour was the slippery political and military pole which noble Roman men sought to climb in order to ennoble themselves, their families and their descendants.

The target was to one day be elected consul; having been consul one would always be known as a consular, in some ways no different from an American President being called 'Mr President' long after leaving office, indeed until his dying day.

A consular might possibly go on to be censor in later life, a role which put him in charge of the senatorial and citizens' rolls and matters relating to morals. By the time of the late republic it was necessary by law to have two censors, one of whom had to be plebeian. Censors often served for eighteen months and no other official could gainsay or veto their decisions, those decisions could only be changed by a subsequent censor, making this a powerful magistracy indeed.

It wasn't unheard of for wealthy families to bribe or get together with other families close to themselves and with similar political views to work together to get their own people elected to important roles, especially that of consul. Nor were the votes of the various tribes entirely equal in weight. In short it was democracy rather like we know it in Britain today, flawed.

The normal processes of the cursus honorum should have led to one becoming consul in one's prime. The various stages took in both military and administrative responsibilities. The first or most junior of these stages was normally to become a quaestor.

This was a financial and administrative position. It could involve organising the games, or being a legion paymaster. In theory a man should have ten years of military service before becoming quaestor, but for most this was too slow. Being a close relative of a general could help in this regard.

Aedile was the next step up and carried greater responsibilities; religious duties, such as maintaining the temples and secular tasks too. Some of the secular responsibilities were of vital importance, such as protecting the food and the water supply for example, but also maintaining roads and regulating the markets. My esteemed brother in law and fellow Jupiter, Appius Claudius Pulcher, had already held the position, without ever having been quaestor. This wasn't so unusual.

Praetor was the final step, before attempting the consulship, were a man to get that far, although following his year as praetor a man might be given the role of governing a province as propraetor.

Praetors were in charge of civil law and were effectively judges. Governors of provinces often taxed as they liked and made vast fortunes at the expense of the people living in those provinces. Of course a certain amount of tax had to find it's way to the treasury, a blind eye was often turned to the surplus. Praetor was a sought after position.

To be consul was the ultimate goal. Two consuls were elected annually, one senior and one junior but they actually held the fasces a bundle of rods containing an axe which symbolised their power to punish or to execute, on alternate months.

Consuls presided over the senate, each had the power of veto, even over the other which could cause problems! Consuls from different factions failing to work in concert would cause Rome many problems down the years.

In the year after being consul the now former consul could also be given a provincc to govern as pro consul. I imagine if you grew up in the system it all seemed pretty obvious and normal. That said noble Romans seemed to me to be fully committed to finding ways around the system or to make it work to their personal advantage.

Bribing voters, smearing opponents, using friends in the people's assembly to pass laws, or bribing tribunes to veto them. Much went on behind closed doors in the noble households.

The senate was in charge of all matters pertaining to war, and international affairs the consuls having imperium over Rome and all its provinces whilst in office. On the other hand, the people's assembly or comitia effectively passed the laws.

By the late republic tribunes of the plebs in the comitia could veto almost anything. This lead to factions, riots and other difficulties. Nonetheless this imperfect, changing system lasted several hundred years and defeated what the Greeks saw as an immutable human law concerning society and governance.

Namely that a king would arise, who would, at some point, be overthrown by his own nobles who would then establish an oligarchy. From this oligarchy a democracy would evolve, or come about by the force of the populace and from that one man would arise to make himself king and start the process anew.

The Roman republican system was destined to survive long after my friend's death although it would be severely shaken by two of his grandchildren, but that as they say is another story.

My friend's career would need to be quite unconventional. Like brother Appius he would need to become aedile quite young and go on to command an army just before his twenty fifth journey around the sun was complete, in short at the tender age of twenty four, going on twenty five, without ever having been praetor.

I knew from my history studies that Scipio would be elected curule aedile this year aged just twenty two alongside his cousin Marcus Cornelius Cethegus. Four aediles were elected annually at this time, two plebeian and two patricians known as curule aediles with greater authority than their plebeian counterparts.

In earlier times there had only been plebeian aediles, but Rome was a strange animal, when an extra day was added to the games and the plebeian aediles didn't want to stump up the cash, the patricians offered to take it on, but on condition of there being two patrician aediles from that time forwards. The patrician or curule aediles then promptly became the senior magistrates.

Eventually curule aediles could be either patrician or plebeian. However, the problem for Scipio and myself was that there was a minimum age requirement of twenty seven years and that stipulation tended to be respected.

All I had to do was try and keep history on track. I already knew how it had happened that Scipio had become an aedile before his time. It was time now for an important conversation alone with my friend in the temple.

"You need to be elected curule aedile this year, within three years you'll need to command an army. That you may achieve, in fact will achieve according to the histories I've read, without ever having been praetor, nonetheless, you must have held some public office so aedile it is and, conventional or not, this is your year!"

"I'm fully five years too young to be admitted to the elections."

"Nonetheless you will be. There is a way to present yourself to the people for election, I'll explain in a moment. You're right, some plebeians may object, but you're liked and respected in the senate and the people adore you. Stand and you win.

"As I understand it your cousin will be elected as the other curule aedile this year. Talk to him, ensure he presents himself as a candidate."

"He's not especially well known or popular, what makes you think he will win?"

"As I've said before it has already happened, we're just keeping events on course. Tell him it's foretold that you will both be curule aediles this year. People like their officials and magistrates to work together, not to compete and try to out manoeuvre each other. He will get in on the back of your popularity.

"Whilst his standing will give you an excuse to present yourself alongside and in support of him. Pomponia will help and we'll go to some lengths, with her help, to make it look like a divinely inspired destiny. You are already regarded as Jupiter's favourite.

"The people will acclaim you, when the objection about your age is raised simply say that a man acclaimed by the people and chosen by the gods cannot be too young.

"The people will elect you and they will elect your cousin too, which may be from sympathy, may be as a support for you, may be because they know you will work together, it doesn't really matter why, trust me, it will happen."

So it was that the Marcus Cornelius Cethegus presented himself with but scant support, my friend donned his toga and presented himself alongside his cousin and as we say in my day and age, the crowd went wild.

The plebeians did raise the matter of his age, Scipio was well prepared with his answer and no one wanted to start their year in office by making themselves deeply unpopular not least the plebeian aediles and so the matter was put to bed, my friend and his cousin returning home with a celebratory crowd on their heels.

The whole successful saga made me very popular with Pomponia too. My own dear Valeria and Aemilia Tertia were thrilled as well. All I had done, as always was to regurgitate what I'd read, but I have to say it felt good to witness it and to feel a part of it.

My friend and his cousin did their work well and at the end of the year left office with everything in the city functioning well, their stock and popularity with the people enhanced, but especially that of my friend who perhaps unfairly was given all the credit given the stories circulating about him which we did nothing to discourage.

CHAPTER 13 MY BROTHER IN LAW THE CONSUL 212BC 542

The first major event of this year was the election of a new pontifex maximus. Surprisingly and perhaps a little suspiciously Publius Licinius Crassus was elected. He'd never been curule aedile, was relatively young, but extremely rich. Indeed it had been considerably more than a hundred years since a pontifex maximus had been elected at such a young age.

In the future one of his descendants would be that Marcus Licinius Crassus, who'd be the victor over Spartacus, Caesar's friend and fellow triumvir who would lose his life and his son's life on an ill fated expeditionary attack against the Parthians.

A future legend, one of several, concerning that particular Crassus would have it that his love of wealth and gold was so great that the Parthians executed him by pouring molten gold down his throat. He in fact almost certainly died when a parley descended into violence, but whatever the truth, no other Romans would have been able to witness or report exactly what happened. A fertile ground for speculation and legend.

This Crassus however, Publius Licinius Crassus would be important in our lives since the pontifex maximus, a priesthood which was normally held for life, did not disbar a man from running for consul. Indeed one of his two opponents in the election, both of whom were far more distinguished and experienced than he, was non other than brother Appius's co consul.

This particular pontifex maximus would go on to be the colleague and co consul of Publius a few years hence. He mattered. Whether he bribed I cannot say with certainty, but the suspicion remains. His descendant mentioned above is also believed to have bribed heavily in his political manoeuvres.

My brother in law was, how can one say this diplomatically about a friend, opinionated would be one option, maybe headstrong. He was also very class conscious. A couple of examples. Early in the year some tax farmers and state contractors were tried by the plebeian assembly.

These corrupt men anticipated being saved by the veto of one of the plebeian tribunes. Casca, the tribune in question, seeing the reaction and righteous indignation of the people wisely did not interpose his veto. When the voting was about to commence the accused men resorted to violence and the meeting was dismissed without a verdict before a full scale riot could ensue.

The consuls did not have jurisdiction over civil law but treason is another matter, brother Appius and his colleague duly arraigned the accused on treason charges, not for the original charges of corruption and thievery of which they were most certainly guilty, but for the violence in the assembly.

Upon this action being taken the accused men went into exile. This I would say was a good move by my brother, if you can't get them one way... A bit like the downfall of Al Capone, a murderer and mobster, on tax evasion charges.

That said I could not agree with my brother's attitude to another matter of concern. After Cannae the surviving consul from that year Varro had received a vote of thanks from the senate for his efforts to salvage the situation. My friend Publius had reaffirmed his own status as a war hero and my brother too had come out of it all smelling of roses.

The captured soldiers had been deemed unworthy of ransom, a decision I've questioned previously, but the common soldiers who survived and escaped were effectively sent abroad to fight and banned from returning to Italy. They were both fighting for Rome and banished from her at the same time, a most unjust juxtaposition with the fate of their officers.

With heavy fighting taking place in Sicily these soldiers, with permission of their commander, sent a deposition with a most eloquent and reasonable plea that they were in no way to blame for the disaster, rather their generals had let them down, whilst they themselves had fought through and continued to fight for the nation, they in no way deserved their exile, or the stain on their reputations.

I agreed wholeheartedly, I had seen these men at Canusium, brother Appius had not only seen them, he'd fought alongside them, endured the same hardships they had. Now he was consul, they exiles. The class system in Rome certainly breeds a sense of entitlement and the idea of superiority through birth. Appius was a prime mover in denying their petition.

Brother Appius's co consul this year was Fulvius Flaccus, this being his third consulship. Another Fulvius Flaccus, actually Gnaeus Fulvius Flaccus the consul's brother was one of this year's praetors! This Fulvius Flaccus would also be at the head of a two legion army.

Here in the city Appius and Fulvius Flaccus the consul raised another two legions. Not without some difficulty and by enlisting boys under seventeen if they appeared sufficiently strong. With the legions newly raised, those raised last year and those in Spain, Sicily, Sardinia, Etruria, Lucania and Gaul, Rome had an astounding twenty three legions in the field.

This would be another year of mixed fortunes and big events largely passed over by historians. Syphax made his alliance with the Romans, military advisors were dispatched by us and Syphax duly made war on the Eastern Numidians or Massylii and their King Gala the allies of Carthage. It struck me as ironic after our many defeats that we should send military advisors. Rome never suffered from a lack of hubris and of course we had our successes too I suppose.

Hasdrubal was ordered, as predicted, to depart from Spain to deal with Syphax, in which task he is not to be entirely successful. Of course this also meant a division of their forces, Spain was too important for Carthage to leave undefended.

Whilst Hasdrubal was absent my friend's father and uncle captured Saguntum, remember Saguntum? The place the war effectively started and which had suffered greatly at Hannibal's hands. Our victory there was too late to help the original Saguntines who had depended upon us, but it was a morale boost and a victory nonetheless.

In Italy my brother in law and his co consul took another huge army to besiege Capua. Rome continually managed to field these armies but some of the legions were still raw and included underage recruits, I knew that success at Capua was still some way off, despite a minor success against Hanno, again near Beneventum.

Hannibal was not at home and Capua did not fall. Hannibal was in fact at Tarentum where our brave legionaries had so annoyed the local people that a conspiracy to oust them had arisen, one which Hannibal almost took full advantage of. With the help of the conspirators a large part of the city was captured, but we managed to hold on to the citadel and, as a result, the crucial harbour.

Hannibal then received a request for aid from the people of Capua, Hannibal's most important possession. He responded immediately by sending two thousand cavalry who could travel swiftly, which with the Carthaginian forces left at Capua and in the region were sufficient that my brother in law and his co consul were defeated. Capua remained in Carthaginian hands but a large part of our forces there also remained intact.

In fact the eight legion army under my brother in law and Flaccus although mauled was still numerically superior to Hannibal's forces and was now blooded and more experienced. Despite this my brother and his colleague decided to split their forces.

Flaccus moved his forces towards Cumae whilst Appius set off for Lucania with Hannibal in pursuit. Clearly, militarily anyway, we were at sixes and sevens. My brother evaded Hannibal but one of his discontented centurions made trouble and sent to Rome declaring that with his knowledge of Campania he could defeat the Carthaginians were he but put in command of an army.

Unfortunately, despite the fact that the consuls should have had the ultimate say, factions in Rome listened to this Marcus Centenius Penula and steps were taken to provide him with an army. Four thousand citizen soldiers and four thousand allies were taken from Gracchus and nearly another eight thousand volunteers were raised so that Centenius found himself in command of around sixteen thousand men, only half of whom were experienced soldiers.

Appius now sought to rejoin his colleague whilst the centurion, Centenius sought battle with a real general. Hannibal secured all possible routes of retreat open to Centenius's men and then defeated them at the battle of Silarus.

As a result of Hannibal's preparations fifteen thousand of our men died in that battle, only about one thousand survived and made good their escape. These men, the smart and effective ones, were then condemned to join the equally, and in my view wrongly condemned, surviving soldiers from Cannae fighting in exile in Sicily.

Hannibal decided not to pursue Appius, but rather to go after the army of the other Flaccus, the praetor not the consul, who was harassing towns under Carthaginian control in Apulia. Hanno based himself once again in Bruttium, modern Calabria and the consuls re-established the siege of Capua. A fine old merry go round and nothing truly decided once again.

In our province of Illyria, modern Albania and Croatia, King Philip of Macedon was making trouble for us, but Roman command in that theatre was in the hands of the very competent Marcus Valerius Laevinus with more than fifty ships and two legions. His fame as an admiral kept the Greeks from using naval warfare, or from crossing the Adriatic, but Philip had some successes in capturing coastal towns.

These actions mirrored to some extent what was happening in Africa. Carthaginian forces there were kept busy which might otherwise have been employed against us in Spain. We on the other hand had great resources tied up on the east coast of Italy that might otherwise have been employed against Hannibal. In that sense his allegiance with Philip was of some help to Hannibal.

Towards the end of the year brother Appius returned to Rome from Capua to organise and oversee the elections. I was sorely tempted, for Valeria's sake as well as his, to urge him not to return to Capua, but his command was prorogued and I held my tongue, next year he would return to the fight outside Capua, to meet his destiny.

The war with Carthage still raged in Sicily although the hugely important port of Syracuse was now in Roman hands. Roman officers had issued an order that the great Greek scientist Archimedes should be spared when the city fell, however in the confusion he had been killed. A great loss to the world.

His use of mirrors to create what amounted to lasers by focussing the sun's rays had caused several of our ships to burn. It would not be until my time that lasers would come into their own again for such diverse uses as cutting steel, through to precision surgery and threatening the reproductive powers of 007 in Goldfinger!

Life for me was perhaps a little too happy and comfortable given all that was going on in the world outside Rome, where I was living in some luxury with my beautiful, much younger wife. I counted my blessings even if no child appeared on the horizon yet, it was fun trying.

CHAPTER 14 BEREAVEMENT UPON BEREAVEMENT 211BC 543

In many ways this would be a most important year, auspicious and yet tragic at the same time for Pomponia, Publius, Valeria and to a lesser extent myself. Knowing what was about to happen weighed heavily on me, Valeria wanted to know what was affecting my mood so, and I decided to do things differently this time. Rather than reveal events to Publius alone in the temple I decided that a family get together was required.

Valeria and I invited Pomponia, Publius and Amelia Tertia to visit and dismissed the servants for the entire day. Snacks had been prepared, I was conscious this could become a long and difficult session with a prodigious number of questions for me to deal with.

Pomponia arrived first and I left her in conversation with Valeria as I did not wish to speak to her about anything important before we were all gathered. Fortunately Publius and Amelia were scant minutes behind her.

We gathered in the Triclinum, dining room to you and me, where we could all be seated on chairs or couches and where food and watered wine had been set out. It was usual in Roman society for men to dine on couches whilst ladies were seated on chairs.

As a family we were somewhat more liberal than conventional and I'd never quite got used to eating whilst reclining on a couch myself anyway. It felt all wrong after so many years of sitting at a dining table and I'm sure my digestion never got used to reclining for all that I was obliged to eat that way more often than not.

Furthermore I couldn't reconcile delivering the messages I had to impart whilst lounging on a couch, it seemed to trivialise what was very far from trivial. In fact I thought maybe I should stand, but that felt too much like a speech or presentation. I wasn't really sure how best to go about it. I suggested people sit wherever they felt most comfortable.

Interestingly everyone chose a chair and so on this occasion we gathered around the table almost like a twenty first century board meeting.

I had forewarned Publius when I sent the invitation that this would be an important gathering rather than a purely social event. He clearly had not conveyed this to Amelia who immediately remarked on the somewhat strange circumstances.

"Where is everyone?"

"The servants have been given the day off, I'm afraid I must ask you to send your people away too, tell them to return in four hours, that should be enough. If not you may have to send them away a second time."

When this had been done I continued.

"Ordinarily I discuss my foretellings with Publius alone at the temple, but this concerns us all and each of us will need support in his or her own way, even me.

"Publius, when we met I told you that you would be the man who would finally and completely defeat Hannibal and rid Rome of this menace. You told me I was crazy and that your father and uncle would do that.

"Later you came to see that my predictions came true and I took another enormous risk in telling you how I knew."

Pomponia, Valeria and Amelia had been watching me intently, now they exchanged glances between themselves, perhaps trying to divine whether one of them had yet found out. I had not revealed how I knew these things to Valeria, nor, I knew, had Publius spoken of it to Amelia.

All three women knew better than to push the matter, yet their looks spoke volumes about the theories and worries they must have mulled over and the discussions they'd had between themselves.

Pomponia as the senior woman present was the only one likely to openly demand an explanation, my wife might try in private, but so far no explanation had been demanded or given. I continued.

"If your father and uncle were not destined to defeat Hannibal and the war was to last some seventeen years, as I also predicted, then the fate of your father and uncle must have worried you. I may have alluded to your avenging them I can't remember everything I've told you, I've written a lot of things down, but even so, I'm sorry."

Pomponia was controlling herself, I was floundering a little, by discussing Publius avenging his father and uncle I had effectively let slip that the love of her life, who she'd not seen for roughly seven years, would never return to her. Amelia, seated next to her clasped Pomponia's hand, and for all her dignitas and seniority Pomponia, uncharacteristically allowed her daughter in law to do so. With all eyes on me and no one interjecting I continued.

"I told you Publius that Cannae would be the high water mark of Hannibal's success and that's true, but I believe I also spoke about further setbacks as well as victories, including the final victory.

"This year will be more disastrous for this family than any other. We've seen so many of our friends and acquaintances grieving over multiple bereavements at Cannae and other battles, from which we escaped unscathed, now I'm sorry to say it's our turn.

"It's because of the events this year Publius that you will receive command of an army, you will take the lessons of the Ticinus, Trebia, Trasymene, Cannae and other battles and you will begin to turn the tide of Rome's affairs. As I told you, you will be the greatest Roman of your generation and one of the greatest Romans of all time."

I knew I was making a mess of it, it's my nature I suppose, so much more comfortable with the good news, so clumsy at imparting the bad. Out with it.

"We will lose three important members of the family this year, I'm sorry dear Valeria, it will start with the loss of your brother. After that we have to bear the loss first of Publius, I'm so sorry Pomponia and then Gnaeus too."

Pomponia looked like she would collapse in tears but with superhuman powers she sat rigidly, looking straight ahead and saying nothing, unawares she had placed her other hand on top of Amelia's and was holding on hard. Amelia did not flinch, such are Roman women. Publius responded after some moments of thought.

"How can it be? We recaptured Saguntum, we've won over many of the tribes, are we not strong in Spain now?"

"Rome has done wonders in raising fresh levies and armies, but Carthage has not been sitting idly by and just watching. Publius and Gnaeus face not one, not two, but three full sized Carthaginian armies and I'm afraid they will make a fatal mistake."

"We must warn them."

"We must not, you know this, we must not change history."

The girls were screaming silently at me to reveal what in hades I meant.

"To achieve your destiny Publius, for Rome to achieve its destiny as ruler of the world we must not interfere with what is already written."

"How will it happen?"

"Hasdrubal has returned to Spain with the men he took away plus extra reinforcements for the forces he left behind, his army is large, experienced and formidable.

"Hannibal's brother Mago is at the head of a second army and Hasdrubal son of Gisgo leads a third. In the face of what appears to be an overwhelming Carthaginian force, our allies will waver and some will betray us.

"Your father and uncle will divide their forces in face of this renewed and widespread threat. I cannot say what the outcome would be were they to face each of the three Carthaginian armies as one united force, but in any event they will split up.

"Your father will be caught by the combined forces of Mago and Hasdrubal son of Gisgo near the Baetis river, he will die nobly fighting against the odds. His army will largely die with him.

"Hasdrubal will defeat Gnaeus soon after at a place called Ilourgeia not far from New Carthage, he will persuade the Spanish fighting with us to change sides at the decisive moment. His victory will also be complete with hardly a Roman escaping.

"The situation in Spain will be the worst for us that it has ever been, Roman arms virtually eradicated, three victorious Carthaginian armies running rampant and no senator, consular or Roman general here willing or wanting to risk their reputation by taking over.

"That's why it is the biggest moment of your life Publius, barring the final victory, this is your moment, your time to emerge from the shadows. You will stand forth and volunteer to take the command in Spain, you will be given the command and an army, I will come with you and Carthaginian power in Iberia will be destroyed. We will even found a city."

Finally Pomponia decided it was time to demand some answers.

" On the one hand you tell me that I will never see my husband or brother in law again and on the other you tell me my son will be the greatest Roman of his generation. Bitter sweet indeed. You say you know these things, you say we should not try to change them whilst there is still time and you expect us to simply accept all this without question?

"Where is he from Publius? He's no merchant, who is he? I like him, I admit it, but when he tells me my husband will die I have a right to know more."

"Mother, if I tell you the truth you will think I'm mad and Caius too, so before I say anything, and I cannot reveal another man's secrets, a man who has been a friend, a right arm and a faithful helper, I cannot reveal his truth without his permission, but to do so without your believing me would be completely wrong of me and counter productive into the bargain. So I ask you, firstly has Caius made a single false or erroneous prediction?"

"I don't think I know all his so called predictions, you meet in secret at the temple, or with your so called Jupiters, but no, everything that has been revealed to me since Caius has arrived has come to pass I agree."

" Have you ever known me to lie to you?"

"Not since you were a child and not often then I admit that too."

"Have you ever known Caius to lie to you?"

"No, when he lived on the Palatine I trusted him completely in my home, I admit that too, but ye gods this is something else."

"Valeria, Amelia, have you ever had cause to doubt my word or that of Caius."

In unison.

"No."

"Caius, should I tell them?"

"Publius, everything I have, I have through you, you probably saved my life, you undoubtedly made me what I am today, you caused me to become a citizen, you made me a landowner, you took me into your family, without you I would not have the wife that I love. I would have and be nothing, without your friendship and support.

"If you feel it is right you may tell them, but remember I was able to show you things to pretty much prove my story, you saw my ship too, the ladies here have only your word and mine, if they think you've been tricked then it's doubtful that I will be able to continue to help you. Your career and reputation are at stake too and they're worth more than my reputation, both to you and to Rome."

"Wife, mother, Valeria, you must swear on Bona Dea two things: one, you will accept what I tell you as fact, indisputable fact, because you have my word on it, as something which even if I cannot prove it to you has been proven to me and I do not lie to my family. Secondly you must swear never to reveal a word of this to anyone.

"You must not discuss it with anyone but Caius or myself, no close friend, no relative, not even the Jupiters. You must even be extremely careful should you discuss it between yourselves lest someone overhear you. Today there are no slaves, no servants present, this is a sacred trust we put in you. Our world could hang by a thread, does in fact hang by a thread."

Desperate for information and explanation Pomponia swore on Bona Dea the Good Mother to trust and believe the word of her son and to reveal nothing to anyone outside this room, Valeria and Amelia swore likewise to believe in the word of their respective husbands and in Valeria's case in the word of Publius too and to hold these facts to themselves only and to discuss with no one not here present.

"Here it is then, Caius has no second sight, everything he has revealed he has read, read in histories that survived for two thousand years. He is not just from far away in distance, he's from another time as well as another place."

"Caius?"

"Valeria, you said you felt the hand of destiny, you believed you were waiting for me, you cannot, I imagine, explain those feelings?"

"No I cannot."

"Nor can I explain how I came to be here. I am from a time some two thousand years hence. Publius will defeat Hannibal, in Africa and later Carthage will be utterly destroyed, her people will be almost entirely wiped from the face of the earth.

"Carthaginian men and women who survive will be few but the men will be sold as slaves at one end of the world, women at the other, in order that their race be totally eliminated. Salt will be ploughed into the land around Carthage to make it barren for years to come and the city itself will be raised to the ground.

"These extreme measures will not be at the hand of Publius, but his victory over Carthage will make these things possible and make Rome the most powerful state on earth. The sea around us will become known as Mare Nostrum, Our Sea and a mighty empire will arise that will last in one form or another for over a thousand years.

"The Roman empire will stretch from the tin islands in the north, to Judea in the east and much of Africa in the south. Spain and the Pillars of Hercules will be at the western end and wealthy, powerful nations such as Egypt and Greece will also submit completely to Roman authority in the end.

"By my time, the time of my birth these events will be ancient history, scholars will study the events I refer to and certain books which will be written soon after the end of this war will miraculously survive to my own time.

"I have always been fascinated by history I have read these books more than once and I carried copies, now lost, on my little ship. In order to save my life I revealed to Publius my knowledge of the future, I demonstrated what I knew and showed him things from the future now no longer working to prove my strange tale. I promised to help him achieve his destiny.

"I started writing everything down whilst it was available to me or fresh in my memory. I did this in my own language which Publius has been learning, a language which does not exist in the world yet except through Publius and myself.

"Pomponia you have seen my writing and puzzled at the language you know that much is true, but actually every word of this is true.

"I have no idea how I was transported here, only that it happened and the circumstances of that I can describe, however, the why is probably the most important thing and that is something I can only surmise. I've come to the conclusion that I am in some way here in order to keep history on the path it has always trodden, but that's speculation I admit.

"In the books I read about this war and about Publius he had a friend called Caius Laelius. I forgot this at first, but when asked for a name I thought that my real name, my modern name would not suit the situation, then it came to me that Publius was assisted by a Caius Laelius, I knew that if I offered that name he ought to reject it or at the least claim to know the real Caius Laelius from school or some such thing.

"He did not react to that name and at that moment I realised that I was the Caius Laelius of history, that my role was to be the right hand of Publius Cornelius Scipio Africanus. My friend will take the cognomen Africanus once he defeats Hannibal in Africa. Like so much else, it is already written.

"Pomponia, you think me cruel for not warning your husband of his impending doom. I understand that, but we all have our destiny. Your husband is a great man, his brother too.

"History, posterity will remember them and what could we say to them in any event? They are great generals thousands of miles away, why would they change their strategy on the strength of advice from a son or nephew in Rome?

"Telling all of you these bad tidings today has been one of the hardest things I've ever done in my life, the fact of it being in advance of the tragedies to come makes it harder still. I grieve with you, truly I do.

"Valeria, we will have a daughter I think and certainly a son, it's not their time yet, but our son has a role to play in this, he will arrive when he's meant to arrive. Truly I've never believed in the gods, but there are things here I cannot explain, they simply are. I have to accept them and for all our sakes you have to accept them as well. Should we seek to change that which for me has already happened we know not what the consequences might be."

"Husband I have always believed in you and trusted in you, you've never given me cause to doubt you. I don't doubt you now, but what you've said opens up so many questions. I know we can talk in private, but you said you can describe the events that brought you here I think the three of us would like to hear that, even if Publius already knows it all."

"Very well, I was travelling alone in a small ship along the coast of what you call Gaul and we in my time call France. Historians have made replicas of historic ships and I saw one come over the horizon towards me. These replicas are extremely rare, when I saw a second come over the horizon I was perturbed to say the least, by the time thirty ships appeared I was terrified and eventually, too late really, but not wanting to believe that I'd voyaged in time I turned my boat around to flee.

"This fleet was the fleet of your husband Pomponia, they failed to capture me because my ship had the means to travel across the wind without oars. I hid in the marshes, thus risking capture. As Publius pointed out to me I had every opportunity to escape which was true, but where would I go in a world so alien to me?

"Not only did I have nowhere to go, but whatever force, or god if you prefer, put me there clearly had a plan, the universe shall we say had a plan, Caius Laelius only exists because he met Publius.

"Your husband's scouts caught up with me lady and although I had thought to flee I went with them as clearly, I know now, I was meant to. Your husband was too busy to question me in great detail and one man with a tiny ship posed small threat compared with Hannibal, by now on his way to the Alps. It was Publius here who took an interest and the rest you might say is history. Wherever that starts and ends!"

Pomponia was not merely an intelligent woman with an enquiring mind she was wise in the deepest sense of the word. My friend Publius came from good stock.

"I thank you Caius Laelius, this must have been as hard for you as for us, maybe more so. I'm sure we will all have more questions but enough for now. My servants will return soon, yours too Publius, we should eat and drink something and think and come to terms with all we've heard.

"I agree with you Caius Laelius, there are forces in this world we do not understand and over which we have no control. I think you are beloved of the gods that they have chosen you for their purposes but others may interpret things differently.

"I would not wish to be you Caius, taken from everything you know. I'm grateful that you have Valeria, as I'm grateful that Publius has Amelia. We will come through this, it will be hard; knowing that loved ones will die ahead of time is hard, very hard and yet those with loved ones suffering from illness suffer the same fate as we every day.

"You promise greatness for my son and you have pledged to go with him, to help him until all he is destined to achieve is achieved. It appears I'm destined to lose my beloved husband after so long apart, I'm destined to lose a brother in law I love and Valeria a much loved brother. We are bound to one another we five. Valeria will lose her brother, but has already gained a husband, I will lose my husband, but tonight I feel as though I have gained another son.

"Greatness will attend you Publius, you father and uncle will be avenged and made proud, the sun will shine on us all once more in time, we will not merely survive, we will prosper. We will eat now and face what we have to face as and when it happens."

We ate in silence and when the servants returned to escort the guests home they departed. As we closed the door Valeria threw her arms around my neck and kissed me gently at first, then passionately.

"A daughter first and then a son?"

"In their right time, I believe so, yes."

"I love you Caius."

"I believe you do, I love you too, more than I can say. I could not have got this far without you, this evening could not have happened without you. I should have seen it immediately, but this is not in the history books. You are my everything Valeria, you complete me, you make me belong here, fit in, you are my reason to go on."

Events moved swiftly. It was a few days later that we received word of brother Appius's wound sustained before Capua.

Publius and I took a small group of retired soldiers and the most comfortable cart we could find to collect Appius, bring him back to Rome where he could put his affairs in order and say goodbye to his loved ones.

"You knew."

"I'm sorry Appius, my heart will break. I'm not sent to change any man's destiny. I will ensure you are remembered, you are a great Roman. I can tell you that Capua will fall and you already know from our meetings that Rome will be victorious, completely and utterly victorious in the end.

"When Capua falls your colleague will make the streets run with blood, that too is a tragedy."

"I will write to him, urge clemency."

"It will make no difference Appius, write what you will, but history is already written. Valeria needs time with you."

We said our goodbyes that evening as dear friends. Not being cut from the same cloth as Pomponia I wept.

Within days we received the news of the death of Publius less than two weeks later word came about the disaster which befell Gnaeus near Cartagena.

There wasn't the same panic in Rome as there had been after Cannae but there was a speculative worrying, what if Hannibal received reinforcements from these victorious armies, what then?

Within the family we mourned each loss for no more that thirty days as another new law post Cannae demanded then, although never forgetting, moved on with our lives and our own destinies.

CHAPTER 15 INTO THE FURNACE 210 BC

The senate met and decided that an election must be held to replace the commanders in Spain. The election to take place on the Campus Martius as early in the year as was possible. It was a cold January day and yet the crowds appeared, although no replacement for the Scipio brothers was found to have come forward. Senators and praetors, tribunes and aediles shuffled around and looked at each other but said not a word.

When despondency seemed to be setting in we made our move. We had found for ourselves an area where there was a small rise in the land, not so much a hill as a bump, but enough to raise Scipio a head or so above the surrounding throng. Publius's speech was rhetoric at its finest. I don't know how, or where he learned it, certainly not from me.

He made use of everything, his experience, his courage, without sounding boastful, his knowledge of how Carthage fought her battles. He reprised his father and his uncle's successes and finally swore vengeance on Carthage and fickle Spaniards. I made sure that elements of his speech were relayed by men paid to pass on the most powerful points to the crowd stretching far and wide, who raised a great chant. Scipio, Scipio, vengeance, vengeance.

It may be true that there were no other candidates willing to lead men into that meat grinder in Spain that had taken so many Roman lives, but in that moment that Scipio was appointed to the command there I think hope re awoke in everyone in the city from highest to lowest. I know it affected me deeply.

Not long after the euphoria of the election a mood of anti climax and worry descended once more upon the populace. What had they done, electing a youth barely twenty four to the command in Spain. We had to move fast.

Scipio spoke sagely to people all that day, reassuring them, lest moves be taken to reconsider his command. I had stories circulated about Scipio's regular communes with Jupiter in the temple after dark, despite believing that we would not fail, that history was already written I still had a voice in the back of my head saying 'make sure, make sure'.

I vaguely knew that Caius Laelius became involved in Scipio's campaigns, but I may have forgotten to quite what an extent I would be involved in the decision making, guiding the fleet and even fighting on land. Indeed when I'd searched the recesses of my mind to provide a Roman name it had been a struggle to even remember Caius Laelius.

Reality, if any of this should be described as reality, was about to come up with me. Of course I knew the main points of the history, I knew that Scipio would move against Cartagena whilst the Carthaginian armies, all three of them were away from base. I knew he'd be successful, albeit next year, but it was the day to day decisions which were largely unknown to me and in many cases I'd be the one having to make them!

Gaius Claudius Nero a former praetor had already been sent to Spain with experienced reinforcements to try to patch up our tenuous position there. His forces largely consisted of soldiers freed up to go to Spain by the very recent fall of Capua.

Knowing of the slaughter that had taken place in Capua I wept inwardly for the civilian population, all men of importance had been executed, many hundreds of them. The lower orders had been sold into slavery.

However, this signal having been sent to other towns and cities roundabout concerning what their fate might be should they too revolt, the walls and houses were left standing and a new population of peasants was effectively moved in to till the soil and keep this most fertile region productive.

Publius appointed Marcus Junius Silanus as his official second in command; I as an oddity had no official rank although I would come to be seen as both admiral and general in due course.

Scipio would entrust me with greater and greater responsibility and the gods know why, with my linguistic difficulties and non-Roman ways, the men came to trust me too. I suppose I was trusted because what I said would happen, happened and given the vagaries of war, no other general could do as much so repeatedly and so consistently.

We sailed from the mouth of the Tiber with thirty quinqueremes. It was summer by the time all the arrangements had been made and sailing conditions were good, nonetheless there would be a limit to what we could achieve this year.

Marcus Junius Silanus had gone ahead of us to relieve Gaius Claudius Nero who had proved ineffective and had at one point been duped by Hasdrubal, who had got himself into a weak position and yet stealthily and successfully withdrew his troops from under Nero's nose whilst ostensibly negotiating.

One of the fogs I feared at sea had aided Hasdrubal's final escape on land from a valley where he had effectively been bottled up, but he'd also been removing forces quietly each night whilst parleying by day. Gaius Claudius Nero could have done us a great service, but had proven gullible and ill equipped for the job.

We had with us some ten thousand foot soldiers to further reinforce our position in Spain and a thousand more cavalry. We coasted as Publius's father had done before, when I had run into him. Spirits were high and the soldiers, always wary of the sea were happy that the land remained in sight. Even the horses remained calm.

Our course involved coasting along the Etruscan shore and then across the Gulf of Lions, I wondered about my boat, was Francesca still afloat in the marshes, we were too far offshore to see, we did not stop at Massilia either, but kept pressing on around the promontory that marks the southern end of the Pyrenees and landed our forces at the small port of Emporiae.

From there Publius would take his forces overland to Tarraco, modern Tarragona. Knowing that his campaign proper would begin next year Publius was anxious to discover all that he could about the local tribes, not least those in our rear and also to learn the lie of the land; an intact army can fight again and Publius had no intention of losing his army, even if forced to retreat. In later years a Roman general could escape censure for most errors and setbacks, so long as he kept his army intact.

To my consternation, although I tried not to show it, and with some success I believe, I was given command of the fleet. As an experienced sailor I had no fear of the sea and the three banks of rowers on each ship were the equivalent of a motor, even if the one square mainsail had its limitations.

I also had prior experience of this coast although it looked more than a little different without high rise hotels, modern fishing boats or tourist resorts.

I paid for sacrifices to Neptune, not for my benefit, but to impress the superstitious sailors that I was a safe pair of hands and I let it be known that I had sailed here previously. Despite these precautions it was the trust displayed by Scipio which really made the captains and officers respond unquestioningly to my orders I think, that and Roman military discipline which was truly something special.

For us the voyage to Tarraco, shadowing Publius's march on land was a relaxed affair. Publius was taking stock and meeting the locals, his progress was slow and therefore there was no pressure on us, we had only to maintain contact. The weather was fine, the sea calm, the visibility good, not a single fog, which I knew from experience could happen here. Something that could easily have caused confusion in a fleet of thirty ships without radar.

I had discussions with my Captains about sound signals and the best ways to avoid collisions yet keep cohesion in the fleet should a fog occur. Fortunately we were not put to the test. It appeared that the normal modus operandi was to cease all movement and sit it out. I made a mental note to equip each of our crews with a single tuba, the Roman trumpet used for signalling during land battles, at the first opportunity.

I would then create a call sign for the lead ship and signals for the avoidance of collisions and for making intentions known. Much like the signals modern sailors use their foghorn for, but simplified.

For all that, thirty ships would be hard to control without sight of one another, the lead ship would provide a periodic signal to follow, all the others would have to hold back from signalling except in the event that ships became close enough to see one another, or hear each other's drum beat used to give the rowers a rhythm, in which case it was imperative to know what each captain had in mind and which way to steer. If everyone signalled at once it would be chaos.

We would row not sail in a fog since the wind which often blows surprisingly hard in a fog can be fickle and the drummers' sticks would be muffled. The drumbeat of another ship would only be audible if it became very close. The tempo of the drums and therefore our speed would be particularly slow to try and minimise the damage should a collision occur. We did after all carry huge bronze rams for the destruction of enemy ships! The modern term 'friendly fire' popped into my head.

That said I was prepared to sit out a fog for a short while were progress not essential and a signal for cease rowing was also be created, this could be passed down the line for fear those at the rear might not hear.

We had rudimentary compasses so maintaining a heading would not be impossible. I mentally debated the conflicting risks of drifting into a dangerous situation by doing nothing, as opposed to setting a safe heading that would keep us away from land, shallows and rocks, but which might risk collisions.

In any event none of my theoretical plans could be put into action until we made port and obtained or had tubas made for us. I felt a manual coming on! After all there were Roman military manuals concerning strategy, tactics, precautions on the march, fort building and so on aplenty, but no nautical manual that I knew of. Not yet anyway.

Of news from Rome there was none as yet, on our arrival at Tarraco I informed Publius that Sicily was largely pacified by now and that Marcellus, the commander there had been granted an Ovation, although he actually celebrated what amounted to something more akin to a triumph.

His procession started on the Alban Mount and proceeded through Rome displaying his spoils. His allied leaders were granted the Roman citizenship and awards of land and they marched in the procession ahead of him. This I knew from my histories, none in Tarraco but Scipio and I knew of these events.

The majority of the Spanish tribes remained loyal to the Carthaginians, possibly because with three armies roaming the countryside and the not so distant victories over the Scipio brothers still fresh in their minds, it seemed to them that the matter was decided. Publius and I, of course, had other ideas, but it wasn't long before all four armies in the theatre were in winter quarters.

Although Gaius Claudius Nero had proven a disappointment Silanus was held in high regard and so was Lucius Marcius who had done an exemplary job in the disastrous, immediate aftermath of the defeat of the two elder Scipios.

If Rome had a military weakness, one which would arise over and over, such as at the future defeat at Arausio, a defeat arguably worse than that at Cannae it was that Roman generals wanted all the glory for themselves. On far too many occasions they simply refused to cooperate with one another.

There are far too many examples, including here in the Spanish province's future, when various generals, including Pompey Magnus, were despatched to deal with the Roman renegade Sertorius and allowed themselves to be repeatedly defeated by refusing to work in concert with one another.

I understood the risks from my studies, but Publius understood them instinctively. He also had the confidence to give praise where praise was due, unlike some leaders not yet born. He kept both Silanus and Marcius close, but not in a, keep your friends close but your enemies closer kind of way. There was a genuine understanding and respect, between Scipio and his officers and all of us shared the same goals.

Publius's father and uncle, being brothers, although even that was no guarantee in some families, had worked together well and effectively for years precisely because they worked in unison, not in competition. Their fate seemed unfair to me, unjust, yet the way that Publius naturally and easily worked with officers who might have wanted personal success and personal glory, boded well.

Of course I knew, or believed at least, that it would turn out well in the end, but there was a great deal of hard fighting to be done and although I believed our success to be preordained it was hard not to feel somewhat overawed by the situation I found myself in. No longer an observer, but a participant. A mistake by me might change history I feared, and then what?

At Tarraco Scipio elected to have the ships drawn up on land for their safety during the stormy winter season. A few quinqueremes which had been donated for our use by the Massilians were sent back with our thanks.

Whilst I agreed with the need to protect the ships from storm damage I also felt it would be good to be able to launch a good few at short notice in an emergency. Therefore with Scipio's blessing I arranged to have slipways built and tested and a system of ropes and pulleys was devised by our engineers, powered by pack animals as well as manpower. Soon after, with practice, we could launch half a dozen ships in under half an hour. Pull them back out in a similar time frame too.

The work kept the men occupied, bored soldiers and sailors often tend towards, gambling, drinking and fighting, especially over women. The work also kept them in condition and I joined in the labour on occasions as I sought to retain not only authority, but also respect.

The Roman navy had learned to overcome the Carthaginian navy, which had more experience of naval warfare and manoeuvring their ships under sail and with oars during the First Punic War, which we had begun without a navy at all.

In the Britain of my youth, the Royal Navy was known as The Senior Service, dating as it did, back to the Saxon Kings. In Rome the army was undoubtedly the senior service and this was reflected in both the pay and the status attached.

A Roman navy had only come into being when a captured Carthaginian ship which had run aground had been dismantled timber by timber, each end and joint being marked to show which timber adjoined it, from this pattern kits of parts had been manufactured, prefabricated as we'd say in my time and warship production took on a speed and scale that would have impressed Henry Ford!

At this early juncture, back in the First Punic War, we still really had no experience of how best to utilise this new weapon at sea and Carthage still had the upper hand. We changed that through the invention of the Corvus which meant crow or raven in Latin. It required coming to close quarters with the enemy ships, which wasn't so difficult at first as they tried to ram us anyway. The Corvus gave us a huge advantage and Carthaginian captains soon learned to try and maintain some distance.

The Corvus itself was a relatively short, but broad boarding device which could be swung around through almost one hundred and eighty degrees It had a huge steel spike on the underside and would be dropped heavily onto the deck of a Carthaginian ship making escape impossible and enabling legionaries to swarm across two or three abreast and effectively turn a sea battle into a land battle. Something we Romans excelled at.

I had known about this and made reference to it earlier when I aimed to keep myself distant from Publius's father's fleet off France, or Gaul as it was then, all those years before. However the Corvus would be of no help to me currently with all our infantry ashore.

So, if I found myself under attack from Carthaginian ships whilst shadowing our soldiers ashore I would have no legionaries to swarm across. The presence of a Corvus on each vessel would give the Carthaginians cause to be cautious, but they'd realise soon enough and then the fight would come down to seamanship and artillery, that is catapults, ballistae and the like. These could be manned by a handful of marines. Those I had.

I commissioned a large number of small floating targets which could be towed a safe distance behind a ship and whenever the weather was good enough, which was very often, I'd take the six ships which could be launched quickly out for exercises and war games. These obviously included sinking the targets but also tests of speed and seamanship.

Those six ships saw a lot of action, and a lot of maintenance to keep them in tip top condition. Records were kept, points awarded and crews were rotated, so that all thirty crews, and their officers, improved markedly. The new tubas were tested, the signals learned, we did not test them in fog it's true, since I had no intention of losing a ship unnecessarily but everyone understood the signals and it became apparent how quickly two ships could take avoiding action and keep their oars intact.

I didn't want to fight a naval battle, but I felt we were prepared should the need arise. I started work on my manual about naval warfare, but I did it in English for now and kept it very quiet. After all, we'd yet to achieve anything, or test my ideas in action. It was all just theoretical for now.

For myself, the first half of winter passed quickly, nor was Scipio sitting back waiting. Different legions were quartered in different places, they stayed in their original units, so some were men who had fought at Capua, some had been in Spain for much longer.

Each legion had some sort of history and Scipio made sure he knew everything there was to know about each before visiting. He built what today we call esprit de corps and an identity for each legion. It wouldn't be until the time of Gaius Marius that each legion would have it's own eagle as a standard.

He met with the men frequently, congratulated them on their successes, made sure he learned about their difficulties, regrets, worries and problems. He ate with them in small groups and lived in no greater comfort than they did.

It wasn't that he had it in his power to change everything or do whatever they might want, a leader has many considerations to balance and certainly he could not change the past, but he did what he could for them. His style of leadership and his simple interest in the men endeared him to them. In some ways these hard men who'd seen death and doled it out too could be quite child like.

It wasn't just our own forces who were congratulated for keeping the Carthaginians south of the Ebro; under the most difficult of conditions Scipio also visited the local tribes who had remained faithful to Rome and built personal relationships there too.

I could understand, knowing him, how it was that he inspired confidence in the local tribes and chieftains, yet I was told later that his presence in Spain had unexpectedly created a certain degree of fear and foreboding, even amongst the Carthaginians as well.

How that might be, when Carthage had three blooded and victorious armies in the field and had defeated both Scipio's father and uncle I found hard to rationalise, yet I believe it was the case. Perhaps there was something of the divine in Publius after all, or maybe it was just a superstitious fear that you cannot go on winning forever.

Hasdrubal Son of Gisgo and his army were quartered at Gades, modern Cadiz, Mago and his forces were in camp above Castulo, the mining town in the interior which was the original home of Imilce, Hannibal's wife, and Hasdrubal son of Hamilcar based himself and his army near Saguntum. Given the dispositions an unexpected winter attack on our position would have been difficult and certainly wasn't something we anticipated.

Nonetheless our spies and scouts kept watch on these distant places and in case they were discovered, captured or cut off from us regular patrols were dispatched locally, whatever the weather. Again this helped to keep men occupied and in fighting condition.

My own small naval exercises also meant that, in effect, a watch was being kept at sea too. Even though I knew from my histories that the Carthaginian fleet was in fact occupied at Tarentum, modern Taranto in southern Italy and nothing I'd read suggested a naval attack here in Spain at this time.

Soon it was Saturnalia once more. The change in the year did not, of course end winter, but after that winter festival minds started to turn increasingly towards the next campaign. How could one relatively small army, albeit experienced and well led, eject three large, equally experienced armies from Spain?

Leadership, it would come down to the leadership of my friend Scipio. This year would be his first big test. Yes he'd charged in as a youth and rescued his father, yes he'd fought at Cannae with a never say die attitude and cut through the Carthaginian lines surrounding our forces even as they were massacring our men at most points. Yes he'd rallied the doubters after that disaster at Cannae and yes he'd made a fine speech that had won him this, his first command at only twenty four. None of these were small achievements, however, now it was time to be the general he was born to be and to deliver results. No longer just a heroic patriot on the battlefield, but now a commander of men, a planner and a decision maker.

For all that I knew the history, for all that I believed his destiny was already written, the enormity of the task awed me.

CHAPTER 16 THE BEGINNING OF THE BEGINNING 209 BC 545

After falling through time and the shock of capture. After so many battles, so much blood and pain, after marriages and bereavements it may seem strange to call this chapter the beginning of the beginning. Yet for Scipio and myself it really was the beginning of at least a new beginning.

For my friend it was the first true test of his leadership and for all that I'd told him he would be the greatest Roman of his generation and one of the greatest Romans of all time, now was the point where he had to prove it. Now it was a time to keep his head when others might lose theirs, to deal with triumph and disaster and treat those two imposters just the same. A time to risk it all with the odds stacked against him numerically, but balanced by his careful planning, his stratagems and his good sense. Not Kipling's coin toss, but a considered weighing of possibilities and outcomes, calculated risks. In fact to defeat the generals of Carthage and one in particular, genius was required, nothing less.

I couldn't remember all my Kipling and I'd no intention of trying to use his words in my conversations with Scipio, these were simply my innermost thoughts. For me too things were changing, Caius Laelius, a footnote in history really, hardly memorable as I knew too well, but involved nonetheless.

Last autumn I had commanded a fleet, but I'd not had to fight. Over winter I'd trained and drilled men, but I'd not had to fight. Truly, I started this year with my fears in check, but with the butterflies ever present. No longer was I soothsayer, a giver of information, an oracle, call it what you will, from now on I was a participant, and that felt very different. Very different indeed.

Injustice is a spectre that haunts us all. Some pass through life without ever feeling its icy touch. Many experience small injustices which rankle and gnaw, but which do no great harm, others have their lives destroyed or ripped from them by injustice.

The original Saguntines, loyal allies left to their fate by an indecisive Rome, injustice. Soldiers who fought bravely at Cannae and Silarus, still fighting for Rome despite their exile, injustice. The Scipio brothers, holding Carthaginian forces in Spain at bay for years, keeping their armies intact, preventing reinforcements reaching Hannibal in Italy, both killed and their armies destroyed within days of each other, injustice.

Injustice makes a man angry it's a powerful motivator it motivated Scipio, it motivated me and we used it to motivate our men, the cornered tiger is the most dangerous. Carthaginian forces were, after all, right to be apprehensive of their new opponent.

In Rome Quintus Fabius Maximus Verrucosus and Quintus Fulvius Flaccus were elected consuls and Roman arms wrested Tarentum back from Hannibal after three years. Marcus Claudius Marcellus fought an inconclusive battle with Hannibal at Canusium, but at least the days of Hannibal wiping out our armies at almost every battle seemed to be coming to an end. However, we in Spain did not overly concern ourselves, we had our own goose to catch and cook, well geese actually.

Come spring my ships were launched and I was ordered to sail down the coast in a south westerly direction to the mouth of the Ebro river. The legions were ordered out of winter quarters to assemble at the river mouth also and Scipio himself had the allies assemble at Tarraco, before he too set off at their head for the mouth of the river.

I alone knew Scipios plan of action. Knowing that I knew what he planned to do, even before he did, there was no reason not to discuss the details with me. Everyone else was in the dark, even Silanus, who would be left to hold our positions north of the Ebro with just three thousand infantry and three hundred cavalry. This was our first calculated risk, that while we went after their most important stronghold, they would not go after ours, seeing our advancing army as the greater threat.

Our second calculated risk was that we could pull off our radical idea before any of the three dispersed armies awoke to the new threat and that when they did they would be panicked into trying to deal with us, not thinking to move on Tarraco and Silanus. If secrecy held they would not know our exact numbers or dispositions anyway.

After leaving such a small force with Silanus we had some twenty five thousand infantry, which included the five thousand allies Scipio had brought to the rallying point himself and two thousand five hundred cavalry.

Some of Scipio's officers wanted him to attack the closest of the three Carthaginian armies, before they could unite, Scipio simply informed them that the plans he had made would be revealed to them when they needed to know and not before.

It made me smile to think that if our own officers could not anticipate our designs it was not likely that Mago and the two Hasdrubals would work it out either. After the resounding defeats of Publius Scipio senior and his brother Gnaeus, who would expect such audacity from their inexperienced son and nephew in his first command?

Prior to setting out on our mission to drive the Carthaginians from Spain my friend made another impassioned speech to the men, of a similar quality to that which gained him his command. Rhetoric is taught as an important subject, from an early age to the young men of noble Roman houses.

Whilst his speech was inspiring and his understanding of rhetoric and its uses was clear to me, I'm of the opinion that the time he spent during the winter, getting to know his men and talking to them in small groups is what really gained their devotion.

For devotion it was, not merely a desire to defeat the enemy or avenge those who'd gone before, that was also a huge motivation as discussed previously, but these hard men took their young man to their hearts. I cannot fully explain it, being somewhat cynical about leaders in my own world and time, it was a little alien to me, but it affected me, I can say that.

Our goal was to pierce the Carthaginian heart, an attack on New Carthage itself. The place was not unguarded and was well fortified, but the three powerful armies in Spain were dispersed and each some distance away. To take New Carthage would send a powerful signal to Carthage herself. It would also shake the Carthaginians in Spain to their core.

New Carthage was the very symbol of Carthaginian resurgence, the symbol of their power, the place established to start over again after the humiliations of the First Punic War. A place of rebirth, a rebirth of power, a rebirth of hope and a rebirth of wealth and influence. Should it fall it would have huge psychological consequences. Hasdrubal The Fair and Hannibal's father would spin powerless and anguished in their graves.

In Italy Hannibal himself would hear the news eventually too. His loss of Capua had made other towns and cities in Italy doubt him, he should have moved mountains to protect it, he failed and his sun was in its downwards trajectory. If we were successful in Spain Hannibal would feel hemmed about in Italy and begin to think more about survival and escape than of ending Rome's power.

I had to hold myself in check. I knew that reinforcements for Hannibal would depart from Spain to Italy despite us in the not too distant future, I knew there was still a long way to go, but I also knew the eventual fate of Hasdrubal's reinforcements and of Hannibal's army too.

Concentrate on the job in hand became my new mantra. The fall of New Carthage would not only be a shocking psychological blow, the Carthaginian war chest was there too and the hostages Hannibal had taken to keep the tribes loyal. Such a victory would have tremendous practical advantages as well as psychological. For all that the taking of New Carthage might be written, the doing of it was for us and we hadn't done it yet. At least, not this time around.

New Carthage in modern times is a Spanish Naval and submarine base, the harbour there was of no less importance to us. It could also, in theory at least, be a staging point for an invasion of Africa although Sicily, Malta and other places such as Sardinia also offered that potential.

The fleet, again under my command was ordered to sail for New Carthage. We were to keep our pace down to that which would mirror the movement of the land forces, however secrecy was more important than ever and so we put well out to sea beyond sight of land. We were all sailors or marines, no superstitious soldiers and no skittish horses to worry about.

I was confident we could stay together, defend ourselves if called upon to do so, attack and capture or sink any vessel that might give us away and that we could appear at the same moment, or as near as dammit the same moment that Scipio and his army appeared to surprise and put fear into the hearts of the inhabitants and garrison alike. In addition no plea for help would escape the place by sea, I would see to that.

About twelve days later the inhabitants of New Carthage awoke to the presence of an enemy fleet, not an insubstantial one, blockading their harbour and an enemy army, not the largest, but also not insubstantial threatening them from the landward side. Surprise is often half the battle, but it breaches no walls.

Scipio placed his camp on the north side of the city where the topography offered a good defence from a frontal attack emanating from the city. He then built substantial fortifications to the rear and on his flanks with a double rampart.

The city itself was protected to the east and the south by the sea, it being situated on a promontory of land jutting out into the water. In effect the city was about a mile from the mainland. On the west the city was, at this time, protected not by the sea so much, as by a shallow lagoon.

The entrance to the harbour was from the south west and was not especially large due to the presence of an island which provided additional weather protection, excepting only when the wind was precisely aligned with the mouth of the harbour.

By not putting fortifications between our troops and the city Scipio was demonstrating that he did not fear the Carthaginians sallying forth. In fact he would have welcomed it, being superior in numbers and keeping in mind that the Carthaginians would probably not have kept themselves in tip top condition, being in what was considered a completely safe spot.

Soldiers can grow lazy in the face of what they see as security and comfort, and a city offers other attractions than military exercises. In addition it was easy for our forces to return to camp each night, the natural defences of the city meant that siege works stretching miles around the circumference were not needed to bottle the place up, nor was there the means to escape or send messages by sea. The scene was set.

When all the fortifications on land had been completed we drew up our vessels in the harbour and Scipio visited every ship with me, talked to the Captains and reminded them that the inhabitants would like nothing more than to fire our vessels. A constant watch was kept day and night and our ballistae were so arranged as to cover attack from any quarter.

His intentions now being clear to all Scipio made another speech to his men, he pointed out as I have above the importance of the city to the enemy, here were hostages from all over Spain, here their war chest, for Carthage relied on mercenaries, here was their grain supply and here their armoury. He claimed that victory here would secure all Spain and cut Carthaginian forces off from Carthage. His claims were somewhat grandiose and exaggerated, but the speech had the desired effect.

The commanding officer supervising the defence put his one thousand troops in two contingents of five hundred, one in the citadel and the other higher still to cover the citadel. It was up to the townsmen to do the initial fighting and foolishly they sallied out of the gate. Although we beat them back easily we had not yet brought all our forces up and so rather than have our keenest soldiers rush through the gates and get cut off Scipio sagely made the signal to retire.

The panic caused when the townsmen tumbled back through the gates worked in our favour for a while, men on the walls abandoned their posts and seeing this my friend brought up his entire force with scaling ladders.

I ordered my marines and some of my sailors to the attack too, holding back enough men to operate the ballistae on the ships and defend against a surprise retaliation. We too had prepared scaling ladders and my men were keen. Sadly this kind of warfare was new to them and our only real effect was to divert some of the defenders away from Scipio's attack.

An attack which Scipio pressed in person with three bodyguards acting as shield men to protect him from the missiles raining down, he pressed right up to the walls in person, encouraging the men and noting each and every act of bravery.

Mago seeing our attack was not meeting with success brought his best troops down to the walls and there was no shortage of missiles stored up, whilst for our part the scaling ladders were proving insufficiently tall or strong so the decision was made to retire.

However, not so many of our troops had been lost due to the narrowness of the front and those not yet entered into the fight were keen to have their go. So even as the citizens rejoiced at repelling the attack and consoled one another that their walls were impregnable the attack started once more.

Scipio had done his homework however, he had spent much time talking secretly to people who knew New Carthage be they merchants, deserters, fishermen, anyone who knew the place had been well rewarded for information.

Knowing the shallowness of the lagoon at low water, which was now approaching Scipio took five hundred men down into the water. With the wind fortuitously blowing in the same direction, that is drawing the lagoon waters out to sea, the water at it's deepest came up to the men's chests, but in no time at all it was knee deep allowing an assault where it was not at all expected. Scipio naturally attributed this to the will of the gods, not to chats with fishermen, thus reinforcing his legend!

The defenders were all attending the main attack which despite being pressed hard by fresh Roman troops was going just as badly as the first assault. However on the lagoon side the walls were lower, without the same fortifications and crucially no one was there to either defend or warn. In short order Scipio and his five hundred picked soldiers were over the wall and marching through the city towards the gate without a single casualty.

As soon as the defenders found Roman troops assaulting them from the rear they scattered, that they outnumbered the invaders no one seemed to take account of, the shock did the job. With the defenders dispersed the gates were soon breached.

Suddenly, with resistance abandoned our men scaling the walls in the frontal attack found they could haul themselves over one at a time and that without too many men on each ladder the ladders held well enough. So, whilst our men swarmed over the walls another body marched in through the gate and there was a general rout. Excepting that is for the best Carthaginian troops who had regrouped in the citadel and on the the high hill.

Scipio recognised the situation for what it was and immediately sent two detachments, one to storm the citadel which he led in person and another to take the hill. The hill being unfortified fell immediately and seeing the entire city in Roman hands excepting only the citadel which was bound to fall too, Mago ordered the surrender.

Scipio had entered the city from the lagoon side at about two in the afternoon, by four it was all over. Which is not to say it was easy, but it in relative terms I suppose it would look that way, it was certainly a tonic for morale and boosted the legend of Scipio immeasurably in the eyes of his men.

Naturally he'd been first atop the wall, although with multiple scaling ladders in use others had made it to the top simultaneously, on the unopposed lagoon side anyway. In the event of being first to surmount the wall of a besieged city a soldier was entitled to claim the award of a mural crown, but Scipio himself wanted no reward for mounting an undefended wall. The outcome was all that mattered. Of course he was not witness to what was happening with the frontal attack.

To take the most important Carthaginian city outside of Carthage, a city fortified and defended by the sea and by the terrain in just one day of real fighting sent a powerful message, in particular to the three commanders in the Spanish countryside and to the three armies that had let it happen.

In my language they'd taken their eye off the ball. Whilst I knew what would happen next, speculation about the reaction of the Carthaginian armies in Spain was all the men could talk about. Those who weren't taking advantage in other ways anyhow.

I found myself in charge of thirty five warships now as there had been five Carthaginian quinqeremes lying idle in the harbour. We also found ourselves the masters of no fewer than sixty three cargo ships, mostly laden too. The cargo ships yielded corn, metals and ores and munitions but the wealth of the city was staggering.

Being Romans everything was duly recorded by the quaestor Caius Flaminius. In addition to the ships, Rome found herself richer to the tune of around three hundred pounds of gold, eighteen thousand three hundred pounds of silver and silver coin, ten thousand bushels of wheat, two hundred and seventy pecks of barley and then there were the weapons.

One hundred and twenty enormous catapults came into our possession plus two hundred and eighty one smaller catapults, of ballistae we found twenty three heavy and fifty two light, plus a vast quantity of scorpions of various sizes and calibres, ideal for picking off enemy officers! The seventy three military standards were of no practical use, but their capture would wound the enemy's pride.

Ten thousand male slaves were taken, the slaughter having stopped swiftly and in a disciplined way as soon as Mago surrendered the citadel. Two thousand artisans were also enslaved, but not for sale, these we would put to work as part of the war effort with eventual emancipation on offer should they make sufficient contribution.

I was gifted, if that's the word, fifteen hundred sturdy slaves to act as rowers now that I had five more warships. Naturally these were dispersed throughout the fleet with captains, men and marines alike ordered to watch them like hawks. They were given the liberty of not being chained upon swearing allegiance, but it was made plain to them that the slightest doubt as to their fealty would lead to their being chained permanently to their oars, or made an example of in more gruesome ways depending upon their actions.

I could not use prisoners as fighting men so the marines were stretched a little thin, fortunately I had lost only three men in the assault with ten wounded, but already recovering.

Scipio in an act of clemency, which I couldn't quite understand, gave the ranking citizens of New Carthage back their freedom. These were not Spaniards but men of and loyal to Carthage whose allegiances were hardly likely to change. I love my friend, but show me a noble Roman and I'll show you a snob! I suppose this respect of rank worked the other way around when our nobles were captured by the other side, well, sometimes anyway. Not in the case of the Germanic tribes, I knew that!

I doubted the system would protect me anyway. I commanded thousands of men and a fleet of ships suddenly, but no one would mistake me for a noble Roman.

The Spanish hostages were treated as allies and like royalty whether they were or not, our aim was to win over the population of Spain, excepting Carthaginians, not cow them into resentful submission and brooding discontent. We understood the wealth and importance of Spain as well as our Carthaginian opponents, but our methods differed.

In the future Roman tax collectors would exceed their authority and make the population bitter, opening the way for the renegade Roman general Quintus Sertorious, a personal hero of mine when I was merely a scholar of things Roman, to take the province out of Roman control and make it his personal fiefdom. In fact some Spaniards even now view him as the first King of Spain.

For the present, as it was to me at the time, Spain could not yet be called a province of Rome and Carthaginian armies still roamed the countryside, but the balance of power was beginning to change. My friend's father and uncle would have been proud, Publius and I celebrated our success, his success really, in their names.

The speed with which Publius made decisions, secured everything and made new dispositions was a wonder to me. Many, in fact most of the men were able, this very day to return to camp, sleep as they usually did, eat as they usually did and rest up.

There was some rotation of duties on the next day, but most of the soldiers had the entire day to recover from their exertions. The medics went about their work and the calmness of it all shocked me. Essentially it was I and my marines who guarded the city that first night and the next day, having done a minimal amount of the fighting.

Just two days after the battle officers, soldiers, marines and sailors paraded to learn their next allotted tasks. Offerings were made to the gods and divine intervention was credited for the fact that the major part of Carthaginian wealth in Iberia had been brought together in one place so that we could capture it. The gods were also credited with keeping the Carthaginian armies away from the city and with opening a passage through the lagoon.

The men believed it anyhow and the idea that Scipio was a favourite of the gods, if not actually the child of Jupiter himself naturally continued to grow. Having dealt, so to speak, with the god's role in events Scipio now turned his attention to heaping praise on his men. Awards were given for bravery during the initial fight when the townsmen had issued forth from the city, to the fight on the hill and the storming of the citadel.

However, the award the men valued the most, the one that had a man's name entered into history, the one he could tell tales to his grandchildren about, should he live long enough and be so blessed, was the mural crown. The award that said I was not just there, but I was first. Scipio could not fail to make such an award but he was loath to claim it or award it to a man who had scaled the walls unopposed.

He announced that he would hear claims and make a judgement. Two men put their case to the assembled army Quintus Trebellius, centurion of the fourth legion and to my consternation, one of my own marines Sextus Digitius. Both men had mounted the wall where the fighting was hot, so far so good. The attack of my marines was something of a sideshow compared with the frontal attack, but it was opposed.

How to tell which man was first, given neither had sight of the other, nor did Scipio have eyes on the fight from the lagoon. This had the potential to turn a celebration into something political, bitter and contentious. Neither of the candidates was unduly pushy as we'd say today, but his fellows were, the fourth legion and the marines rallied to the cause of their champion.

As commander of the fleet I felt it incumbent upon me to support the claim of my man. To say nothing at all would be almost as bad as to support the other. Men fought for their commanders, which meant they were fighting for Scipio really but I couldn't escape the fact that I was directly in command of Sextus Digitius and the men supporting his claim.

Our attack on the walls had been ineffective and chaotic but I had been aware that one of my men had mounted the wall quite early on. Now that his comrades supported his case I knew who that man was. He hadn't progressed into the city at that point, but then neither did the frontal attack succeed in doing that until Scipio and his five hundred appeared in the defender's rear.

Having spoken up for my man Marcus Sempronius Tudianus spoke up for the side of the legionaries and his centurion. The men were becoming increasingly unruly and a riot threatened. The candidates were withdrawn from the dais but rather than calming things down, as had been the intention, the men on parade felt the matter was now in their gift to decide by violence and became even more agitated naturally my marines were heavily outnumbered.

Scipio announced that the decision should be made by myself, Tudianus and Publius Claudius Caudinus who was effectively independent. I pointed out to the other two that we had no time to debate before this turned into a disgraceful internal fight that could only benefit our enemies, we decided to say that both men had surmounted the wall to the exact same moment in different places and that accordingly two mural crowns should be awarded.

It was decided that I should be the one to present this solution to Scipio. That bothered me not one bit, I approached my friend and appealed to him, urging him in a whisper to prevent this getting out of hand, stating that we had found that both men had stood atop the wall at the exact same moment in different locations and that it could not be ascertained in the chaos of battle which of them entered into the city first, therefore the award should be given to both men.

Scipio understood, of course, what I was doing and standing, demanded silence and spoke to the men making this perjury sound, just and honest. It's hard to say you were first when another has the same award, but it was announced and calm settled once again. For this even I thanked the gods, I already had too many ships for my contingent of marines who would have come of worst in a fight, a bit like a dozen artillerymen in hand to hand combat with the entire SAS!

The awards continued, which revived the celebratory atmosphere. It never ceased to amaze me how childlike our soldiers were, excepting, thankfully, most of the officers. To my great embarrassment I was personally awarded a gold crown and thirty oxen. My friend making it sound as if my paltry contribution were on a par with his own!

Again, being Roman all was duly recorded and the thirty oxen were written down in my name and slaves were appointed to look after them for me whilst I went on with the war. Not once in my entire life did I ever set eyes on the beasts, or profit from their existence to the extent of a single denarius!

Later, in my political life I did benefit from being the recipient of a golden crown at the event that came to symbolise the emergence of the great and ultimately victorious Scipio Africanus and as the turning point in the war.

The addition of the oxen to my award, even if only in name, did signal to all that Scipio held me in the highest esteem, valued my counsel, my leadership, my decision making abilities and that was worth ten thousand oxen in my eyes. Men would be content to follow my orders, on land as well as at sea and that was Scipio's intent. Not only was I now a participant, I was a major component in the war effort.

After the awards, the hostages, previously taken by Hannibal and his brothers to secure the allegiance of the tribes from across the Iberian peninsular, were paraded in order that all present might know their fate and if required work to ensure that the general's wishes were carried out to the letter.

There were some three hundred male hostages, mostly the sons of chieftains, but there were also a substantial number of ladies of rank and not forgetting a number of princesses who had largely been held in comfort and security, but of course without their liberty or extended family.

Scipio spoke to all about the difference in character between the Romans and Carthaginians before setting out to prove his point. Caius Flaminius our untiring quaestor was given the task of recording everything and overseeing the safe return of hostages to their rightful families, tribes, wives, husbands or betrothed as the case may be.

Two incidents are of some note during this somewhat long and bureaucratic, but entirely necessary, state and alliance building exercise. An elderly but noble matron, aunt to the princesses of the Ilergetes threw herself at Scipio's feet to urge that he should protect the honour of her younger companions, fearing that our soldiers would steal their virtue at the first opportunity. Scipio duly undertook to ensure the safety of all the female hostages, from any and all kinds of wrongdoing. Telling the quaestor to ensure their modesty and innocence as though he were a doting parent himself.

He assured her that the Ilergetes were not unknown to him. He respected their fierce independence and noted that they had opposed both Carthage and Rome equally. He hoped in time to be able to cultivate a friendship with her people and award them the status of friends and allies of the Roman people. I am not sure that this last appealed greatly, but she was a born diplomat and a wise woman, she had achieved her goal and was gracious if not effusive in her thanks, to this another invader of her ancient lands.

The men were aware, the officers were aware and the quaestor was aware that any failure would rebound on him that either did wrong or failed in his duty to protect the sanctity of these Spanish maidens, who, collectively were a part of Scipio's statecraft and strategy. This was not a matter of mere discipline, or for the avoidance of fights amongst the men.

Another young maiden was then brought before Scipio whose beauty was so outstanding and conspicuous that a hush fell on the proceedings. She was not in fact a hostage, but had been taken prisoner and such was her effect on the men that she was brought untouched before the general, being considered, by the standards of the age, a prize of great financial value.

It was learned that she was betrothed to a young Celtiberian noble by the name of Aluccius. Messengers were despatched to bring both her parents and her betrothed before Scipio which was achieved a few days later, but I will reveal his actions here. Her parents received the girl back with joy and wonder. Aluccius was assured that the marriage could go ahead and that his betrothed was unharmed.

The parents insisted on buying their daughter's freedom with a not inconsequential amount of gold that they had set aside more in hope than expectation. Scipio declined to take payment but her parents laid the gold at his feet in a state of high emotion. Scipio then took up the gold and gave it to Aluccius to, in his words, supplement her dowry. By these actions and others did Scipio win hearts and minds without need of hostages on our side.

Messengers having been sent into the lands of each and every hostage, almost all were restored to the bosom of their families and to their friends within a few weeks. No enemy force appeared in the few days that I remained in New Carthage with my friend and I enjoyed assisting Scipio with administrative matters for a few days but I was soon assigned a task I'd forgotten about despite it being mentioned by both Livy and Polybius and one which was hugely daunting to me.

More daunting than leading men. I was assigned to return to Rome with a fleet of six quinqueremes for my protection and that of my prisoners. That in itself did not worry me, I love the sea. My cargo was Mago, the captured Carthaginian commander (not that Mago who was Hannibal's youngest brother) and fifteen Carthaginian senators of New Carthage who had been taken alive.

My mission, should I choose to accept it, not accepting it wasn't really an option, was to report our victory in Rome. In fact Scipio was doing me yet another huge kindness. In the first case it demonstrated, perhaps not for the first time, but it demonstrated a trust, even greater than putting me in charge of the fleet I felt.

Secondly it raised my status and profile in Rome, he was in fact laying the foundations for me to have a political career and lastly, whilst he himself was separated from his dear Aemilia, I would enjoy a brief time with my own dear Valeria, a gift worth more to me than my golden crown.

Scipio further assisted me by drafting the report himself and talking me through it. In effect I would simply read his words and answer questions if required.

After my departure Scipio repaired the walls and improved the defences with artillery and other devices, whilst the artisans were put to work making military equipment of every kind. For a few days he exercised both the soldiers and the fleet with mock battles and when they weren't exercising they were sharpening weapons and burnishing armour. I like to think that my own previous exercises with the fleet, led to their impressing him with their skilled manoeuvring and marksmanship.

When all the hostages we were able to had been restored, even to the provinces furthest away, and having ensured that the city could not fall to another the way it had fallen to him Scipio retuned with both the army and the fleet to Taracco. He left a garrison sufficient to defend the improved walls and summoned all the tribes of the peninsular to meet with him at Taracco. Most would answer the call.

The three Carthaginian commanders tried to instigate a campaign of misinformation, at first denying that New Carthage had fallen and when this proved untenable they endeavoured to minimise its importance. They ascribed the victory to beginners luck and stated that the smile would be wiped from Scipio's face when three mighty armies descended on him to dole out to him the fate that had befallen his father and uncle.

Yet actions speak louder than words and in action they were pitifully unconvincing. Although we were unaware, until the chieftains came to Tarraco, indeed, I was unaware until my return from Rome in March next year, two Spanish chieftains had already deserted Hasdrubal's army one night as news of the restoration of the hostages and of Roman attitudes passed, as these things inevitably do, around the tribes.

For my part I enjoyed being back at sea, albeit almost always in sight of land. We took a straight course between headlands to make good speed which put us quite a way offshore on occasions and we did cut straight across the Gulf of Lions on a compass heading. Both my captain and myself knew the coast well enough to recognise where we were once we re-established sight of it and then headed south for the port of Rome. The remaining escorts were simply to follow us although all knew our plan in the event that we became separated by fog or any other misadventure. All carried a compass and tuba.

I sent word ahead from the mouth of the Tiber by fast courier to say that I would be arriving and to arrange suitable and secure transportation for sixteen high ranking prisoners.

Respecters of rank as ranking Romans are, Mago himself was taken into the home of a leading Roman senator. Effectively under house arrest this enemy of the state whose countrymen still had an army at large in Italy as well as three in Spain was nonetheless treated as something of an honoured guest. The senators of New Carthage were likewise dispersed into various private homes. I declined to host one!

I kept my thoughts on the class system to myself, not least because I knew, and was saddened by the knowledge, of what the eventual fate of Carthage would be. At the first opportunity, having made all the necessary arrangements for my ship, my crew and my prisoners I once more fell gratefully into Valeria's arms. Although she insisted on talking half the night trying to extract every detail of the news which I was honour bound to report first in the senate chamber.

The senate was crowded for my report, yet I was greeted by a respectful silence and having read my friend's report of his actions, and of the successful capture of New Carthage in such a short time, a vote of thanks was conveyed to me.

It now being almost winter I would in fact remain in Rome until the spring. Although it would be very early spring when I returned I would enjoy some three months with my beloved and of course celebrate the Saturnalia with her. Equating this festival with the Christmas celebrations I had enjoyed from childhood this meant a great deal to me. It reminded me and saddened me that we still had no children and I wondered if Valeria trusted my assurances that they would eventually come.

We entertained Pomponia and Aemilia Tertia frequently, both of whom were happy that things had progressed as I said they would. My sources for my 'predictions', as you know dear reader, were primarily Polybius and Livy. Polybius being closer in time to these events ought to be completely reliable, however, neither is completely accurate, there even appear to be discrepancies about which year things happened in!

For this reason I tried in my notes to simply record which event followed which and to predict the next when the previous one had come to pass. I didn't want to make early predictions anyway for fear that someone would try to change the course of events. I sometimes think Polybius, who would one day be a friend of my son, thought more highly of Scipio than even I did.

According to Polybius, after departing from Tarraco, the army of Scipio appeared before New Carthage some seven days later. The idea that an army, encumbered with weapons, large and small, siege equipment and supplies could march forty eight miles each day for a week, prepare food, eat, sleep create even a modestly defensible camp each night is of course preposterous and Scipio was naturally protective of his men, for whilst he had scouts and spies, he did not want to be tricked into losing his army or his life.

For this reason a proper marching camp was built each night on the march and although some of the siege equipment and the ladders were transported on my ships, much also went overland. I personally regard the thirty five miles per day actually achieved over most of the march to have been a superhuman effort.

In fact Scipio and I had agreed that I should sail into New Carthage on the twelfth day after departing, he was confident he could achieve this. In point of fact he could have done it in ten just about, but he slowed things down on the last couple of days in order that the men should arrive ready to fight immediately if required and also to stick to our agreement and to coordinate our arrival.

The fact that many of the men went into battle scant hours after arriving before New Carthage is also testament to their condition, courage and determination, but also to Scipio's wisdom. I can't believe that they would have been in any condition to fight had they already achieved that which Polybius ascribes to them. His motivation it seems to me is to make the achievements of my friend Scipio seem all the more remarkable, when in reality no gilding of the lily is required.

I gave Pomponia and Aemilia a true account of Scipio's achievements, his planning, his powerful rhetoric, his leadership and his statecraft. They seemed to think that I was in some way being modest when in fact I'd had a leisurely cruise down the coast and given a few orders and directions. Both Pomponia and Aemilia were delighted to hear that I would be returning as early as seemed possible in spring, having a view to the weather and the winds.

The two of them seemed to believe that I was in some way Scipio's luck and Romans put great store by Fortuna. Valeria was less keen that I should go, all the more so when I told her that I believed I had a role to play in the fighting on land.

"But, I'm not with child yet, you cannot go."

"I must go, I've told you, a daughter and a son will come, but it's not their time yet."

"What if you get killed, I couldn't go on."

"Oh you can go on all right!"

"What does that mean?"

"I'm sorry my love, an English failing we love a little play on words, a double meaning, but I meant it in jest I couldn't wish for more than I have with you.

"Don't be dramatic, that's all, it's not the Roman way, it is written that I will return, it is written that we will have a family and a life together, I've said many times it is not my part to change events, rather to see them through, which I have every intention of doing. If events go other than I believe they always have then anything could happen, anything, so long as everything remains as it should then our future, Scipio's future and Rome's future are all assured.

"Trust me, you know that patience is a virtue, Aemilia has not even had a visit, support her, we will all of us be fine in the end."

CHAPTER 17 THE BATTLE OF BAECULA 208 BC

Those three and a bit months rattled by, it seemed like no time at all and I was getting my crews back together for the return voyage to Spain. Our voyage to Tarraco was about nine hundred and thirty miles, maybe a little less depending how soon we left the Etruscan coast and struck out west above Corsica, likewise we would cut across the Gulf of Lions but both of these short cuts were weather dependent.

The strait between Sardinia and Corsica funnelled and concentrated the wind and was not considered an appropriate route at all. Actually I personally felt safer out at sea, away from rocks and sand banks and the like, whilst most of my men liked to have eyes on the shore and ports of refuge should the weather cut up rough.

In any event we left towards the end of February and two weeks and two days later sailed into Tarraco to a rapturous welcome, not just from Scipio but from the men too. It seemed they also laboured under the superstition that I in some way represented their leader's luck. They would have followed him anywhere, without me, but they preferred he carried his luck with him!

I wasn't there for long however. I spent a couple of days with Scipio sharing what I knew, which aligned with the ideas he already had, perhaps unsurprisingly. It was clear he wanted to move against Hasdrubal Barca. Defeating the brother of Hannibal would send another powerful message.

At this juncture Hasdrubal had more men than we, even if we sent almost our entire force plus my sailors and marines. By returning hostages and by virtue of Scipio's diplomacy we had recruited some Spanish warriors, but there was still a deficit, even without the nightmare scenario of one, or both, of the other Carthaginian armies uniting with Hasdrubal before we managed to take him out of the equation.

In my own time football fans regard certain matches as key. If towards the end of the season the two teams at the top of the table play one another the match is often referred to as a six pointer. Not only does the victorious team win three points but they deny the other team three points as well.

Following this logic, every Spanish warrior we could detach from Hasdrubal and bring into our camp was worth two. Provided they could be trusted of course. Although we had returned most of the hostages to the Spanish tribes we still held, well looked after of course, the daughters of two of the chieftains attached to and aiding Hasdrubal. Three Spanish Chieftains still adhered to Hasdrubal but we had Spanish warriors who could take messages and return with replies.

Embassies were sent to Edeco, Andobales and Mandonius, the latter two were offered their daughters back unmolested and in good health. Word had already spread about the return of the other hostages released after the fall of New Carthage.

We weren't sure we could persuade Edeco, but possibly if Andobales and Mandonius entered into treaties with us then he would see which way the wind was blowing despite the two other Carthaginian armies in Iberia. Rome certainly possessed more energy and determination, or at least Scipio did.

Not knowing yet what the outcome of these embassies would be, at least not that we could admit to, every man still counted and if my sailors and marines were to fight as infantry they would need a soldier's armour and weapons. The armouries in New Carthage and the craftsmen and artisans there had been working non stop. All I had to do was sail down the coast as rapidly as possible load the weapons and armour and get back. Every day mattered since we did not know how long the Carthaginians would remain indolent. Aside from my own private predictions of course.

In my other life I had briefly dated the daughter of a major working in logistics for the British army and he and I had discussed mistakes that had been made. It might be easier to load all the guns on one ship or aircraft, all the food on another, all the ammunition, on a third, all the medical supplies on a fourth and so on, but lose one of those vessels and you lose all of one vital supply. Split your supplies up spread them around and if one ship or aircraft goes down you still have something of everything.

One quinquereme was adequate to load all the arms and armour we needed and the sea seemed to be clear of Carthaginian ships. So I took three quinqueremes, better odds in the unlikely event of a naval engagement and we could spread swords, armour, pila, sandals and some scorpions and other heavier weapons around each of the three ships against the risk that one should founder for any reason, regardless of enemy action. It also allowed me to take more men to work shifts should we need to row the whole time.

The distance was about two hundred and ninety nautical miles each way, call it three hundred to be safe even though it's a relatively straight coast. If we could maintain five knots for one hundred and twenty hours that would cover the return journey and I estimated eight hours to load everything, if it was ready and waiting on the quayside properly packed for shipping.

Men from the garrison and or men from the town could do the loading so that my men could rest, but I would need to supervise everything in order to spread things as I wanted them spread, get the weight distribution right and make sure everything was properly secure against the risk of storm damage and a shifting cargo compromising any of the ships. In theory using the night hours as well as the daylight hours it could be done in around five and a half days.

In summer the heat tends to cause thermals on the land the hot air rises and the cold air rushes in causing an onshore wind which reverses as the temperature falls away in the evening. Of course weather systems and particular winds such as the Tramontana or the Levante can disrupt these patterns and in spring things are pretty variable. I didn't want to make a commitment but I thought we could do the job quicker than an overland expedition and more subtly too.

Fortunately we did not encounter any storms or high seas. We did however have to row into a slight headwind almost the entire time on the first leg of the journey although things were quieter in the night hours and the men didn't get quite so hot then either.

It took longer to load than I'd hoped, but we turned it around in roughly ten hours. I was exhausted but happy that everything was done correctly, records kept, all properly Roman. The men were rested, I stayed awake long enough to see us safely offshore once more, sails raised and then left things to my senior Captain.

The wind on the return journey was rarely strong enough to stop rowing completely but we made our five knots and managed a couple of rest periods when the wind obliged. In the event the entire job, including the unloading and hauling the ships ashore was completed in under a week. Given a land expedition would have halted overnight, we saved time and proved the worth of the fleet and the crews. The navy always being regarded as second in importance to the army in Roman society and politics.

My crews would now have to function as infantry, they had forty eight hours to acquaint themselves with their equipment and practice throwing javelins and learning the drills. Then we'd be off. At least the men were in peak condition and surprisingly keen.

When I had re-read my Polybius and Livy and one or two other items I'd downloaded to my tablet and made my notes I'd realised that Caius Laelius was going to be put in charge of land forces and be involved in the fighting. That had been back in 218BC or 536, take your pick.

At that time my main concern had been to make notes about everything of importance before the battery in the tablet died, secondly it was too late to change my name or the strategy that had kept me alive to that point and thirdly ten years seemed a long way off back then.

Even so, I knew then that this year would eventually come and many thoughts were spinning around my head without me at the helm of them. I remembered in my youth hearing on the television about American planes bombing guerillas in Vietnam. At that age the word guerilla was unknown to me and I wondered why the Americans thought they needed to bomb gorillas.

I didn't know much then and I didn't understand war. I knew a lot more by this time and I still didn't understand war, although I had some idea about how to conduct it. I tried to imagine being involved in hand to hand combat, tried to imagine a sword entering my ribs, my throat slashed, an arrow or slingshot in my face.

Worse, I tried to imagine having to impale another human being on my gladius or hurling a pila at someone. It was horrific. My value was in my knowledge not in my non existent hand to hand combat skills yet I knew I was destined to lead the heavy infantry on our left flank, the enemy's right flank and lead my men in an uphill battle.

When Scipio had approached the walls of Carthago Nova three shield men had been assigned to protect him from missiles. I would be accorded the same protection by three of our most renowned fighters. My unit of heavy infantry however would include our least experienced fighters, my rowers and sailors, although my marines had some idea of what they were about in combat. There still not being enough of us we were to be assigned a chunk of regular legionaries too. A mixed bag then.

It was normal in the legions to place the hastati in the first rank, that is to say young keen soldiers, but of limited experience. These then were at the front of the formation, the principes or best soldiers were placed in the second rank and the triarii behind them, often men coming to the end of their time in the service.

With so many disasters in this war the triarii weren't necessarily so common, so old or anywhere near discharge but they were considered the third best shall we say, the last line of defence, even though Romans saw themselves more as conquering warriors than defenders. Until Hannibal anyway! Perhaps that should be the last line of attack.

There was even a saying in Roman society about being down to the triarii which meant you were in dire straits. I mentally classified my regulars as principes, marines as hastati and sailors as triarii.

However it was in my mind to lead with the principes, hit hard and hit fast, but I was planning on the basis that I knew how the battle would unfold from Polybius and Livy. That is I knew the big picture but I couldn't see every brush stroke, the exact shape of all the events to come in every detail.

I also realised I was getting ahead of myself. In the morning we would set out from Taracco, the battle itself was hardly imminent. We knew that Hasdrubal was encamped at the town of Baecula on the Baetis River, the modern Guadilquivir, more or less north from Almeria and just a trifle west until you meet that body of water. Scipio and I knew that he would move his encampment to a more defensible position but not far away from his current location.

The distance was approximately four hundred Roman miles, twenty Roman miles a day would take twenty days marching and twenty miles per day was about normal given that a Roman army built a fortified encampment every night and dismantled or burned it the following morning.

In terms a modern reader will understand there would have been a day or two of March remaining when we left, a journey of twenty days or so would take us just past mid April, then we'd need a day or two to scout out the routes by which we would attack Hasdrubal and all this time we risked the appearance of the armies of Mago and Hamilcar.

Furthermore the Carthaginian armies could move swiftly, not building the kind of fortifications we did each night when they were on the move and with large contingents of cavalry, often they would ride two up as well if the horses could manage.

We also knew that burning anything each morning would be a certain giveaway. We wouldn't exactly break the rules by which Roman armies operated in the field but we would bend them. We'd aim to make twenty five or even thirty miles in a day. We'd burn nothing and try to carry our wooden walls with us, no tree felling to do and no ditches or earthworks to dig, if possible just a wooden palisade that could be erected and dismantled in under two hours.

We were very particular about sending out plenty of scouting parties and obtaining intelligence from settlements along the way though, using our Spaniards to talk to the locals. This did not slow down the march and was the sort of precaution expected of every Roman general.

It was very easy going as far as Saguntum, then the route took us further inland to places less well known by us. We managed to get ourselves within a couple of miles of Hasdrubal's new position in sixteen days, a considerable achievement, which left us a little on the tired side, but we'd take two days to scout out the terrain and rest the men. Something some historians, probably taking their cue from armchair generals in Rome have referred to as indecision. It was nothing of the sort.

By now enough Spanish tribesmen had come over to us that Hasdrubal's army was down to around thirty thousand and our own army of thirty thousand Romans was augmented by ten thousand Spaniards. The mathematics looked good, but here the numerical advantage was offset by the strength of Hasdrubal's position and our desire to send detachments around to his rear to at least try and interfere with, if not cut off any retreat. Two detachments were needed there being two possible valleys he might employ to get away.

Marcus Silanus was holding our possessions in the north with a tiny force of around three thousand infantry and three hundred cavalrymen and it behoved us to get the job done here and return lest the other two Carthaginian armies in the field, rather than reinforce Hasdrubal chose to do to us what we had done to them at New Carthage, that is take away our base of operations. In fact either Carthaginian general would probably have been able to do that had they possessed the required initiative.

The detachments we sent around to the rear would need to be undetected, be disciplined, be well led and act independently, reacting to circumstances as they occurred. In short they needed to be Romans led by Roman officers. They needed to be secreted, in position ahead of time. They left the morning after we arrived whilst our scouts examined the sides of the plateau Hasdrubal had occupied for routes up which would not lead to a mass slaughter of our men.

Planning and detailed preparation, were the order of the day not indecision and not just senior officers but centurions too were involved, knowledge of the plan was vital to all in every sector. With our small army split into so many groups it was also imperative that every group knew what it had to achieve and could act, or react I should say, according to events as they unfolded. Failure of one part of the machine could lead to a total meltdown.

I already knew that my infantry would be on the left side of our formation and that we would have the longest route around in order to attain a path up on to the upper plateau, in short we'd be the last to enter the fight. It was no surprise to me then when the scouts reported the distance and details of the route we'd take, they'd come with us but the point at which we could ascend was still tricky and not as wide as I'd have liked.

The enemy was in a defensible position then, but only if the Carthaginians were both prepared and thought through how best to defend it. I knew from my histories that Hasdrubal would be late deploying his main forces and I believed we'd be facing scant opposition on the way up.

I say upper plateau, because there was a kind of shelf directly in front of our position, or it might be more accurate to say that the plateau was stepped. Hasdrubal deployed his light troops javelin men and slingers on the lower plateau, but our light armed more mobile troops would still have to climb this under a hail of missiles from above. They were to do an outstanding job and when Hasdrubal's men ran out of missiles our light troops routed them.

This happened so fast that Hasdrubal would bring his infantry out of camp too late to even form up properly before Scipio with his heavy infantry fell on their left flank. In the chaos and confusion the Carthaginian lost many men and turning away from Sicpio, Hasdrubal's men found my infantry mounting the plateau on the opposite side, just in time from our perspective.

At this point the only option for the Carthaginians was to fight where they were, in no particular formation, or flee to the rear. This was something Hasdrubal had already commenced doing with some alacrity, taking his treasure and his elephants and effectively sacrificing a large swathe of his army.

Some of those ahead of Hasdrubal, or perhaps I should say behind him since he'd turned his back on his front facing troops, chose to fight whilst others chose to follow their leader's example and flee. Consequently, although some Carthaginians fought valiantly, the result was not in question. The Carthaginians were in chaos, each man choosing his own course of action, discipline and cohesion were lost completely.

CHAPTER 18 I LEARN THE TRUE MEANING OF COMBAT 208 BC 546

Those are the essential facts of the battle, my own experience was an emotional roller coaster. I was a little on the old side for this kind of thing, but fit enough. I'd done plenty of hill walking and some climbing in my previous life. I'd climbed mountains like Foinavon and Arkle in Sutherland, forded rivers and the like. The terrain held no worries for me.

Early in the day, as our light armed attacked Hasdrubal's skirmishers directly ahead on the lower plateau, I, together with my three shield men and three scouts, set out to lead my heavy infantry around the enemy's right flank.

Scipio led his men around the opposite flank at the same time, knowing that he had the shorter distance to cover and that he would fall on Hasdrubal's main force before my forces arrived. One scout might have been enough for me, but in case of casualties, I wanted someone alive who knew the proposed route, so three it was.

As I led out the heavy infantry assigned to me. I had no qualms about the march or the climb, but I didn't really want to lug a huge, cumbersome, heavy and unfamiliar shield with me and so I had requested and been given a much smaller circular cavalry shield.

I was agile enough and taller actually than many of my somewhat squat men, but I couldn't hold a candle to them for toughness or brute strength, especially in the arms and shoulders. I wanted something in my left hand, which wasn't too heavy for me to wield, with which to fend off blows and I also wanted to feel balanced, being right handed, when I drew my sword it would be in my right hand.

The last part of my logic was that my marines and sailors, if not the regulars were a superstitious lot who saw me as felix, that is lucky, or more to the point their luck! I think they also understood that I wanted to keep them alive as much as I wanted to keep myself alive! Maybe, just maybe, despite me being something of an oddity, some even saw me as something of a father figure.

Anyhow, the atypical circular shield marked me out to them, without really signifying much to the enemy. If anyone in my detachment saw the guy with the circular shield in difficulty they'd know it was their officer.

My previous thoughts on whether to place principes in the front rank had proven academic. In an open battlefield situation we'd have been arranged in maniples of one hundred and twenty men with forty hastati in the front row forty principes in the second rank and forty triarii in the third rank. This might be augmented by a fourth rank of reserves on occasion if such reserves existed. However, this wasn't a flat battlefield.

My marines were happy to be in the front rank closest to me so I let that be. However this wouldn't be a broad front, so it wouldn't mean very much. We set off with a front line just four maniples wide, that is to say a front line of only one hundred and sixty men. Furthermore, the centurions had been briefed to narrow even this not very broad front if the terrain, especially where we intended to ascend proved too restrictive to allow even this size of formation to remain cohesive. The men had been drilled and knew which maniple would fall in where whenever there might be a need to narrow the line, or conversely widen it.

I have visited the site in modern times and memory plays tricks I know but it seems to me to be less imposing and less stepped today, two thousand years can alter the topography as well I suppose.

We marched in silence. This wasn't unusual, nor did the men normally make any sound in the build up to battle unless ordered to do so. This could be ordered for the purpose of, for example, encouraging an enemy to attack, usually when we held the high ground, or if it meant them crossing water, in these eventualities we'd hurl insults to make them act foolishly and attack our stronger position.

The other use of noise would be to cow an enemy and instil uncertainty, or better yet real fear in them as they charged us, in these instances pila and swords might be clashed against shields making a terrifying sound. These tactics weren't called for today, silence allowed commands to be issued as quietly as possible and mitigated against early detection.

We possessed trumpeters if commands were needed later once the noise of battle ensued. Our route to the plateau meant us marching a little over two and a half Roman miles, about an hour. I knew that our light armed would make remarkably quick progress and that Scipio's men would probably enter the fray about a quarter of an hour before us.

Having grown up in post war Britain I'd experienced fifty one years of peace in Europe before suddenly arriving in another time. There was too much violence even in my time, but many people would live their entire lives without seeing any. In ancient Rome violence was an every day fact of life, even in peacetime, in the city itself, however many young men couldn't wait to learn the arts of war, go off to fight for their city, gain what they saw as glory.

I didn't hesitate; after ten years, bereavements and having absorbed cultural attitudes, as if by osmosis I knew we had to arrive on the scene of battle as swiftly as possible and play our part. I did not want to kill anyone, but I knew it might come to kill or be killed, or that I might need to kill a man in order to save one of my own. Fortunately we moved too swiftly to really dwell on things.

We could hear the sounds of fighting almost from the off, but of course the yells and cries grew louder as we climbed until suddenly the gory, distressing scene unfolded in front of me. I had to press forward to allow the maniples behind me to attain the plateau and I did. My shield men were disciplined and efficient, those suicidal Carthaginians who chose to fight might make a run at us but none got near me.

I saw my men thrust swords into bellies; the normal way to use the Roman short sword was a thrusting movement as raising the arm to strike down exposed a man to a thrust below the arm. A sword in the belly would take a man out of the fight, but it wasn't a quick, clean death. Oft times guts were spilled on the ground, I saw one man hopelessly trying to push his back into the gaping bloody slash across his body.

I wanted to vomit, knew that I must not. I don't know how long I walked, I'd like to think strode, but walked, maybe staggered would be more accurate, through the maelstrom, my shield men allowing me to keep my sword unblooded and my small shield undented.

Scipio's men and our valiant light armed troops who stormed the hill front on must take most of the credit, but my men had played their part, even the sailors. All our men were jubilant, our losses were around two thousand, mostly from the men who joined the fight first. I couldn't celebrate that.

I wanted to weep at the folly of mankind, but succeeded in keeping a stiff upper lip, just about. No jubilation for me, although the men's joy was infectious in a way. However, the horror of close, hand to hand combat with blades had affected me. I returned my sword to its scabbard so that its clean condition would not be noticed as soon as I was decently able.

Scipio met me in the centre of the field and embraced me, one look at my face and he decided to postpone conversation until later. The blood, mud, screams and moans, the abandoned bloody weapons the posture of the bodies and the groans of men still in agony, clinging desperately to life were not new to my friend. That day changed me forever.

CHAPTER 19 THE AFTERMATH OF BAECULA 208BC

Baecula seems to me to have become a footnote in the history of the life of my friend Scipio Africanus. Ilipa may have been sheer genius and in some ways more important. Zama earned him his cognomen, but the importance of Baecula should not be overlooked or minimised.

There is a legend that the secret name of Rome is Roma spelled backwards. Rome was not love; it was many things: politics, rivalry, murder and corruption, but not love, albeit I found my love there.

Rome was also a birthing pool of brilliance; for nigh on a thousand years when Rome needed a man of superior ability one would arise, from Cincinnatus, through Scipio, Marius, Sulla, Sertorius, Pompey, Caesar, Augustus, Vespasian and Constantine, Rome spawned brilliant men. However it was politics, faction and rivalry which sought to belittle our achievement, Scipio's achievement actually at Baecula.

Hasdrubal escaped it is said with two thirds of his army. In fact we killed eight thousand and took twelve thousand prisoners to sell into slavery and boost our coffers. Paying the legions is a vital part of the equation but to my mind if Hasdrubal started with thirty thousand men and we killed or captured twenty thousand he escaped with only one third of his army to cross the western Pyrenees and seek to reinforce Hannibal. Of course he recruited en route where he could.

Armchair generals and factions in Rome criticised us bitterly for allowing Hasdrubal to escape, so let us look at some other simple facts. In the first place, when Scipio asked for the command in Spain, not one of those armchair generals or rival factions wanted the impossible task.

Secondly thirty thousand Roman soldiers had to secure twelve thousand prisoners, the Spanish troops were of limited use in these matters, that's a mammoth undertaking, twelve thousand men may be unarmed, but it's not long before their minds turn to thoughts of escape with slavery in prospect and these were hardened warriors, disarmed or not.

Furthermore we had secured Taracco, Saguntum, New Carthage, we'd taken an entire Carthaginian army out of the war in Spain and we'd brought all the most powerful and significant tribes of the peninsular into our fold. Indeed the Spanish character and culture being somewhat different from Roman ideas our new allies would happily have proclaimed Scipio king as they did some years later in the case of Sertorius.

Spain was rich in resources which we were well on the way to securing for Rome. It would be one of the most lucrative provinces for years to come once the job was complete.

To have chased after Hasdrubal into unfamiliar territory, with the armies of Mago and Hamilcar still on the loose would have been military incompetence of some magnitude. In addition our spies suggested Hasdrubal was moving north and west, our base of operations was well to the east, too far, what we needed to do was sell our captives and re-secure what we already had a tenuous hold on. For Mago and Hamilcar, their day of reckoning would come.

Naturally the job was very much incomplete at this juncture, but everything was moving in the right direction and given the rapidity with which we'd secured Carthago Nova at the end of last year and then taken Hannibal's brother out of the fight in Spain before summer of this year, I'd say we were doing pretty well.

We'd laid strong foundations for our future success in Spain and done so without delay. Of course I'm not impartial. Nonetheless, we did not need less able rivals in Rome trying to lessen Scipio's reputation or weaken an aura that made his enemies nervous.

At a suggestion from me Scipio instructed the quaestors in charge of selling the captives, now officially property of the state, to look out for one particular captive of some value, he being Numidian royalty. Massiva was the nephew of the future king Massinissa of the Massylii who led the Numidian cavalry loyal to Carthage.

Massinissa was a born warrior he'd live into his eighties and despite a civil war that would go against him he remained a warrior even into old age. However, at this time Massinissa was at the height of his personal powers and his men loved him.

It's even possible that my friend's father might have survived the battle of Castulo and that his uncle might have survived the battle of Ilorca were it not for the role played in both battles by Massinissa's skilled Numidian cavalry.

The future king's young nephew Massiva had, I knew from my histories, disobeyed his uncle's clear instruction not to enter the battle. The impetuosity of youth caused him to disobey. That his horse stumbled and threw him was the gift to us that led him to be in our power. His release and return to Massinissa would not bring the powerful leader to our side, indeed we would face him again at Ilipa, but eventually, when Massinissa saw the tide start to turn he would come to us and the release of the youngster might well have played a part in bringing that day forward.

In any event Scipio gifted the youth a beautiful Spanish cloak and other rich clothes, a gold ring and a gold brooch to secure the cloak plus a fine horse caparisoned and decorated to the same degree as the young royal himself. A body of our own cavalry was assigned to escort the young man in the direction of the enemy and to stay and protect him for as long as he wished to be escorted.

For us it was the long march back to Tarraco to relieve Marcus Silanus and his three thousand three hundred men upon whom so much still rested. We would stop at Saguntum en route and review our defences and arrangements there, question the commander and ensure all was well.

Before we set out messengers were despatched to Rome with our account of events and others were sent to Carthago Nova to check on the state of affairs, issue instructions from Scipio to the commander there and to bring his reports back to us at Tarraco.

Oft times prior knowledge of events weighed on me, but now it was a relief to know what would occur. Hasdrubal son of Gisgo and Mago Barca commanding the other two Carthaginian armies in Spain would hear of Hasdrubal Barca's defeat and come to their senses. The three generals had not been working in accord, now the two armies which had done so little this year would march out to meet Hasdrubal Barca and agree their next course of action.

This would see all three Carthaginian armies heading towards the far end of the Pyrenees well away from our base. They would be no threat or nuisance to us and we would spend the rest of this year dealing with administrative affairs and continuing to woo the Spanish tribes and their leaders.

Knowing this I could personally enjoy the march back. Our speed was dictated by the infantry and so I chose to ride some of the time, or walk as the mood took me. I think one should not be too familiar with the men, or even with what in my time would be described as NCOs, but I did talk to them. Officers too of course, but I was, even ten years in, still learning as much as I could.

Evenings I naturally spent in the society of Scipio and his immediate circle. On occasion the two of us would spend the evening together with no other company than the servants. This special treatment protected me from the potential error of becoming one of the men and whilst I was one of them in a way, I was also something else. I'm, not sure what exactly, I felt both accepted and yet apart at one and the same time.

CHAPTER 20 THE BATTLE OF THE METAURUS RIVER IN ITALY CONSOLIDATION AND PREPARATION IN SPAIN 207BC

War is an abomination, I've always thought so. witnessing bloody hand to hand fighting where men looked into the faces of other men as they killed them and often stepped on them to reach the next victim, or to meet their own end, perhaps slipping on blood and guts as they did so, did nothing to disabuse me of my long held opinion.

I knew enough about the life of Caius Laelius now, from what I'd read, to know that if I were really him, that even if a return to my own time were possible it would not happen for many years yet, that Caius Laelius still had a role to play and it would be one that involved more battles.

I realised that destiny, fate, the universe, some force greater than me and beyond my understanding had put me in this position. I had grown up in peace and now must fight. I realised that human beings had found themselves forced to kill or be killed, protect themselves or submit to invasion, slavery, rape, torture and loss for millennia.

Why does humanity allow itself to be led in this way? For led it is. In this time and culture, that is to say what we today call antiquity, war was more the norm than the exception and yet there were still many who would have preferred peace. A kind of peace would be brought to Europe by the future Emperor Augustus, probably the longest European peace right up until the time of my birth in 1956.

Violence and war always beget more war until one or both sides are exhausted it seems, viz the hopeless defence of Berlin in 1945. The First Punic War led to the second and the third, just as the Franco Prussian War was one of the causes which led to World War One which together with the Treaty of Versailles created the conditions which led to World War Two.

It was ever thus. My mind wandered onto treaties and how men manipulated them, created them not so much for peace as for advantage; national and even personal.

I considered how Rome had abused the treaty it made with Carthage at the end of the first Punic War and the treaty made by Hasdrubal the Fair as a delaying tactic. I suppose I thought about these things because I knew our return to Tarraco would pass unmolested and I was left alone to my thoughts for much of the time as I walked or rode alongside my men. My men, strange expression.

My knowledge weighed on me once more, not so heavily as when I'd had to tell Scipio and Pomponia about the loss of father, uncle, husband and brother in law, or my own sweet Valeria about the impending death of her beloved brother, but I knew now that Hasdrubal Barca was marching to meet his destiny, that Hannibal would shortly lose his brother.

As cruel and ruthless as Hannibal could undoubtedly be I doubted he was without any human feeling. Had history taught me that Carthage had won I might have chosen the other side, in fact I'm sure I would, the history of the world subsequently would have been entirely different.

The three Carthaginian generals held their meeting, probably around the same time that we arrived back in Tarraco, or possibly even sooner. Had we pursued Hasdrubal we would have found ourselves in an entirely untenable position.

They seem to have made the following decisions, firstly that Mago Barca, the youngest of the brothers would transfer his forces over to the recently defeated Hasdrubal Barca his older brother. This may be why Rome thought that Hasdrubal had escaped with two thirds of his army intact, but the numbers for that assertion do not add up.

Mago himself would repair to the Ballearic islands and recruit anew. Just as Hasdrubal would attempt to recruit on his march into Italy, by which action he also hoped that his Spanish survivors being further from home would resist the temptation to desert. Finally Hasdrubal son of Gisgo would return to Gades, modern Cadiz in what was known as Lusitania then, Andalusia today, an area where Carthage still had adherents.

So it was that even as we reinforced our friendly relations with the Spanish tribes, kings and princes so Carthage made fresh preparations to carry the seemingly never ending war forwards and 546 slipped inexorably into 547, Saturnalia and all that.

The consuls for 547 were Claudius Nero and Marcus Livius. Nero was based in the south, Livius in the north. Hannibal, in Bruttium was somewhat reduced in power, but yet formidable. Nero with forty thousand men was forced to play a cat and mouse game with Hannibal who declined to meet him in open battle, which suggested to me that Hannibal was also suffering a loss of confidence.

For Hasdrubal Barca Fortuna appeared to be smiling. He had put together another formidable army. He'd recruited Celtiberian mercenaries on the first part of his journey then crossed the Alps in spring. Unlike the tortuous crossing made by Hannibal eleven years prior Hasrdubal had an easy time of things. The Gauls had been impressed by Carthaginian successes and where they had previously opposed Hannibal they flocked to join his brother.

Hasdrubal again brought elephants across the Alps, this time elephants raised in what we called Hispania, that is to say Spain. He must have felt confident that once united with Hannibal Carthage would once again have very much the upper hand.

Meanwhile Nero had won what might be termed a major skirmish and a minor skirmish against Hannibal's forces near Grumentum and the western end of Lago del Pertusillo as it's known today. Nero claimed to have killed some eight thousand Carthaginians and four elephants with two elephants captured and seven hundred prisoners taken in the larger engagement and another two thousand Carthaginians killed in the second, smaller engagement.

He put his own losses at five hundred. Roman generals had a habit of exaggerating their successes against Hannibal for their own career prospects whenever they could, but it did no harm to the public mood.

Marcus Livius, the one later to be called Salinator after a dispute involving a law concerning salt taxes when he was censor was currently falling back, but preserving his forces, in face of the threat presented by the rejuvenated Hasdrubal.

The career of Marcus Livius was quite remarkable given he'd been found guilty of misconduct concerning spoils in the earlier Illyrian war yet came back to be consul for a second time and then censor. That of course is, once again, another story.

Nero took seven thousand of his best men, that is six thousand foot and one thousand cavalry, leaving around thirty three thousand men under the command of his legate Quintus Catius to hold Hannibal in check and hurried north to join Livius and deal with the threat from Hasdrubal before he could effect an alliance with his brother. Emissaries from Hasdrubal to Hannibal having been captured we were at least ahead in the intelligence war.

Nero moved fast, his men carried only their arms and armour and the cavalry went ahead to the Roman settlements en route to arrange food and shelter for the foot soldiers marching as rapidly as possible in their wake.

Livius together with the praetor Porcius Licinius had fallen back on the town of Sena, modern Senigallia. Nero arrived in the night, but trumpets heralding his arrival gave away the fact that Livius had been reinforced. Hasdrubal was not to know that Nero had brought just seven thousand men, although admittedly his best.

Had Hasdrubal elected to fight a pitched battle, and had he possessed the genius of either Hannibal or Scipio, he might have defeated Livius and Nero, but believing he faced two full Roman armies he elected to retreat. This proved his undoing. The following night he led his men out of camp to retreat further. He may have been betrayed by his guides, but whether that be so or not, he found himself in an unfavourable position, unable to ford the Metaurus River. Now he had to stand and fight.

In addition his undisciplined Gauls had had rather too much access to alcohol and were not in the best state for a fight, unless with each other.

Reluctantly Hasdrubal prepared for battle he faced two legions assigned to Livius and two legions previously assigned to Porcius Licinius plus the seven thousand men brought by Nero. With auxiliaries that's approaching thirty thousand men.

Appian claims Hasdrubal's force consisted of forty eight thousand infantry eight thousand cavalry and fifteen elephants. That's an army of fifty six thousand to our near thirty thousand. Romans do love to exaggerate their achievements. The colourful and dramatic Livy goes further still, he claims sixty one thousand four hundred enemies were slain that day! What size the initial army of Hasdrubal in his eyes one wonders.

Whatever the precise statistics the threat from Hasdrubal was neutralised that day. Hannibal's brother was slain and Nero together with the resurgent Livius, on account of the victory, were awarded a full Roman triumph the following year.

I knew these events would unfold albeit the numbers are somewhat vague and had naturally informed Scipio of the location and outcome, those particular facts not being vague. So, back to us in Spain.

Carthage was proving itself to be almost as resourceful as Rome. Another general with a familiar name Hanno had arrived in Spain from Carthage with yet another new army and Mago also returned from recruiting in the Balearics, augmenting his forces still further with yet more Celtiberians and mercenaries.

Joined in Spain by Hanno and his new army we faced a considerable threat once more and although I knew we would not come to the same end as my friend's father and uncle it was still very tiring from my perspective. Of course there was still Hasdrubal son of Gisgo down in Cadiz as well. If we took our entire force to deal with Hanno and Mago we risked being cut off or surprised by Hasdrubal's army.

In addition Massinissa, (remember him?) was out and about, popping up here there and everywhere with his fast moving cavalry making life very uncomfortable for the native population which we hoped to keep on our side, something that would become increasingly unlikely were we unable to protect them.

Next we decided, although it was also the action dictated by history as I already knew, to despatch Junius Silanus with ten thousand infantry and five hundred horse to see what he could do about Hanno and Mago whilst we kept watch on Hasdrubal.

It was at this point that we were joined by my friend's younger brother Lucius. You may well ask why I've not mentioned him before. This is how it fell out. Publius undoubtedly loved his brother. However, Lucius had been born in 228BC or 526 to us. When I met Publius, Lucius was nine going on ten years old. We were in Gaul and then northern Italy, Lucius still a boy, in Rome. In 537 when we arrived in Rome he was eleven. Still too young to be a member of the Jupiter Club or fight in the battles soon to come at that juncture.

When I stayed with Pomponia Lucius was hardly to be seen, between attending classes and spending time with his own group of friends, mostly school friends he was absent a great deal. In addition, when he was at home, Pomponia did not want him to be distracted by me or to be involved in our deep and oft times worrisome conversations.

It was 544 when Publius had been given the command in Spain and Lucius was eighteen that year. He was commencing his own try at the cursus honorum, something I explained earlier, but the disasters which helped Publius achieve power before his time did not assist Lucius. In fact Lucius had a cousin, born the same year as himself Scipio Nasica and they found themselves chasing the same positions on each rung of the ladder in the same year.

Publius had not had the same problems, indeed despite the love between the two brothers their personalities and life experiences had been quite different up to this time, although both would encounter very similar political problems and envy later in life.

Publius was indeed happy to see his brother despite the superstition it engendered regarding history repeating itself and what had happened to his father and uncle.

Lucius requested that he be part of the expedition to be led by Silanus and Publius granted this request, little suspecting that Lucius would kill a feared Cantabrian mercenary leader named Larus in hand to hand combat. Larus may have been the last man standing in that area of the engagement at the time, tired and injured, but he was a large man and the incident did no harm to Lucius's image and standing with the men.

Again I'm getting ahead. Another Roman seeking a name and glory, Junius Silanus moved with great alacrity to attack Hanno and Mago. Despite impenetrable forests, supposedly, viz the Ardennes in world war two and rocky terrain Silanus came upon the enemy before there was even any rumour of his departure.

Although he commanded a much inferior force overall, he was able to deal considerable blows to the enemy in stages. The Celtiberian camp was separate from that of the African forces and without an adequate lookout Silanus routed the Spaniards before the Carthaginians could come to their aid. Thus creating the opportunity for Lucius to distinguish himself. Those Carthaginians who did come to aid their allies were too late and also went down to defeat.

Mago with a considerable body of cavalry and around two thousand infantry immediately fled towards Gades that is Cadiz to join Hasdrubal. Hanno having come to the aid of the Celtiberians too late was captured along with several other noble Carthaginians. Some of the Celtiberians did escape, however this may have been to our advantage as the defeat would weaken the Carthaginian PR campaign with the Hipanics and strengthen ours!

Scipio, as was his nature was unstinting in his praise for Silanus. I've always thought it tragic the course my friend's life would take with others so keen to belittle his achievements when he was so generous in his praise of the achievements of others.

Lucius, was also rewarded for his part in events. Men were happy to follow him now and he was given an important task to fulfil, one we both believed he could achieve and one that would give him an added aura of success and help his career.

He would in fact be curule aedile at age thirty three, but be beaten to the consulship by one year by his cousin. However, I'm getting ahead yet again as he and I would stand for office together one day, but that is another story, although I will get around to it.

Lucius's task was to capture the town of Orinx, modern Jaen to the east of Cordoba, which was being used by the Carthaginians commanded by Hasdrubal son of Gisgo and held some strategic value it must be said as a jumping off point for raids. This time Lucius was put at the head of ten thousand infantry and an additional one thousand cavalry.

Initially Lucius tried to negotiate with the townsfolk and that having failed built a ditch and rampart, his intention being to split his force into three parts so that one part could carry on the attack whilst two parts rested safely behind these defences and awaited their turn in the rotation. The first attack being repulsed, he decided to attack again with a full two divisions whilst the first rested.

The defenders being tired after beating off just one third of the Roman force were dismayed to see twice as many men as before attempting to scale their walls and in the chaos and dismay caused by this development some of the townspeople deserted, believing that to resist was to invite retribution on themselves.

Sadly these were killed by the Romans before their purpose was clear, probably because they carried shields to defend themselves from projectiles as they exited the town and were viewed as hostiles, however the Romans were able to enter through the open gate. The cavalry took the forum rapidly and soon all the gates were opened or broken and Roman troops occupied every quarter of the city taking the Carthaginians therein prisoner.

Some three hundred of the townsfolk who had supported the Carthaginians were also put under guard, but the other Spaniards were left in possession of their property, there was no looting and no wanton killing although some two thousand Carthaginians are claimed to have been killed, possibly another exaggeration, Lucius caught on fast! Importantly our own losses were no more than one hundred.

Scipio heaped praise on Lucius and his men, even to the extent of comparing it with his own conquest of Carthago Nova. Thus 547 drew to a close and we all returned to winter quarters. Affairs in Spain could not be said to be settled with Hasdrubal son of Gisgo and Massinissa still in the field, but it had been another year that had been better for us and worse for Carthage.

Lucius sailed for Rome with Hanno and the other notable Carthaginian captives. A good opportunity for him to establish his name and his own political career.

Overshadowed by his older brother he may forever be, yet his achievements in this and other conflicts were of considerable significance. He, like my friend, his sibling was a great man, one I would enjoy working with in the future.

CHAPTER 21 THE BATTLE OF ILIPA 206BC

This would be our final year in Spain or Hispania as we knew it. The year of the consuls Lucius Veturius Philo and Quintus Caecilius Metellus, not the greatest consuls we ever produced, but more than adequate. Both men had fought under Nero at the Metaurus and Philo would one day join Scipio and myself on our expedition to Africa.

Quintus Caecilius Metellus had grown since despairing at Cannae and though not a Jupiter would become an ally and friend of Scipio despite the earlier history between the two men. He would also go on to distinguish himself militarily.

Scipio too had grown greatly from the youth I had met almost twelve years ago. After I had convinced him that the events happening at that time were truly history for me, he had come to rely on my 'prophesies'.

My role was somewhat different now. Scipio was his own man a great leader, a great orator and an accomplished politician. He no longer needed me to tell him what his plan should be. We had reached a largely, albeit not entirely, unspoken agreement. If he asked, I'd tell what I knew, if he didn't ask I'd keep quiet, unless I saw some major deviation from the way things ought to have been according to what was written.

This last possibility did not happen. If the universe had put me here to ensure continuity then the period where history might have diverted from it's intended course must surely have been when Scipio was but a youth, not truly believing that he would be the hero of this, Rome's greatest test to date. Possibly its greatest test of all time, although that might be debated regarding the time of Gaius Marius.

It's still entirely possible though, if one also excludes the dangers posed by Roman on Roman, that Hannibal was the greatest threat Rome ever overcame. It certainly set Rome on course for Empire.

The size of the armies of Rome and of Carthage in this year depends upon whom one believes. Polybius has the Carthaginians fielding an army of seventy thousand infantry, four thousand cavalry and thirty two war elephants. For once it is Livy who is the more conservative.

Choosing between these two was ever a difficulty back when I had to make predictions to Scipio to prove my worth. Not so now. Livy says the Carthaginian forces consisted of fifty thousand infantry, four thousand five hundred cavalry and an unknown number of elephants.

I can talk with confidence as to the size and composition of our own forces and having seen both armies in the field I would say that we were certainly outnumbered although not as heavily as some have suggested, especially Polybius who is usually quite accurate.

We were however disadvantaged with regards to cavalry, something the African commanders failed to capitalise on. How Carthage continued to acquire such large armies is something incredible, but with so many mercenaries it speaks more to their wealth than to a martial philosophy.

That said the Carthaginians were making a huge, albeit final, effort to wrest back control of Hispania. In Carthage itself this theatre almost certainly held more import to the politicians and powers that be than poor old Hannibal bottled up in what you and I know as Calabria.

Our own forces in Spain, by this time consisted of six crack legions and as every true Roman will tell you that's more than enough to take on any enemy! A belief which came about after the demise of Hannibal and Carthage and not before. Nor did it always hold good even then.

We had near three thousand cavalry, some half of which were allied and less to be trusted than our own. The balance of our infantry, which brought our total number up to approximately fifty thousand men were Spaniards and a few Gaulish mercenaries and journeymen.

The Carthaginians came out from Gades quite early in the year; the calendar being somewhat unreliable I'd say mid March in modern terms and marched in the direction of modern Seville known then as Hisbaal after the Phoenician and Carthaginian god Baal. Having spies keeping watch we received news of their departure some seventeen days after they left Gades.

Our spies achieving an average of forty Roman miles per day over all terrain wore out several sets of horses to bring us the news. We, well, most of us, were like a coiled spring waiting for the off. I can't quite put myself in that number but we were prepared and able to depart the very day the news came in. Our spies were immediately turned around and sent ahead to monitor the enemy.

Our march to confront the enemy was around six hundred Roman miles and it was important that we arrived in good condition. Of course we did not know how fast the enemy would move or what exactly his plans were, but we saw him moving into the interior to try and show a display of strength to the tribes and possibly recruit. Carthage, excepting for Hannibal himself ever placing too much store on numbers.

We moved in what we took to be the right direction generally, sent scouts out in various directions to mitigate against unpleasant surprises and hoped our original spies would be able to report back before too long. We covered roughly twenty five Roman miles a day depending on the terrain and roughly four weeks later found ourselves encamped across a valley from the combined forces of Mago Barca and Hasdrubal son of Gisgo.

Massinissa and the Numidian cavalry attacked us even as we began constructing our camp, however, having scouted the area before arriving at the defensible site chosen for our camp we had secreted our own cavalry in nearby woodland. As the Carthaginian cavalry attacked uphill our own cavalry took them partly in flank and partly from above.

Instantly the fight began to go our way, but our Spanish cavalry at least were not the best, Massinissa and his Numidians were experienced, skilled and not easily put down. As the tide started to turn against us our infantrymen downed tools and rather than continue to build the camp marched out to sweep the Numidians from the field. This did not take long and it was back to building and digging! I've often though that the Roman Empire was built as much with the spade as with the sword.

As was the case with so many, although not all ancient battles, a game of cat and mouse commenced, skirmishes, probing and testing. Again Hannibal was an exception to this rule, however the game we played on this occasion was specifically planned to create a false impression with our enemies. It had nothing to do with reluctance.

Hasdrubal and Mago daily led their forces out of camp in the early afternoon and lined up, offering battle always in the same formation, which we took careful note of. We led our own forces out also, always after them but we held our position on our side of the valley and did not attack allowing the Carthaginians to study our own dispositions also, the crack Roman legions in the centre, Spanish allies on both wings and cavalry behind in reserve.

Each day the Carthaginians would return to camp close to sundown after a tiring afternoon standing, in full armour for many of them. Only once they quit the field did we do likewise. Having created this routine stand off over a period of days we prepared to attack. Scipio ordered that the men retire early and rise early, well before sun up and be well fed, armed ready and that the horses be saddled.

At the very break of day, the cavalry and velites would attack the Carthaginian outposts and guards causing alarm in the Carthaginian camp and a hurried exit to form up for battle. We also had formed up and demonstrated our intent by positioning ourselves in a slightly more advanced position than had become usual.

The Carthaginians might have done better to stay in their camp and defend it but their reaction, as predicted, was to form up in their habitual way, not noticing in the dim early light that we had changed our line of battle. They did notice that we had moved forwards more than usual in a clear show of intent devised to hurry them. Whereupon we stopped and waited, making no further advance until the effects of fatigue and hunger began to work upon them.

This was not the Trebia there was no sleet and snow to weary the enemy as it had wearied us that day, but disturbed sleep, no food, the adrenaline of impending battle followed by anticlimax and inaction, a stiffening of the limbs and fatigue, these things affect a man. Publius had learned from Hannibal, his own brother and brother officers had not.

With our crack legions three on each wing and the Spaniards in centre our cavalry and skirmishers were sent out to keep the enemy on his toes. Hasdrubal and Mago could not rearrange their line of battle for fear that we would attack them mid manoeuvre from our advanced position. The skirmishing was indecisive, nor was it expected to be otherwise and although we were in a position slightly more forward than on previous days we were still marginally raised up on our side of the valley.

After harassing the enemy for some hours at no great risk to ourselves we sounded the retreat and brought the cavalry and skirmishers in good order back behind the army. The cavalry riding around our own wings after the velites had retired through the gaps left for them in the Roman maniples. On our wings then we had heavy infantry and behind them the velites, a little tired but not overstretched and behind them the cavalry likewise.

The centre was wholly Spanish, Gaulish and rag tag allies we'd collected here and there. Their only task for most of the day was to hold position and by the threat that they posed anchor the Africans in place whilst our crack troops fell upon the enemy's wings. Silanus and Marcius commanded our left wing, Publius and myself the right.

The cohorts of heavy Roman infantry spread out and advanced against the Spaniards on the Carthaginian wings which until now had presented the broader front. As our infantry spread out and advanced in a prearranged choreography so our velites and cavalry enjoying a second wind, for they had known not to over exert themselves earlier, took an even wider path which would enable them to press the Spaniards fighting for Carthage from the flanks, the cavalry could even get behind them to some degree. The legionaries inexorably advanced in formation, push with the shield, thrust with the sword, push, stab and repeat.

The Carthaginians and their Spanish and mercenary allies had stood, with no food in their bellies for some seven hours before facing this highly organised, disciplined attack from men, who, having the upper hand pressed their advantage somewhat gleefully.

The enemy's wings crumbled quickly into chaos. Both wings could only fall backwards, trying to dodge our less numerous cavalry as they did so, each wing having Romans to the front of them Romans to one side of them and their own African colleagues to the other side of them, who finally, finally were to join the fight.

These, the best of Hasdrubal and Mago's army were without room to manoeuvre and our cavalry attack, which had in part got behind the enemy so startled their elephants that the mahouts could not control them and they were of no use whatsoever. Their handlers worked wonders in preventing them from actually trampling their own men.

At first the tired and hungry Carthaginian centre lived up to its reputation, but it was in no position to turn the battle and although it initially fell back in good order it soon became the rout that always ensues when men decide it's every man for himself. As soon as they showed signs of disorder our own Spaniards were given leave to charge forwards.

The Carthaginians fled to their fortified camp, some twenty thousand may have made it including most of the Numidian cavalry, both Carthaginian generals and Massinissa of course. We were unable to follow as quickly as we should have liked owing to a sudden torrential downpour making conditions slippery and hazardous underfoot.

Carthaginian power in Spain was shattered that day, we had killed or captured, mostly killed, some forty thousand of the enemy. If twenty thousand had made it back to the Carthaginian camp it did not stay that way for long. It being inevitable that we would attack in the morning, tired hungry and bloody wounded men endeavoured to strengthen their fortifications by night. Excepting that is all those who had hope of shelter and succour in Spain. The remaining Spaniards duly deserted.

Seeing the hopelessness of defending the camp Hasdrubal and Mago attempted to slip away whilst it was still dark. Next morning our cavalry caught them first and the slaughter began again, by the time the remnant made high ground they were down to just six thousand survivors. Even these had been used as a decoy, whilst we followed them Hasdrubal and Mago slipped away, with the merest handful of adherents.

On their defensible but waterless, foodless hilltop the last few thousand men, after a couple of days, submitted to capture. We had blocked the overland route to Gades but by some circular route, or more likely sailing from some other place Hasdrubal and Mago managed to make it to the sea and to take ship, thence to return to Gades before we eventually took that final vestige of Carthage in Spain.

From Gades Mago ultimately sailed for the traditional Carthaginian recruiting grounds of the Balearics, more of that later, whilst Hasdrubal fairly promptly sailed for North Africa although I outdistanced him.

Immediately after Ilipa I had been sent to endeavour to make a formal treaty with King Syphax, who recently and not so long ago, had been warring with Carthage. Now however he was being wooed by Carthage and menacing the neighbouring kingdom of Eastern Numidia.

The kingdom of the Massaesylians ruled over by King Syphax roughly equates to modern Algeria, they were, if you like, the western Numidians, the kingdom of Eastern Numidia that is the kingdom of King Gala, the father of Massinissa lay immediately to the east. Syphax was a bit of an unknown at this point but he was tending now to favour Carthage, largely on account of Sapanbaal who you'll meet shortly, although not so long ago he'd pledged loyalty to us. The perfidy of kings.

Carthage had made much use of Eastern Numidian cavalry, led by Massinissa, as you already know, at the behest of his father, Carthage's near neighbour, King Gala of Eastern Numidia. However, when King Gala died Syphax had seen the opportunity to invade and expand his own realm. Rather than fight the advancing Syphax as well as Rome, Carthage had chosen diplomacy.

Hasdrubal son of Gisgo had a young, beautiful, educated and charming daughter by the name of Sapanbaal, known in modern times as Sophonisba. Hasdrubal had promised her hand to Massinissa, whilst he needed Massinissa's loyalty and cavalry in Spain and I suspect he had also promised her to Syphax, although that decision may well have been made by the government in Carthage without the knowledge of Hasdrubal.

When Syphax started expanding his kingdom in Africa he was probably seen as more useful than Massinissa. The perfidy of governments.

Events moved quickly. I as a strange, un-Roman Roman tried and failed to persuade Syphax that he was better off allied to a victorious Scipio and Rome than a failing and doomed Carthage. Syphax volunteered to treat with Scipio and discuss a treaty, but only in person.

I had no choice but to send despatches to this effect by fast trireme to my friend, together with a warning that I suspected treachery and capture should he choose to come. To capture Scipio would be quite a coup for a king tending towards alliance with Carthage and hoping to marry a Carthaginian princess, or at least noblewoman. Especially after all the successes my friend had achieved.

Of course Publius came, however, scant hours before his arrival Hasdrubal, en route to Carthage from Gades, with seven triremes anchored in the supposedly neutral harbour! Fortunately an onshore wind allowed Scipio to rapidly sail in, before the Carthaginians could row out with their seven more manoeuvrable triremes and try to sink Scipio's two quinqueremes at sea. Once in the harbour belonging to Syphax there would be no fighting.

Syphax, puffed up with his own importance invited both contingents to dine with him that evening. What a performance!

I took a back seat as both Scipio and Hasdrubal made their respective cases to Syphax. Publicly at least Syphax chose to make an alliance with Scipio, however there was still the Sapanbaal effect in the background and we left to return to Spain with the bones of an agreement hardly worth the paper it was written on before Hasdrubal left on his journey to Carthage, with what promises we knew not.

Shortly thereafter Sapanbaal married Syphax, making our expedition a largely wasted effort. Not to mention a risky one.

The Carthaginians still had some semblance of a garrison left in Gades at this time. However other matters needed to be resolved first. It was at this juncture that Massinissa, remember him? Having sailed to Numidia after Ilipa and finding both his father's brother Oezalces and King Syphax had designs on his newly inherited kingdom, and that the latter also had designs, now realised, on his betrothed decided it might be better for him to be allied to Rome and Scipio after all!

His arrival on our side of the straits was a surprise to all but myself and Scipio. He returned to Africa as our man in waiting. The hell with Syphax.

My friend's priority at this time was to secure all of Spain, as far as that was possible, as a Roman province and to punish those Spanish tribes and chieftains who had assisted Carthage in the destruction of his father, his uncle and their Roman armies. Prime amongst them were the cities of Castulo and Iliturgis.

Africa may be key to all, but our recent diplomatic expedition there, which had greater success on paper than in reality shall we say, had given these two cities, now expecting retribution, time to prepare their defences. Both cities were in the general region of Baecula and not far from what we today know as the Guadilquivir River.

Marcius was sent with the smaller force to deal with Castulo, my friend and I together moved with a larger force, comprising around half of our still fit men against the Iliturgi. This was a major offensive commitment again when you consider that we had to keep various garrisons in different locations and had yet to rid Gades of its Carthaginian survivors.

Our men, jubilant after Ilipa, yet tired and depleted were less than enthusiastic to be campaigning again. Publius made a speech which was to his normal high rhetorical standard, largely about the men we had lost before and the perfidy of Spaniards, but I think the promise of discharge and land possibly held more appeal, although in my experience most retired soldiers make poor farmers!

Whilst our men had, had enough, the defenders knew full well they were fighting for their very lives and fought with that exact desperation, repulsing our attacks. Our own forces had been divided in two. I was given the responsibility of trying to breach, or mount the walls in one place whilst Scipio attempted another.

This divided the defenders, but it was not yet enough for success. Finally Scipio decided it was necessary to lead by example and at considerable personal risk approached the walls himself and made to scale one of the ladders.

Knowing he meant to do this and the timing of it I pressed the attack hard in a new area of the wall to distract the defenders as much as possible just ahead of time. Our men fighting with Scipio, not wishing to lose a leader who had never personally lost a battle went to it properly this time.

The walls were seized and even the citadel itself was taken. I knew what would happen next but chose not to witness it in so far as that was possible. Of course it was not entirely possible. Scipio, in my opinion and perhaps I'm giving too much credit here, or making excuses, did not so much seek vengeance as to make an example of the town. It was a massacre, no other way to put it and the city was razed to the ground. Barbarity and waste, but it was hard to be a pacifist in war in antiquity.

Unbeknownst to us Castulo had received some Carthaginian survivors which bolstered the Spanish defence there, however on hearing of the fate of the Iligurti the Spanish treated with Marcius behind the backs of the Carthaginians.

Marcius duly took the city with far fewer casualties than might have been the case and likewise set an example. This time the example was play fair with us and we'll play fair with you. Castulo and its Spanish inhabitants were treated more kindly and the town itself remained standing. The Carthaginians were mostly taken prisoner to be sold into slavery. A few preferred death.

To all intents and purposes that just left Gades. We returned to Cartagena, where as luck would have it deserters from Gades awaited us with promises of assistance. Gades still held some Carthaginian ships, some Carthaginian soldiers who had made their way there from other garrisons no longer worth trying to defend and some auxiliaries and mercenaries as well as Hannibal's remaining brother, Mago.

Publius wanted to take advantage and quickly, which precluded the usual slow march of the legions, the distance being just shy of four hundred Roman miles. I was despatched with seven triremes and one quinquereme as my flagship to attack from the sea. Lucius Marcius Septimus was sent with a fast moving body of velites to attack from the land.

Had the deserters been more effective we may have succeeded, however the plot had been discovered and the plotters sent as prisoners to Carthage already, this meant it was full on siege warfare now, or nothing, and we weren't equipped for a siege so we returned the way we'd come.

I did surprise and partially destroy a small Carthaginian fleet of eight triremes off Carteia commanded by one Adherbal who escaped with just half his squadron. My own ship sunk two of the enemy and destroyed the oars on one side of a third. Meanwhile, on land, Marcius defeated a Carthaginian recruiting party commanded by another Hanno that he unexpectedly came upon.

The Roman velites killed at least half of the Spaniards recruited by this Hanno, so the expedition wasn't a complete waste. These large skirmishes really have both come to be known as the battle of Carteia. However, it was fortunate in a way that we did return to Publius in Carthago Nova as soon as we did.

After we'd left Publius had fallen ill. I'm no doctor so I cannot say if it was food poisoning, a virus, a bacteria or something more sinister but he nearly died. I may have had antibiotics on my boat, but that had been donkeys years ago now. I knew enough to make sure that he was properly hydrated, that water was boiled, that sanitary conditions were maintained and I controlled what he ate.

In truth his own determination saved him, but the rumour that he had died did us great harm. The Carthaginians had long had a love, hate relationship with the Spanish who were in no way sorry to see the back of them despite they had fought against them, then with them, rinse and repeat many times.

Now we were regarded as the new thorn in the Spanish side and with Scipio believed dead the revolts started immediately and even, something I had not dreamed of, a mutiny in our own ranks!

Mandonius and Andobales, recently come into alliance with us after we returned their daughters to them, were more allies in theory than practice. They were first to take advantage, not by attacking us, but by attacking their neighbours who were more faithful in their alliance to us. Opportunistic land and property grab really, tribe on tribe.

More serious was what happened in the town of Sucro. We had used this town as a staging post for communications, it being roughly half way between our initial base at Taracco and the captured Carthago Nova. The garrison there had not seen much fighting, lucky them, nor had they seen much plunder either, too bad.

With Scipio apparently dead, some bright spark started to convince his friends that they could take plunder or tribute from the Spanish roundabout to make up for the pecuniary losses inflicted on them by their general, now, thanks to Fortuna, deceased. It might be admitted that with so much going on, Ilipa, expeditions to Africa and Gades that pay had fallen behind, however these guys had had a comfortable time and the pay would have been made up. Treason was not called for.

Nonetheless the tribunes had been ejected and the common soldiers who had fomented the mutiny took command, if that's the word for it. On hearing of Scipio's miraculous recovery, Mandonius and Andobales, I often wonder if those two had a hand in poisoning him, swiftly withdrew back within their own borders and sat tight.

We made it known that we were preparing an attack on the two trouble makers and messaged Sucro to advise the garrison that they should remove themselves to Carthago Nova to receive their pay and to garrison this richer, more attractive city since we were marching out.

Of course it was a ploy, we marched straight back in as soon as the mutineers arrived. Scipio made another stirring speech, one that might have turned the heads of educated senators in Rome but which probably made little effect on the mutineers. Livy has added to it to his book for posterity, although largely invented! However the mutineers were affected when the sorry looking ringleaders were paraded before them naked, to be scourged and then beheaded.

Anyone seen to so much as murmur disapproval amongst the mutineers was likewise despatched. The troops who fought at Baecula and Ilipa and elsewhere had no truck with those who'd had it easy in the garrison at Sucro and they showed it by pressing around them swords drawn and beating their shields. After the executions, the rest were readmitted as Roman soldiers, more than happened to our gallant survivors after Cannae I might add and were paid up in full.

Andobales and Mandonius still had to be dealt with. They were in fact brothers and if they couldn't be relied on by us, they could be relied upon to help one another. Our victory at Ilipa was far from being a pyrrhic victory, but we had lost men and our remaining men, excepting those at Sucro had worked hard, marched hard and fought hard all year, including dealing with two troublesome Spanish cities already.

It must have seemed to many, myself included, that 549 and the fighting would never end. The Spanish rebels were close to the river Ebro, remember the Ebro, the one time border, supposedly, between the Roman and the Carthaginian sphere. Another three hundred plus Roman miles to march, or in my case ride and in under two weeks we were encamped facing yet another enemy. Albeit the last for this momentous year.

My friend undoubtedly had more faith in me than I had in myself. I had been admiral of a small fleet, commander of infantry and cavalry too, to a lesser extent in previous engagements and this time I was to command our cavalry with not one, but two important tasks to accomplish. Me, who had yet to kill a man in combat and had no wish so to do. Not something I spoke about.

We faced the Spanish across a valley, a bit like we'd faced the Carthaginians across a valley however this valley had the spur of a hill jutting out into it which made an ideal hiding place. It was also steeper sided and more restrictive that the site at Ilipa.

On the first day I was to hide my cavalry behind the spur. Scipio would then pasture our cattle in the valley under guard of a small force of light armed velites; how a Roman army fed itself is another topic but food that walks by itself can be useful, in this case for more than just food! By the way, remember Hannibal using oxen with torches on their horns to mislead the Romans at night. Innovation and cunning belonged to us this time.

Scipio anticipated that the Spanish would try to steal our cattle and that to do so would deploy a force greater than the one guarding them, in which they duly obliged. As soon as our outnumbered velites were engaged I swept down on them with the cavalry. The charge was admittedly exhilarating, however I again kept my sword clean and my shield undented, but my men inflicted substantial casualties on those Spaniards who had come down into the valley to drive away our herd.

The Spanish were sufficiently enraged that the following day they formed up in the valley and offered battle. The steep sided valley protected both sides from a flank attack. Indeed the front, if you like to call it that, was, from our perspective, just four cohorts wide. Given our expertise at close quarters infantry fighting face on in a pitched battle this suited us just fine.

In addition we were adept at swapping ranks in mid battle to give the men at the front a break. The Spanish were not used to this method of fighting, many of their men would be unused at all until their comrades immediately in front of them had been slain. Not as encouraging as swapping places! Meanwhile the Spanish cavalry were left redundant behind their foot soldiers. We had another idea entirely.

One thing cavalry can do is to cover distance. Thank goodness I learned to ride on Chingford Plains in my last year at school. My force took a long and circuitous route, but one which would allow us to attack the enemy, somewhat unexpectedly from their point of view, from the rear. It wasn't even genius, it just required a little forethought and planning.

By the time I was able to attack the Spaniards from behind our legions had largely cut the enemy foot to pieces in the usual way, shove with that enormous shield, stab, step and shove again, stab, step and shove until it's time to swap with the rank behind and take a rest. When I surprised the Spanish horse their own tattered remnants of foot were trying to retreat into them. In the chaos some dismounted, others wheeled and tried to charge us, but we had all the momentum required to sweep the enemy from the field.

For me there was no joy in victory. One cannot lead from the back and I was in the thick of it. A Spaniard who rode at me was despatched within what seemed inches of my face by one of my assigned shield men. As he turned to ensure the job was finished another Spaniard was upon me, the blow to my shield felt like it ought to have broken my arm, somehow it did not.

In delivering that blow the Spaniard lost his balance for a moment, or maybe his horse stumbled. My own horse turned away just enough that I had a clear moment to strike before my assailant regained his balance, not wanting to rely on someone else, or to die of course, I swung at the man's exposed neck and his blood spurted into my face.

My shield men were back in position either side of me in what can only have been a few seconds. The battle was decided and I was bloodied. I didn't feel good about it. The horror of it wakes me at times.

Apart from some light armed Spaniards who'd been in an untenable position on the side of the valley and who as a result were forced to watch impotently the slaughter of their comrades, the Spanish foot and cavalry died almost to a man. Our own losses were not debilitating, but were more than either I or Publius were happy about, more than a thousand dead yet again and near three times that number were wounded.

In contrast to the fate of the Iligirti both Andobales and Mandonius were spared. Killing them would not make their tribes love us and someone else would simply take over. We showed them they were no longer to be feared by leaving the survivors not only in possession of their lives, but also their weapons. Promises were of course extracted.

That only left the port of Gades, supposedly impregnable, but the same had been thought of Carthago Nova and we'd taken that. I knew from my earlier expedition to Gades by sea that had Scipio followed up with the legions rather than falling ill we'd still probably have been bogged down there a while, although knowing him I expect he'd have come up with something.

Fate however overcame this remaining problem for us. Mago used his initiative whilst we were away fighting Mandonius and Andobales, and chanced an attack on Carthago Nova. He didn't really have enough men for the job, but probably thought that with the benefit of surprise he might achieve something.

Our garrison there easily disabused him of the idea and he cut his own anchors away in his haste to retreat back to Gades. The population there, seeing the way things were going refused him re entry and as mentioned earlier he finally sailed away for the Balearics. Although not before tricking senior representatives from Gades into coming out to parley with him and promptly crucifying them.

Even the trip to the Balearics did not go well for him. In Pityusa, Ibiza to you and me, there were Carthaginians to welcome him, but he received a hostile reception from the native slingers of what we call Majorca, whom he'd hoped to recruit and was forced to overwinter on what is now known as Menorca.

Despite our diplomacy and crushing victories various Spanish tribes would revolt again after Scipio and I left for Rome, but our forces left behind dealt with them easily enough. They would rebel periodically here and there, but Rome basically remained in control of Spain until virtually the end of empire.

Indeed, many fine legions were raised there in what was at that time still the future. The renegade Roman general Sertorious, who I've always admired personally from what I've read about the man, took over for a while, but basically Spain became Roman. Some Spaniards in the twenty first century even regard Sertorius as the first real king of Spain!

Our forces had been depleted at, Baecula, at Ilipa and again in the various battles with the Spanish, we had not been reinforced and although we had enough strength to hold the now pacified and Carthaginian free peninsular we had many thousands of wounded men and men coming to the end of their service and frankly worn out. So this is how victory looks I thought and again said nothing.

It was Scipio's final act in Spain to make the field hospital, established on the banks of The Guadilquivir River, the Baetis River to us at that time into a town and colony in its own right. It's not far from the city you and I know today as Seville. The hospital was established after Ilipa, but now building work started in earnest on a new town.

Those veterans who wished to settle in the fledgling colony were given land and work building a properly Roman town which would be known as Italica after its inhabitants. Shades of Alexander the Great I thought to myself, but Scipio by contrast did not name the town he founded after himself.

I told my friend that the town he established there would one day be crucially important, but I could not, or chose not to tell him the details. Although both he and his brother Lucius would fall foul of Roman republican politics and jealousies, Publius was a republican to the core and kingship was anathema to him.

I could not tell him that one day the empire he would effectively found, when he finally destroyed Carthaginian power, even in Africa, so that Rome should inherit the entire Mediterranean world, would one day be ruled over by only one man. He had no need to know that two of Rome's greatest rulers maybe three in total of the 'Emperors' would be born in Italica, possibly even descendants of his own men. These being Trajan, Hadrian and later Theodosius.

Having made all necessary arrangements for security, for our men and for the future, it was time for us to turn our attention once more to Italy. Before the weather turned we sailed for home, Saturnalia and all that.

Lucius Cornelius Lentulus and Lucius Manlius Acidius we left in command of the new province. We sailed in a fleet of ten ships, bringing with us fourteen thousand, three hundred and forty two pounds of Spanish silver for the Roman treasury.

If anyone ever deserved a Roman triumph it should have been Publius Cornelius Scipio on his return from Spain. A triumph had never been awarded to a man who had not held a major magistracy with imperium. This could have been worked around. Rome did work around its own rules when it wanted to, but egos in the senate did not want Scipio acknowledged in that way. He'd taken on an impossible task no one else wanted and come out on top.

Scipio requested a meeting of the senate in the temple of Bellona, she being the goddess of war, but more importantly the temple was outside the sacred boundary of the pomerium. Having crossed said boundary a triumphal entry was no longer an option. It was here that Scipio made his report of the war in Spain. I'd warned him that a triumph would not happen for the above mentioned reason, or excuse in my view.

For Cato and others it was all too much, young upstart, but the people, yes the people understood.

CHAPTER 22 MY FRIEND THE CONSUL 205BC

Before the Roman Republic made way once more for rule by one man, after some five hundred years as a republic, the ultimate goal for any noble Roman be he patrician or plebeian was to be consul. Two consuls were elected every year and in normal circumstances ruled on alternate months although it was largely meant to be first amongst equals. Effectively the senate controlled foreign policy and the assembly of the plebs proposed the laws at home.

Having been consul a man was forever after known as a consular and many would ultimately become censor and in charge of the citizen rolls. However, consul was what a Roman nobleman aspired to. In those five hundred years one family spawned more consuls than any other, that was the family of my dear friend Publius Cornelius Scipio and this would be his year, albeit he was still younger than was normal for the position, his co consul too technically.

Most former consuls also went on to be pro consular provincial governors, although provinces could be and were allotted to consuls in office. Some abused their position as governor of a province for self enrichment at the expense of the people in said province, others did a good job. Being consul brought many advantages and opportunities. It was originally intended that a man be consul just once but several gained the distinction more than once and a rare few multiple times.

Scipio and I knew that the war must be transferred to Africa. Many in the senate would oppose that as they had opposed any mention of a triumph.

Before slipping through time I'd formed the opinion that Hannibal, operating far from home and far from resupply had run rings around the Romans for nigh on seventeen years, but, being there I'd modified that opinion somewhat.

After Cannae Hannibal had failed to capitalise, he'd failed to establish a sea port and had failed to make Capua the capital of Italy. He'd failed to break most of our alliances and for our part we overcame incredible shortages of man power and more besides. We simply refused to lie down.

In recent years Hannibal had been bottled up in Bruttium, his strength withering. It was strange that Rome had happily despatched my friend's father and uncle to fight Hannibal far from Italy and had been dismayed to say the least when Hannibal sped past us and brought the war to our homeland.

Now the senate would prove reluctant to move the war to the homeland of the enemy. In view of Hannibal's position here in Italy, the destruction of his base in Spain and his brother Hasdrubal Barca's failure to reinforce him I could understand the senate's reluctance, they were wrong, but I could understand it.

I knew, although they did not, that a threat would also soon emerge in the north of Italy. From my point of view all the more reason to move the war to Africa, but the woolly old senate might have seen things differently. Scipio agreed with me, but then he would.

I knew we were in for a year of politics and preparations, and for me a preliminary trip to North Africa too, but I was so happy we'd returned to Italy before the end of last year. I found genuine solace and love, after that oh so hard year, in the arms of Valeria.

Not only that but Valeria and I conceived our first child in that moment. Seventeen when I married her my twenty six year old wife was beside herself with joy.

Had a Roman general on campaign satisfied his lusts with a slave or a prisoner no one would have turned a hair. A Roman wife would not dream of asking what her husband had got up to whilst he was away; an affair with another noblewoman, that would be a betrayal, satisfying one's desires on a slave a mere bodily function! That may have been the accepted position, but I'd been faithful to Valeria and every moment together was precious to me, in bed and out of it.

I'd warned Publius not to expect a triumph for Spain and he, as I've said, wisely did not push for one. What he did do was announce his candidacy for the consulship. Veturius Philo one of the outgoing consuls had returned from Bruttium to organise and oversee the elections and Scipio was voted in first by every century. The people expressed their love rather more than the senate, by making Publius the senior consul by a country mile.

The day of this election was very different from the day when Publius had sought the command in Spain. Joy this time, not fear after the loss of the elder Scipio brothers and their armies. Aside from what I already knew, everyone else also knew the result was a foregone conclusion this time around.

My beautiful, pregnant and blooming wife Valeria and I went early to the house of Publius and Aemilia, Pomponia was there too. Valeria, Pomponia and Aemilia would wait together for our return, the two younger Roman matrons bubbling over with excitement and supervising the servants in preparation of a celebratory party. I would accompany Publius to the Campus Martius, the space there would be needed, more people turned out for this election than any other throughout the entire war.

Even though we left early a huge crowd of well wishers followed us cheerfully shouting encouragement, without ever becoming rowdy, this was to be a most happy day where the people expressed their love and appreciation for my best friend Scipio.

The crowd which followed us home after the election was even larger. Somewhat disconcertingly from my point of view I seemed to be a war hero too. I was recognised as a man Scipio had trusted to bring despatches to the senate. Furthermore, everyone was hungry for every detail about the war and Scipio's reports had been fully complimentary about the part played by his brother and all his officers. He was never one to hog the glory.

The well informed crowd was aware that I had led infantry, that I'd been involved in siege warfare, that I had led more than one cavalry charge and been in the thick of the fighting, possibly as a result they even interpreted my very minor naval engagement as a major victory. Instead of being seen as a Jack of all trades, or a man who could follow orders and little more, which is how I saw myself, in twenty first century parlance I was viewed by them as a consummate all rounder!

The crowd was not aware that I'd only ever killed one opponent and reluctantly at that, and in self defence too, not valiantly attacking and cutting down the enemy on my gallant charger, as they imagined me. Nonetheless Valeria was bursting with pride and I could not take that away from her. In addition to her pride, it justified her decision to wed the strange un-Roman Roman.

Most Roman women have little or no say in who they marry, but Valeria assuredly had. Not only that but she had convinced herself that I was her destiny. She wanted to count and for that her husband had to count and here he was, war hero, general and admiral close friend and confidant of the new consul.

Anyhow, the more I tried to down play my role, the more my supposed modesty caused my standing to go up. Even Pomponia believed fully in me now that I'd fought shoulder to shoulder, as she saw it, alongside her beloved first born son and shared his perils!

So eventually I just said as little as possible and graciously accepted the congratulations that came my way. I just wanted to hug Valeria but public displays like that did not happen in our circle at gatherings like this. How different a twentieth or twenty first century celebratory party would have been.

I loved Valeria so much, but I felt it most deeply and passionately in that moment and at other times like this one when every other emotion was also at fever pitch. I cannot adequately describe the way I felt or the physical sensation it gave me, it made me shiver inside is the only way I can describe it. I think Valeria understood and I believe that the lady, now ecstatically expectant, felt the same, which was far more than I deserved.

Those Jupiters who were present in Rome at that time and other special friends were admitted to the house, the good natured crowd did not try to barge in, respect was present in addition to love. The party went on very late.

It was a party befitting a consul too, designed to impress Scipio's guests as much as feed them! Personally there was much for me to miss, bourbon and rum for example, but also butter, chocolate and coffee. I did not eat snails, mice or whole songbirds personally either.

However, oysters, lobster and wild boar I adore, venison and peacock not bad either. The wine and olive oil were of course superlative, not to mention simpler fare such as the breads, sausages and olives. There was not so much by way of healthy vegetables, but I am partial to asparagus which we did have and a multitude of fruits and nuts, there was even a kind of iced cream.

Much has been written about Roman banquets, mostly probably to titillate the reader, dancing girls, prostitutes, acrobats, the descent into orgy. That was not the case in the period or society I was in. We did have some musicians playing quietly in the background and the tableware, the gold and silver, the way the food was displayed was certainly designed to impress, but it was tasteful let's say.

After campaign food, often stale bread, lentils, salted or smoked meats preserved for travelling, that kind of thing the food in Rome was a joy, one diet fed the body, the other the soul. Of course we did do some cooking on campaign, mostly when in camp for more than just one night, however only when there was time to do so.

Publius's colleague in the consulship I've mentioned before, one Publius Licinius Crassus, the man who had been elected as pontifex maximus, Rome's most senior priest some years before. At that time he'd really been seen as too young for that role as well and then, as now, had possibly been up against more suitable candidates, yet he won then and he won now. Bribes, no doubt of it, the perfidy of voters. Still, he did come second to Publius, so achievements still counted for more than mere money where the voters were concerned it seemed.

Publius Licinius Crassus would later be known as dives, which doesn't mean divine or anything like that, for all he was the Roman equivalent of the pope, it means rich and his family would stay that way.

In modern parlance you'd call him a wide boy. I couldn't help liking him though, amiable sort of plebeian villain! I had more time for him than I have for the leaders of organised religion in what one might call my own time.

As Rome's most senior priest he was not allowed to leave Italy. A handy thing if you don't wish to risk your person in foreign wars. Scipio was under no such restriction or reluctance and was itching to take an army into Africa.

Scipio made his feelings known about invading Africa and was swiftly opposed, primarily by Quintus Fabius Maximus Verrucosus Cunctator he of fabian tactics fame. That there was jealousy regarding my friend's successes in Spain I have no doubt. The gods forbid he should have yet more success.

They also seemed to have handily forgotten that at the beginning of the war the senate had wanted the consul Tiberius Sempronius Longus, the loser of the battle of the Trebia to invade Africa.

To his great discredit Quintus Fabius even brought up the subject of the Sucro mutiny in the senate to try and belittle Publius. He further tried to deny jealousy by implying that Scipio's achievements compared modestly to his own and remarking that Scipio was younger than his own son.

By denying jealousy without it ever having been alleged the Cunctator demonstrated that very thing to anyone with eyes to see, ears to hear and a modicum of intelligence. Something Scipio alluded to in his retort, however he endeavoured to be a little diplomatic knowing the elder senators were with Fabius and the man was revered.

Unfortunately though my friend nearly lost his temper and there was the suggestion made that if the senate did not approve his taking an army to Africa that he might seek a law in the people's assembly, that is to say the plebs. Not a wise move given the ever present rivalry betwixt patricians and plebeians.

Throughout the Republican period there was a power war between the patrician senate and the plebeian assembly with tribunes of the plebs ultimately obtaining the power of veto over senatorial decrees. Senators were often more concerned to protect the political power of their own assembly than to protect their nation!

A bit like Brexit really.

The senate, rather than debate the issue demanded that Scipio state unequivocally that he would abide by the conscript fathers' decision, before they would vote on what he was allowed to do! Oh, the freedom we'd enjoyed in Spain, to act in the best interests of the nation! The perfidy of senators!

Publius returned to diplomacy and agreed that he would accept the decision of the senate after a quick tete a tete with his amiable colleague who did not want to go and fight. He once more held himself in check with commendable self control. In the end the senate decided on one of its crazy compromises, but we took what we could get. The consul who was assigned Sicily would be given leave to cross into Africa should he deem it in the best interests of the Roman state.

Provinces were assigned by lot, however, with the covert assistance of the ever flexible Crassus, Scipio was assigned Sicily as his province, thus he was given leave to cross over to Africa, but no army was to be provided for him to take with him!

Before we left for Sicily I would have a little more time with my wife as Scipio was allowed to organise and hold games to honour his father and uncle which he paid for from his own share of the spoils brought back to Rome from Spain. In addition he made sacrifice of one hundred oxen to the god forever associated with him – Jupiter. The next thing to do, before leaving was to start raising some sort of force. We could not officially levy troops for the state, but volunteers were another matter and Rome loved Scipio!

Seven thousand men volunteered to come with us and we built thirty new ships, again Publius used his own money. They were built quickly from green unseasoned timber unfortunately, but we did what we could, building twenty quinqeremes and ten quadriremes.

The quadriremes had just two levels of rowers, two men to each oar. They had less freeboard, which basically means the hull wasn't as high as a ship with three decks of oars. As a result they are less affected by crosswinds. They also have a lower draft than a quinquereme and most triremes, that's the depth under the water, so they can operate in shallower water, they're fast and manoeuvrable, although a quinquereme in particular carries a greater punch when it comes to ramming.

They were still sixty ton ships and could comfortably carry more than seventy marines and a cargo. Horses for courses as they say and all navies in my own time have different types of craft for different purposes.

Not long after we sailed for Sicily and perhaps unexpectedly, although of course Scipio and I knew it would happen but didn't want to be distracted from our own designs, Mago Barca attacked northern Italy by sea from Menorca. He arrived with thirty quinqueremes and fifteen thousand men.

One cannot fault his commitment he succeeded in taking Genoa in the early summer and not long after he took Savona, assisted by a Ligurian tribe, the Ingauni. By which time Publius and I were recruiting still more volunteers, including men still trying to re-establish their good names, that is survivors from Cannae no less, in Sicily.

So, we had permission to act, but no functioning army as yet, although a small one was taking shape. Meanwhile in Africa Massinissa, without our help, was making no inroads in winning back his kingdom, he would need us and we him, we just weren't ready yet.

One nice little anecdote that I have from this time however is this. From our initial seven thousand volunteers Publius selected three hundred who he considered the cream of the crop, they were taken aside and unlike the rest, perplexingly for them, were not provided with arms.

Next he instructed the Sicilian nobility to demonstrate their loyalty by providing three hundred equites, knights or cavalrymen if you prefer from amongst their own youth for the prosecution of the war on African soil. These reluctantly arrived into our camp. Publius noted their reluctance to cross into Africa and told them that no harm would be done to them if they openly admitted their feelings. An unwilling horse and all that.

One youth took Publius at his word and was told he need not go to Africa, but that he should leave his horse, it's trappings and his arms behind for one who was braver than he. Livy suggests he also had to take his replacement home and train him, but this is a nonsense. You can't train an infantry force if they're strung out across three hundred different homesteads.

Anyhow, an avalanche followed as the noble Sicilian youngsters, rich enough and propertied enough that they didn't want to take risks with their persons, barring only a handful keen for adventure, handed over their horses and arms and walked away returning to their relieved parents. Thus were our three hundred volunteers made knights, armed and formed into the nucleus of our new cavalry. Livy says the youngsters left to a man, but a few sought adventure and glory. Likes a good story does Livy.

Our Roman forces in the north failed, if indeed they really tried to push Mago back into the sea and were content to bottle him up in the region so he, like his other brother before him would fail to reinforce Hannibal. From our point of view, that is to say Publius and myself, it made an attack on Carthage even more urgent. Were Carthage under serious threat it would certainly recall its two best generals and their armies, both Hannibal and Mago would have to quit Italy.

The situation in northern Italy was indeed serious. Mago sent twenty of his ships back to Carthage, whether to protect the African coast from us, or whether to return with even more soldiers I cannot say with certainty, but I strongly suspect the latter.

However, even without reinforcements from home, which he did ultimately receive, to the tune of seven thousand, a certain symmetry there with our seven thousand volunteers, Gauls were flocking to his standards and his army was growing to the point where a breakout was distinctly possible. The perfidy of Gauls.

The senate wasn't asleep at least. Marcus Livius was ordered to march his slave volunteers, the army we'd raised some years before in dire straits but now a seasoned fighting force, from Etruria to Ariminum. Marcus Valerius Laevinus also marched two regular Roman legions to Ariminum. These combined forces would succeed in preventing a breakout and the linking up of the two Carthaginian armies now on Italian soil, but it wasn't a comfortable position, yet again.

Here in Sicily, some nine hundred Roman miles from the troubles in the north Scipio was alive to every eventuality. We had brought grain with us, but he secured more from the Sicilian and Sardinian farmers against future need. He had old ships repaired and the new ones, made of unseasoned timber drawn up on the land to dry out.

Then, with me being not much of an asset at training warriors, I was despatched to Africa to establish the lie of the land and what was happening there and maybe stir things up a bit with a raid or two. Admiral, general, cavalryman, spy. Oh well, in for a penny and I'd read that I'd live which was something good at least!

Whilst I was away Scipio would test and blood his small army. Those who'd fought at Cannae were of course blooded already, several times over. Most of the seven thousand volunteers from Rome were not. The town of Locri, on the eastern side of the toe of Italy had long been a base of operations for Hannibal and the general populace had had a bellyful of their Carthaginian masters.

Although the consular army opposing Hannibal was not really taking the fight to him, it had captured a handful of citizens from Locri who had ventured forth beyond the walls and these had been taken as prisoners to Rhegium, that is modern Reggio Calabria a little south of the narrowest part of the straits of Messina on the Italian side.

This was also the place that Locrian noblemen loyal to Rome had escaped to when Hannibal first moved into their town. Recognising the prisoners, mostly artisans, some of whom had done work for the nobles now at Rhegium, they conferred with them and having confirmed that they would be prepared to open the gates if ransomed home the Locrians made the beginnings of a plan.

The plan was duly relayed to Scipio; a man more likely to take action than the Roman legions in Bruttium who were essentially sticking to fabian tactics like those in the north. In reality it was only Scipio who advanced the Roman cause now.

Scipio received these men from Locri, anxious that the town return to the Roman fold and prepared to throw open the gates at an appropriate time and agreed to take the requisite action. The Carthaginian garrison at Locri was in any case quite small when Hannibal himself was not there in person with the larger part of his remaining army.

Scipio made his plans and despatched a force adequate to the job whilst many others in the volunteer army, not yet seen as ready, remained in training. He could really only spare three thousand men under the command of two tribunes, but judged it adequate, they being either fully trained or in fact veterans.

The plan largely worked, however enough Carthaginians made it to the citadel, in fact, unusually the town more or less had two defensible citadels, in any event, in a nutshell we found ourselves with partial rather than complete control. Both commanders having received reports Hannibal marched to rescue his possession and Scipio sailed with more men in the new ships to finish the job and secure the safety of the valuable men who had gone ahead.

All our men were precious, but especially the more experienced ones, we were creating an army from out of thin air with Scipio's fame, rhetoric and frankly, his money! I had taken the older, repaired vessels to Africa at this time so I'd further reduced the size of the fledgling army in Sicily as well, albeit temporarily.

Hannibal arrived marginally ahead of Scipio, but with the townspeople firmly on our side and lending aid to our expeditionary force it was able to hang on. Scipio's appearance when it came, shortly after, combined with the assistance of the population gained him both entry and the subsequent opportunity to then sally forth, in command, in person and defeat the Carthaginians there present. This led Hannibal to swiftly abandon the place, sending word to the Carthaginians in the citadel to escape if they could. Most could not.

Many of Scipio's men, saw action for the first time in this engagement and gaining a victory, even a small one, over the old Carthaginian with the cunning of a fox, the bogey man and lion of Carthage was hugely good for morale and future confidence.

Unfortunately Scipio trusted one Quintus Pleminius to govern the place when he left. Despite appearances to the contrary he was one of the most rapacious crooked Romans you could ever hope to meet. The poor citizens at Locri must have wondered whether they'd chosen the right side after all and why they'd bothered.

I might have warned Scipio before I left, but, for one thing I had vowed not to try and change history and for another Scipio was now very much his own man. I was supposed only to say something in the event that he deviated greatly from what was written and this episode was written about.

On my return I did warn Scipio to be prepared to face charges from his enemies in Rome, claiming that he was in league with Pleminius for personal profit and in that regard at least forewarned was forearmed. I felt it to be very important that Scipio not be distracted by politics at this vital moment in our preparations.

Quintus Fabius Maximus tried to have Scipio condemned in absentia, where that man found the gall is beyond me. Cato who had briefly served with us, who wasn't liked in our circles, nor in the army when he served, and who also had ideas above his station backed Fabius up. A deputation from Rome was sent to make inquiries first to Locri and then to Scipio himself in Syracuse.

The townspeople of Locri confirmed that the thefts and corruption practised by Pleminius had all occurred in Scipio's absence. Unfortunately Scipio had confirmed Pleminius in his role after our two tribunes who had been wronged and threatened with a scourging by Pleminius roused their men and took it upon themselves to mutilate the man. Wrongs on both sides and the tribunes who were basically in the right of it, excepting their methods, paid with their lives after Pleminius recovered.

Nothing about it was good, but Fabius had also charged, in the senate, on the flimsiest of reports, that Scipio was simply living a life of Greek style luxury and inaction in Syracuse rather than pursuing the war. Inconsistent with events at Locri I know, and inconsistent with Scipio raising an army on his own initiative too, but that was the nature of the old man.

Scipio had in fact exceeded his authority by acting in a place that was not within his province. Many years later Caesar would face similar criticism. However, it couldn't really be argued that a victory over Hannibal was a bad thing, when Fabius had previously demanded Scipio stay in Italy and fight Hannibal on our soil.

When the deputation to check the facts visited Syracuse and saw the preparations there, all undertaken by Scipio without permission to levy troops for the state, they returned with most favourable reports and there was no more the bitter and twisted old Quintus Fabius and his equally jealous and disgruntled ally Cato could do. The perfidy of Quintus Fabius Maximus etc etc.

In addition, whilst I was away Scipio won hearts and minds in Sicily by restoring property plundered after the siege of Syracuse to its rightful owners, something which the Roman senate had promised previously and repeatedly to do but had not delivered on.

Now, back to my story for a bit. My main aim was to link up with Massinissa, find out what was happening and reassure him that we would come to his aid as soon as we were prepared. Syphax was still taking full advantage of the situation in Africa, that is to say acting with impunity and taking all he could since Carthage had two armies and most of its available resources focussed on Italy and Numidia was divided and unprepared.

Any ideas that Syphax would support us had long since gone out of mine and Scipio's minds given he was clearly only out for himself and Sapanbaal was likely to keep him at least partially, if not wholly, on the side of Carthage. The ancient writers are a bit confusing as to what exactly happened when.

We'd not made public our distrust of Syphax in case it affected morale, but really we knew, even before he sent envoys to warn us he was now no longer neutral. He'd probably been put up to this by his bride ,or father in law, or both. The envoys were swiftly sent on their way and since their arrival had been seen, we did what you have to do in these situations, we lied and put out that we were being urged to invade. The perfidy of Scipio and myself.

I sailed with thirty quinqueremes, a few soldiers, as many as could be spared and of course my marines and sailors, around twelve thousand men in total although naturally we could not all go ashore and leave the ships unattended. I planned a raid with around five thousand men, leaving a full complement of rowers on each ship and a couple of officers in case the ships needed to be moved in a hurry.

Scouts mounted on the few horses we carried with us went out ahead immediately to search out Massinissa. It wasn't difficult, he likewise was looking for us, having loyal men at various points along the coast briefed to report the minute they saw Roman ships. Although he was hoping for a full invasion force this year, not a raiding and reconnaissance party.

Being dispossessed of so much he'd been praying to the gods, quite naturally of course, that Scipio would cross over with his army this year. He but little understood Roman politics. He'd not have believed that Scipio would have to create his own army out of thin air after his achievements in driving all Carthaginian armies out of Spain and him now being a consul. I admit Roman politics could quite often be baffling.

My men and I landed at Hippo Regius what is now Annaba in north east Algeria, about two hundred Roman miles from the city of Carthage. I've seen it suggested by some historians that we landed at Hippo Diarrhytus, modern Bizerta, which is indeed an easy place to land and far closer to Sicily. However I considered it far too close to Carthage itself for safety and subsequent events show I was right!

With Massinissa's help we raided several settlements in the area and took enough plunder to make a worthwhile contribution to Publius's depleted war chest and pay our troops. I gave some of the profits on my own initiative to Massinissa, we both needed resources badly and he'd played his part even if he was down to a mere couple of hundred horsemen at this juncture.

I didn't enjoy what really amounted to thievery inflicted on a largely civilian population, in my own time a war crime. I did instruct my men that we were looking for gold, silver and valuables to pay them and to expand the army. We did not want to further inspire hatred in the population through rape and murder since we intended to return. However, money was badly needed since we received no assistance from the treasury at Rome, itself somewhat depleted by the war also.

It wasn't strictly true about the intention to return, since our eventual return was planned to be at a spot much closer to Carthage itself, but there was some truth in it since we hoped eventually to establish Massinissa as a client king in the region. In any event there was no blood bath, my men were disciplined and followed orders.

In Carthage there had at first been great alarm the government there believing that Scipio had landed in Africa whilst their best armies were abroad in Italy and they at home were relying on, by comparison, very few possibly unreliable mercenaries. They'd even shipped the seven thousand men mentioned previously to Mago by this time, who was indeed a major and growing threat in northern Italy.

Carthage, in a panic sent a deputation with two hundred talents of silver to King Philip in Greece and urged him to attack Sicily, messages were also sent to Mago and Hannibal to urge them to take the offensive and divert attention away from Africa. Livy reports it was at this time that Carthage sent reinforcements to Mago, but in fact they had already gone. If Carthage had still had those men she'd have hung onto them for her own defence.

As soon as the Carthaginians had reports that it was just Caius Laelius, whoever he was, with a few thousand men they heaved a great sigh of relief and gleefully despatched a fleet to capture me and mine. The scouts Massinissa had strung out along the coast reported the departure of the Carthaginian fleet from the cothon, that is the inner harbour of the great harbour at Carthage, truly a wonder of the ancient world. No better protection for warships could be wished for, right up to the time of Hitler's concrete submarine pens.

Anyhow, before the Carthaginian fleet could travel the two hundred plus miles west, it not being a straight coast, we happily slipped away, taking our plunder and intelligence back to Publius in Sicily with us. Fortunate that I did not land at modern Bizerta. One to Livy this time, who got it right on this occasion.

I reported all to Scipio and the men were allowed to know at least that the renowned warrior Massinissa was urging on the invasion. In addition they were shown the plunder I had brought back from what had really been a small raid and nothing excites a Roman army more than the thought of plunder. If this could be garnered from small outlying towns two hundred miles from Carthage what could be brought back from the legendary city itself?

This was no idle speculation, Carthage had been founded around six hundred years before by Phoenicians from the city of Tyre and although Utica pre-dated Carthage she had become the world's leading city state whilst Rome was yet in her infancy. In my time, that is modern times, Carthaginian art is more or less forgotten and unknown. That's largely because Rome plundered it all, spread it around and then largely lost it having wiped out its makers.

Carthage produced fine furniture and soft furnishings even if her jewellery and ornamental pieces were not to my taste, although I did rather like their lion motifs. Like Rome, Carthage also had her own foundation myths, in Carthage's case based around queen Dido and Carthage naturally had her own gods, Baal and Tanit particularly, but Dido also came to be worshipped. A great deal, so much in fact, has been lost. Her influences were largely from the Egyptian and Canaanite civilisations although her own influence once covered almost all of North Africa, Spain, Sardinia, Corsica and the Balearic islands plus half of Sicily.

I say influence because Carthage was ever a mix between conquest and trade. I've mentioned the Carthaginian gods, but what Carthage worshipped most was money, if you're making enough money why fight? Especially when you don't fight yourself, but rely on mercenaries and they cost money. In many ways the family of Hannibal , being true warriors, were not typical. The point however is that our men could smell the plunder and this inspired them more than speeches ever could.

Greater to me than all the plunder I'd brought back and all the riches yet to come, was the news brought in a despatch from Rome that I was father to a daughter my wife had named Laelia Julia. I had to remove myself from the company and wept. I had attended the birth of Francesca, my daughter in modern times and our once close relationship had foundered. I was somehow certain it wouldn't happen that way this time but it was at one and the same time a great joy and a great sadness that I'd not been there this time. It also reminded me of my other daughter and all the pain that entailed.

This then was the position when the elections started to get close once again. Dear old Marcus Licinius Crassus reported that a pandemic had broken out and that he was too ill to supervise the elections himself and that his army should be dispersed to stop the infection spreading and wiping them out. Somewhat counters modern thinking on controlling the spread of disease but still. The senate gave him leave to do as he felt best.

Quintus Caecilius Metellus was named as dictator, basically just to arrange the elections and the Sibylline books were consulted, largely on account of the disease problem.

A prophesy was duly found, as one always was; I'm such a cynic. Anyhow, the prophesy found talked about a foreign enemy on Roman soil and that this enemy would be driven out if the goddess Cybele the Idean mother of the gods were brought from Pessinus in Asia Minor, that is Turkey to us today, to Rome. She would ever after be Magna Mater the great earth mother to Romans, a major part of our pantheon, often worshipped by the female part of Roman society.

Suddenly there was optimism that the Carthaginians would be forced to depart Italy, despite sickness in the army, a growing threat in the north and the ever present threat of Hannibal in the deep south. The power of prophesy and superstition, not perfidy this time.

It's funny the way things work because the only other person, of note anyway, who had demonstrated optimism that the war could be brought to a successful conclusion was my good friend Publius Cornelius Scipio and suddenly people wondered, even senators, if perhaps he'd been right all along.

And so 205BC 549 drew to a close, Saturnalia and all that.

CHAPTER 23 THE INVASION OF AFRICA BEGINS 204BC 550

Marcus Cornelius Cethegus who had been curule aedile in 213 alongside Publius, to whom he was obviously related and Publius Sempronius Tuditanus were elected as consuls, Tuditanus, unusually, in absentia. The latter had proven himself a hero at Cannae and would be given Bruttium as his province this year where he would inflict further damage on Hannibal without actually destroying his forces there. He had, as per convention, also been curule aedile and praetor previously.

More importantly from our perspective Scipio's command in Sicily was prorogued, that is extended in modern parlance and our preparations continued apace. With the new and the old ships we now had a fleet of forty warships, quite insufficient to transport all we needed for an invasion and so we acquired some four hundred merchant vessels as transports.

Thank the gods for the Sibylline books, for without official assistance we'd have struggled, but now that it was prophesied and people in high places had started to believe in Scipio things happened. Even though in theory you can't get much higher than consul and pro consul!

In fact Publius had been obliged to make a trip to Rome, he'd sailed out from the port of Ostia to take possession of the goddess Cybele as she sailed in. Once transferred to Publius's ship he then brought the Magna Mater to the matrons of Rome and handed her over. This bit of theatre, attended by my darling Valeria, Pomponia and of course Aemilia did no harm to Publius's standing with the people of Rome, most especially the women of Rome.

Lilybaeum was the obvious harbour to depart from in order to attack Carthage, ironically it had been founded by Carthage. It had a considerable harbour, even so, not strictly large enough for our now enormous fleet, certainly not without the risk of collisions or restricting the possibility to use oars, so some of the transports had to be loaded and then put at anchor just outside, which wasn't without it's risks, for all that I considered myself something an expert on anchoring. None of the actual warships were exposed to this particular risk.

Back in 218BC when my friend Publius and I were first meeting in Massilia, Lilybaeum had been the scene of a naval battle. Marcus Aemilius Lepidus with twenty quinqueremes had defeated a force of thirty five Carthaginian quinqueremes. That's another story, but thank the gods that we held the place.

It was spring when we set sail, not sure the date exactly with the calendar still being so haphazard, but fairly early spring. The townspeople and our forces left behind to protect Sicily all came out to see us off.

In different quarters we've been criticised for not attacking Africa soon enough and then again for attacking with too small a force. Partial I may be, but I believe we took the time we needed to create the best force we could.

With such a vast fleet to worry about I created ships lights to distinguish one another at night three lights for the flagship, commanded by Publius, and two for every other ship of war. The transports all displayed a single light at night. I should have liked to employ ships lights as used in my own time which give rather more information regarding port and starboard and direction of travel, but it was too much to try and change the way things were done to that degree. Our warships were disposed so as to protect our transports, much like a World War Two convoy, a column on each side, one column led and commanded by Publius, the other by myself.

In addition all Captains had been briefed on the audible signals I'd devised years before for use in fog, which turned out to be just as well. However, we left with fine weather and a strong, but not too strong following wind.

We also left with a strong sense of optimism too, which was fitting and how one should set out on a new venture. No one but me knew that, according to Polybius, Syphax alone would bring some sixty thousand men against us in support of Hasdrubal son of Gisgo, father in law to Syphax, who himself commanded an army of another thirty plus thousand men.

Our own forces comprised four full legions with auxiliary cavalry bringing each legion up to a little over six thousand men. In addition I still had fifteen hundred marines who'd been with me through thick and thin already and many of the sailors, that is to say rowers primarily, would be up for a fight if it came to it as well.

Anyhow, in terms of fighting men we had near twenty six thousand foot and four thousand cavalry. The fighting ships, being a mixture of quinqueremes, triremes and quadriremes, but mostly quinqueremes and quadriremes had a total of about ten thousand tough hardy rowers, but removing these from the ships to fight on land would make our precious vessels vulnerable.

The transports were a hotchpotch ranging from about sixty tons to a hundred and fifty tons each, but apart from a couple of biremes none had oars, they relied entirely upon one large square sail on the mast and one smaller example on the bowsprit.

Some seven thousand fighting men, our best, were boarded across the forty ships of war in case of a naval battle when we would aim to use the Corvus on each warship to board the enemy. The rest of the troops were distributed across the transports which also carried food, water, horses, siege equipment and spares of all sorts, weapons, shields, projectiles, armour, clothing, shoes, cooking utensils, tack for horses, nails and tools, everything the mobile Roman army might need.

As before I ensured that items were well distributed so that the loss of any one ship should not mean the loss of all of one item. Scipio and I supervised the loading and embarkation personally.

On the day of departure Publius led prayers, made a sacrifice and of course made a speech, this was history in the making.

In the first year or so of our friendship Publius, I know harboured doubts as to the veracity of my claim that he would be the man to defeat Hannibal, that he would be the greatest Roman of his generation and one, at least, of the greatest Romans of all time. It's been said before, but I make no apology for repeating it, that Scipio unlike almost any general you can think of never lost a battle.

Now that we were embarking on the final chapter of this great war, albeit that the final battle was not to be this year, or even the next my friend was entirely comfortable with the belief that this was indeed his destiny. We left in the morning, not as early as I'd have liked, but the formalities had to be observed.

By next morning we were in sight of land. It was a good omen, with by far the majority of the transports being oarless we all had to sail with our speed governed by the slowest to keep the convoy in shape, yet here we were, in sight of the promontory of Mercury. The promontory being named after the god of commerce and trickery, how fitting for Carthage!

In modern times this promontory is known as Cape Bon and of course today it's in Tunisia. We determined on a landing point to the west, but were soon engulfed in a thick fog. Being close to land this was especially hazardous regarding rocks, not to mention the risk of collisions amongst the huge fleet, as well as potential groundings and so loth as I am to anchor without adequate shelter, the soundings being adequately shallow I gave the order to all ships to anchor knowing that in nautical matters Scipio would defer to me.

Thank the gods yet again for agreed audible signals and tubas or trumpets on every vessel to ensure the message reached every captain.

It was not until the next morning that we had sufficient light and visibility to proceed, but no damage had been occasioned and the entire fleet was in good order. We were soon able to begin the long process of disembarkation on what was then known as the fair promontory and today is Cape Farina, not far from the very ancient city of Utica.

I have visited in modern times and the topography seems to have changed a little in two thousand years, however we could bring ships close to shore on both sides of the promontory, Roman soldiers do not swim as a rule! Wading is fine. The disembarkation took all day it not being a regular port.

The transports were disembarked first, keeping the warships ready in case of any surprise naval attack from the Carthaginians. The first troops ashore began laying out and building a fortified camp on the nearest high ground, which was still on the promontory, making attack really only possible from one direction and so naturally that ditch was dug first and that rampart too was erected first, but as more and more men came ashore so the pace of the work was increased.

A Roman army on the march can throw up a defensible camp in three hours, but we wanted this to be more than just a marching camp, it was to be our security and escape in times of trouble and our first established outpost in Carthaginian territory.

By the time the last men had disembarked the camp was complete and food was being prepared. Not that all the men were disembarked, we still needed protection from the sea and so seventy or so fighting men remained on each warship as well as rowers. There was a general air of satisfaction and Publius and myself were well pleased with the work done and the safe arrival of every last man and beast, plus all our supplies.

Our first strategic objective was to take the town of Utica, more defensible than our camp, with better facilities for storage, that is to say a proper base of operations. I sailed with half our warships and all my marines to attack from the sea, three of our four legions set off to march overland preceded by almost all the cavalry, a legion was left to defend the camp and the transports from the land and a cavalry detachment was left behind in case urgent despatches or a mobile force were to be needed.

Carthage we were to learn later had been more concerned to bolster its own defences and farmers and others from outlying regions were hurrying to the relative safety of the city. They had sent out a cavalry force to reconnoitre our landing, but far too late to interfere with our disembarkation or defensive arrangements. This despite the establishment of a line of lookout towers along the coast. Slack I'd call it.

Our cavalry en route to Utica came upon theirs. There were some five hundred of them at an educated estimate, so even though we had left some cavalry behind in camp we substantially outnumbered them. Even so, that they chose to flee without so much as an arrow being fired was another good omen and good for morale.

Another good thing to happen that day was the arrival of Massinissa. With many Numidians being paid to fight for Carthage and with his kingdom largely invaded by Syphax he did not bring as many horsemen with him as we'd have liked. However the men who were with him were loyal, dedicated, experienced and warlike, not just paid mercenaries. In addition Massinissa and his men knew the country well.

Massinissa's life would make an interesting book in its own right. His fortunes waxed and waned and he remained a true warrior into his eighties when many would be happy just to live so long. His uncle Oezalces had usurped the kingdom on the death of Massinissa's father King Gala, he too was an old man who died and left the kingdom to his young son. I think Massinissa with all his experience allied to a just claim, could relatively easily have taken his kingdom back were it not for his avaricious and powerful neighbour King Syphax. In the end though, that worked to our advantage. Massinissa was firmly with us now.

Massinissa might have fairly born a grudge against Publius and myself in relation to Sapanbaal, more of that later, but he remained a loyal ally of Rome and we were pleased to receive him. His little force of near three hundred punched way above its weight in modern language, to us they were worth perhaps another thousand men.

Publius put Massinissa to good use immediately. Carthage placed four thousand Numidian mercenary cavalry under command of one Hanno. Yes I know there are a lot of Hannos and Hasdrubals in this book, they were popular Carthaginian names.

Hanno based his force at Salaeca a town about fifteen miles from our camp. It's reported that Scipio made a joke about cavalry being housed in a town in summer, probably apocryphal since it was still spring, however Livy who liked to dress things up says that Publius remarked along the lines that with leaders like that let them send more men. Perhaps he tempted the gods, because they certainly did send more men.

If he said it at all I must have been aboard ship at the time threatening Utica and I forgot to ask him about it, no one reported it to me.

Publius sent Massinissa's small force to tempt Hanno out, which it did, even so Massinissa had to dart backwards and forwards, now attacking with javelins, now retreating then threatening again before Hanno, in frustration, led all his men out.

Massinissa gradually withdrew along a line behind two adjacent hills in the region of the tower of Agathocles, built by the one time tyrant of Syracuse around a century before, whilst Scipio and the Roman cavalry were hidden in the valley between the hills.

When the time was right Scipio was able to sweep out from the valley to take Hanno's men in the flank and rear and Massinissa turned for the last time to charge them head on. Of the four thousand Numidians in service to Carthage one thousand were slain, two thousand were captured and roughly a thousand, those who fled most precipitously and were therefore the least to be feared anyway, escaped.

Massinissa himself gave chase and captured Hanno alive and was shortly after able to exchange the prisoner for his own mother who was being held by Syphax as a result of his invasion of Numidia. For the next week our forces ravaged the countryside roundabouts, taking supplies of food for our men and at the same time of course denying these resources to the enemy.

I was still at Utica as these events unfolded and having removed the threat of Hanno and taken what was of use from the surrounding area Publius now pressed the siege of Utica in person. It was a difficult nut to crack. We would have taken it in time, if only by starvation, but time was not on our side.

Syphax and Hasdrubal son of Gisgo were bearing down on us with huge numbers of men. Remembering the maulings he had received from us in Spain, Hasdrubal had waited for the security of numbers, and Syphax, encouraged by the beautiful Sapanbaal, had not disappointed.

Polybius states that Syphax arrived with fifty thousand infantry and ten thousand cavalry, whilst Hasdrubal brought thirty thousand infantry and three thousand cavalry. Now Polybius was not one to wantonly exaggerate. He got his information from Publius's son and mine. I may have exaggerated in my notes, but again, not purposefully.

It's easy to state the size of a Roman army I served with. Our enemies rarely formed up in the formations we used, although a few copied us naively thinking that was all there was to Roman success. Anyhow I always gauged the size of an enemy force by comparing it to ours and that's not completely accurate, they may be more spread out and the ranks may not be so deep. However, this was overwhelming force, no doubt of it. A pitched battle was out of the question, we needed to withdraw to a properly defensible position.

We prudently withdrew from Utica in good order, without loss and built a new fortified camp in a very defensible position on a small peninsular connected to the mainland by a narrow isthmus. This negated any enemy advantage of numbers on land since the approach was so narrow.

We also still had warships and a good few transports. Many, but far from all of the transports had been allowed to return to being normal merchant ships doing trade. Some of the warships had accompanied them, but we had the capacity for an emergency evacuation of everyone should an emergency arise and we could defend ourselves from a naval attack too. We were heavily outnumbered, but well provisioned and secure.

We also largely blocked the approach of any forces sent from Carthage to Utica. Our camp came to be called Castra Cornelia and our enemies chose to camp to the east near the Bagradas river. They also built two camps, very different from ours and somewhat dissimilar from each other. One for Syphax and his army, the other for Hasdrubal and his. However, both camps had a fatal weakness and they were too far apart. Complacent I call it.

So it was that both sides settled down for winter, for us a somewhat smaller Saturnalia than we'd have enjoyed at home, but the men enjoyed it. I missed Valeria, but held my tongue, not a thing one expresses on campaign.

CHAPTER 24 BATTLES AT UTICA AND GREAT PLAINS 203BC

At home there was still optimism. We had won some small victories and despite overwhelming numbers opposing us our losses were next to nothing. The senate decided to reinforce Sicily so that our remaining men there could join us as soon as springtime made sailing relatively safe. We received reinforcements then by sea and more grain from Sardinia and whatever supplies we needed, although we'd lost none of what we brought with us.

The news from home was that Gnaeus Servilius Caepio, aedile in 207 and praetor in 205 had been elected as senior consul. Thanks to us he'd be the last Roman consul to have to fight Hannibal in Italy, his province being Bruttium. He'd acquit himself well there, however being a man solely out for himself he would try to usurp my friend's position in North Africa after Publius and I had done most of the work there in order to take the glory for himself. The perfidy of politicians.

His colleague was Gaius Servilius Geminus, aedile 209 and praetor 206, he too had largely followed the conventional cursus honorum. He would be named dictator briefly next year, to hold the elections, when his younger brother would also be elected as junior consul. In addition in 183BC he'd go on to replace dear old Crassus as pontifex maximus a post that was held for life.

Our thoughts now turned to dealing with the overwhelming numbers ranged against us. We decided to turn their overconfidence against them and sued for a peace treaty. Our tactics were a bit on the, how shall I say this, dirty side.

We opened negotiations first with Syphax; there being some distance between his camp and that of Hasdrubal an approach was not difficult. Publius hoped that Syphax might have grown bored of Sapanbaal by now, but she wasn't the kind of bride a man soon loses interest in. Unable to separate Syphax from Carthage we listened to the counter proposal that Carthage should quit Italy and we should quit Africa.

This was not on our agenda but we kept the negotiations going. The officers sent to negotiate took their personal servants with them, or so it appeared, however, the men dressed as servants were in fact other officers and centurions. Whilst the negotiations were going on they ambled about aimless and bored ostensibly, but actually making mental notes about the layout of the camp and more besides.

Every time a conference took place different 'servants' would go and familiarise themselves first hand with the layout of the camp, the guard posts, how often the guards changed and anything they could usefully observe or find out. By observation from inside and out we learned that Hasdrubal's men had built wooden huts, Syphax's men had built their dwellings from interwoven reeds, matting and the like.

The layout was haphazard and some dwellings were even outside the not very impressive ramparts. In part because new levies arrived after the ditch and, let's call it a fence rather than a rampart had been built and Syphax and his men were too lazy to redo the thing.

Overconfidence in the extreme. After a series of conferences with Syphax, Scipio messaged that the business must be brought to a close and Hasdrubal was drawn in. An agreement was reached, but we instantly repudiated it by adding further stipulations. Publius used the excuse that although he was inclined to accept personally, his council of officers was not. We were of course being entirely disingenuous.

By rejecting the truce, at the eleventh hour as we say post World War One, Publius was able to attack without losing his honour by breaking a truce, but it was painfully close, not quite Pearl Harbour, but not our finest hour.

The fatal weakness of both camps was their flammability and the lack of space between the buildings if one can call them that. Our men were fed early and the trumpets that sounded the night watch were sounded as usual in case any enemy should hear.

The enemy camps were, as I've said about seven miles distant, they were also about one mile apart from each other. We marched out after dark, leaving very few men to guard our own camp and arrived stealthily in the vicinity of the enemy encampments around midnight.

Of course all the planning and briefing had been done previously with the intelligence gained from the false negotiations.

Everyone knew his role. I was to attack the camp of Syphax with half our legionaries and Massinissa and his men. There were a greater number of enemies here, but the camp was less well built and more poorly defended than that of Hasdrubal. Scipio would attack the more robust camp of Hasdrubal without the benefit of surprise after we had fired the camp of Syphax.

In fact Publius did have the benefit of surprise, and chaos too, something he'd hoped for but not assumed, because when the flames a mile off were seen in the night sky it was also assumed in Hasdrubal's camp to have been an accidental conflagration. As a result many men rushed out of this second camp, unarmed to go to the aid of their comrades and fight the fire. There being no way of course that our small force would attack a concentration of around eighty thousand!

In fact attack might not be a fair term for it. Although my men set fires at several places, to be certain it would take hold they were all clumped close together on the upwind side of the camp and Syphax and his men also assumed a terrible accident had occurred.

The fire spread quickly through the densely packed wooden framed reed huts. Many were asleep, some probably died in their sleep from smoke inhalation. Others may have been trampled by men or horses, others were cut down by us as they fled the intense heat, many were too badly burned to ever fight again even if they survived long afterwards.

With Massinissa on one side of the camp and myself and my infantry spread around the other we covered all the existing exits. The men who managed to get out from those exits had little chance, the flames illuminating them as if it were day so intense was the fire, some may have eluded us, but probably very few if any who fled individually in fact. Of course as the fences burned new escape routes did open up.

Shortly thereafter we saw the flames and heard the sounds of distress from Hasdrubal's camp as well. The destruction of Syphax's camp was more complete than at the camp of Hasdrubal from where we did obtain weapons, later burned as an offering to Vulcan and some plunder and some noble Carthaginian prisoners.

When men from Hasdrubal's camp had rushed out to help the army of Syphax extinguish the flames, believing us some seven miles distant, Publius and his men had cut them down and then stormed in through the now unguarded open gates and fired that camp too.

Naturally when Hasdrubal realised that both camps were ablaze he discounted any thoughts of it being an accident and thinking mainly of himself, fled with as much of an escort as he could hurriedly put together. This consisted of two thousand foot and five hundred cavalry from his initial thirty thousand foot and three thousand cavalry who found a way out as a unified force.

Hasdrubal took refuge in a nearby town, but the townspeople there did not like it nor were they willing to offer any support and so he swiftly continued to retreat to Carthage where the news would cause great alarm and fear. My ancient sources also suggest that he hurried on to Carthage to quell the fear there and stiffen the senate, in which he was successful, at least regarding the latter.

Syphax also escaped, he too managed to group a few thousand men around him, he probably kept some sort of elite bodyguard. Neither I nor Massinissa engaged him as he fled, our own men being too thinly spread out around the vast circumference of the huge camp and too few in number to take on several thousand armed men in some sort of order, at least in any one spot. Mind you the lightly constructed camp burned so quickly that anywhere on that circumference soon became a possible exit. It was as if the whole edifice were no more than kindling.

We had done enough damage for one night and sustained no losses at all. Soldiers appreciate generals who keep them alive.

This event has been called by some the battle of Utica, but it was no battle in the conventional sense, it was a horror show and a massacre. Possibly as many as fifty thousand men lost their lives from the camp of Syphax alone, at least another twenty thousand died at the camp of Hasdrubal although prisoners were captured there, including Carthaginian nobility as noted. I've talked before about Roman snobbishness regarding so called nobility. In addition we captured many horses and even a few elephants. Without skill in the use of war elephants we had no use for them. I'll leave it there.

I personally witnessed men fleeing naked from the camp of Syphax, men who'd been asleep moments before, only to be cut down by my own fully armed, fully prepared and wide awake soldiers. The ancient writers regard that as a dishonourable death, to die naked. Personally I harboured doubts about our own honour, but we could not sit idly by in the face of such odds. In the morning the smouldering remains and the stench were sickening. I hope never ever to see the like again.

Syphax and Hasdrubal made no attempt to link up, with Hasdrubal fleeing as fast as he could in the direction of Carthage, Syphax took refuge in another nearby town named Abba, no, really. I'd like to say in Abba did Syphax then surrender and set it to the tune of Waterloo, but it didn't quite happen like that. Abba was a fortified and defensible town.

Despite the dismay in Carthage from the turning of the tables and where it had been assumed that Scipio would remain bottled up on his little isthmus and that in this very spring they would launch a joint sea and land offensive to finish him off, it was nonetheless the Barcine faction led by Hasdrubal son of Gisgo that carried the day. They would carry on fighting and would not yet recall either Hannibal or Mago.

Embassies were sent from Carthage to Abba to convince Syphax not to abandon the fight and together with the pleadings of his young wife he wavered as to what to do.

In addition some four thousand Celtiberian mercenaries who had come over from Spain looking for payment and revenge to assist in the defeat of the Romans happened, handily, to arrive at this very moment, as did reinforcements from Syphax's own kingdom.

Syphax of course fell for it, and puffed himself up in front of the embassies from his wife's home town, much as he had done when entertaining Scipio and Hasdrubal, and according to reports said something along the lines of 'look I'm already raising fresh levies' when of course those men lately arrived from his own kingdom had obviously been recruited well before. He was a foolish and proud man.

Regarding the four thousand Celtiberian warriors who had made the journey to Africa, their number was exaggerated to ten thousand for propaganda value back in Carthage to help calm the people. The perfidy of propaganda.

Just thirty days later Syphax with his survivors, the Celtiberians and the new levies from his own kingdom met with Hasdrubal who had also been recruiting, and of course his few survivors. They made camp on the great plain with one united army of a little over thirty thousand.

The Celtiberians and some of the survivors from the firing of the camps were fully trained soldiers, but more than two thirds of this new army were green, untrained, unbloodied and untested recruits. Syphax seems to have thought that forming them up Roman style was going to be enough to make the difference!

Publius had initially decided not to pursue Syphax believing he would probably return to his own country and ideas about supporting Carthage would fizzle out. However after this latest development he determined that he must attack this new force immediately, before there was time to train or stiffen the new recruits.

We had at this juncture renewed our siege of Utica and Roman merchants who had been short changing our troops when buying booty from them had been sent packing by order of the commander. Not only was this better for the men in the long run, but it meant they stayed focussed on the job in hand.

In order to go after Syphax and Hasdrubal and maintain the element of surprise it was necessary to maintain the illusion that the siege of Utica was still being pressed. Of itself this was of no huge difficulty, but in case it be discovered that there were far fewer troops at Utica than previously Scipio involved himself in long discussions and briefings with the officers to be left behind to cover what should be done in any likely, or foreseeable scenario. Any kind of loss was unaffordable to us, not to mention it would raise spirits in Carthage.

Speed being of the essence we set out for the Great Plain as it was known in light marching order, having slipped away under cover of darkness less our departure be discovered. The ships menacing Utica also remained in place with adequate crews and marines for both appearances sake and for their safety.

Within five days we fortified a camp a little over three miles from the enemy camp and for the next couple of days we harassed them until on the third day they succumbed to temptation and offered battle. The four thousand Celtiberians, their best troops took their centre and the Carthaginian survivors from the burning bulked them out shall we say.

Syphax and his Numidians were positioned on their left wing, the bulk of the Carthaginians including cavalry were on their right wing. In essence the centre was quite strong, the wings almost entirely comprised of inexperienced , raw new recruits.

For our part we formed up in a pretty conventional way, legionary infantry in the centre hastati to the front, then principes and finally triarii, the conventional way of fighting for a Roman army, but it wouldn't stay that way and the tribunes and centurions had their orders and had passed the plan down to the men so that they could all work to the plan, even if their officers should fall.

We had Roman and Italian Cavalry on our right wing facing Syphax and his Numidians, Massinissa and his cavalry took our left wing facing the Carthaginians, but Massinissa's little force had grown over time as Numidians loyal to the true king had come to his standard and horses for them had been captured at the so called battle of Utica.

Given our recent successes, our men were in good spirits and were up for another victory. The enemy survivors from Utica on the other side wanted revenge but probably had less optimism. The enemy's new recruits simply did not know what was about to hit them when our cavalry crashed into both of their wings simultaneously.

With the wings of this new army in complete disarray within minutes the centre at first met our infantry in a staunch defence. The Celtiberians in particular knowing they would be most severely punished for crossing over from Spain in the event of defeat and also that they had nowhere to retreat to in this foreign land. They put up a stiff fight, but there were too few of them and once the hastati became engaged, instead of waiting their turn as was normal in a Roman battle the principies and the triarii spread outwards and ultimately surrounded the enemy centre. Hasdrubal and Syphax lost their best soldiers almost to a man.

The resistance put up by their centre lasted long enough that it allowed both Syphax and Hasdrubal each with a small body of cavalry to flee, each, once again aiming to make it to his own city, Hasrubal to Carthage and Syphax to Cirta. The last of the fighting and mopping up only really ended shortly before night fell, even so our losses were very minor. Yet again our tactics had largely kept our small force intact and safe.

At this point the story again divides. Our forces at the battle on the plain had been just over eighteen thousand men and we still had nearly eighteen thousand men. I took half the infantry together with Massinissa and his cavalry in pursuit of Syphax, but also with a view to finally confirming Massinissa in his kingdom as a client king and friend and ally of Rome for the longer term.

Publius intended to take plunder from the settlements in the region of the battle then march on and invest the city, or town really at that time, of Tunis a mere fifteen miles from Carthage and in plain sight of Carthage. I will tell his story first before returning to my own.

Scipio found the surrounding settlements disgruntled with Carthage on account of the heavy taxes they had been forced to endure, ostensibly to pay for the war with us. Carthage had huge wealth, not just from trade, but from silver mines in North Africa and until recently from silver mines in Spain too.

I doubt they needed to heavily tax the outlying towns but Carthage was ever greedy and avaricious. Scipio took plunder to reward his troops, and supplies as needed, but he did not punish the local civilian population with violence for the sake of it, or commit murder or anything of that sort.

Having secured the area and fortified a few strategic places he set out for Tunis which was a much easier place to invest than Utica. Meanwhile the Carthaginian senate had decided to send a fleet to destroy our ships at Utica. Which as you know were not without marines, but by normal standards were lightly manned.

Unbeknownst to us at that time the Carthaginian senate finally also sent recall messages to both Mago and Hannibal. Mago had recently been defeated by our legions in the lands of the Insubres in what today is known as Lombardy. Defeated, but not wiped out Mago had been wounded personally in the battle and the wound festered. He obeyed the recall and sailed with as many of his men as he could for Carthage, but died of his wounds on the journey, not far from Sardinia.

Hannibal also made the best arrangements he could to get his men out and he too sailed for Carthage. One of our major objectives had finally been achieved, the rest of the fighting would take place in Africa.

Publius left our spoils in the safest place he could by leaving it in the camp on the isthmus near Utica. Shortly after arriving in Tunis he witnessed a Carthaginian fleet, reportedly thirty quinqueremes, sailing past his new position in the direction of Utica and without a moments hesitation marched his forces back the way they had come to support the infantry, marines and sailors still harassing Utica even if they were too few in number to actually take the town.

Even with this swift action, we were spread very thin what with me being off in pursuit of Syphax with a chunk of our infantry accompanied by Massinissa and his men. I've often wondered that we didn't get more credit for what we achieved with so few. No reference to Churchill intended.

Rather than risk his foot soldiers in the usual form of naval battle which would have meant sailing out to meet the Carthaginian fleet and endeavouring to board their ships by means of the Corvus, thus turning a naval battle into an infantry engagement Publius decided to build a defensive wall around our valuable warships by lashing four rows of transports across the access to make a kind of wall four ships deep. This was a wise decision, even the loss of one warship with infantry aboard at sea could have meant many drownings, many of our men don't swim and armour drags a man down.

Not only were the ships lashed together to form this barricade, but planks were laid between them for mobility and a store of missiles such as javelins was brought up. The transports were high sided compared to the Carthaginian warships meaning their missiles would have to be thrown up at us, ours could be rained down on them.

I've often thought that the Roman empire was built as much by labour and downright hard work as by fighting or anything else. Caesar's circumvallation at Alesia, well in the future for us at this point and something only I knew about, being a good example.

However the preparation of this defensive barricade, a full four vessels deep, our properly fortified camps compared with the flimsy huts, inadequately protected, employed by Hasdrubal and Syphax also demonstrate the difference in attitude, application, planning and energy, compared with complacency, sloth and a lack of foresight in very many of our enemies.

Beneath the gangways between our transport ships there was space for small boats to sally forth like cavalry or velites issuing out between the maniples as in a land battle. This idea backfired somewhat as the small boats with our men in them were brushed aside by the large Carthaginian warships and obstructed the line of fire for a while actually hindering our own javelin throwers on the transports. Nonetheless it was an experiment and a lesson was learned. The small boats were also able to withdraw the same way they had gone forth, so no great harm done.

After forming up for a naval battle offshore, only to realise after wasting a lot of time that no one was coming out to meet them, the Carthaginians approached. They attacked wholeheartedly and adapted quite well to this new kind of fighting. After being repulsed initially by the hand picked one thousand men on the barricade, they resorted to grappling equipment, poles hooks and chains to try and break up the barricade.

After a very hard fight they managed to separate part of the outer line of transports from the second line which our men, we'd sustained very few casualties due to the height advantage, simply fell back on.

Faced with having to start again, from scratch effectively and seeing the same thing could happen twice more, even if they could succeed in detaching our second line the Carthaginians simply called it a day, they towed off a few empty transports to show back home and claim a victory and off they went.

They did not return for another such victory! We lost half a dozen old ships, naturally the least valuable had been put in the outer barricade. Polybius suggests we lost sixty transports, I'm sure this is a genuine error, he certainly didn't get it from me or my notes, or from my son.

Thirty quinqueremes do not tow away sixty transports rowing, it's preposterous. Nor could all the Carthaginian ships be brought to bear at the same time. In addition they could not put skeleton crews aboard and sail them since in the preparation of the blockade we'd removed the masts and rigging lest they be an obstruction to our javelin throwers. Six is more like it, a few others may have drifted away.

In addition, the Carthaginians lost a considerable number of men. Some might call it a draw, I'd say men are more valuable. Rome could replace the ships easily enough. Of course some military people and even historians see men as disposable too. I do not, nor did my friend.

So, we go back to my story and that of Massinissa. I liked him and there's a part of the events which happened next which saddened me greatly and still does.

We pursued Syphax for fifteen long days, but his energy in wishing to preserve his own life and his horses kept him ahead of us. After fifteen days on the march we came into the kingdom rightfully belonging to Massinissa and the garrisons Syphax had left to hold his ill gotten gains in the towns nearest the border were easily mopped up. Indeed the populace welcomed Massinissa and myself, and our men much like the French and Dutch welcomed the allies during the liberation.

Syphax himself had fallen back on the great city of Cirta which had been the capital in the kingdom of King Gala but which Syphax regarded as his capital city at this point, for all that the larger part of his kingdom actually lay to the west in modern Algeria.

On a plateau by a gorge Cirta has a great and naturally defensible position. However encouraged no doubt, yet again, by Sapanbaal, Syphax quickly raised another army from the seemingly endless pool of manpower in what was for the moment anyway ostensibly his kingdom.

Yet again, it was no small army and despite men rallying to Massinissa I was leading a force one third the size of Syphax's new army. Fortunately more than six thousand of my men were true soldiers, hardened experienced and disciplined and the core of Massinissa's cavalry were of like calibre.

Once again numbers caused Syphax to throw caution to the winds, he marched on us, when he had a perfectly defensible fortress in Cirta. The engagement began with the cavalry and at first numbers were a problem, even for Massinissa's expert horsemen, however, they knew better than to sell their lives cheaply and remained intact. They fell back as our infantry advanced and soon Syphax's inexperienced army, for all that it had copied our Roman formation was in disarray.

It's hard to believe Syphax had not learned anything. This time however, instead of fleeing yet again, he rode forward to try and rally his hopelessly outclassed, unseasoned men and was duly un-horsed and captured. With such leadership as there had been gone his army fled and we didn't really have the manpower or will to pursue them, better to hold our shape.

With Syphax captured we could put Massinissa on the throne and the almost unlimited pool of manpower in Numidia would be ours. The difference would be that if and when we recruited men they would be properly trained, used carefully and not simply sacrificed.

I knew what would happen next and it saddened me, I'd pledged to myself, to Scipio, to the universe I suppose that I would serve destiny and history, not endeavour to change it. I still cannot get the guilt and sadness to leave me though, I think about it often.

Massinissa asked leave of me to go on to what would now be his capital at Cirta. I assented as I must and he took Syphax in chains with him in order to show the magistrates in that city that to open the gates was not to betray Syphax, he had already lost and they were looking upon their new and rightful king the son of Gala.

Who knows what the outcome might have been had Syphax defended the city instead of marching out to meet us. If Utica was a tough ask with all our forces on hand Cirta would have been an utter impossibility for my very small force.

It was now that Massinissa met his former betrothed and Sapanbaal had lost nothing of her charm, indeed she was probably at her most beautiful at around twenty two years of age I think. Massinissa knew that he would be expected to surrender her, but he couldn't bear it and knowing how I felt and still feel about Valeria I understood him well enough. Before I could arrive with the infantry he'd married the girl, hoping that we would not see fit to deprive him of his queen.

With Syphax still in the land of the living I have no idea what he did about annulment or divorce, just decreed it I suppose. I knew I was supposed to be angry, but it was really just an act, what I really felt was a deep sense of pity, regret, tragedy at what I knew would play out.

Sapanbaal's appearance has been the subject of much speculation down the ages, some even suggesting a blonde haired, blue eyed beauty. Carthage was a cosmopolitan city and so no doubt it had Spanish and other European genes, Punic and Semitic genes, African genes, it was a melting pot. I'd liken it to modern Rio de Janeiro in many ways a great variety of people and some very beautiful people.

Being of the nobility Sapanbaal was essentially Punic, she had a light olive unblemished complexion. Her eyes were large, brown and doe like is as good a description as any I suppose. Her features were soft and framed, when it was down, by long very dark brown hair, not quite black.

Beauty comes in many shapes and forms and people have differing ideas, but occasionally there are people of such obvious beauty that none would deny it. Her lips were as perfect and as appealing as all her features, she was slim yet shapely, lithe I would say and of course always beautifully dressed.

The beauty of Cleopatra has been debated, some say it was her education and charm that made her so attractive rather than her looks. Sapanbaal was not lacking these qualities either and she spoke always in a soft almost musical voice. If ever a siren existed it was she.

As the agent of Scipio I had to pretend anger and when this pretend anger had died down I seemingly relented and agreed that Sapanbaal could remain in Cirta. Massinissa and I would then return to Scipio with the other prisoners, as much plunder as we could transport and then Massinissa could take his case in person to Scipio, that he be allowed to keep his queen and that she as a noblewoman of Carthage and wife of a defeated enemy in King Syphax should not be taken, humiliated in chains, to Rome.

I knew the outcome and I wept inwardly. On our arrival in Castra Cornelia, as it was called much later, our fortified camp near Utica, Scipio first interviewed Syphax. Our men all flocked to see him a prisoner, the story of both Hasdrubal and Scipio courting a once powerful king, thought to hold the balance of power in Africa, at no small risk to themselves was well known.

Syphax bewailed his errors of judgement, as well he might! Of course he blamed the fair maiden for all his ills, siren voice and all that, weak bastard.

My friend spared his life, he would die later as a prisoner in Italy. He was held in Tibur to be precise, modern Tivoli, not far from Rome. He died in 201BC that is 553 a couple of years after his capture. I know not what ailed him, perhaps loss of face, but he was not executed.

Fearing that Massinissa would fall for the blandishments of Sapanbaal, he listened to Massinissa, but insisted that Sapanbaal be brought to him as a prisoner for onward transmission to Rome. Whether he harboured thoughts of displaying her in a triumph I cannot say. I did not ask as I would like to think better of him, but a different culture, a different upbringing, he may well have thought as Octavian would do in relation to Cleopatra in the future.

Massinissa was publicly thanked in front of the assembled army, his kingship was confirmed and he was gifted a curule chair, an ivory sceptre and much besides, but not before he had sent a trusted man with poison and a message for Sapanbaal that he was unable to protect her.

Sapanbaal took the poison after instructing the man to tell Massinissa that she'd have been better unmarried if this was the only wedding present he could provide. There was more according to the ancient writers, but that anyway was the essence of the message I believe, effectively calling Massinissa a coward. Only Massinissa knows exactly what the message said, so the ancient writers used supposition.

I've often wondered how things would have turned out had Massinissa ever found happiness. Maybe Sapanbaal would have turned him into our enemy, maybe Scipio was right. I'll never know, which is why I feel I cannot interfere with what is written, but the sadness not only for Sapanbaal, but for Massinissa who was a great and unhappy man in many ways never leaves me, even now.

After publicly honouring Massinissa my friend also publicly honoured and recognised my achievements, after which he gave me a gift most precious and one I'd not have asked for. He announced that I was to escort the prisoner Syphax and take his own dispatches too back to Rome. I would be with Valeria if only for a short while and our son would be conceived.

So ended another year Saturnalia and all that, in Rome for myself. I imagine it has more to do with menstrual cycles and that sort of thing, but all my children have been conceived, in that time and this, at moments of extreme high emotion. I'm not referring just to the act itself, but to my mental state at the time. I cannot help but wonder if it plays a part.

As I sailed away, Publius prepared to return to Tunis.

The Roman senate was well pleased with the reports I brought and the main prisoner, a man who had caused us much opposition, at least in numbers if not in efficacy. He would walk in my friend's triumph when it finally came, he'd not the courage of Sapanbaal.

Four days of celebrations were decreed in Rome and all the shrines were to be open for the populace to thank the gods on account of the news I had brought. Accompanied by the praetor Publius Aelius I even mounted the rostra and repeated my news to the jubilant crowd.

The senate was also pleased to receive emissaries from Massinissa the following day and to confirm him in his kingship and friend and ally of the Roman people status. Yet more gifts were sent to him. These consisted of a consul's campaign tent, horses and other insignia and clothes more normally seen adorning a Roman consul, a very symbolic event. The emissaries asked that Numidian prisoners in Rome be sent back to Massinissa to help him cement his position with his people. This too was agreed and even his emissaries were given most generous gifts and payments for themselves.

I was more than well pleased to see my wife and daughter. Of course my daughter barely knew me, but she would come to. Valeria was ecstatic, but controlled herself when in the company of Aemila or Pomponia, what with Publius still being overseas on active duty so to speak. After my appearance on the rostra Valeria even joked that I might be consul one day.

There's little to be gained from describing my happiness in Rome; that Caius Laelius, later to be known as Sapiens was conceived then says all that needs to be said and the time of my departure came around far too soon, although not as soon as it might have.

About this time envoys arrived from Saguntum where all this started. They had captured some Carthaginians once again endeavouring to recruit mercenaries in Spain. They brought with them two hundred and fifty pounds of gold and eight hundred pounds of silver confiscated from the recruiters and laid it before the senate. The money was given straight back to Saguntum with thanks and the envoys had a ship provided to them to take them home the easy way. Optimism thrived, everyone was in a good mood, even the senate.

The senate decided I should stay longer than originally envisaged in view of my experience and knowledge of affairs in Africa and then hear the representations of the peace envoys from Carthage and take part in the debate. Recognition indeed.

Valeria once again blooming, proud of her husband who was both present and lauded, and in fine health herself found the pregnancy delightful apparently. Perhaps that too was a good omen. I was beginning to become truly Roman with this belief in omens.

Once my friend had established himself at Tunis the Carthaginian Council of Elders had sued for peace. A body supposedly senior even to their senate. I believe the Council of Elders were sincere, they even went so far as to prostrate themselves before the conqueror. Had Scipio wanted personal glory for himself, more than he wanted what was best for Rome he might have offered outrageous terms in order to bring on a final battle. In fact his terms were more than reasonable.

Unfortunately the war faction in Carthage was planning to use the peace negotiations to gain time, as disingenuous as we'd been before Utica. With the armies of Hannibal and Mago returning, and as they thought at the time both generals too, they believed they could scupper the peace later and win, at least on home soil, despite what should have been several object lessons by now.

Being in Rome at the time and trying to piece things together afterwards it's hard to be precise about the order of events and which events overlapped with which.

However Hasdrubal son of Gisgo was accused of treason. Largely on account of losing the battle of the Great Plains I believe. The idea that Hasdrubal was a traitor to his city is laughable. He might not have been the greatest general but he was a fighter through and through. He never gave up, almost Roman actually in that sense. He'd used his daughter to gain diplomatic advantage for Carthage, soldiers too and now he had lost her.

History records that he too killed himself, in his case to avoid lynching by the mob. I believe this happened late in 203BC 551 but it could have been early in 202BC 552. Once back in Rome I also learned of the passing of Quintus Fabius Maximus I didn't mourn him personally.

The terms my friend laid down to end the war were as follows. Carthage was to hand over all prisoners of war and deserters, there were not so many of the latter I can assure you. She should withdraw her armies from Italy and Cisalpine Gaul as we called it, he was referring to the army of Mago in what today is northern Italy. Scipio was of course unaware that Carthage had already sent to recall these armies for the continuance of the war.

In addition, Carthage must repudiate any claim on Hispania, that is Spain and she must evacuate all the islands between Sicily and Africa. The largest of these being Malta of course but there are several smaller islands too. She should surrender all her warships excepting twenty for her own defence and supply Rome with five hundred thousand measures of wheat and three hundred thousand measures of barley. Finally he demanded five thousand talents of silver as war reparations.

These terms were not harsh in my view, particularly with regard to the amount of the monies to be paid given the wealth of Carthage. He gave the Council of Elders three days to accept or not, stating that if they accepted there should be an immediate truce and that envoys should be sent to Rome to ratify the peace treaty.

Not only did Carthage accept but she immediately released prisoners as a sign of good faith and sent a deputation to Rome to ratify the treaty. Really that should have been the end of the matter and Carthage might have remained on sufficiently good terms and sufficiently strong to avoid a third Punic War but fate, the universe, or perhaps it was just the weather had other ideas.

CHAPTER 25   ZAMA 202BC 552

This being the year of the consulship of Tiberius Claudius Nero and Marcus Servilius Pulex Geminus whose older brother had been consul last year. Pulex means flea, but he wasn't so terribly small, maybe someone found him irritating! His family renounced patrician status and his older brother would be a tribune of plebs. Strange family, still, they did me no harm personally. Geminus did attempt to take something from Scipio, but spectacularly failed, more of that later.

Early in the year, both sides having technically accepted the terms devised by my friend, Livy denies this, but Polybius confirms my version, as he would, getting his information from my son, a Roman fleet was sent on a supply mission to Scipio.

In fact two fleets were sent, one from Sardinia which arrived safely and shortly after another from Sicily with more supplies and reinforcements.

Having left in good weather for the short voyage from Sicily the second fleet after being becalmed was driven, by the onset of a sudden gale, onto the island of Aegimurus in the bay of Carthage. With the treaty agreed, but technically not ratified yet Carthage, or people within Carthage who wanted the war to continue could not resist attacking the damaged ships and stealing their cargoes. Some surviving ships were captured too and were sailed or towed into the great harbour at Carthage.

Livy suggests that Hasdrubal was behind this, but Hasdrubal was a common name and Livy does not specify Hasdrubal who. Being in Rome at the time I can't be certain if Hasdrubal son of Gisgo was still alive at this point, or whether this was another Hasdrubal, or whether Livy was just plain wrong. Livy was, after all, not even born yet. The more reliable Polybius does not mention Hasdrubal.

As mentioned before, an earlier resupply fleet from Sardinia had arrived safely and the warships attending the fleet from Sicily were able to escape by means of their oars. Most of the reinforcing troops were on the warships not the transports, therefore the situation could have been worse for us. However the two hundred transports, all fully laden and dependent solely on square sails, and therefore unable to tack out of danger were lost to Carthage.

My friend sent emissaries to complain to the Carthaginian senate about these warlike actions whilst suing for peace, the tribunes' language might have been more diplomatic, but I doubt it would have changed anything. With Hannibal now returned the war mongers in Carthage once again had the upper hand not to say complete control. Nor was Carthage in a frame of mind to return what she had opportunistically stolen.

Feelings in Rome were mixed about the return of Hannibal to Africa our forces in Bruttium had been ordered to harry him and keep him occupied until matters in Africa were fully resolved, but of course the old fox, lion, call him what you will, had slipped away with the best of his men leaving the worst of them to garrison a few places and lead us astray.

Ridiculously the envoys from Carthage laid the whole blame for all the events which began with Hannibal's attack on Saguntum at Hannibal's door, they had never supported him, not ever! They had clung to the peace negotiated at the end of the first war. Patently untrue.

In Africa, our envoys returning to Scipio by sea from Carthage were attacked by Carthaginian quadriremes and forced to run their ship to shore and escape on foot. Undoubtedly the war faction had the upper hand in Carthaginian politics, regardless of anything the envoys in Rome might say. Of course news travelled slowly in the ancient world.

Massinissa was at this juncture seeking to expand his own kingdom by conquering the territories once belonging to Syphax that is to say further west than the kingdom of Gala, his now dead father.

Massinissa had also been loaned ten cohorts of Roman infantry to assist him in his quest. With war looming urgent dispatches were sent to Massinissa that he should return with all haste. It was a long way to go however, there and back. Nor was Scipio's force in any sense sufficient to besiege the city of Carthage itself even with the men now accompanying Massinissa.

Leaving as few men as he dare to protect his base, under a legate named Baebius my friend marched his remaining forces into the fertile Bagradas river valley to cut Carthage off from its supplies, to threaten the interior and ravage the towns and settlements therein.

While this was going on I sailed back to Africa with the Carthaginian peace envoys. I'd participated in the debate, which was as usual heated with many different views.

Some senators said the peace envoy was a sham, some said we should accept, some said let Scipio decide. I pointed out that Scipio, despite our plan to relocate the war to Africa, had until recently envisaged Hannibal and Mago being bottled up at either end of Italy whilst he concluded matters overseas. However you look at it, it was a mess.

We'd taken the war to Africa in the first place in order to get the Carthaginians out of Italy, so we could hardly complain if it worked. However, given the limited support we'd had from the state and the large number of troops tied up in Italy pretty soon the odds in North Africa would start to turn against us and in favour of Carthage.

By the time I arrived at Castra Cornelia, Scipio had started his operations in the Bagradas Valley, but he returned in person to discuss everything with me and to interview the Carthaginians I'd brought with me. Upon hearing how our envoys had been attacked on their return voyage from Carthage, not to mention the advantage taken of our supply fleet the Carthaginian peace envoys imagined the worst for themselves and their short term life expectancy. In fact they were let go without rancour, but clearly the war would be resolved by force of arms, not by negotiation.

By this time Servilius Caepio had set off for Sicily intending to progress with his army to Africa to usurp my friend and win the glory for himself, in what he imagined would be the final battle. It would be the final battle but it may well not have been had Caepio been in charge.

He wasn't the only one looking for personal glory either. Both of this year's consuls Tiberius Claudius Nero and Marcus Servilius Pulex Geminus also wanted the command in Africa.

The decision about the command in Africa had been put to the people and the tribes had voted, naturally and overwhelmingly, for the man who kept winning, that is my friend Publius Cornelius Scipio. This did not stop the consuls drawing the lots anyway, Geminus the flea won and was awarded joint command with Scipio. Utterly crazy, war by committee, the perfidy of committees and the perfidy of Romans seeking all the glory for themselves.

Geminus was given fifty quinqueremes and happily went off to make his arrangements. He did this very slowly and when he eventually set off a storm blew him and his forces to Sardinia. The flea never made the hop to Africa at all. This was far better for the command structure, but the numbers did not look so good. As mentioned above the odds were now favouring Hannibal.

Hannibal landed at Leptis in the Gulf of Hammamet, modern Lamta just south of Monastir if you know Tunisia. From the landing site he moved his forces to Hadrumetum, a Phoenician town pre dating Carthage. This is modern Susa today, just north of Monastir with the ancient remains of this once important city being in the northern suburbs of the modern town.

He had with him an army of twenty four thousand very experienced warriors. He then recruited a Numidian chieftain related to Syphax who came to him with two thousand very good cavalrymen. Next to arrive was the remnant of Mago's army, also all experienced veterans, twelve thousand of them and for the icing on the cake King Philip from Greece sent him four thousand Macedonian infantrymen. As to their quality I cannot say but Alexander the Great had done very well with Macedonian warriors and King Philip being wealthy, it meant they came very well equipped too.

Hannibal now had forty two thousand men at his disposal, none of them raw recruits like the men of Syphax. Hannibal of course was a much respected general with many victories to his name for all that in recent years he'd not achieved so very much. Most of his men had the blood of many a Roman on their hands. It was actually a most formidable force.

With Scipio raiding the Bagradas valley Hannibal found himself under pressure from Carthage to move into the interior and end the devastation now being wrought on his homeland. So the final chapter, of the war anyway, begins with Hannibal setting out for Zama, a name that has gone down in history.

Zama is about five days march south west of Carthage. In the meantime Hannibal sent spies or scouts, call them what you will to inform him about Scipio's strength, our dispositions and our exact whereabouts.

My friend's men caught said spies and brought them before the commander. They may well have expected execution, just as the peace envoys had a right to expect harsher treatment than they received.

My friend, instead, appointed a tribune to show them around his camp, answer any and all questions and invited them to inspect everything. Having asked them if they had seen everything they wanted to see and having been answered in the affirmative he ensured they were safely escorted as far as necessary to make absolutely certain they got safely back to Hannibal. Fortuitously that very day Massinissa returned with the ten cohorts loaned to him, six thousand foot soldiers of his own and four thousand mounted warriors. The spies witnessed this too.

I have my own thoughts on Hannibal's state of mind, but this display of supreme confidence by my friend no doubt played on Hannibal's thoughts.

Our push up the Bagradas valley had forced Hannibal to operate far from his support in Carthage and shortened the distance by which Massinissa had had to return to us. All of this had already borne fruit. Nonetheless at this juncture Hannibal was receiving more support from his government and state than we from ours. He was also receiving hurry up and get on with it messages from Carthage, but replied that he'd choose his own time and place to attack us.

It has been suggested that the act of showing the spies around our camp inspired Hannibal to want to meet Scipio in person. I personally think there was rather more to it than that. Cannae had happened fourteen years previously and Hannibal had precious little to show for it. Further, Scipio had cleared Carthaginian forces, frequently reinforced or replaced, completely from Spain, a land Carthage had held dear.

Hannibal sent messengers requesting a personal meeting with Scipio, and my friend, unsurprisingly given the history with Syphax agreed. We moved our camp near to the town of Margaron, a town no longer extant. This was done in order to be closer to Hannibal and to facilitate the proposed meeting. At this time our chosen position was both defensible and crucially we also had essential supplies of water.

Hannibal occupied a nearby hill, near four miles away but to attack us he'd have to come down on to the plain and he was under greater pressure than we. Not only was he under pressure from Carthage but his defensible hill lacked the water we had in abundance, he could not stay there long. Once on the plain we could exploit our one advantage, although we were the smaller army, we did at least have superiority in cavalry despite the contingent supplied to Hannibal by the kinsman of Syphax, the chieftain Tychaeus.

A tent was erected by us, we were ever better at this kind of thing, in the midst of the plain, where both armies had plain sight and were equidistant. I dearly wanted to attend this historic event, to see Hannibal in person, to look into his eyes, sorry, eye, and hear what was said, but my friend put me in command of all our forces, lest any treachery should befall him and so I have only his testimony to rely on and he was less forthcoming than he sometimes was, lost in his own thoughts I suspect.

It seems to me, reading between the lines, that Hannibal did not really want this battle. He was prepared for it certainly, he had his tactics clear in his own mind I'm sure and yet he spoke about how fickle fortune and war can be essentially he tried to warn my friend off bringing things to an end by a clash of arms. He stated, I believe, that Publius had done a lot of winning, why risk his perfect record when a peace could be negotiated now. That from a throw away comment my friend made before retiring for the night.

I'm no psychiatrist, but I believe the fears that Hannibal tried to imbue in my friend were actually a reflection of the fears he himself felt. I've already alluded to the amount of time that had passed since the apogee of his success. Further, at Cannae the smaller army had engulfed the larger, I wonder if he was anxious to avoid a similar legacy whereby Scipio might defeat him and destroy the larger force with the smaller, however it was achieved.

Polybius and Livy were, like me, story tellers, they could not let this moment pass unremarked. However, as with the messages exchanged between Sapanbaal and Massinissa there is much that I think only the two people personally involved really knew and much that was unspoken about to others not there present.

It's been suggested that Hannibal was an old man, nonsense, he was in his early forties by my calculations. However, that his best was behind him was undeniable in light of the outcome, that he was tired mentally I personally have no doubt.

The essential facts are that the terms Hannibal offered in order to avoid battle were not dissimilar to those of the treaty already violated and Scipio's terms now were unconditional surrender, terms Hannibal could not accept.

Polybius and Livy relate much more, but it is largely their own supposition. I'm sure that past events, treaties made and treaties broken, and battles won and battles lost, although not lost by Scipio who had not endured that humiliation, were discussed, soldiers cannot help themselves, but the real details are known only to my friend and to Hannibal.

So the die was cast. Both generals led their forces out onto the plain the next morning to conquer or be conquered. We had Massinissa's four thousand cavalry and by this time we had a little over two thousand Roman cavalry. In addition to the six thousand foot soldiers furnished by Massinissa we had around eighteen thousand Roman legionaries, equivalent to three full strength or very slightly over strength legions. We technically had four legions in Africa at the time, but we had to hold a few other key positions so not all were at the Battle of Zama as it's come to be called.

Our total force amounted to around thirty thousand men. Facing us were, by my estimate forty five thousand infantry, three to four thousand cavalry and about eighty elephants. Not quite two to one, but we were quite possibly outnumbered by near twenty thousand.

We drew our legions up in the centre in near usual formation, hastati to the front, then principes and triarii, but we left greater gaps between the maniples than was usual to allow elephants to pass through or at least give men a chance to get out of the way.

I was personally given command of the Italian and Roman cavalry on our left wing, Massinissa had command of the entire Numidian contingent, foot and horse on our right wing. Our velites were initially positioned in the corridors left for the elephants as they would begin the attack and could use these same corridors to withdraw. Any velites who were overtaken during the withdrawal, who yet lived, would seek sanctuary in the wings of the army if they could make it.

Both Livy and Polybius maximise the theatre by stories of the speeches made by one or both generals. Livy has Scipio making his speech from horseback riding up and down the line. In fact all the preparatory orders and oration had been taken care of in camp where the commander could be heard, or at least his words could be accurately relayed to ensure that all heard. For Hannibal I cannot say.

My friend did point out that being in a foreign land there were limited options for retreat and that any captured alive could harbour little hopes for their future. However, he also pointed to their past successes and although it may be win or die, winning was the outcome every man should anticipate as well as work towards. He did show himself on his horse at the head of the army as an example of leadership after taking the field, but not for the purpose of an oratory that would have been lost on the breeze.

The battle commenced with a testing advance by our skirmishers the velites which drew a swift response in the form of a charge by the elephants. We had prepared for this by bringing all my trumpets and tubas used otherwise for signalling on board ship in poor visibility. These instruments were dispersed along the line together with the men who knew best how to blow them. As the elephants approached we let out an unholy din which turned many of the poor beasts around and saw them charging back towards their own lines.

I've often thought the use of elephants was self defeating.

Those elephants which did continue took the line of least resistance and went straight through the open corridors where they were either dispatched with javelins or simply encouraged to keep going. Massinissa's cavalrymen, having more experience of elephants, drove those elephants which had turned back on towards the enemy at speed by following up with projectiles.

Naturally the Carthaginians and their allies could not attack their own elephants and so the intelligent animals again took the line of least resistance and ran into the lines which were not hurling projectiles at them.

Hannibal's Cavalry on his left wing, facing Massinissa on our right wing had been preparing to charge when their own elephants came charging back on them and Massinissa's cavalry, already in hot pursuit decimated the confused and disordered cavalry of Hannibal's left wing to the extent that the survivors fled leaving Hannibal's wing on that side completely exposed.

It was now my turn to lead a cavalry charge again and thank all the gods, for the last time in my life. My charge against the Carthaginian cavalry on my side of the field was more successful than I could have dreamed of. Perhaps the business of the Carthaginians, being in their own land and having places to flee to, whilst for us it was win or die really did have a bearing. Maybe it was due to what happened on the other wing, but whatever the reason, even if it was just our superiority in numbers as regards cavalry the Carthaginian horse promptly wheeled and fled.

It was the loss of cavalry support on both wings that really decided the battle in my opinion, but not yet, it must have been a little like Cannae in reverse although we were not exactly able to surround our foe. Our infantry advanced, theirs did not. Hannibal had his sacrificial Gauls and Ligurians in the front line, the Carthaginians behind them gave them no help and scant encouragement, they simply held their formation.

After losing many men the Gauls and Ligurians endeavoured to fall back, but the solid massed ranks of the Carthaginians behind them left no escape routes and the Carthaginians themselves, intent on keeping their shape even drove off their own allies.

Those Gauls and Ligurains who were able to, fled towards whichever wing was easiest for them to reach. Most did not make it to safety being tired, greatly dispirited by this time and by the actions of their own side. Soon they just gave up the unequal struggle.

Our own infantry were hampered by having to advance over the bodies of the fallen Gauls and at the same time fight the Carthaginian troops which were the cream of Hannibal's experienced and much tested army. The hastati were having a hard time of it and swapped, as is our custom, with the principes, these too found the going hard, but eventually managed to make progress.

When the Carthaginian line, effectively the second line after the Gauls and Ligurians tried to retire they found themselves confronted by a hedge of spears from the third line which had been kept some way behind the fighting, they too being intent, as ordered by Hannibal, on keeping their formation tight. In short they did to their comrades and countrymen what the second line had done to their allies. Again the survivors from Hannibal's second line tried to make it to the wings seeking safety, but most were unable to escape our advancing line.

By now the numbers were nearly equal but Hannibal's third line represented what might be called the old guard, the most experienced men who had been with him the longest and there were still twenty thousand of them, maybe more. Our men had been victorious over the first two lines, but not without losses and they were beginning to fatigue too. Hannibal's old guard were just at this moment getting started. That was Hannibal's strategy.

I knew what I had to do, not least because I had read up on the battle. I heard the trumpets sound recall and knew that Scipio would pull his men back and extend his line with both hastati and triarii spreading left and right of the principes to create a line that could envelop the Carthaginian wings as my cavalry and that of Massinissa charged the Carthaginians in rear. In short the smaller army finally surrounded what had been the larger force and cut it to pieces.

It was bloody and it was ghastly and it brought the Second Punic War to a close. I've never liked that we as a species have used animals in war, be they horses, beasts of burden, elephants or dogs. I wasn't at Cannae, but I imagine the result must have looked much the same. The sounds and smells too. From this ghastly scene and the previous one at the burning of the camps I would never quite fully recover my peace of mind I think.

I had thought at one time to finish my book with the end of the war, but of course it's not the end of the story. It's not the end of the story for my friend Scipio, or for Hannibal and nor is it the end of the story for Caius Laelius, and of course as you have worked out, this could not have been written at all had I not returned one day. That day was unlooked for, unexpected and in many ways unwanted, because now I could live in peace with my wife and children and my friends. Well, largely in peace at least.

Hannibal lost some twenty thousand men killed and the same again captured. Others were scattered. Hannibal himself quit the field at the last, having directed his troops for as long as he harboured any hope at all, he rode away with a handful of horsemen and made for Hadrumentum.

We had lost in the region of two thousand killed and perhaps twice that injured. This was a testament to Roman discipline, methods and equipment, for much of the day had been a slogging match of brutal hand to hand fighting.

Polybius and Livy are complimentary about Hannibal's actions as a general that day, but I think their motive is to make our success, or Scipio's anyway seem all the greater. The lily does not need gilding. I have my own criticisms of Hannibal's tactics, but I'm no great or distinguished commander so I'll keep my personal thoughts about his errors to myself.

It was important that, Carthage being militarily exhausted, was not given a breathing space. We had not the forces to besiege so great a city but we had the power now that Carthage was bereft of all military means to bring about a peace on our terms.

To impress on Carthage just what its true position was Gnaeus Octavius was given command of the legions and told to march them to, and place them before the city in plain sight of the residents. My friend and I with a large body of cavalry made for Utica where, with our old fleet and a new one brought by Lentulus, we were able, in a considerable show of naval superiority, to sail for the harbour of Carthage looking for a bloodless capitulation.

Vermina, son of Syphax had raised a force and was en route to assist Carthage. Too late to the party he was intercepted and defeated by Gnaeus Octavius without difficulty. As we sailed for Carthage we were met by a single Carthaginian ship bedecked with olive branches containing elders and deputies sent by order of Hannibal to sue for peace yet again.

No answer was given them other than that they must follow us to our camp before Carthage. At the camp itself thirty more envoys arrived to beg terms. These likewise were kept waiting a full day to increase their fears.

When the conference did take place on the morrow Scipio told the Carthaginian representatives that having broken a truce already agreed, having started the war in the first place and having invaded Italy they must expect the harshest of terms. In actual fact, in view of all that, his terms were unbelievably lenient.

It interests me that the terms of the Treaty of Versailles were so harsh that, in my view, it created the conditions which led to the second world war and so I have to believe that my friend exhibited greater wisdom. Yet his terms allowed Carthage to recover and such would be the Carthaginian recovery that Rome would eventually see fit to destroy the rival city utterly.

Rome would plough salt in the fields, and sell male and female civilians captured in that city as slaves at the far ends of the known world so that no Carthaginian man should ever come together with a Carthaginian woman and continue the race. Some years after that Rome would build a Roman city on the ancient site.

That was after my time, but my friend's adoptive grandson, my own son and indeed even Polybius would have a hand in it. That is largely beyond the scope of my story barring a few comments on the subject.

Hannibal was also allowed to live and to return to his city where he was elected suffete, a kind of judge but effectively the most senior position in the government in a Phoenician city. He became an effective reforming politician until eventually he was driven out.

He remained faithful to his oath and a passionate enemy of Rome until his dying day, offering his services, after leaving Carthage, to any foreign king or adversary who opposed us. His good management of the city's finances after this war were a large part of the reason Carthage did recover, he stamped out corruption and embezzlement which enabled Carthage to both pay us and prosper once more, but in so doing he made many enemies.

Scipio's terms then. Carthage was now only allowed ten triremes as a navy, all other warships to be surrendered to Rome. She obviously had to return all prisoners and all the ships and supplies taken in the incident in the bay of Carthage as well. She was allowed to retain her own laws and customs and would not be garrisoned by Rome, but must surrender her elephants and train no more.

Carthage must not wage war on anyone within or outside Africa without the permission of Rome, she could keep her traditional lands, but must accept Massinissa as king of Eastern Numida and beyond, exact borders to be agreed.

The intention was that all of Numidia, to include the former realm of Syphax would be united under King Massinissa. This threat would keep any ambitions Carthage might aspire to in the future in check. In fact Massinissa would steal bits of Carthaginian territory from time to time and eventually they would respond militarily giving the hawks in Rome the excuse for the third and final Punic war.

Envoys should be despatched to Rome for the ratification of the new treaty and Carthage must pay and feed the Roman troops in situ here in Africa until the peace was concluded. That brings us to the financial reparations and tribute. I don't believe my friend Publius appreciated the true wealth of Carthage. Even Hannibal may not have realised it until faced with the problem of how to make the payments, which it seems weren't as arduous as they were perhaps intended to be. At least, not once embezzlement and corruption within the city had been dealt with.

Ten thousand talents of silver were demanded to be paid in equal instalments over the next fifty years. Scipio was also to personally choose one hundred hostages from amongst the young of the Carthaginian nobility to be transported to Rome. Restitution of the fleet opportunistically taken by Carthage was to be immediate, otherwise hostilities would begin again forthwith.

These terms led to a fifty year peace and were it not for the perfidy of another Cato, Marcus Porcius Cato, known as Cato the elder, but not the first bitter old man in his line, who finished every speech he made in the senate with the words 'delenda est Carthago' Carthage must be destroyed, it might have endured indefinitely.

Once back at the coast I was despatched to Rome to report the victory. That my friend continued to honour me so, and facilitate my spending time with my beloved wife and children whilst he could not spend time with his is one of the greatest debts I owe him. I would also ride at the head of my cavalry unit from Zama in his long overdue triumph when it came.

Lentulus, wanted to continue the war in Africa in order to obtain personal glory, yet again Romans do this and would continue to do so for years to come. Anyhow, he was the main, if not the only real opponent to making peace, but the people had had enough of war and he was voted down.

I will now continue the story by telling you first about the life of Publius after the war, then Hannibal and finally my own story.

CHAPTER 26 AFRICANUS COMMENCING 201BC

It was in 201 then that Scipio finally returned to Rome having put affairs in Africa in order to his satisfaction. He sailed first to Sicily where the crowds thronged to see him and cheer him. They called him Africanus, literally 'the African' after the people he had conquered.

In later times it became not uncommon for victorious Romans to take the name of a race or country they had been victorious over as a cognomen. However, this was a new idea at this time, Scipio took the cognomen Africanus, the first Roman ever to take such a name.

Before leaving, those Carthaginian ships for which Rome had no use were towed out to sea and burned within sight of the city of Carthage. This was done in order to remind the populace that this was both an end and a new beginning. Effectively it was a signal that Carthage was more or less a province, or at least a vassal state of Rome, never again would she be a major military player on the world stage.

Our prisoners were released and welcomed back into the Roman fold. Our few deserters were sent to us and were duly executed for treason.

Before burning the warships their great bronze prows were removed to be displayed in Scipio's triumph. After that they would be mounted on the rostra in the comitium alongside the ships beaks as they were known, which had been captured during the Latin war and mounted there back in 338BC by the then consul Gaeus Maenius. It was from this decoration, that the rostra, used for public oration took its name in fact.

Scipio's triumphal entry into Rome when it came was a procession of magnificence such as I had never before witnessed. Even before the triumphal parade itself people thronged to see their hero and cheer him. A Roman triumph is a bit like a carnival with floats and people in fancy dress, although they are not in fancy dress, just dressed in the clothes or armour of their homeland.

Some people ride on floats, others ride horses, some walk or march, there are dancers and musicians and gifts are tossed to the crowd. However, the purpose is to show to the people the magnificence of the achievement of the triumphator or vir triumphalis.

Having been denied a triumph for the Spanish campaign those achievements could not be represented, however there were great artworks mounted on huge floats which depicted the burning of the camps, the battle of Zama and the battles against Syphax. The defeated king was dressed regally with a mock crown and forced to walk, chained behind a chariot.

The practice of executing prisoners after a triumph had not yet begun thankfully and Syphax was imprisoned at Tibur, now modern Tivoli, where he died a year or so later. I'm not conversant with the conditions in which he was held. His men who'd been taken prisoner, likewise were not executed, but they were sold into slavery after the triumph.

Enemies were displayed at a Roman triumph so as to both stress their strength and importance before being conquered and their abject state afterwards, a difficult balance to strike. Prisoners taken from the armies of Syphax walked in their fighting clothes and armour where we had it, yet in chains and naturally without weapons.

A great store of captured weapons was displayed on another float and there were several floats which displayed plunder, from gold and silver to artworks, furniture, rich fabrics, jewellery and more.

Publius himself led the parade in a gilded chariot pulled by four magnificent white stallions. At his side was a slave detailed to constantly remind him that he was just a man, not a god, although the legend or fantasy that the man was descended from, or was specially favoured by, Jupiter had already taken hold.

Publius's popularity, especially amongst the ordinary plebs, but also amongst the higher ranking plebs, was already causing jealousy in patrician circles. It's funny, they all love a triumph and they're all jealous of the trimuphator, unless it's themselves. The perfidy of patricians.

Behind Scipio came the floats with the scenes of his victories, followed by the prisoners, flanked by armed Roman soldiers despite the chains. After them came the store of weapons and then the plunder, then came our own forces. To the delight of my darling wife I rode at the head of the cavalry and finally the legions marched into the city singing ribald songs to delight the crowds.

This, the day itself and the parade were the highest honour a Roman general could receive. It all began at the triumphal gate and afterwards the procession wended its way through the streets of Rome, in order that all citizens should be able to witness it. It concluded, fortuitously, at the temple of Jupiter where this supposed son of Jupiter made sacrifice of a pure white bull.

After the parade the feasting began, for ourselves and for every free born Roman, no slaves or freed men were allowed to take part. The following day the games began, they lasted for many days, all paid for by Publius, but his share of the spoils was vast. My own wasn't so bad either, but more of that another time.

Scipio's first son had been conceived and born in 205BC. Conceived early in the year when Scipio was home and standing for election. Publius Cornelius Scipio; as the first born he took his father's name, was ever a sickly child. He would never be a warrior but he was to be made augur in 180BC. He had no children of his own, but adopted his cousin, who in effect became my friend's grandson by adoption. He would take the world stage in his time and would also become a good friend to my own son.

I wonder if young Publius remembered his father's triumphal parade, his mother Aemilia took him to see it with my family but perhaps he was too young, although it should have made a huge impression.

Publius senior, as he was now, would have two more sons and two daughters, his younger daughter being Cornelia, mother of the Gracchi, possibly the most famous Roman noblewoman of the republican era. The family would continue to matter in Roman society and in Roman politics for many generations to come.

Two years after celebrating his triumph, that is in 199BC my friend became censor and princeps senatus, that is to say titular head of the senate. A bit like father of the house in modern British politics, since it was the consuls who theoretically held the power. Not that you'd think so the way old Fabius Maximus had interfered when my friend had been consul.

Publius had become consul in extraordinary circumstances without holding all the normal preceding magistracies on the cursus honorum, but now he had held the two most important positions any Roman could aspire to.

Roman convention had it, at this time, that ten years should pass before a former consul should stand again. In the future this convention would not hold. Men like Gaius Marius and Sulla would get around it, a bit like Putin coming back repeatedly as president of Russia, with a little assistance from others of course, despite the supposed constitution banning it.

In 194BC Scipio was elected consul once more, coming in as the senior consul ahead of Tiberius Sempronius Longus. My friend hoped to replace Titus Quinctius Flaminius as governor of our province in Greece and strengthen our position there, believing that the growing strength of King Antiochus III would become a problem. It did become a problem, my friend was prescient himself for once. His jealous rivals in the senate ensured he did not get the position he sought.

Instead my friend was sent to northern Italy to suppress the Boii and Ligurians, who had not given up their campaigns against Rome despite the heavy losses they suffered supporting Hannibal, Mago and even fighting for Carthage in Africa some of them. How that worked out for them at Zama has already been recorded here.

My friend probably thought this campaign beneath him and largely allowed his colleague Flaminius to run it, himself returning to Rome at the first opportunity to organise the next elections.

In 193BC, early in the year, my friend led an embassy to Africa to adjudicate a boundary dispute between Carthage and our old friend Massinissa. Naturally he decided in favour of Massinissa, but this may have sown the seeds for future conflict.

Later in the year my friend also led an embassy to the court of King Antiochus III, then at Ephesus, a city which is now in what we call western Turkey. It has been said by some modern historians that my friend could not have attended both Africa and Turkey, Asia Minor to us, in the same year. Absolute nonsense, clearly they are not sailors and Ephesus was a port city.

By this time King Antiochus III had received Hannibal into his court as a military advisor. The king, in some ways like Syphax was now overconfident and full of his own self importance. To be fair to him though, he'd enjoyed more success than Syphax ever did. Antiochus, like Pompey in the future gave himself the self congratulatory, egoistic title of 'The Great'.

He had inherited the Seleucid kingdom from his murdered brother. Antiochus had been in Babylon at the time of the killing, always good to be far away if you don't want to be implicated. After an unpromising start he had recovered much territory lost to that empire and put down various rebels and rivals.

With Hannibal encouraging him he saw himself as the self styled defender of the Greek world against the Romans. Not that the Greeks, largely left to their own devices by Rome at this time, wanted defending. War was all but inevitable. However, although ultimately unsuccessful the trip did lead to a second meeting between Hannibal and Scipio. Although denied by some historians, more than one of the ancient writers made note of it, primarily Livy and Appian. They may have embellished, but they didn't entirely invent everything.

Publius found himself having a discussion with his old enemy. He told me they discussed the record of various generals and kings in war.

It appears to have been a good humoured exchange. I think there was a genuine respect between the two men at the minimum and in some ways they had things in common. Had Hannibal been Roman, or Scipio Carthaginian, I think they could have worked together. That is a terrifying thought indeed.

Ignoring the speculation and embellishments of Livy and Appian, Scipio apparently asked Hannibal who he thought were the greatest generals. Hannibal gave first place to Alexander the Great, something Publius agreed with, no other man had travelled so far and conquered so much and with such a small army as well. Hannibal placed Pyrrhus of Epirus second. We, today have a somewhat different view of his victories on account of his losses in winning them, which ultimately confounded his plans.

When Publius encouraged Hannibal to say who was third he jokingly gave that position to himself and Scipio laughing asked him where he would rank had he defeated the man sat before him.

"Ah, then I should rank myself first above all ." Came the now famous reply.

Punic humour is an acquired taste and some have suggested it was sarcasm. I think not, I've already alluded to Hannibal's state of mind before Zama, I think his vow and his hatred of Rome prevented him naming a Roman general, but that, in fact, his respect for Scipio as a man and a leader was entirely genuine.

As a means to stave off yet another war the embassy was a failure, but for its interest in telling us about the nature of Hannibal it's something remarkable and for those who did not know my friend Publius it is also quite telling.

In 192BC Antiochus, as expected, attacked Greece. He was not welcomed as a liberator and had to take Greek cities one by one through siege warfare. Rome immediately declared war on Antiochus but was not so precipitate in taking meaningful action. A bit like Saguntum all over again really.

However Manius Acilius Glabrio, the senior consul in 191BC did cross over and defeat Antiochus at the Battle of Thermopylae. Obviously not the much earlier one with the Spartans taking on the Persians, or the World War Two battle of Thermopylae, the 1941 tussle with the Germans.

Antiochus was forced back across the Aegean, returning to Ephesus, but he was not yet a spent force. The senior consul of 190BC was non other than my friend's brother Lucius Cornelius Scipio. Even more remarkable was who would be elected as his junior colleague, but we'll get to that in due course.

Lucius was assigned Greece as his province with permission to cross over into Asia. Why am I telling you this when I'm supposed to be recording the life of my friend Publius after he concluded the Second Punic War?

It's because Lucius, who I also consider a great friend, appointed his brother Publius as his legate, in order that Publius would finally get to confront Antiochus, having been denied that opportunity as consul due to the vagaries and perfidies of Roman politics.

It was a convention in Roman republican times that the commander always got the credit, even if a subordinate were to achieve a victory. For example Sulla would one day capture the illegitimate King Jurgutha, a later successor to Massinissa, yet his commander at the time Gaius Marius would take the accolade.

Lucius and his brother weren't able to reach the theatre of war until late summer or early autumn, by which time our fleet as well as our army had significantly weakened Antiochus who promptly offered peace terms and reparations. The second lot of Cornelian Scipiones brothers to fight together were having none of it.

Wishing to reshape the map somewhat the brothers insisted that Antiochus retreat to the far side of the Taurus mountains and pay an indemnity sufficient to cover the entire cost of the war, not just cede a few towns and pay a bit of money.

The terms were of course unacceptable to a king who still commanded an army of sixty thousand men and negotiations ceased forthwith. The brothers Scipio met Antiochus in battle at Magnesia where the king's army was routed. Publius had in fact deferred to his brother as commander and Lucius quite rightly took the credit. Following on from his brother's example Lucius took the cognomen Asiagenes.

Antiochus was now forced to retreat beyond the Taurus mountains and had to pay an eye watering indemnity of fifteen thousand talents. Further, he had to hand over twenty hostages, including his own youngest son and none other than his military advisor Hannibal.

Taking on the youngest sons of enemies, as hostages, educating them in Rome and romanising them, would, in the future become a recognised way of making the known world, as far as was possible, Roman.

Despite opposition in the senate, due to jealousy and fear that the Scipio brothers were becoming too powerful Lucius was awarded the triumph he rightfully deserved, even if there wasn't a defeated king present to walk in it. His plunder was however more than a little impressive. He exhibited one hundred and thirty seven thousand, four hundred and twenty pounds weight of silver, two hundred and twenty four thousand tetradrachms, these being large silver Greek coins, each being worth four Roman drachmas.

Of gold, in addition, there were one hundred and forty thousand gold coins and two hundred and thirty four gold crowns. One thousand two hundred and thirty one ivory tusks completed the most valuable part of the plunder. There were of course weapons, armour and other items, furniture and trappings removed from the possession of the defeated king.

All of this was handed over to the Roman treasury, each soldier received a bonus of twenty five denarii and officers and equites received rather more. The triumph probably rivalled that some years before of Publius and this time I was able to sit and watch it. The usual sacrifice, feasting and games followed, paid for naturally, by the triumphator.

Clearly, the treasury had done very well out of the war with Antiochus, but Cato, the Caecilii and others jealous of the Scipiones almost predictably started rumours of corruption and bribery against both Publius and Lucius. I was personally outraged.

There was little I could do to help and in 189BC Lucius was put on trial in the courts. Despite having proper accounts he was found guilty and fined, which was better than being exiled, but it was a terrible slur on his good name.

He duly refused to pay the fine, pleading poverty. He wasn't actually in poverty at all, it was more the principle of the thing. The tribune of the plebs Tiberius Sempronius Gracchus interceded and the matter was dropped before, despite Lucius being patrician, it could become a patrician against plebian battle. Plebs like Tiberius generally loved the Scipios and loved to annoy their patrician colleagues.

Tiberius Sempronius Gracchus, of course, would go on to be consul twice, be awarded two triumphs, marry the younger Cornelia, Publius's daughter, and father the rather more famous, but ultimately somewhat less successful Gracchi brothers. They, ironically, are remembered by posterity far more than he.

Publius himself was arraigned in the senate on corruption charges for the same invented offence of profiteering and taking bribes. He tore up the account books in front of the outraged senators and reminded them how much he and Lucius had paid into the Roman Treasury from Spain, Africa and now Asia.

In the end Cato and the others embarrassed no one but themselves, such were the achievements of the brothers and the love they engendered in the people. Had my friend been minded to lead and uprising I believe he could have done so but it was not in his nature. Publius was a Roman of the republic to his core. Had Cato and his evil minded conspirators succeeded in obtaining a guilty verdict, or worse, exile for Scipio, I believe the mob would have bodily torn them to pieces.

Publius and Amelia retired to their villa at Liternum on the coast of Campagnia, not far from modern Naples and ancient Cumae. It's been suggested by some that my friend was a bitter and broken man. Nonsense, he may have had enough of politics especially, and even of campaigning, however, a man more confident in his position, his legacy and the love of the people it is hard to imagine. He wouldn't let a little toad like Cato, or a small minded family like the Caecili get the better of him.

With five children and a wonderful wife, from whom he'd been separated by duty on far too many occasions family life suited him. I wondered if he'd adapt having been a man of action for so long, but he just slotted right in, often doing manual farm labour to keep in shape and, I think, because he just enjoyed growing things. I do not enjoy growing things. Shades of Cincinnatus in his case. Valeria, Caius, Julia and I visited frequently, his villa was always fun and laughter filled, Valeria and Aemilia remained incredibly close to the end.

I say that, but I wasn't strictly there at the end, however their bond was unbreakable by anything other than death. Publius died in 183BC, my life in Rome continued beyond that time, but we'll come to that. I attended my friend's funeral, bade him farewell and hugged each member of his family. There was debate about whether to bury him in the tomb of the Scipios in Rome, but Aemilia intended to remain in the villa and wanted her beloved to be close by, so he was interred there.

Aemilia herself would live a long life, her eldest son Publius, now with the inherited cognomen Africanus, which would pass on through his adopted son down the generations would predecease her in 170BC.

CHAPTER 27 HANNIBAL

Hannibal's first task, having lost at Zama, was to ensure that Carthage accepted the peace terms and did not try to fight on. Such a decision might well have brought the destruction of Carthage forward by many years. He actually threw a senator arguing to continue the struggle off the podium. Dissent was silenced, but a new enemy was made.

In fact Hannibal at forty six or thereabouts was a very different man from the youth, indoctrinated by his father to make war on Rome. We, in the modern world, think of crucifixion as a Roman invention, largely because of one particular crucifixion that caused the cross to become a religious symbol.

In fact, in the ancient world, thousands were crucified, from the pirates captured by Caesar to the slaves who rebelled with Spartacus. I mention this because the method, if it wasn't invented by Carthage can only have been older still. Carthage had used crucifixion for decades already and had been known to crucify defeated generals.

Imagine then, the courage it must have taken to return to Carthage and, having lost the war and been blamed for all of Carthage's ills, to return and try to win the peace. Roman writers stress the cruelty of Hannibal and he was cruel. He used what we would describe as atrocity and terror to instil fear in others and encourage capitulation of the next town or city. Speaking now as a Roman, our own treatment of Capua was no better but it doesn't get written about so much.

Scipio had tacitly supported Hannibal in becoming suffete in Carthage in 201BC, recognising his abilities as more than just a military man. Hannibal swiftly overcame the existing oligarchy and with the end of the embezzlement and corruption practised by the power brokers in Carthage was able to both pay the indemnity and see trade grow once more. He actually became a reforming politician and an accomplished statesman.

In this role Hannibal changed the constitution of Carthage; the hundred and four as they were known, the ruling council or senate of Carthage now had to be elected, not co-opted by their wealthy friends, and their term in office was also limited to a maximum of two successive years. They had to win that second year too, since elections were now, as in Rome, annual events.

Six years after becoming suffete and seven years after the Battle of Zama Hannibal's enemies were circling. A worried Rome, especially worried when Hannibal made the mistake of offering to pay off the indemnity early, sent a deputation accusing Hannibal of supporting a foreign enemy, that is to say Antiochus. I don't personally believe that he was at that stage, be careful what you wish for!

Hannibal's enemies amongst the rich and powerful, would probably have handed him over there and then if he hadn't chosen voluntary exile, it was 195BC when he slipped aboard a ship heading east and departed for the even more ancient Phoenician city of Tyre. The city that had given Carthage birth in fact. Now in his early fifties Hannibal would never again set eyes, sorry eye, on the city he had devoted so much of his life to.

He lived quietly in Tyre for a number of years, disappearing from the pages of history, if not from memory. Indeed, he would never be erased from Roman memory, the expression Hannibal ad portas, Hannibal at the gates passed into the language as a well used expression presaging disaster or catastrophe.

From Tyre he would eventually travel to the Seleucid city of Antioch, an ancient Greek city, founded in 307BC by one of the generals of Alexander, Antigonus Monophthalmus. It became the capital of ancient Syria after being captured by Seleucus I Nicator in 301 and was effectively at the heart of the Seleucid empire he founded.

Today Antioch is known as Antakya and lies just within the borders of modern Turkey. From there Hannibal would eventually travel to the western end of Asia Minor, modern Turkey, to the court of Antiochus III the current king of that empire at this time based in the port of Ephesus.

As already recounted it was during Hannibal's stay in Antioch that he once again met his nemesis, my old friend Publius Cornelius Scipio Africanus. In his war with Rome Antiochus made precious little use of Hannibal, believing he knew best. It was only after being defeated at the battle of Thermopyae and having been driven back to Ephesus that he gave this famous general, famous for his exploits on land that is, a small fleet to command.

In 190BC this fleet was engaged by the Rhodian navy, that is to say a fleet from the island of Rhodes. This was called the Battle of Eurymedon, or, by others the Battle of Side, which I prefer. There was another battle of Eurymedon more than two centuries before, between the Greeks and the Persians. One of those places I suppose, a bit like Thermopylae, battle prone on account of its position.

Hannibal bravely attacked the Rhodian fleet in the mouth of the Eurymedon river and initially the surprise attack started well, but quality always tells and soon the Rhodians had the upper hand.

The Rhodians were famous seafarers and down the years their navy was greatly to be feared by any seafarer on the wrong side of it. Naturally the small Seleucid fleet was defeated by the Rhodians and as a result, despite Hannibal escaping yet again, he and his remaining ships were unable to link up with the rest of the Seleucid navy at Ephesus.

This made life easier for Lucius and Publius when they went after Antiochus. Having defeated Antiochus Lucius and Publius included in the peace terms the condition that Hannibal be handed over, but anticipating this eventuality Hannibal was again too quick to be caught out and slipped away once more.

He escaped first to Armenia, where he served King Artashes I and helped found the city of Artashat on the banks of the Arat River, which would become the capital city of Armenia. The river is now known as the Azat River and Artashat is now modern Artaxata. Another town nearby called Artashat today is much newer and completely unconnected.

From Armenia Hannibal continued his odyssey and went next to the court of King Prusias I of Bithynia which was on the southern shore of the Black Sea, the northern part of modern Turkey.

Prusias was at war with King Eumenes II of Pergamon. Eumenes being allied to us at the time, that is to say Rome. Pergamon is within the boundaries of the modern city of Bergama in Izmir province in NW Turkey about sixteen kilometres from the sea.

Prusias made better use of Hannibal than Antiochus had and Hannibal defeated forces belonging to Eumenes on several occasions. Naturally Rome could not tolerate this and demanded that Prusias hand over Hannibal. Hannibal died in 183BC, 571 to me. The exact nature of his death is disputed and I was far away in Rome. Some say he died from an infected cut finger, others say he poisoned himself, the poison having long been carried secreted in his finger ring against the possibility of capture.

I personally think he did die of poison but not self administered, I think he was tricked by Prusias lest he slipped away as he'd done so many times before when he'd appeared to be cornered. In this way Prusias could hand Hannibal over to Rome without risk. Perhaps it's better we never know for sure.

Hannibal's life involved the deaths of hundreds of thousands of Romans, Gauls, Carthaginians, Insubrians, Numidians and more. He was ruthless, as indeed he was brought up to be. He also turned into a remarkable statesman, politician and reformer and even a town planner as well as general and warrior.

He lost two brothers and his own eye in the war and remained true to his youthful oath. Not a good man certainly, but a remarkable one nonetheless. His corpse was not taken to Rome, he was buried in Libyssa on the road between Nicea and Chalcydon in Bithynia. The town ceased to exist, even in antiquity but Hannibal's grave is not far from modern Izmit, itself ancient Nicomedia in north west Anatolia, Turkey.

Carthage herself would survive for another thirty seven years. In a strange symmetry my friend Publius Cornelius Scipio Africanus, the man who finally defeated Hannibal died the same year.

CHAPTER 28 CAIUS LAELIUS

So, we return, for the final time to the year 201BC, or as I remember it 553. After the drama of riding in Scipio's triumph at the head of my cavalry and having shared in the adulation of vast crowds of people I had partaken of the feast in the evening and I attended the opening of the games alongside my friend, the Ludi Magni, known as such because these were exceptional games vowed by a commander, not the annual Ludi Romani.

I personally had little desire to watch gladiatorial contests after all these years of war. Wild beast hunts, thankfully were not a feature of the games in my time. I did not object to chariot racing, it could be brutal and charioteers did get killed from time to time, but again I think it became more brutal with the passage of time.

It amused me to support the reds since I remembered seeing Formula One and Sports Prototype Championship Ferraris in my youth, red and of course with a prancing horse as the symbol. I didn't try to explain the reasons for my choice to anyone in Rome!

I did enjoy the theatre once I started to understand the language well and also the idioms and humour. By day three after the triumph I just wanted to be at home with Valeria and that's what I did.

As a result of my dispatches to the senate of Rome on behalf of Publius I had had to become a senator, much to Valeria's delight and I was so entered on the rolls. I barely qualified as regards the ownership of land stipulation, so in order to avoid a challenge later I used some of my spoils from the war to purchase the farm adjacent to the one we already owned.

Senators were obliged, by law, not just convention to make their money from land, trade was completely disallowed, which included being a merchant or ship owner. Of course many senators broke the law behind the scenes with nominees and what we would call shell companies, nothing changes.

Not being a Roman of the Romans myself I could take no chances, but I did not consider myself to be a career politician any more than I considered myself to be a career general or admiral. I was happy to be a sleepy backbench nobody, make no enemies, that kind of thing. I did vote the way my feelings led me to vote and very, very occasionally I'd speak in support of something or other. I did try to avoid controversy and I did not inspire the jealousy that accrued to the Scipios.

Not long after I was elected quaestor, I stood because Valeria wanted me to, never dreaming I'd get in. It seems my stock with the public after seventeen years as Scipio's right hand man still counted for something. Scipio and my friends in the Jupiter Club possibly conspired with Valeria to advance my career in spite of my lack of ambition.

In 197BC 557 I was elected as plebeian aedile and in the following year I was made praetor of Sicily. Valeria accompanied me part of the way, it wasn't the done thing for her to be there when I was working, another reason for my lack of ambition. On the way she fell in love with a small place in Bruttium. I thought little of it at the time.

At least my role as plebeian aedile had kept me at home in Rome. My three colleagues were all very much younger and following the traditional path up the cursus honorum, however I kept my real age to myself. I always celebrated my birthday as close to the actual day as possible, but by 197BC I was theoretically seventy two years of age.

Back when Valeria and I had been discussing marriage I had expressed doubts about the age difference, without actually daring to tell her exactly how much older I was. In my fifties back then. The strange thing was that falling backwards in time had seemed to give me a new energy and vitality and I still didn't feel my age even now. Maybe it did make me younger.

Valeria would tease me that the age difference cannot have been as wide as I'd inferred, I countered that she kept me young, but I did worry that the years would suddenly catch up with me somehow, that I'd age overnight. As aedile I was in charge of maintaining public buildings such as temples, the temple of Jupiter being especially close to my heart. My colleagues regulated festivals, public order, roads and suchlike. We got along very well.

Aedile wasn't absolutely essential to the cursus honorum, but it showed a level of public service and people appreciated it. Therefore it would stand one in good stead for future elections.

As plebeian aedile I also had to look after the interests of the plebs and the temple of Ceres which was exclusively plebeian. My colleagues organised the Ludi Romani games, which made one even more popular with the general populace. They were welcome to that and they were happy that I was more than happy to take on the more mundane role.

The popularity which accrued to me, despite not being the organiser of the games, was borne out when I became praetor, another unlooked for thing, basically taking the line of least resistance. I loved Sicily and still do, I have friends in Licata in the modern age.

My role there was basically judge and governor. Now that it was no longer a base for the war Sicily was delightful, but I'd rather have been at home with my family. I'm sure Valeria would have liked me to be at home too, but she had ambitions that had to be lived out through me.

She had me run for the consulship in 192BC that's 562, I didn't get in and I myself put it down to my age, surely I'd done enough anyway, but no, two years later she had me try again. My friend's brother Lucius was also standing and maybe that reminded people about the war, his role in it and mine. Whatever the reason Lucius got in as senior consul and I as junior consul.

Junior consul is still consul, one is still a consular for ever afterwards Valeria was finally satisfied, indeed her cup had runneth over. Her best friend Aemilia had been married to a consul and whilst I would never achieve what he had, we were now in the club too so to speak.

For me it was ridiculous, when I had met Publius there had been talk of him justifying my presence by being his slave. I'd salvaged my dignity and built up a friendship. That he'd worked to make me a citizen was beyond all I could have hoped for, then he trusted me with ships and men, then with dispatches to the senate. He'd helped me marry, gifted me land, smoothed the way for me to enter the senate and then three magistracies, including the most important of all, consul. In fact it was beyond ridiculous.

I believe I'd helped him too I knew a bit about seamanship and I'd developed signals for the fleet to cope in fog. I had reluctantly led men in battle, but he was the architect of the strategies and the success. I found that once again I was also in a position to help my friend, friends actually because Lucius had also become a dear and trusted friend.

It has been suggested that I wanted the command against Antiochus III in order to enrich myself. Nothing could be further from the truth, I'd had a bellyful of war. My friends and I hatched a little conspiracy to ensure that the command went to Lucius in order that he could appoint Publius as his legate.

Rather than drawing lots as was the usual system I announced in the senate that the conscript fathers should decide who had the command in Asia. In so doing I flattered them of course and at this point Publius announced that if Lucius was given the command he would assist him.

The Scipios had their enemies in the senate, but what the senators wanted most was success in the war and the record of Scipio Africanus was unsurpassed. Lucius got his command and I got peace, plus the satisfaction of having helped my friends to get what they wanted after all that Publius had done for me.

When my year as consul was done I heaved a huge sigh of relief and told Valeria I was now retired, she'd just have to put up with me being at home.

I didn't get under her feet, I spent much time in my study writing, much as I do now. I enjoyed entertaining our friends and spending time with our children. I wasn't sure what the future held for Julia, little was written about women unfortunately, but I knew that my son would be a successful politician and earn his own cognomen Sapiens, the wise. What more can one hope for in a son?

He too would go to war, with his friend Scipio Aemilianus, during the Third Punic War, the conflict that would see the utter destruction of Carthage. I was not happy about that, but, as always, I regarded history as having been written a long time ago, even if I was living it at that moment, it was not my place to interfere.

My son would also meet the Greek writer Polybius who had been held hostage in Rome. Some people think I met him, but no, my son would meet him in 160BC. Too late for me.

I hoped that Julia would be safe and happy and worked to ensure that was the case. Caius would be consul himself some thirty years after losing me, not that I knew what the fates had in store for me. I expected to live out my life in antiquity, to die in Rome with my family around me and was more than content with that fate.

In 174BC at the theoretical age of ninety five I was asked to go on an official embassy to King Perseus of Macedon. No one new my official, theoretical age and I still felt like a man in his sixties so I agreed to go.

I must have done a good job because still looking and feeling fit and still of an indeterminate age I was asked to go on another embassy to Transalpine Gaul in 170BC. In theory I was ninety nine, but I still felt more like a man in his late sixties. Valeria was just sixty two, she'd kept fit and she'd kept her looks although I'd had to ban both her and Julia from using cosmetics containing arsenic.

What the hell eh. One last trip. Transalpine Gaul was, as the name suggests, across the Alps. In republican times northern Italy adjacent to the Alps was known as nearer Gaul or Cisalpine Gaul. A trip to France then and my curiosity was piqued. France was, after all, where it had all begun, for me anyway, so many years ago.

CHAPTER 29 LEGACY

So it was that the universe, with a mind of its own nudged me back to Massilia. Like the rich, foolish old man that I was I headed out on horseback alone. For old times sake I headed out into the marshes to see what was left, if anything of my old boat.

Remarkably she was still afloat. Maybe the silt had built up underneath and that supported her, but she appeared no higher or lower in the water than she ought. I walked my horse forward and was able to clamber aboard without so much as getting a foot wet. I tied the reins to the handrail and ventured inside.

The doors had been left open when I'd been captured, I'd hardly been able to ask to lock up. The canopy behind the front section of the wheelhouse had long since rotted away, rain had got in, but not so very much, maybe it had dried out each summer, who knows.

When at anchor, or in harbour I'd normally slept in the large triangular double bed at the bow and being furthest from the now exposed wheelhouse this was the driest least mouldy and least smelly part of the boat.

A great weariness suddenly came upon me. Is this how I die at ninety nine, so far from my wife. 'You stupid old man. No one will find you, a rich old fool goes off into the marshes on horseback on his own. Anything could have happened from heart attack, to drowning, to bandits.'

I laid myself down, hopefully to rest and recover, not in fact to die.

A strange noise awoke me, it was the noise of jet engines, a passenger plane on final approach to Marseilles airport. Sometimes I feel bitter at the universe for what she put me through. I miss Valeria, Julia, Sapiens. I know what became of my son, but not what became of my wife and daughter and I know they will have suffered not knowing what happened to me.

My relationship with my daughter in this day and age is not what I would like it to be. Yes, I admit it, I'd go back in a heartbeat, for all that I suddenly appeared to be fifty one again when I returned. Now I find myself living once more in a world with dentists, chocolate, coffee, tomatoes, cars and motorcycles, electric guitars and other things I'd missed, butter for example, which was considered a barbarian thing in ancient Rome.

My boat was floating happily, the keys were in the ignition, the tender was on the davits and the canopy was like new once more. Did I dream it you ask. One cannot dream for forty eight years. As is my habit I started writing it all down, even as I resumed my travels. I didn't know what else to do. For a while I must have been in shock and I felt bereaved, I cut myself off from humanity, but the loneliness of that brought me low.

I stopped writing, I went back to the UK that Christmas and visited friends, what a contrast with Saturnalia. I kept my mouth shut, my friends at dancing had seen me only twelve months before, how could I explain I'd been away for forty eight years.

Friends started to visit the boat once more. My girlfriend brought my daughter to see me in Elba. I tried to make it fun. From Elba I sailed to Pisa, Fiumicino, Sicily, the Aeolian islands, by the time I'd finished I'd visited half the Roman Empire, including what remained of Rome, Carthage and Utica.

I wrote books on other subjects in order to take my mind off things and when the money ran low I eventually returned on my boat to London. It was in London that my boat was burgled and almost everything I had left to show was taken.

I sold the boat as a knee jerk reaction to the theft and broke up with my girlfriend. For a while I lived with a lady I'd been to school with, that too came to an end. Browsing the internet I found a house for sale in Calabria, ancient Bruttium and bought it after one visit. I wrote other books here, but in 2024 I returned to this book.

I don't know if I should have finished it, but it's been cathartic for me at least.

APPENDIX

When one reads Polybius and Livy one comes across certain contradictions. Is Polybius the more reliable source, or is Livy correcting the errors of Polybius? These are questions for the reader to decide.

Alternatively, perhaps my account is the most definitive. Were I to claim overtly to have travelled in time I might become a laughing stock, again it is for the reader to decide. If you are an accidental visitor to the twenty first century from some future or indeed past time then maybe only you will understand.

Today I have a home in what in ancient times we knew as northern Bruttium, it's in the mountains, in a place Valeria once told me she would go to spend her final years should anything befall me, which in fact was a near certainty given our age difference.

Whether Valeria did come here I cannot know. I endeavoured with the help of a friend to trace the family trees of both of my parents. Both the Snook and the Keates family lines seem always to lead to ancestors in London, and only in London, despite the Snook name's association with Sevenoaks in Kent.

Despite the fact that I'm clearly a Londoner through and through people here in Calabria have accepted me in a way I could never have expected as an outsider. A complete outsider with no history whatsoever in this tiny community. They could have closed ranks, but I've rarely felt so welcome. People here have large and warm hearts.

The house I purchased, although very ancient is certainly not Roman, however the moment I first viewed it I knew it had appeared to me in dreams. What lies beneath it I don't know but something does as a hole opened up near the door of my garage when the Comune decided to pave the courtyard. There also seems to be a section through an ancient pillar set into one of my walls.

Am I now spending time where Valeria lived out her life? I don't know, but I do know that I experience a serenity, a calmness and a sense of belonging in this place, so far from London the birthplace of my ancestors and the place where I experienced a very happy childhood that should have rooted me there.

CONCERNING MY ROLE IN EVENTS

I spend a great deal of time pondering what happened to me. How could one not? Attitudes in the Twenty First Century are immeasurably different. Even the word genocide is a relatively new invention and whilst the, so called, ancients fully understood homosexuality and transvestism, gender transition and how to deal with it sensitively was not an issue for obvious reasons.

The ultimate fate of Carthage was genocide, no doubt of it. I'm glad to say I had no role in the decision to try and eradicate Carthaginian genes entirely from the world, to salt their lands or to poison Hannibal. I don't really believe the accepted version that Hannibal poisoned himself although I admit the possibility.

Hannibal wasn't one to take the easy way out though, I admit the possibility because he would not have allowed himself to be taken as a prisoner to Rome. I do think though that he would have found a way to slip past us yet again, unless maybe he was simply too tired of it all and set on accepting the inevitable.

I cannot escape the fact that I played a part in these events, as did my friend, his father, his uncle, his grandson and indeed my own son. I could discuss pacifism with my son alone in our Tablinum, but I could not give him the experience of life in the Twenty First Century, he was Roman, grew up Roman with Roman contemporaries. That he acquired the cognomen Sapiens is a matter of some pride to me. That Carthaginian culture and achievements were obliterated from the earth, is a matter of profound regret and sadness.

My friend's grandson Scipio Aemilianus adopted by my friend's first born son, they were in fact cousins, did unfortunately play the leading role in the destruction of the city of Carthage. Perhaps we all have a destiny, perhaps it's pre ordained, I don't know. Due to its strategic position Rome would rebuild Carthage many years later, but not in the Carthaginian form. Even that Roman version of the city is all but invisible now.

In the entire war I killed one man, it was him or me, a decision made in an instant, I fight to not let it haunt me and yet I don't feel a sense of moral guilt just a detestation of war.

Normally in a book like this there is a disclaimer stating that none of the characters are real. I leave that for the reader to decide. I hope I have not libelled anyone, or offended anyone, nothing was further from my aim as I wrote this.

I would naturally like to thank Polybius and Livy especially for their amazing works of literature and in a smaller way Appian and Cassius Dio.

Any mistakes are mine and mine alone, the lady who helped check and edit my first novel sadly died as I was finishing this one, as a result I've endeavoured to edit my own work.

I had a comprehensive school education in the east end of London in the 1970s, so I'm aware my English isn't always perfect! As regards the events themselves all I can say is that when you live so long memory plays tricks, but I've tried hard to be as accurate as possible.

Sapanbaal

Copyright Malcolm Snook 2007 and 2024

Printed in Great Britain
by Amazon